SHOW ME THE ASHES

Previously published Worldwide Mystery titles by
CAROLYN MULFORD

SHOW ME THE MURDER
SHOW ME THE DEADLY DEER
SHOW ME THE GOLD

SHOW ME THE ASHES

CAROLYN MULFORD

W⊕RLDWIDE®

TORONTO • NEW YORK • LONDON
AMSTERDAM • PARIS • SYDNEY • HAMBURG
STOCKHOLM • ATHENS • TOKYO • MILAN
MADRID • WARSAW • BUDAPEST • AUCKLAND

Recycling programs
for this product may
not exist in your area.

Show Me the Ashes

A Worldwide Mystery/March 2019

First published by Five Star™ Publishing, a part of
Cengage Learning, Inc.

ISBN-13: 978-1-335-45534-5

Printed in U.S.A.

ACKNOWLEDGMENTS

Each manuscript presents special challenges to the writer, and knowledgeable readers provide indispensable feedback on the various drafts. As usual, other mystery writers—Maya Corrigan (Reston, Virginia) and Helen Schwartz (Chevy Chase, Maryland)—critiqued most of the first draft chapter by chapter and the penultimate draft in one gulp. Mystery readers Joyce Campbell (Chattanooga, Tennessee), Joy Finnegan (New Windsor, New York), Blenda and Donald Marquardt (Rocheport, Missouri), and Fatima Thomas (Columbia, Missouri) gave valuable comments on the penultimate draft. Fatima also shared her expertise on childhood trauma.

Others sharing special knowledge included Gerald DeMenna (New York) on arson, Ellis Bramblett (Adairsville, Georgia) and Larry O'Rear (Chattanooga) on firefighting, Kim Clark (Columbia) on beauty salons, Jon Cook (Kirksville, Missouri) on firearms, and Kevin Marquardt (Columbia) on Harleys. Any errors, of course, are mine.

It takes a village to complete a book.

ONE

ACHILLES TROTTED INTO my office, reared back to put his front paws on my desk, and lobbed his tennis ball onto my keyboard.

I hit Undo and confiscated the ball. "Later. After my 'urgent' four o'clock appointment." I glanced down at my sage-green silk dress, my standard office attire in Vienna six months ago but a rare departure from my jeans and t-shirt in Laycock, Missouri. "And after I change. Go check on your hummingbirds." Worrying that he would take it personally when the hummingbirds fled northern Missouri for a warmer winter climate, I rose to go let him out.

He turned right toward the back door and then whirled and sniffed. When the front doorbell rang, he looked to me for instructions, a sign the visitor's scent disturbed him.

My hand automatically moved to my right hip, but I'd put my Glock 27 in my desk drawer. I studied Achilles. He appeared more puzzled than alarmed. I stepped back to my desk and brought up the view from the front security camera on my computer monitor. A sandy-haired, middle-aged woman, surely my four o'clock, stood on the bottom step beside a small child obscured by a big black-and-white stuffed dog. They posed no threat. Leaving my Glock in the desk, I went down the hall and through the house-wide front room to unlock the door and let them in. I smiled a welcome as I opened the storm door. "Come in, please. I'm Phoenix Smith, the foundation's chief financial officer."

"Beatrix Hew," the woman said, stepping toward me.

The little girl, her complexion like Halle Berry's, held back. Loosely braided black pigtails fell over the toy she clutched against her red flannel shirt. Her brown eyes widened and her pink mouth rounded when she saw my Belgian Malinois behind me.

He sat down and lifted his paw for her to shake.

"Achilles says hello," I told her.

She rushed up the steps, thrust out the stuffed animal's leg to meet Achilles' paw, and then held the toy in one arm and shook the paw herself.

The petite woman, who had the same heart-shaped face as the child, reached out a restraining, manicured hand. "She's crazy about dogs. Is he safe?"

"Yes, Achilles enjoys children." Or hides from them. I pointed to a yellow Frisbee he'd left on the piano bench. "They can play fetch in the backyard while we discuss your problem."

"I'd rather they play inside." The woman glanced to her right at the sparsely furnished reception room, once my parents' living room. "This is Hermione Hew, my granddaughter."

The child pointed to the scruffy stuffed dog.

"And that's Harvey Hew." The woman stepped to her left to put a red tote bag on the conference table that had replaced the dining-room table.

"A pleasure to meet all of you," I said. "Please come into my office, Beatrix."

She followed me slowly, adjusting a lovely hand-woven blue and gray shawl over the shoulders of her navy blue dress and watching the child stroke Achilles. I guessed the grandmother to be close to fifty, a few years younger than I. Skillfully applied makeup didn't quite conceal her pallor.

In the office, I motioned her to the chair in front of my desk and took my place behind it. I anticipated hearing about a real problem rather than the fraud and frivolity that had frustrated me during the foundation's first two weeks.

She licked her lips. "Did you recognize my name? Do you know why I contacted you?"

"Sorry, no. I grew up in Laycock, but I came back only last May."

"That's good. You can be objective." She spoke quickly in the local border-state drawl and knotted her fingers in her lap. "I've heard how generous you are, how you came to visit Annalynn and stayed to help her learn the truth about her husband's passing, how you started the Coping After Crime Foundation to help crime victims." She paused for breath.

I didn't correct her overestimation of my character. I'd learned to take credit even when I hadn't earned it.

"I desperately need your help." She placed her hands together in the traditional attitude of prayer. "You're my last hope of proving my daughter is innocent and getting her released from prison."

The woman had misunderstood the foundation's function. And mine. Why hadn't she gone straight to Annalynn, the temporary sheriff and a permanent do-gooder? Beatrix Hew's intensity cautioned me to keep my face neutral and my voice businesslike. "What was the charge against your daughter?"

"Manslaughter and arson. She didn't kill him, and she

didn't set the fire." Beatrix waited a moment for my reaction. Getting none, she continued, "The sheriff's department questioned Jolene when she was addled by drugs and scared her into a false confession. They wouldn't let me see her, and the public defender talked her into accepting a plea deal for six to eight years. That was more than a year ago. She has almost five years to serve."

Cynicism kicked in. This well-dressed, well-spoken woman had expressed a mother's wishes, not necessarily the facts. Besides, she was accusing Annalynn's late husband, an incompetent sheriff but a caring man, of railroading a young woman. "I'm afraid you've misinterpreted what the foundation, and I, can do. You need an experienced criminal lawyer."

"Good criminal lawyers charge much more money than I can raise. I've already gone to special groups who clear people wrongly convicted, but they won't even consider the case for another six months, and I'm running out of time." She reached into her bag and placed a large white envelope on the desk. "Here's my application for assistance and all the information I could bring together on Jolene's case. You've solved three crimes that baffled local and federal officers since you came back to Laycock. I'm sure you can prove that Hermione's mother couldn't have killed that awful man." She leaned forward and shoved the envelope toward me. "Believe me, I wouldn't come to you if I knew of any other possibility."

"I'm sorry," I said, surprised at my genuine regret. "The Coping After Crime Foundation doesn't investigate crimes. We provide short-term assistance to help victims and their families deal with the aftermath."

She slumped in her chair. Then she straightened.

"My daughter was a crime victim. She was drugged and assaulted. My granddaughter is a victim. She cries for her mother every night. The child barely speaks outside our house. I scramble to earn enough to feed and clothe her. Oh, yes, Ms. Smith, my family meets the foundation's criteria for assistance. Every single one of them." She reached into her bag and withdrew a printout from our website. "I went through your guidelines carefully to be sure. Please. Hear me out."

"Certainly, and call me Phoenix." No one else had cited the criteria. "Fair warning: If I'm to consider your application, you'll have to convince me your daughter didn't commit a crime."

"Thank you." She pitched forward, barely cushioning her head with her hand before it hit the desk.

Suspecting theatrics, I clasped her wrist to check the pulse. Fast and thready. Hard to fake that. "Should I call 9-1-1?"

"No. Give me a moment," she said, her voice muffled. "Could I have a glass of water, please?"

I hurried to the kitchen and filled glasses for the woman and the child, now sitting on the floor stroking Achilles and humming in his bullet-scarred right ear.

Beatrix raised her head from between her knees as I came back into the office. She'd dropped the shawl from her shoulders to the back of the chair. Perspiration had smudged her makeup. I recognized her effort to stay conscious. After being wounded during a mission in Istanbul, I'd spent weeks doing the same. Even now, six months later, sudden pain sometimes rendered me dizzy and breathless. I handed the water to her and opened a bottle of pills she'd put on the desk, strong pills. I shook one, and then another, onto the desk.

She dropped one back in the bottle with a trembling hand. "If I take two, I won't be able to drive back to Green Springs." She washed down the pill.

"You're quite ill," I said matter-of-factly.

"Please, promise me you won't tell anyone, not even Annalynn." She waited until I nodded. "Two weeks ago I learned that I have pancreatic cancer. The doctor gives me only a few months. No one else knows yet." She blinked rapidly. "I'm the sole support of both my disabled mother and my granddaughter. I'm desperate to free Hermione's mother right away."

Hermione's mother, not Beatrix's daughter. The illness and responsibilities certainly made a compelling argument for investigating in the foundation's name, but not one for letting emotion override reason. "Why weren't you desperate when your daughter was arrested?"

The woman sipped the water and avoided eye contact. "I never imagined they would send her to prison. When they sentenced her, I couldn't get anyone—the sheriff, the prosecutor, the public defender—to listen to me. Jolene wouldn't talk to me. She wrote a note saying that going to prison would atone for her sins and that I could take care of Hermione better than she could." Beatrix lowered her forehead to the desk.

A soap-opera tale of mother-daughter tensions lay behind her words, but I could delve into that later if necessary. More important, that little girl clinging to Achilles had lost her mother for years and would soon lose her grandmother forever. Everything else on my boring schedule paled beside this. I returned to my desk chair and waited for her to raise her head. When she did,

I said, "Tell me what happened, how you know your daughter is innocent."

She nodded and leaned her elbows on the desk for support. "Jolene worked as a waitress at the Bush-whacker's Den in Green Springs. That's where it all happened. The owner, Cork Klang, closed at one that night and left Jolene to clean up. A man named Edwin Wiler had been hitting on her earlier, and off and on other nights. After Cork was gone, Wiler came back and insisted she have a drink with him. She poured herself a beer and him a vodka. He slipped one of those date-rape drugs into her drink."

Finally a fact we could verify. "You have a toxicology report proving that?"

"No, the police tested only for alcohol." She took a deep, tremulous breath. "I saw how out of it she was that night. A beer wouldn't make her that groggy."

Any tests would be in the department's case files. Annalynn could pull them. "Go on."

"Edwin Wiler attacked her—cut her lip and yanked off her bra. She fought back. She scratched his cheek with a ballpoint pen, and he knocked her out." She paused. "That's in the police report. Nobody disputes that he attacked her."

Clear self-defense. "I don't understand why she was charged."

"He died from blunt force trauma. The confession she signed said she hit him on the head with the vodka bottle, went home, and came back and set a fire to cover up what she'd done." Beatrix raised her right hand, palm out. "I swear on the blood of my Savior that's not true."

I nodded even as my skepticism mounted. Ninety percent of the agents I'd encountered in Eastern Europe had sworn to blatant lies. The international bankers and entrepreneurs I'd dealt with in my cover and post-CIA jobs had been little more truthful. "How do you know her confession is false?"

"I was at the Den." She pulled a tissue from her bag and patted perspiration from her forehead. "Hermione woke me at one fifteen, the time Jolene usually got home. I put the baby in bed with my mother, threw on some clothes, and walked to the Den. It's less than two blocks away. I saw candlelight inside." Her voice had quickened. "I opened the door. Jolene lay on the floor right in front of the bar, her mouth bleeding. Wiler was crouched over her on his knees. He drew back his fist. I threw my flashlight at him, and he turned toward me. I picked up a chair to hit him. He pulled it out of my hands and flung it behind the bar." She closed her eyes. "He yelled at me, 'Take your slut home.' Somehow I got her up."

The way she'd repeated his insult convinced me she could be telling the truth. "So he was alive when you left the bar."

"I swear to God." She cleared her throat and sipped the water. "I half carried her home. I could smell alcohol on her, so I thought she was drunk. I didn't realize he'd drugged her. I couldn't get her up the stairs to her bedroom, so I put her on the living-room couch and cleaned the blood off her face. I should have called the police right then, but I was afraid people would blame her. There'd been a lot of nasty talk when she came home with a dark-skinned baby and no wedding ring. She's never told me who the father is."

I guessed that Beatrix had chastised her daughter

but doted on the child. "Did you or your daughter go back to the Den?"

"No. Jolene fell into a deep sleep. I stretched out in the recliner and dozed until I heard the volunteer fire department's siren about four thirty. I went out into the front yard and saw flames at the Den. I was glad the awful place would be gone. I had no idea that man was still in there."

Her story had some huge gaps. "Why did the officers arrest Jolene?"

"I didn't know it then, but they found a bra with the body. They came and woke her up to see if it was hers and then took her to Laycock. I'd already gone to work. When I heard, I thought they wanted to ask her about how he got into the bar, not how he died. I went to the jail as soon as my mother learned they were holding her. They wouldn't let me see her. They said she had a lawyer. I finally cornered Boom—he was sheriff then—in the parking lot as he left that afternoon and told him what happened."

Scheisse! Annalynn's good ol' boy husband had been an administrator, not an investigator. Surely he hadn't handled this case himself. "Did Boom believe you?"

"No. He claimed Jolene had confessed to killing Edwin Wiler and to starting the fire. Boom said he understood how a mother would lie to protect her child and he wouldn't report it. He said I could go to prison for perjury."

I pushed my concern about Boom's role aside. "Surely you told Jolene's defense attorney what happened."

She grimaced. "Yes, two days later when he finally 'had time' to see me. He was a public defender just out of law school. He told me Jolene swore no one else was there. He bragged that he'd gotten her a great plea deal. He said to keep my mouth shut or I'd make it worse for her."

I weighed her claims. Could Boom and the public defender both have been so sure of the young woman's guilt that they refused to investigate her mother's story? Of course they could. They, like the dead man, probably viewed the unwed mother of a biracial child as fair game. Any accused person's mother lacked credibility as a defense witness. Besides, prosecution and defense undoubtedly were pleased to close the case quickly. Jolene Hew may well have received a raw deal, but I had to have the facts before I offended my best friend by questioning her late husband's handling of the case. "I'll have to go over the file and make other inquiries before I decide whether to accept your application."

"Of course." She stood up. "I feel stronger now. I need to go home while I'm able to drive. Call me there or at my beauty salon when you're ready to talk again. My numbers are on my application."

"You'll hear from me in two or three days." I went around the desk in case she needed an arm to lean on. "If I can verify your story, I'll do what I can to get the case reopened. For now, I have one more question: Who killed Edwin Wiler?"

She smiled for the first time. "When you answer that question, Jolene can come home to her daughter, and I can go home to my Heavenly Father."

TWO

I REWARDED ACHILLES for his stellar babysitting by changing into the jeans and t-shirt stashed in the supply room, once my two brothers' bedroom, and playing fetch. The mindless activity allowed me to evaluate the meeting. No lies had pinged on my radar, but observers' accounts tend to be inaccurate or incomplete. Her story gained credibility because Annalynn's husband had demonstrated a fatal lack of judgment during his short term as sheriff. I itched to dig in and find out what happened at Bushwhacker's Den.

Hold on. If Boom had induced a false confession, I wouldn't be able to hide that from Annalynn the way I had some of his other transgressions. Besides, part of my eagerness to investigate sprang from boredom with the misspelled and poorly reasoned applications for financial assistance. Reviewing those fell to me until Annalynn's term as sheriff expired and she took over as Coping After Crime's executive director.

The foundation gave me no authority to investigate a crime. Neither did the reserve deputy card Annalynn had issued to me after she wangled the appointment of acting sheriff in order to investigate her husband's death. More troubling, my CIA tradecraft didn't include investigating arson or murder. But if I didn't, who would?

Achilles nudged my hand with his drool-soaked tennis ball.

"Last throw. Monday is my night to cook dinner." I heaved the ball into the orchard in Annalynn's back lot, picked up Beatrix's envelope from the patio table, and carried it into the castle, Annalynn's nineteenth-century limestone house. I was the woman who came to dinner and stayed to mend our shattered lives.

Leaving the file on the kitchen's granite island, I whipped up a ham-and-spinach quiche and poured it into a store-bought piecrust. Then I allowed myself to open the envelope and pull out about twenty sheets of paper. On top was Beatrix's application for assistance and a single-spaced account of what she'd told me. I checked her income—well above the poverty line but a good $10,000 less than I'd expected. I flipped through the rest—mostly photocopies of articles from Laycock's *Daily Advertiser*. The top article, "Woman Arrested After Firefighters Find Body in Burning Building," carried Jolene Hew's sweet-faced high school graduation picture and a photo of a blond bodybuilder posing during a competition. The caption identified him as the victim, Edwin Wiler, twenty-eight, the manager of Laycock Storage & RV Parking.

I skimmed the straightforward news article. It reported the arrest and quoted Sheriff Boom Keyser as saying Jolene Hew, twenty-two, had confessed to striking Wiler after he attacked her and starting a fire to conceal her action. The next three pages showed a series of indistinct photos of the fire burning during the night, the damaged interior in dawn's dim light, and the body being removed from the scene in bright sun. Captions identified the people and listed the time each photo was taken.

Times ranged from five to nine. The credit line listed the photographer as Vernon Kann, the newspaper's retired publisher and Annalynn's good friend.

My spirits lifted. Vernon would know what happened and how seriously to take Beatrix Hew's story. He could also provide the original images, sure to be much clearer than the photocopied newspaper photos.

A separate article reported on the fire. A passerby had seen the flames at four twenty and called both the Laycock Fire Department and the Green Springs volunteers. Three volunteers arrived within ten minutes and sprayed the building and surrounding area with foam from portable extinguishers and water from garden hoses. Volunteer chief Leo Klang entered the building briefly but left because of the dangerous conditions. The LFD took over at four forty. No one entered the building until two hours later, at which time firefighters discovered the body.

Hmm. The guy could have been unconscious—from a blow or alcohol—and died from smoke inhalation. Odd the article didn't say that, or maybe not. The police, and the newspaper, would wait for the autopsy report. I flipped through the sheets.

Three days later a headline stated, "Blow to Head Caused Wiler's Death." Again the article carried little information, stating only that the autopsy confirmed that Wiler died as a result of blunt force trauma. The alleged weapon was a vodka bottle. The article also quoted the LFD chief: "The fire was no accident. Someone applied an accelerant to both the floor and the ceiling."

I skimmed the other articles from the *Advertiser* and short ones from St. Louis, Kansas City, and Sedalia newspapers. None gave more information about the fatal blow or the arson.

No one had spouted off the way they usually do in sensational cases. It appeared the prosecution and defense both had stonewalled the press. I didn't find any interviews of the Hews or the victim's family. Did Vernon and other reporters deliberately play down the case? Or did everyone stonewall?

I glanced at the final article: "Jolene Hew Pleads Guilty, Accepts Prison Sentence." Sheriff Boom Keyser's handsome face beamed in a close-up. He praised his officers for obtaining a confession and the prosecutor for negotiating a plea agreement that saved the county the cost of a jury trial. *Scheisse!* Annalynn would demand absolute proof if I proposed changing the ending of Boom's success story.

I checked the dates: four weeks—mid-July to mid-August—from arrest to sentencing. The county must have set a record. That alone argued for examining Beatrix's claims.

The doorbell rang. A nanosecond later, the front door opened and the intruder called, "Don't shoot. I brought wedding cake for dessert."

Connie Diamante. She often irritated me by using her key before I had time to answer—or ignore—the door. Let it go. Keep the truce. I called, "The main course is ready to go in the oven." Then Connie's timing struck me. "You sang at a *Monday* wedding?"

"No, I went to Kirksville to meet with the bride's mother and choose songs for the rehearsal dinner *and* the wedding *and* the reception." Connie waltzed into the kitchen and put a white cardboard cake box on the island. As usual, she wore a skin-tight dress, this one turquoise, with matching dangly earrings—pretty, but not real turquoise. "She was tasting cakes and wanted temptation out of the house." Connie ran her fingers through her short blond curls. "Get this: The wedding's on Halloween. The bridesmaids are wearing orange dresses with black trim, their school colors." She shuddered.

Annoying as the soprano in our high school trio could be, I was glad Connie would be here as a buffer when I told Annalynn about my visitor. Maybe Connie knew the story. "I received an application today from Beatrix Hew. She lives in Green Springs, that spot in the road in southern Vandiver County. Do you know her?"

"Well enough to nod, not well enough to ask her how her daughter likes prison. Annalynn knows Beatrix pretty well, or used to. Why did she come to the foundation?"

"She asked me to prove Jolene is innocent. Beatrix claims that the sheriff's department coerced her daughter into confessing that she killed a man in self-defense and set a fire to cover it up." I slid the papers back in the envelope to finish in private.

"That happened a couple of weeks after my mother died. I didn't pay a lot of attention, but I must have been the only one in the county who didn't." Connie took a glass from the cupboard and opened the refrigerator door. "I remember people saying Jolene would have gotten off on self-defense if she hadn't tried to burn the place. Raleigh, my cousin Trudy's son, was part of the crew that went out to fight the fire. Trudy grilled him for weeks, but he refused to talk about it." Connie poured herself a glass of lemonade. "Annalynn will be terribly upset if you question the confession. She was really proud of the way Boom handled that case. I vote the foundation turn down the application. Beatrix can hire someone to investigate."

Connie's vote carried little weight with me. I couldn't ignore the desperate woman's plea. I hedged. "I didn't approve the application, but Beatrix was convincing enough that I agreed to consider it."

The phone rang. It was Annalynn.

"Can you please meet me at 1010 West Hays? Laycock Police answered a call about a burglary at the Carmetti house. That's the fifth break-in since late August. Jim hopes Achilles can pick up a scent."

"Did Jim forget the DEA trained Achilles to find drugs, not people?"

"Achilles is the only dog in town trained to find anything except ducks or coons. Let's see what he can do. Is Connie there yet?"

"Yes." I hit the Speaker button so Connie could hear.

"Tell her we—or at least you—will be there in time for dinner. She can go home or stay as she likes."

"I'll check my email here," Connie said. "Call when you want me to put in the quiche."

"Oh, good grief," Annalynn said. "Hurry, Phoenix. The front yard is swarming with boys." She cut the connection.

Connie said, "I'll call Achilles while you grab your keys and your gun."

Two minutes later Achilles and I jumped into my banged-up, white Camry. Five minutes after that we pulled into a long driveway lined with dense shrubbery. I couldn't see the old two-story brick house until we reached the end of the drive. Annalynn's black SUV, which she used as her official car, and a white LPD squad car were parked in front of a detached two-car garage.

In the big front yard, a blue-clad LPD officer was talking to an excited bunch of adolescent boys dressed in mud-stained football uniforms. I waved to Michael Moniteau, the town's only black cop, and went up the front steps onto a spacious porch.

Annalynn came out the door, her beige uniform still fresh, her brown, chestnut-highlighted hair still in an elegant French roll. She pulled off rubber gloves and petted Achilles. "It's no use to take him inside. The kids ran all over the house searching for clues before the LPD got here. They also roamed around out back. I doubt Achilles can distinguish the burglar's scent from that of the boys."

"We're here, so we may as well try. Is this burglary the same M.O. as the two you investigated earlier?"

"Looks like it—afternoon, house back from the street, no sign of where they broke in, an older resident. The owner left at two to coach an after-school game and brought the kids home for refreshments. One of the boys noticed Mr. Carmetti's shotgun, rifle, and an antique six-shooter were missing from his gun cabinet."

I didn't like the idea of armed burglars. "Have they taken firearms before?"

"No, but they always choose items easy to sell. They've taken everything from a unicycle to silverware. Never a television or other electronics, oddly enough." She led the way around the corner of the house. "We think they parked in the alley and entered through the back door. With the burglaries on the county side of the line, I thought teenagers were walking in unlocked doors and grabbing items at random. This time they knocked half a dozen souvenir beer mugs off the mantel and broke them. That seems personal."

"Yes, so maybe that burglar knew where to find a key." I paused at a side door and studied the lock. I could open it in five seconds with my handy-dandy picks. "A career burglar wouldn't need a key."

"We don't have career burglars in Laycock."

Achilles raced toward the back of the house barking.

Annalynn ran after him. I followed, drawing my Glock.

She stopped right in front of me. "He's treed a squirrel. We might as well give up."

I veered to the side and holstered my gun. "Not yet. Come, Achilles." He trotted to me as I walked toward the back door. Kneeling beside the bottom step, I pushed his nose down. "Find, please."

He sniffed, sneezed, and went up the three steps with his nose in the air. He walked back and forth across the porch a couple of times and then down the steps and toward a little white shed near the back alley. He hesitated at a partly open door and moved on.

"He's searching for drugs," I said. "He probably smelled fertilizer." I watched him make a quick circuit of the backyard and head back to the tree where the squirrel had taken refuge.

A moment later, Annalynn drew her gun, racked it, and crept toward the shed. "Police," she called. "Come out with your hands up." No one emerged. After half a minute she edged forward and stuck her head in the door. "Fall lawn fertilizer."

Achilles trotted away from the tree to sniff red roses.

She holstered her gun and touched her Bluetooth earpiece to answer her phone. "Sheriff Keyser." She listened. "That's great, Jim. We may be able to match even a partial print." Pause. "No, I'm sending Achilles and Phoenix home. Bye."

"You have partials?"

"Possibly on one of the broken mugs. I'll come home as soon as I talk to Jim about a joint operation." She smiled. "I know you've been bored with all that paperwork for the foundation. Maybe we can provide a little excitement."

THREE

WHEN I REACHED my car, I called Connie. "I'm heading home, and Annalynn won't be far behind. Go ahead and put in the quiche."

"Sure. Umm, I read the application and the articles you left on the counter. You were right, Phoenix. We have to check it out. I called Trudy to refresh my memory on the cast of characters and the plot."

Anger that Connie had called her busybody cousin rendered me speechless.

"I can hear you exploding," Connie said. "Relax. I never mentioned the Hews or the fire. I asked Trudy if the Family Fish House—that's what the Bushwhacker's Den used to be—is still open. I know better than you not to give her any hint of what we're investigating."

We are investigating? My own fault. I should never have mentioned the application. I forced a smile to soften my tone. "What did Trudy say? The short version."

"You always say that, right before you demand every tiny detail. Okay. The Den never reopened. As for the Hews, they're a classic American family: saintly mother, wayward father, self-righteous brother, wild-child daughter. The community consensus is that Jolene killed a rotten guy in self-defense but lost her head and tried to destroy the evidence." Connie paused. "I'm waiting to hear a thanks."

Courtesy costs nothing. "Thank you."

"We shouldn't say anything to Annalynn until I talk to Raleigh, Trudy's oldest, about the fire and you find out who benefited financially from the death."

Suggestions inspired, no doubt, by the mysteries Connie had devoured since Annalynn became acting sheriff. What I hated most was that Connie made good sense. "Agreed. Let's talk about your wedding client at dinner. Bye." That should keep both her and Annalynn happy.

When I started up the castle's front steps, Connie opened the door with the envelope in her hand. "I remembered that one of my voice students said Jolene left for Sedalia the minute she graduated from high school. She dated several African-American men stationed at Whiteman Air Force Base. Apparently one of them is the little girl's father, but no one—maybe not even Jolene—knows which one." Connie handed me the envelope. "I'll fix the salad and set the table while you digest the file. Be sure to read Beatrix's notes on Wiler on the back of an article."

"Right. Slice some tomatoes, please." I hurried up the grand stairs in the wide central hall to my bedroom, the one that had been Annalynn's as a child. I sat cross-legged in the middle of her antique four-poster canopy bed, pulled out the papers, and found the handwritten note. "Edwin Wiler pled guilty to drunk and disorderly conduct at a bar in Springfield, Missouri. Martina Pelben paid $7,478 in damages to prevent an assault charge against him."

Wiler's propensity for violence supported the self-defense story. I read on. "Right after that they moved to Laycock and ran Laycock Storage and RV Parking, which she inherited. He took part in bodybuilding competitions. He usually went to the Den alone and sang karaoke. That night he came with Martina, left, and came back alone."

Add cheating to Wiler's rap sheet. I turned the page over to an article with a photo of a longhaired young woman screaming at Jolene Hew in a squad car. The caption identified the screamer as Martina Pelben. Wiler's beneficiary? Perhaps I should visit Laycock Storage and inquire about storing some boxes. The article reported Jolene would be incarcerated at the Chillicothe Correctional Center.

I moved on to a photo of a long white frame building streaked with black. On the left, a section of the roof had fallen in. Above the entrance, which no longer had a door, a metal Confederate flag dangled from a crudely lettered Bushwhacker's Den sign. The flag stirred memories of the Family Fish House. During the summer my father had taken us kids to Green Springs to catch our supper in a big pond. We carried our trout and bass to the kitchen to be cleaned and fried while we drank pop and ate green onions and little squares of hot cornbread dripping with butter. Dad always joked with the couple who owned it. The Bells? No, the Klangs. Leo, the firefighter, and Cork, the Den's owner, must be their sons or grandsons.

On the next sheet, three photos—probably taken through the entry—showed the inside of the building. In the largest, the end of an Old West bar and empty shelves behind it appeared unscathed. A superimposed rectangle marked the spot where the body had been. Right by the bar where Beatrix claimed she found the man beating her daughter.

The second photo showed holes in the floor and the ceiling and remnants of tables and chairs encased in ashes and debris. No curtains on the windows and no cloth anywhere. The third photo offered a stark contrast: a cloth-covered pool table and several ash-strewn but whole tables and chairs. So one section of the building had sustained little damage. I strained my eyes studying the grainy photographs but saw no sprinkler system. Why, then, did so much of the place escape the flames? With all that dry wood as fuel, I'd expect the whole building to burn.

A brick wall between the kitchen and the tables flashed into my memory. The bar and the shelves behind it had not been there. Mrs. Klang had passed heaping plates through empty window frames to the servers. The white frame structure had been built around an older brick one that served as the kitchen.

I needed to see the original photos on a computer screen where I could zoom in on details. The *Daily Advertiser* would have removed the photos from its website but not from its archives. I'd have to persuade Vernon to give me his take on what happened and access to the archives. I'd abhorred the press all my professional life, but Annalynn's friend had proved himself trustworthy during our death-by-deer investigation.

"Annalynn's here," Connie called from downstairs. She greeted Annalynn at the door and started a conversation, giving me a little more time.

I stuffed everything but one day-after article back into the envelope and read: "Sheriff Frederick 'Boom' Keyser named Jolene Hew, 22, Green Springs, a person of interest in the death of Edwin Wiler, 28. Firefighters found the Laycock man in the smoking ruins of

Bushwhacker's Den at 6:45 a.m. Sunday. Sheriff Keyser said the cause and time of death have not yet been determined."

I skipped down to witnesses' accounts. "Green Springs volunteer firefighter Leo Klang reached the scene first. He said, 'I thought the whole place would go. I emptied out our chemical fire extinguishers on the inside. The others sprayed water on the roof and around the building to keep the fire from spreading.'"

Downstairs, Annalynn laughed heartily, a sound too rarely heard these last five months. I skimmed the other interviews. No one said anything useful. I noted that no Laycock firefighter or police officer, other than Boom, had been quoted. That couldn't be because Vernon didn't question them. They'd clammed up.

"What are you concentrating on so hard, Phoenix?" Annalynn turned from the stairs toward my door, a smile lingering on her lips.

"A new application to the foundation," I said casually, slipping the article into the envelope. "You're in a good mood. What did Jim and Michael turn up?"

She leaned against the doorframe. "A partial print. It may be enough to confirm a theory I've developed because of what we found at the Lassiter burglary scene today."

"Really? You said yesterday that the place was clean." I swung around to dangle my feet over the edge of the high bed.

Annalynn's eyes shone. "This morning Mrs. Lassiter noticed that the toilet seat was down in the downstairs powder room. She cleaned Saturday, and she's positive that she left the seat up and no one had been in there. Gillian and I found a smudged print."

"A seat print," Connie called from downstairs. "Every ass is unique."

Annalynn rolled her eyes. "We can't identify the partials in the database, but we may be able to match them with any suspects' prints."

"Is going to the bathroom during a burglary a sign of tension or of confidence?"

"I have no idea." She walked in, perched on the bed beside me, and said softly, "Either way, that lowered seat supports my theory that we're looking for a woman."

"Do I need to remind you that men occasionally put down the toilet seat?"

"Men also tend to steal TVs, not small pieces of furniture or collectibles they can conceal in a towel." She smiled almost smugly. "Besides, Gillian says the loops visible in the partial are more common among women." She whispered, "Jim and I agreed that I'll show you what we have—after Connie goes home."

That was a switch. Usually Annalynn insisted on telling Connie everything. Laycock Police Chief and candidate for sheriff Jim Falstaff must have vetoed that.

"Five minutes," Connie called.

The phone rang the double ring signaling a department call. Annalynn hurried toward her room. "Maybe that's Jim. Don't wait dinner."

I washed my hands and went downstairs to the dining room.

Connie, putting white wine at her and Annalynn's plates, arched an eyebrow. "Well?"

I shrugged. "The files don't give enough information. Vernon covered the story. Let me quiz him before we talk to your firefighting cousin. How well do you know him?"

"Not very well. Raleigh was a little kid when I left for college. When I moved back after my divorce to help Mama, he was a busy father and firefighter. He's a quiet, goodhearted guy, closemouthed like his father. I can get more out of him than you would."

"Okay." I hated to leave anything critical to Connie, but she'd pried information from people without their noticing before. "I'll call you after my morning run."

"I'm giving a piano lesson at nine. After that, I'm free until two."

Annalynn came into the dining room wearing royal-blue slacks and a matching turtleneck. "What are you two planning tomorrow?"

Connie answered without a nanosecond's hesitation: "Phoenix is going over the contract Laycock Community College offered me to direct two musicals of my choosing, as long as they don't cost more to produce than a high school play."

"Congratulations!" Annalynn kissed Connie on the cheek. "They've asked you to direct again because your *Oklahoma!* got rave reviews."

All through dinner we chatted about musicals feasible for college students who worked part or full time. Preparing after-dinner coffee, I wondered if this pleasant meal was our quiet before the Hew investigation stirred up a storm.

Connie sliced off two-bite samplings of three kinds of cake and placed them on a plate. "I prefer the white cake with orange-flavored icing myself. The orange-tinted white cake with the dark-chocolate frosting tastes good, but the model had the visual appeal of a mud pie. They'll probably choose the carrot cake frosted with orange-and-black stripes." She closed the cake box. "I'll skip dessert and take the rest of the cake to Trudy on my way home."

I recognized the cake as an excuse to visit gossip central. "I wouldn't mention the contract," I cautioned, sure Connie would know I meant the Hew case. "We don't want everybody in town knowing you plan to negotiate terms."

"Connie knows better than to tell Trudy anything confidential," Annalynn said quickly.

Hmm. So Jim feared Connie would let slip details of the burglary investigation. "Of course," I said. "One thing we've all learned in the last few months is to keep quiet and listen." Usually Annalynn stepped between Connie and me to keep the peace. Hiding the burglary information from Connie and the Hew application from Annalynn put me in the middle this time. I didn't like it there. I carried our coffees to the table and chose a sliver of white cake.

Achilles, who'd been chewing on a nutritious fake bone while we ate quiche, whined and focused pleading eyes on Annalynn.

She glanced at me. "Sorry, Achilles, but cake isn't good for you."

I took Connie to the door so Annalynn could slip him a crumb of icing-free cake. That would satisfy them both. When I'd found the half-starved, wounded dog on a creek bank and brought him into her elegant house last May, I'd pushed her to feed him in order to overcome her fear of dogs and his distrust of people. Now they adored each other.

Annalynn picked up our napkins and coffee mugs. "Let's work in the ladies' parlor."

I carried in the cake plate and put it on the coffee

table in the cozy sitting area of the long, narrow room. A carved Indian screen blocked the view of Annalynn's home office—an antique roll-top desk, a computer, and a low bookshelf that held papers, reference books, and a printer.

She went behind the screen. "I'll print out the files. Would you open the county map on the table to the Laycock side, please?"

She knew that map as well as I knew the multiplication tables. I spread it out. The addresses of the burgled houses had stuck in my mind, as numbers always did, but I couldn't spot two of the streets. They had been added since I left Laycock.

Annalynn sat beside me on the love seat and circled five places on the east and north sides of town with red ink. Then she numbered them. "Do you see a pattern?"

I studied them: city, county, city, county, city. "Not really. Most people don't even know where the city's boundaries are. I doubt the burglar purposely alternated jurisdictions."

She placed papers with photos of the front and back of the houses at the top of the map. "Do you see any pattern here?"

Two-story yellow Victorian, sprawling ranch, two-story vinyl and brick, one-story white frame, two-story brick. The architecture didn't matter. The surroundings did. All the houses stood well back from the street and had trees or fences, or both, on at least two sides. "They chose houses where passersby wouldn't see them. Do you have photos of the door locks?"

Annalynn handed me several sheets, each with close-ups of two to four locks.

I glanced through them. None would take a pro more

than half a minute. I searched for scratches or gouges and saw none. "You can buy tools to open these online, but using them without leaving any marks takes practice." I pointed to the locks on the first house, the most challenging. "Unless the owner left a door unlocked, this one was no impulse break-in."

Annalynn handed me more papers. "These list the items stolen at each house."

I shuffled them so the burglaries fell in chronological order, starting with late August, and went through them one by one. No single item was valued at more than four hundred dollars. The lists varied widely, but the take always included cash and small collectibles. The last two included towels. "They're either really short on towels or using them to wrap up and carry the stolen items." I studied the lists side by side. "They must have a van or a car with a big trunk. Each time they've taken one fairly large item—a portable sewing machine, a unicycle, an antique rocker, a marble-topped end table, and this time the guns. Each time the total estimated value has gone up." She knew all this. What did she expect me to see that she didn't? Maybe she simply wanted confirmation of her own conclusions. "The burglars are getting bolder, more confident."

She massaged her temples. "This is the first time they've hit on consecutive days. The first time they've done any damage. The first time they've taken guns."

"Are the guns what's spooking you?"

She nodded. "I have a bad feeling about this. Phoenix, I'd like for you to put the foundation work on hold. We have to catch these burglars before they hurt someone."

FOUR

THE GRANDFATHER CLOCK'S chimes woke me from a dream of swooping up Hermione Hew and running with her out of a burning saloon. I threw back the flannel sheet to cool off and tried to reconstruct the dream. I couldn't recall why I was in a saloon with the four-year-old or why a horseman with a towel-covered head had tossed a Molotov cocktail through a window. Obviously my subconscious urged me to rescue the child even though nothing I'd read substantiated Beatrix's claim of a false confession.

Achilles had abandoned the grungy green blanket he slept on by my bed. I got up and looked across the hall. Annalynn's bed was made. I chose running shorts and a t-shirt and turned on the local radio station's seven o'clock news.

"Did the burglar take anything besides money?"

I recognized the reporter's voice as that of M. L. Moniteau, LPD officer Michael Moniteau's seventeen-year-old brother and an aspiring crime reporter.

"Guns," a boy said. "They broke the cabinet glass with a poker. We think the burglars wrapped them in a towel they stole from the toilet. That lady deputy with the Belgian shepherd went out back to look for a trail."

Scheisse! Anywhere I took Achilles people would assume we were tracking burglars.

M. L. said, "Police Chief Jim Falstaff would not

comment on how the burglars entered the home. We'll continue to follow this breaking story."

I turned off the radio and hurried downstairs.

Annalynn sat at the dining room table in her beige uniform with an open newspaper, a no-no in her father's household and in hers. That paper had to contain important news.

She looked up. "The Sunday paper had an article on volunteers coaching after-school football games, including a schedule of games." She turned the page. "And an announcement that Mrs. Lassiter was leading a discussion on modern wedding vows at her church Sunday afternoon. The burglar used the newspaper to choose victims." She closed the paper. "I made a pot of English breakfast tea."

I lifted the knitted blue cozy from the white china teapot and poured a cup. "Any newspaper connection to the earlier burglaries?"

"I don't think so. Those owners had run errands—the grocery store, a dental appointment, the beauty shop." She frowned. "The burglars are planning better. We'll ask the first three homeowners whether towels were taken. They may not have noticed that right away. Now, thanks to M. L.'s interview, any copycat will grab a towel."

The phone rang. I arched an eyebrow at Annalynn.

"Would you answer it, please? I'm probably not here."

I went to the kitchen phone. "Keyser residence."

"Good morning, Phoenix," said Vernon's slightly loud tenor voice. "How about joining me for waffles and French breakfast coffee during your morning run?"

He wanted info on the burglaries. Perfect. I'd slide in

questions on the fire. "Thanks, Vernon." Don't sound eager. "I'm sure you have no ulterior motive."

Annalynn waved frantically at me.

"Just a sec." I covered the receiver. "Breakfast with Vernon."

"Say yes. Ask to search the paper's archives for mentions of the victims and the items taken. Find out if he knows of any links between victims."

Perfect. I could research both cases at once. "Vernon, would eight fifteen be okay?"

"The coffee will be fresh, and the waffle batter ready to pour."

I hung up. "I'll run one of my regular routes today. Tonight let's map out routes on streets where homes are likely to appeal to the burglars. I'll start running those tomorrow."

I went upstairs to belt on the Glock and tie the sleeves of a light jacket around my waist to cover the weapon. I debated a moment before putting on my billed cap with rearview cameras. The boy's mention of Achilles and me on the radio had heightened my caution, or exacerbated my paranoia.

Opening the window, I whistled for Achilles. He raced from the orchard toward the front of the house. He loved our morning run, two miles for me and, I estimated, six for him. He grew restive if he didn't run off some of his abundant energy.

I called good-bye to Annalynn on my way out. I considered untying my jacket and putting it on against the morning chill, but I'd warm up in a couple of blocks.

Achilles sniffed his way along the row of evergreen trees bordering the lot's north side, alert for animal or human intruders. I paused at the sidewalk and checked the street while I stretched. I felt a little silly, but I'd had more people try to kill me during my five months back in my little hometown than I had in twenty-five years as a covert operative. Nothing moved on the quiet residential street. All the houses had been built before 1929, and half the residents had lived here at least thirty years.

Turning to my right to go past my small brick childhood home, I settled into an easy jog. In the tiny screen in the bill of my cap, my cameras showed me a dark SUV backing from a parking place at the end of the block. Rather than pull forward, it backed around the corner and out of sight. Not normal. "Achilles, come," I said softly. I positioned myself so I could watch the corner and pretended to check his collar. A motor accelerated, but the SUV didn't appear. I slid my jacket around to allow easy access to my Glock.

Achilles searched for the source of my unease with his eyes and nose.

"Stay alert," I said softly, stroking his back. "Let's go straight and see if that SUV reappears."

He trotted behind me until we reached the corner and crossed the street onto another quiet residential block. Then he darted in and out of the spacious yards I ran past.

When we were a half block from the next corner, a black SUV stopped on the cross street. That street had no stop sign. A hooded head, face invisible, turned toward Achilles. The driver's window was up. With no threat of being fired upon, I waved a greeting. The SUV leapt forward and raced down the street.

I ran full tilt in hopes of seeing the make and license number. By the time I reached the corner, the SUV had disappeared. I looked around, hoping someone else had seen the vehicle. I was alone.

Alarmed at my sudden sprint, Achilles pressed his shoulder against my left leg. He was shivering.

"It's okay, boy." For now. I stroked his head to reassure him. He shared my paranoia. Being dognapped and shot had taught him to beware of strangers, especially men, and to fear guns. "Let's go."

Achilles at my side, I picked up the pace. This block offered little protection from a drive-by shooter, so I turned right onto a block lined with trees. With no danger in sight and no squirrels chattering alarms, I thought about my possible stalker. Someone not trained in surveillance—the masses. Someone who knew I lived in the Carr castle and ran each morning—hundreds. Someone who hated or feared me—a couple of dozen? Nobody local would have the guts to face my Glock. No one from my dual careers as an undercover operative and a financial adviser in Eastern Europe hated me enough to wend their way to rural Missouri.

Who did that leave? Someone concerned about what I was working on right now. Did the burglars hear the radio broadcast and worry that Achilles and I would sniff them out? Hard to believe. My only other project was the Hew case. Had the real arsonist seen Beatrix's car in my drive and feared I would believe her story? A lot of people must know she claimed her daughter didn't set that fire. So farfetched that I dismissed the possibility. I couldn't think of another.

More likely, I'd overreacted. Maybe a homebuyer was checking out the neighborhood. Maybe a roofer was searching for clients. The driver had stared at Achilles. Maybe he wanted a good look at the only Belgian shepherd in the county.

Not reasonable explanations. I'd survived as an operative because I'd accepted the worst possibility as the most likely and guarded against it. I'd gone against my gut in the Istanbul spice bazaar and almost died. I had to assume that someone was stalking me. I'd watch for him, or her, in the block-square park where I could see in all directions and take cover.

Achilles spotted an abandoned Frisbee as we ran onto the grass and picked it up. I positioned myself between a large maple and a metal trash receptacle and played fetch with him for fifteen minutes, amusing a baby in a stroller and annoying the squirrels. The black SUV didn't show. Neither did anyone else except a grandmother with a toddler determined to ride Achilles. We retreated, Achilles ranging around me but never more than twenty feet away. I wished I could call Stuart in St. Louis for an objective reading on the incident, but my wannabe sweetheart had left Sunday to lead a week-long no-contact DEA training exercise.

When I turned onto the circular driveway leading to Vernon's blue Victorian, Achilles trotted ahead to scout the shrubs separating the property from the neighbors' yards.

Vernon waved from his table on the front porch. He watched Achilles a moment before closing his laptop, picking up an old thermos, and pouring coffee into delicate gold-rimmed white cups. He rapped on the window beside him, his signal to the housekeeper to put the waffles on.

Achilles completed his circuit and ran up the steps ahead of me to greet Vernon and lap water from a bowl.

Vernon wore green fleece pants and jacket. The collar of a white business shirt and a red bow tie showed above the jacket's zipper. He cocked his silver-haired head at me. "He's reconnoitering. What's wrong?"

Damn! The man was observant. "He's restless this morning." Divert him. "I heard you got scooped by a seventeen-year-old interviewing on a smart phone."

He grimaced. "I said a few choice words when I heard M. L.'s interview. Then I gave thanks that we're still producing real reporters, not just entertainers who spout uninformed opinions."

A car turned the nearby corner. I dropped my hand to my holster and raised it again as a navy sedan went by.

"Good God, Phoenix. Who's after you now? Should we go inside?"

"Relax." I picked up the pitcher and poured real cream in my coffee. "I'm being—alert." I told him about the black SUV, concluding, "Do you suppose my stalker is connected to the burglaries?"

He closed his eyes in thought for several seconds. "I doubt it, but I see a connection between our news items and the burglars' last two victims."

So he'd invited me over for a private chat about the burglaries. "Annalynn thinks so, too. She'd like your permission for me to check your archives—unofficially— for similar links to the three earlier burglaries."

He touched his laptop. "I searched last night. I found no mention of any of them in the last three months."

Damn. That destroyed my reason for needing access.

He leaned forward. "Phoenix, you have to catch these burglars fast. Unsolved cases will hurt Jim in the sheriff's race now and Annalynn in the House primary next summer."

"Really? Surely these penny-ante thefts will be forgotten months before the primary."

"Believe me, if Annalynn doesn't close these cases before she completes her appointment, they'll haunt her. Besides, the stolen guns increase the probability of violence. The thief can sell the Stevens crackshot .22 rifle and the Winchester 97 pump shotgun pretty easily, but that .44-40 Colt is so rare that Carmetti loads his own cartridges rather than buying ammunition. I'm afraid the burglar will carry it, break into an occupied home by mistake, and shoot someone. I suggest you forget the foundation until he's caught."

"The national odds against catching a burglar are roughly six to one. What do you expect *me* to do the police can't?"

"The same thing you always do—investigate on the sly. Use your unique analytical intelligence. Follow leads Annalynn can't."

The door opened, and the housekeeper came out with a tray bearing our breakfast. "Mornin', Phoenix. If you're cold, you tell this old coot to come inside." She put a plate of waffles covered with raspberries in front of me. "How's Rin-Tin-Tin today? I'm glad Annalynn finally put you two on the case."

I needed to stop that talk right now. "We'll leave this one to the LPD."

She winked at me. "Sure you will."

Scheisse! The whole town was watching every move I made. I resigned myself to that and asked Patty the expected question: "How's your husband's arthritis these days?"

"Bad. He's about ready to turn into one of them

Texas snowbirds." She finished emptying the tray and ambled back inside. She left the door open.

She had big ears. I sprang up to close the door. "So much for investigating on the sly." This was a covert operative's worst nightmare, but I'd never been outed in Eastern Europe. I returned to my seat and took a big bite of waffle and raspberries.

Vernon stroked his laptop. "After your last shootout, people decided you must be a retired federal marshal. Maybe you can use their expectations that you're after the burglar to hide your other investigation."

What? I finished chewing, swallowed, and took a sip of coffee. "That would be a great idea, if I were investigating anything."

He shook his head in mock sorrow. "Then you don't need access to my photos and notes on Jolene Hew's case."

That explained the application. "You sent Beatrix Hew to me."

He nodded and smiled, obviously pleased that I hadn't known. "I'm counting on you digging up information no one bothered to look for. Have you talked it over with Annalynn?"

"No, and I'm not going to unless I can verify Beatrix's story. And, yes, I would appreciate having access to your files, including the photos."

He opened the laptop. "I'll ask my daughter to assign you a password. She's a tough editor. She'll expect you to give us story leads in exchange for our help."

"You know damned well I won't agree to that."

He chuckled. "Worth a try. Take it easy, Phoenix. Enjoy your breakfast. I pulled you into the Hew situation. I'll help you any way I can with that and the burglaries."

The raspberries were delicious with the waffle. I took another bite. "What convinced you Jolene is innocent?"

"I'm not convinced, but the sheriff's department conducted a sloppy investigation. If she hadn't confessed, they'd have done a much better job. Annalynn's going to be crushed if you find Boom mishandled the case, but she won't allow a mistake to go uncorrected. Besides, if an opponent exposes a miscarriage of justice during the campaign, Annalynn will lose support."

"Jeez. Everything has become political. Is the threat to Annalynn's future campaign the real reason you sent Beatrix to me?"

"No, no! I suggested she approach you before that occurred to me." He pushed the laptop to one side and picked up his fork. "I've known Beatrix for years. She asked me for help right after Jolene confessed. I couldn't do a thing." He sighed. "Maybe I didn't try hard enough. The girl had a bad reputation, and the legal establishment was bragging about a just solution."

"What changed your mind?"

"Beatrix came to see me Sunday afternoon. She'd said she'd exhausted every possible resource." He shifted nervously in his chair. "She's a very together, disciplined woman. Sunday she verged on hysteria."

"So naturally you thought of me."

"Yes. For two reasons." He counted them off on his fingers. "First, you follow leads like an investigative reporter. Second, you care deeply about justice, and you don't equate it with the law." He held up a hand to forestall an insincere denial. "It's been more than a year, so the trail is cold. You're the only person I know capable of finding out what really happened at Bush-whacker's Den."

FIVE

VERNON'S ATTEMPT TO rope me in with flattery dismayed me. "Do you really expect me to fall for that 'only you can save her' garbage?"

"Yes. Because it's true. I know it. You know it." He ducked his head. "It galls me that I can't do it myself."

That I believed. "Then tell me where to start. What aroused your suspicions?"

"The lack of detail, especially about the fire," he said promptly. "The arson charge is what mandated a prison sentence, but the fire department never issued a public report." He stroked the laptop. "I got out there before the LFD firefighters went inside, before they knew about the body. I watched with a bunch of people from across the road. Somebody said Cork Klang probably started the fire himself for the insurance. Nobody laughed, nobody disagreed. You can't print that, but you don't forget it." He balanced raspberries on a square of waffle. "That's in my notes. I'll send you a password and links to all my notes this afternoon." He took his first bite of breakfast.

My phone buzzed twice, the signal Annalynn was calling. I excused myself. "Hi, Annalynn. Vernon and I are finishing breakfast."

"Would it be convenient for me to pick you up there in five minutes? The LPD just received a report of a vehicle stolen on the east side of town. I'm going to cruise along the city-county boundary line in case someone took it to use in a burglary."

"Okay. See you in five." I disconnected. No need to tip Vernon off about the theft. "Annalynn wants me to ask you what the owners of the burglarized houses have in common."

He shook his head. "Other than being past sixty and fairly well off, nothing that I can think of. Annalynn knows the first three better than I do."

I concentrated on the waffles. Manslaughter and arson interested me more than minor property crimes. Jim Falstaff, a competent and conscientious police chief, could handle burglaries better than Annalynn and I.

My phone buzzed. Annalynn again.

"Never mind," she said. "The owner found his SUV. The odometer shows four extra miles, and the spare key he'd taped under a fender is gone. He lives two blocks south of the high school. Probably some kid found the key and couldn't resist taking a joy ride."

I had a hunch. "Description, please."

"What? Oh. Vern's listening. A black 2007 Chevy Trailblazer. License plate W5L-6W2."

"See you at dinner." I disconnected and picked up my fork, debating whether to excuse myself and call her about my suspicion that the stolen black SUV had followed me. I could see Vernon's reportorial antenna waving. The call could wait. "Sorry for the interruption. She can't come by after all. Back to the Hews. I'm going out to Green Springs this morning to see the Bushwhacker's Den. It will help me interpret the reports and photos. I'd also like to talk to someone who suspected the Den's owner."

"I'm ashamed to admit that I don't know who they

were." He reflected a moment. "That may not matter. You're likely to find out more in casual conversations with whomever you come across than during formal appointments." He ran his hand over the closed laptop. "Beatrix spent three years raising grant money to renovate the defunct depot as a mixed-use community center. It opened right after the fire. I'd look for talkative people there."

I agreed on the value of an informal approach. Any stranger in Green Springs, especially one with a big dog, would be conspicuous. I'd leave Achilles at home.

Vernon opened his laptop and typed. "The town website says the Green Springs Depot is home to the C-h-e-w-Chew Café. It features daily lunch specials and take-home pies."

"I hope their pies are better than their puns. What kind of pie would you like?"

"Coconut meringue. I haven't had one since my wife died five years ago."

With our meeting and my breakfast finished, I jogged home, showered, dressed in jeans and a blue t-shirt, and went through the tunnel—a 1950s conversion of our storm cellars into a bomb shelter—connecting the basements of our houses. No phone or email messages demanded attention, so I went to Green Springs' simple but attractive website to find other likely places for initiating conversations on the fire. I skimmed the history: founded in 1851 by migrants from Kentucky, a center for southern sympathizers during the Civil War, a busy railroad junction and coal-mining center from the 1880s through the 1920s. The population peaked at 3,142 in 1910, double Laycock's population that year. The closing of the mines and subsequent cutbacks in rail traffic had doomed Green Springs. Its population had dropped to 1,624 in 1950 and 462 in 2000.

Those stats aroused the economist in me. Many rural towns had declined as small family farms became unviable and young people left for the cities. Laycock, the county seat, had grown to almost 10,000, a good-sized town in northern Missouri. The town faltered during the 1980s as its small factories and mom-and-pop businesses closed. The major new employer since 2000 was Laycock Community College.

I clicked on "Historic Depot Reopens." A photo showed Mayor Beatrix Hew and other dignitaries at the opening last year. I found the date in small type. The opening came a few days after the fire. Had Beatrix put the event ahead of her daughter's welfare? Typically a small-town mayor received no pay and little thanks. I wondered whether Beatrix shared Annalynn's commitment to public service or became mayor to satisfy ego. I clicked on the site's business link. A half dozen local businesses, including Bea for Beauty, popped up. I opened Quick Fix. It claimed to repair anything around the house. The owner's name caught my eye: Leo Klang, volunteer firefighter and, most likely, the brother of Den owner Cork. I had plenty of things that needed fixing before I could sell my house. I clicked on Chew-Chew Café. You had to order the pies a day in advance. Baker: Wanda Sue Klang. Surely Leo or Cork's wife. The Green Springs expedition held promise.

My cell rang. Connie. "Hi," I said. "I'm inviting you to lunch at the Chew-Chew Café in the historic Green Springs Depot. Did you learn anything more about Jolene Hew or the fire from Trudy?"

"No. She didn't want to talk about anything but the

burglaries. The one yesterday afternoon really upset people. Annalynn and Jim need our help."

Damn. I had to keep Connie out of that investigation without hurting her feelings. "They have officers working on the burglaries. You and I are the only ones investigating the Green Springs case. Let's focus on it."

"I, for one, can sing and dance at the same time. Besides, the girl has already been in prison more than a year. A few more weeks won't matter. Annalynn has little more than a month to wrap up the burglaries and leave with a perfect record."

"And she will." After decades of leading a double life, I was tired of glib lies, but I'd promised secrecy to Annalynn and to Beatrix. "I'm giving priority to manslaughter and arson."

"You never give priority to anything over Annalynn," Connie said skeptically. "Okay, smartass, keep me in the dark and do what you want, as usual. Your car or mine today?"

Great. She blamed me for shutting her out of the burglary investigation. "Let's take yours. I'll leave Achilles here."

"Okay. I'll email my contract to you now and pick you up in half an hour. We can discuss it in the car."

I went out the back door to make sure Achilles had plenty of water.

He usually came running the instant I stepped outside. Instead, tail wagging gently, he stared through the wire fence separating my yard from the neighbor's garden. He turned his head to acknowledge me and returned his gaze to a mangy brown mongrel chewing on a bone in the shade of one of the towering tomato plants.

I'd seen the pathetic animal there a few days ago.

Then, as now, it dragged itself away on arthritic haunches as soon as I approached the fence. When I'd asked my neighbor about the stray, he speculated that someone had dumped a dying animal rather than pay to have it put down. I knelt by Achilles and gave him a reassuring chest and shoulder rub before going back to download Connie's email.

The scope of Connie's duties and responsibilities in directing a musical production and the paucity of her pay as an adjunct faculty member appalled me. The rest of the contract dealt mostly with parking, LCC policies, and faculty conduct. Amid this boilerplate one paragraph stood out. It gave control of the choreography to the elfin dance instructor with whom Connie and I had tangled during *Oklahoma!* rehearsals.

Turning my mind from the disgusting exploitation of talent, I put my Glock in my leather handbag and went out to the end of my driveway to meet her. No cars were parked on the street. Three houses down a neighbor trimmed her roses.

Achilles raced up to me with a Frisbee in his mouth.

I sent it sailing across our driveways into Annalynn's front yard several times before Connie drove up in her yellow Beetle. Achilles dropped the Frisbee and ran to her car.

"Achilles, backyard," I ordered as I opened the door.

He whined and danced in place, begging to go with us.

"Sorry. Not this time. We'll be back soon. Backyard, please. Go watch the birds."

He tried one more whine, but gave up when I pointed toward Annalynn's spacious backyard.

"He's anxious today," Connie said. "Maybe we should take him."

I closed the car door. "No, if he's along, people will assume I'm on deputy duty."

She pulled out. "What did you think of the contract?"

"Awful. Only a fool would sign it."

Her expression didn't change, but her cheeks colored. I'd been too blunt. I backed off. "The college obviously doesn't understand the amount of work involved. You made directing look too easy." And she'd undervalued her own talent and expertise. I'd seen dozens of women, but few men, make that mistake. "Were the other two contracts this bad?"

"Yes, except for that bit giving the dance instructor the power of no. When LCC offered me *Annie Get Your Gun*, I was so happy to get a chance to direct that the pay didn't matter. They offered me *Oklahoma!* the day after *Annie Get Your Gun* closed. I signed the contract without thinking. Now that I've proved myself twice, I'd expected a raise."

"They won't give it to you unless you ask."

She smiled ruefully. "I'm afraid they won't give me the job if I ask for more money. I really want to do more shows, Phoenix. I love directing almost as much as performing. Directing makes all those years in summer stock and community theater worthwhile."

"I understand that, but you have to think like a businesswoman." Not a sucker. "You can't afford to work for half minimum wage. You'd actually lose money because of the engagements you wouldn't have time to do."

She gripped the steering wheel so tightly that her knuckles went white. "Tell me something I don't know,

Dr. Smith. Like how to persuade the Arts Department to pay me for two classes rather than one."

"You should ask for more than that. Remind them that LCC made a nice profit on the tickets and an even bigger one, I'd bet, by attracting new students."

"I hate negotiating. When I ask for more money, I feel like Oliver Twist holding out his bowl and begging for more."

"Asking for a fair wage isn't begging." Still, LCC might well say no. People here earned low salaries, and the old attitudes about paying women less than men lived on. "In my experience, you can't win in a contract negotiation unless you know what they're prepared to offer, and you're willing to walk if they won't offer what you want."

"The problem is, I have no place else to walk to."

True, and I couldn't provide an alternative. "By the same token, the college has no one else with your experience to recruit."

"I doubt that they care." She turned left onto Green Springs Road, a two-lane, blacktop strip. "Enough about the contract. What's our plan for today?"

"Use our memories of the Family Fish House to start people talking about what happened at Bushwhacker's Den. Vernon said some suspected Cork Klang started the fire for the insurance. We have to be careful not to tip people off that we're investigating. I also want to see the inside of the Den, try to figure out what the paper didn't report about the fire."

"How do we get in? Trudy says the Den never reopened. In a town that small, somebody's going to notice anyone fooling around the place."

"Let's keep it simple. We're curious about a burnt-out restaurant." And if no one was around, I'd unlock the door. "Maybe we'll be able to walk in."

By now we were driving past corn and soybeans ready for harvest and Holsteins grazing on close-cropped grass. A few of the trees near the shoulderless road showed flashes of autumn yellow. I leaned back to enjoy the late-September scenery.

"Phoenix, if Beatrix Hew told the truth about Wiler telling them to leave, Jolene didn't kill him."

I pictured Hermione's sweet face. I hoped her mother was innocent, but I doubted it. "Jolene might have hit him with a bottle before Beatrix got there. Head injuries don't always show up right away. Besides, why would the girl confess if she didn't whack him?"

Connie frowned. "Fear. Confusion. Fatigue. I Googled 'false confessions' last night. They happen a lot more than you'd think, especially with young people. Remember when four teenage boys confessed to a vicious 'wilding' attack on a jogger in Central Park in 1989? They denied it later, but they were convicted despite a lack of evidence. The real attacker confessed in 2002. DNA evidence proved he did it. The boys—young men—sued and won a huge settlement. I say we look into the possibility someone else killed the bodybuilder and set the fire."

I knew physical torture elicited many false confessions. I hadn't realized that modern police interrogations did the same. "We'll deal with how the bodybuilder died later. Our first step is to determine whether she set the fire. That's what turned self-defense into manslaughter. If she's guilty of arson, we drop it. If she's not, we'll persuade Annalynn to investigate the arson and the death."

We rounded a curve. A white doublewide trailer rested far back in a wide, well-kept yard. Right by the road on the next lot sat the filthy, forlorn Bushwhacker's Den. Blue tarps covered one end of the front roof. Tall weeds grew in scattered clumps amid the gravel of the empty parking lot, almost obscuring the phone number on a For Sale by Owner sign stenciled in red on a yard-square white board.

"Pull over," I said. "I'm going in."

SIX

Connie turned into the Den's small front parking lot. "The place is boarded up. We won't be able to see a thing."

"Maybe on the sides or the back." I pulled out my iPhone as I got out of the car and took a series of photos to record a panoramic view of the building. Two large overlapped blue tarps covered most of the front roof's left side. Plywood covered the doorframe and the eight front windows. The metal Confederate flag was gone.

"Funny." Connie said, "I could have sworn this place was brick. I remember the cook passing the plates through a window in a brick wall."

"The original building was brick." The smell of fish frying flooded back. "Dad said the Klangs built on to it." I headed around the left corner of the building. "Maybe we can get in through the kitchen." A double-headed faucet extended from the rear corner. "The volunteers, or at least Leo Klang, knew where to hook up to water. Maybe that's why they were able to keep the fire from spreading."

Connie peered in a filthy side window. "Empty, but what a mess! If we sneak in there, everyone will know it from the dirt on our clothes."

I shaded my eyes to peer through a relatively clean spot. "I see a couple of chair legs, but most of the debris

came from the ceiling. The worst of the fire must have
been in the roof."

"If Jolene set a fire to disguise how Wiler died, she
put the fuel in the wrong place." Connie stepped back
from the window. "I can't tell what's black from smoke
and what's charred. I'll get my flashlight."

"It won't help from out here." I needed to get inside
without Connie seeing me unlock the door. "Let's walk
down to the pond."

"I thought you—"

I put my finger to my lips and walked to the back of
the building. "The path is still here. We always fished
from the dock on the far side where the water was deep-
est." I whispered, "Go on to the pond and keep talking
in case whoever lives in that trailer behind the trees
heard us pull in and wonders where we are. I'll try the
back door."

Connie nodded. "We usually fished from the closest dock." She continued her monologue, projecting as
though on stage, as she walked down the path.

I hurried to the big metal door. The cement slab
where Mr. Klang had cleaned fish still stood by it. So
did a water faucet. So even with no water hydrants, the
volunteer firemen had three faucets for their hoses. The
big, old-fashioned keyhole stopped me for a moment,
but I soon tripped the lock. I opened the door, slipped
inside, and pulled out my powerful mini flashlight.

The empty kitchen was clean. Holes marked where
water and electrical connections had been. The smell
of rancid cooking oil mingled with the odor of burnt
wood. The tin ceiling and flaking white paint on the
brick walls showed smoke marks behind cobwebs, but
some of the dark streaks may have come from the years

of cooking. I studied the ceiling for signs the heat had melted the tin, but the square patterns appeared intact. So the fire started in the front and never reached the kitchen. Sweeping the light back and forth over the ceiling, I spotted a panel about two feet square near the inner wall to my right. If I had a ladder or tall stepladder, I could see the ceiling from above and the roof from below. Later perhaps.

A car slowed on the road outside, and I prepared to leave fast. The car went on by.

A swinging door led into the restaurant. I pushed it open but stayed in the doorway so I wouldn't leave footprints on the filthy floor. Keeping my flashlight beam low, I focused on the only relatively clean spot in the room—an eight-foot-long rectangle where the bar had been. I calculated where the newspaper photo had placed Wiler's body and directed the beam to that spot and then to the ceiling above it. Black but whole. I moved the beam across the floor to study a semicircular hole at least six feet away from the rectangle. The rough-edged semicircle was more than five feet wide at its longest edge and a yard wide at the broadest point.

I focused the flashlight on the ceiling above the hole in the floor. The fire had burned a much bigger oval hole overhead to the right, but the two barely overlapped. I moved the light back and forth across the ceiling. Near the front windows to my right, charred beams—eight by eight?—showed through. The plywood nailed over the windows obscured the damage to the front wall, but from what I could see, the wall appeared black, not burned. So the fire hadn't traveled up or down the wall to link floor and ceiling. I went over the same areas again, frustrated by my inability to interpret what I saw. Surely the arsonist had set two fires, one on the floor and one on the ceiling. How do you ignite a ceiling?

The door obscured part of the restaurant on my left even when I craned my neck. This side had suffered considerable smoke and water damage, but the ceiling and floor appeared whole. Streaks where people had walked or dragged away furniture marred a layer of muck—soot and water-soaked ashes? Perhaps the chemical foam and water sprayed on the fire explained the lack of gray ashes like those in my apartment's fireplace.

I took photos with my iPhone as a memory aid and hurried out. The back door wouldn't lock. I wiped off my fingerprints and sprinted down the narrow dirt path to the pond, where Connie was still talking.

She met me on the path. "You didn't get dirty. I'll take a look. Flashlight, please."

I handed my keychain over reluctantly. "Use a tissue on the door so you don't leave any prints. Stay in the kitchen, push open the swinging door, and peek in. One minute."

She nodded and ran up the path.

I ambled to the only dock remaining and looked down several feet at ugly green algae. It covered everything except the cattails. "Yuck! Not even a frog could live in this muck. I'll have to tell my brothers that our favorite fishing hole has turned into a bog."

Time to go. As I followed the path lined with thigh-high grass and weeds, I studied the back roof. The tarps came down over the ridge, but the back roof appeared undamaged.

Connie slipped through the back door and wiped the

part she'd touched with a tissue. "Two fires, for sure," she whispered. She pirouetted in her A-line, salmon-colored skirt. "Did I get any dirt on my clothes?"

"No. Now that we've seen *the pond*, let's go." Walking back to the car, I looked at the long-closed one-pump filling station next door. The dead grass and weeds surrounding it and flanking the Bushwhacker's Den could easily have caught fire. The volunteers may have worried more about keeping the fire from spreading than saving the Den. I thought aloud, "Leo Klang got here first. He probably went in the back door and sprayed from the kitchen. He wouldn't have seen the body lying next to the bar."

Connie walked backward toward her car, studying the building. "I can't visualize Jolene, drugged and beaten, walking back here to burn the place on the spur of the moment. How do you start a fire? Maybe the arsonist splashed liquor on the ceiling and the floor and lit it. You know, like you light brandy on a baked Alaska."

Was liquor a good accelerant? It burned fast. The accelerant in Molotov cocktails is gasoline or kerosene or some such, not vodka. "Ask your firefighting cousin."

"I will." She frowned. "If Jolene didn't set the fire, who did? The obvious suspect would be the owner. The police and the insurance company surely eliminated him. Somebody who really hated Wiler must have tried to burn the place down."

"No one knew he would be there after hours, let alone that he'd be dead."

"Maybe the arsonist also killed Wiler."

"You're guessing, Connie. We need facts."

She grinned. "And Phoenix, the Laycock Sherlock, is ready to dig to China to find them."

I ignored the gibe and replied with my own literary reference: "That pond isn't the only thing rotten in Green Springs." I intended to figure out what was.

SEVEN

Connie turned on the motor. "It's too early for lunch. Where to now?"

I glanced at the long, tree-filled yard across the road where Vernon had watched the fire. Through the leaves I could see a one-story white house. If whoever lived there had seen anything, Vernon would have quoted them in his article. "Leo Klang reached the fire first. I'll visit the Quick Fix, his business. It's on Robert E. Lee Avenue."

"That's the main street. My Diamante grandparents lived on Lee Avenue a year or two." Connie pulled out into the road. "My great-grandfather came here in nineteen oh three to work in the mines. My grandparents moved to Laycock to escape the mines."

We passed the filling station and an empty little blue house with a faded For Sale sign in the front window. In sharp contrast, a sparkling white sign with green calligraphy welcomed us to Historic Green Springs. Beyond the sign to our right, towering oaks shaded deep, well-kept lawns and substantial two-story frame houses, evidence that Green Springs had prospered a century ago. On our left, a rusting Quonset hut housed DIY Used Auto Parts. Beyond that were two overgrown empty lots.

The two-lane road had wide shoulders but no sidewalks or streetlights. Beatrix would have needed physical strength and determination to drag her daughter home. People find both when their loved ones are threatened.

I spotted a house number. "The Hews live two houses down. Pull over and I'll check her view of the Den."

Connie parked at the end of the neighboring driveway. "She owns a beautiful place."

A nicely landscaped lawn led the eye to a white, plantation-style home with two-story front columns. A child's red car sat under an aging dogwood near the long driveway. One would assume the house's owner could afford a good lawyer. I should check her claims of an empty bank account and a fatal illness. I hopped out and strolled to a crape myrtle in the neighbor's yard. Admiring the pink flowers, I looked toward the Den and saw nothing but trees and bushes. Disappointed, I got back in the car. "The vegetation blocked my view of the Den. Beatrix said she went outside to look when the fire siren went off. If she lies about little things, she'll lie about big ones."

Connie pulled out and turned left opposite the Hews' house. "Flames coming out of the roof would show through the trees, and the Den is closer to the street than any of the houses."

On the corner to my right stood a two-story brick building with giant windows. Etched in cement over the door was Green Springs High School. A wood sign by the door proclaimed it Green Springs Senior Center. That switch from serving youth to serving the aged pretty much summarized the town's recent history.

On our left stood a baseball diamond and a soccer field with a little wood concession stand and a line of pole lights between them. Behind the fields were three attached two-story brick commercial buildings. Over the door of the center one, a wood Quick Fix sign hung from an iron rod.

"There's the volunteer firefighter's shop. Just the man I need to ask about doing some work on my kitchen."

Connie parked across the street in front of Golden Oldies. "I'll check their vinyl collection. We'll see who finds out the most."

I swallowed a warning about being obvious. She'd shown a talent for leading people to divulge useful information. "The depot is only half a block away. Let's meet at the café."

"Break a leg," Connie said as we opened our doors.

Suppressing my annoyance that she treated clandestine interrogations as improv, I crossed the street. A bell rang when I opened the framed-glass door. No one moved behind the polished wood counter where a row of metal shelves bore red, blue, and green plastic bins. An easel on one end of the counter held a miniature blackboard with a chalked note: "Be with you in a minute." I peeked into a room to my right at a jumble of used bathtubs, sinks, and toilets. The tub closest to the door was an antique claw-foot model.

A man cleared his throat at the counter.

I turned and smiled at a short, muscular man in his late twenties. He wore his brown hair in a crew cut that would have looked old-fashioned on most civilians but suited his square-jawed face. "Hi. I need to update a bathroom from the eighties. Do you sell new fixtures?"

He didn't return my smile. "No, ma'am, but I install them."

"I'll keep that in mind." I approached the counter. He didn't appear hostile, but his grave face didn't welcome a potential customer. "My priority is my kitchen cabinets. They're beautiful old wood, but the doors don't open right. I hope all they need is rehanging with new hinges."

He stared at me several seconds. "I charge for mileage and travel time."

He'd recognized me. For the hundredth time, I cursed YouTube for making my face and my ever-ready gun known. I wondered whether Beatrix had told him she'd approached me. "Laycock isn't all that far." I extended my hand. "My name is Phoenix Smith. I'm preparing my late parents' house to go on the market."

He shook my hand but said nothing.

"Are you one of the Klangs whose family owned the Family Fish House?"

"Yes, my grandparents built it, and my parents ran it." His voice held no emotion.

"My brothers and I loved that place." I was getting nowhere. I had to substantiate my excuse for being here. I took out my iPhone. "I have some pictures of my cabinets." I pulled up the photos. "Perhaps you can tell what I need by looking at them."

He reached for the phone and thumbed through the pictures. "You definitely need new hinges. The cabinets may need remounting, too." His posture more relaxed, he handed the phone back to me. "I'm booked the next two weeks. I'll be in Laycock this afternoon. I could take a look and give you an estimate a little after five."

"Excellent. Thank you."

He looked out the front window. "That your yellow VW?"

"A friend's. Why?"

His face didn't change. "I heard it was parked at the Fish House."

Talk about instant messaging. "That's right. I was so sorry to see there'd been a fire. My friend and I walked down to the pond where we used to fish for our supper. The water was so clear then. What on earth happened to it?"

"The spring dried up."

"Is that why the Fish House closed?"

"Ask Cork. He owns it."

"Cork. Is he your brother or a cousin?"

"Brother." He crossed his arms over his chest.

Apparently some sibling tension. He'd called the place the Fish House, not Bushwhacker's Den. I needed to build some trust with this taciturn guy. "It's none of my business, but I'm really curious about what you're going to do with those old bathtubs."

"I'm restoring the hotel." He smiled, showing a fine set of white teeth. "Just in case the springs rise again on Robert E. Lee Avenue."

I laughed, surprised to discover a sense of humor and history lurked behind the solemn face. "How many springs were there?"

"Three big ones and a dozen or so little ones." He reached under the counter and handed me a spiral-bound calendar with a white cover and the same green calligraphy as the welcome sign. "We sell this historical calendar as a fundraiser for our volunteer fire department."

I opened it to January and saw an old black-and-white photo of a woman in a shawl and long skirt holding a wood bucket under a pipe protruding from a snow-covered bank. The caption read, "Greta Klang used an oaken bucket to carry water for cooking from a spring in 1905 or 1906."

"Interesting." I turned to February, a photo of miners, faces filthy, emerging from a tunnel. The caption said, "Immigrants from Italy worked in the coal mines from the 1880s until the largest mines closed in the 1920s." I stared at the faces, looking for any resemblance to Connie. I saw none, but she took after her mother's Swedish line rather her father's Italian ancestors.

I flipped on through, pausing at the May photo, the two-story stone-front Western Trails Hotel in 1912. "Is this the place you're restoring?"

"Yes." His brow furrowed and his jaw jutted.

I gathered he'd received disparaging comments about this undertaking. That gave me an opening. "A destination hotel could be a major economic asset to the town, the whole county."

His eyes widened in surprise. "That's what our mayor says."

"It's an ambitious project." High risk. "Are you receiving financial help from a state economic development program? Or grants from historic restoration groups?"

"Not yet. Mrs. Hew, the mayor, promised to help me with that."

But she hadn't, and now she couldn't. An opportunity to win him over. "I'm an economist. Let me know if you need some help pulling together figures and putting in the right jargon to make your case."

"Thanks. I'll tell her you volunteered."

I hadn't reeled him in yet, but he was nibbling at the bait. I leafed on through historic photos to December, the only color photo. Hermione Hew, riding a beautifully restored rocking horse, gazed straight into the camera, eyes and mouth round in wonder and delight. In the background was a Christmas tree decorated with antique ornaments. "A beautiful photo of a beautiful child," I said. "But how does it fit with the calendar's historic theme?"

"The nineteenth-century ornaments and rocking horse," Leo said defensively.

Hmm. A personal connection to the child? "Restoring it must have been a big job. Did you do it?"

"Yes. It belonged to Jolene's great-grandmother."

Not Hermione's great-great-grandmother or Beatrix's grandmother but Jolene's great-grandmother. Wrapped presents sat under the tree. "Did you take the picture?"

"Yes."

He had spent Christmas eve or morning with Hermione. He couldn't be her father, but he could be in love with Jolene. Enough to kill the man who had attacked her and to burn the building around the body? That would surely be first-degree murder and a prison term much longer than the one Jolene received. She might have taken the fall for him.

Facts, Phoenix, get the facts. But first build trust. "I'll take a calendar for my friend. Her great-grandfather worked in the mines." I found a ten. "See you this afternoon."

That gave me five hours to learn enough about Leo Klang to figure out whether to approach him as a likely suspect or as a nice guy who brought joy to a sad little girl.

EIGHT

COMING OUT OF Quick Fix onto the uneven sidewalk, I glanced around but saw no sign of Connie or anyone else on the street or in the long narrow park between Golden Oldies and the railroad tracks. The park had probably replaced warehouses.

I followed the sidewalk across the tracks to the hotel, brick on the sides, rough-cut limestone on the front. The stone looked like that of the Carr castle, Annalynn's ancestral home. Curtains covered the windows of the first-floor rooms, and a red geranium flourished on one sill. Someone—Leo?—lived there.

I turned to cross Robert E. Lee Avenue to the depot and recognized the same limestone on the depot's front and in little square towers on its front corners. How could I have forgotten the limestone glowing in the sun? Perhaps because it used to be dark with smoke and grime.

Big wood double doors, recessed some ten feet from the front wall, stood open. A shop with large glass windows and a glass side door stood on each side of the main entry. A green calligraphic sign identified the shop on my right as Bea for Beauty. To the left, matching calligraphy spelled out Chew-Chew Café.

I'd never gone inside the depot as a child. Passenger trains hadn't stopped here even then. I crossed the street and paused at the café's glass door. Connie wasn't there yet, so I walked into the depot. Sunlight poured through a row of high windows on the center left to light what had been a waiting room. Behind the brick wall separating the café from the waiting room, a male mannequin wearing a railroad cap and overalls posed at the ticket window. Above its head, a board announced destinations and prices in 1922. On my right, the favored green calligraphy proclaimed Knit Bits. The name fit, for the shop—now closed—was little bigger than the ticket office. The high-ceilinged building stretched back another forty feet. At the far end was a stage with a long conference table, five chairs, and a polished upright piano.

Connie waved to me and played an arpeggio. She moved toward the steps and began to sing "Hello, Dolly." She went into full stage mode, dancing up and down the four steps until she sang the final note.

Applause sounded behind me, and I looked back to see a half dozen women.

I felt a pat on my left arm.

Hermione Hew gazed up at me, an expectant smile on her lips and her bedraggled stuffed dog under her left arm.

I patted the dog's head. "Hi, *Liebchen*. Did you like the singing?"

She nodded and pivoted slowly, her eyes searching every corner of the room.

"Achilles couldn't come with me today."

Her lower lip trembled.

"I'll bring him the next time." Little kids live only in the present. I knelt beside her. "If you give me a hug, I'll hug him for you when I get home."

She nodded and put her dog-free arm around my neck. I hugged her and the dog for a moment and pulled back, concerned that contact would frighten the shy child.

She ran her hand through my short black hair several times. "You could use a trim."

Connie's trilling laugh startled the child. She ran toward her grandmother, who stood leaning against the back entrance to her shop. They both waved as Beatrix closed the door behind them.

The rest of Connie's audience disappeared into the café or out the front door.

"What a beautiful child," Connie said, projecting her voice to be heard inside the shops. "I'm ready for lunch," she whispered. "I hit pay dirt. I'll tell you later."

We went into the café. Two sixty-something, pleasant-faced women wearing bright floral blouses occupied one of the square wood-veneer tables. They both smiled and nodded a greeting.

At the far side of the room was a counter identical to the one in Leo's shop. A matching blackboard on an easel listed the day's menu: chicken vegetable soup, chili, cornbread, tossed salad, pie, iced tea, coffee.

"Cornbread!" Memories of the Family Fish House treat made me salivate.

A middle-aged woman wearing a chef's hat and green apron with a Wanda Sue label stepped from behind an old office partition. She forced a smile on her too-red lips. "What would you ladies like?"

From her age, I gathered the baker was Cork's wife, not Leo's. "Do you use the wonderful cornbread recipe Mrs. Klang made at the Family Fish House years ago? The one served with green onions?"

The fake smile disappeared. "No. I put onions and bacon in mine."

Bad start. "That sounds good. I'll have the vegetable soup, cornbread, and iced tea. What kind of pie do you have?"

"Cherry. With whipped cream or vanilla ice cream."

The woman's voice was so flat and uninflected that I wondered if she suffered from depression. Dark circles under her light-blue eyes indicated a lack of sleep.

"I'll decide about pie later." I stepped back to make room for Connie.

"The same for me," she said.

The woman scribbled on a scrap of paper. "On the same ticket?"

"Yes." She didn't move, so I pulled out my billfold. "How much is it?"

"Nine dollars."

She underpriced her products. I gave her a ten and waved away the change. Connie and I took a table.

The other two customers rose to pick up food. One stopped at our table. "Ms. Diamante, I'm Louise Tidwall, the music and activities director at the senior center. Your *Oklahoma!* was the best college musical production I've ever seen."

"Thank you." Connie shook her hand. "I was fortunate to have an outstanding voice as the lead."

The fan smiled. "Yes, and you made the most of her talent."

"Hear, hear," I said. The woman could be a source. "Would you care to join us?"

"Thanks, but I have to get back." Ignoring me, she handed Connie a card. "Please let me treat you to lunch the next time you come out this way. The mayor and I have been talking about applying for an arts grant to start a community choral group. I'd appreciate your advice." She hurried to the counter and left with a plastic bag.

I sighed. Another project Beatrix wouldn't live to bring to fruition.

Connie raised an eyebrow. "What's the matter with you? Can't stand not to be the center of attention?"

I overcame the temptation to tell her I'd spent years perfecting the art of being inconspicuous in Eastern Europe and tried, with less success, to do the same here. Wanda Sue spared me the need to answer by placing a tray with our food on the counter. She ducked back behind the partition.

I brought the tray to the table and unloaded our ample servings.

"We'll get zip from the arsonist's wife," Connie muttered.

Facts never interfered with her conclusions. "We'll see," I replied *sotto voce*. I broke off a corner of the lukewarm cornbread and tasted it. Good. It would have been better hot from the oven. I raised my voice to reach behind the partition: "This cornbread is delicious."

Connie winked at me. "The soup is good, too."

I took a few bites of the adequate soup and called, "Mrs. Klang?"

She stuck her head out. "You want some pie?"

"What I'd really love is a pan of your cornbread to take home."

She came to the counter. "I didn't make enough to sell you a whole pan. I have to keep most of it for my regulars." She furrowed her brow and counted on her fingers. "I can sell you five pieces."

What a terrible businesswoman. "I wouldn't want to make you run short. I'll settle for three pieces. Judging from your cornbread, your pies must be very good." For the first time, her frown disappeared. So she took pride in her pies. I played to that. "I have dinner guests coming. Could I buy a pie to take home?"

"Sorry. You have to order a day in advance." She studied her painfully short, radically red fingernails. "I do have a cherry pie in the freezer."

"Good. Please box that and the cornbread up for me." I stepped to the counter and handed her two tens, almost certainly an overpayment.

She gazed at the bills a moment and put them under the counter.

"Do you ever make coconut meringue pie?"

"Every Saturday morning." She smiled. "That's my specialty. I've won prizes at the fair for that pie. People buy them for Sunday dinner."

"Put me down for two, please. What do you charge for a coconut meringue pie? Fifteen?"

She ducked her head a moment before replying, "Two for twenty-five. You can pick them up any time between ten and two Saturday."

She desperately wanted the money but was afraid to cheat in an obvious way. Calculating I could pry information out of her if she thought she'd taken advantage of me, I handed her a hundred and said, "Sorry, I have nothing but fifties."

She covered the bill with her hand, licked her lips, handed me back a twenty and a five, and hurried behind the partition.

I rejoined Connie and dug into my soup and cornbread. I'd primed the pump, but I had no idea what Wanda Sue, the Den owner's wife, could tell me.

Connie muttered, "So far you have nothing to show for your money but calories."

"I will. Stay alert."

Wanda Sue brought a clear plastic grocery bag holding a foil-wrapped square of cornbread and a pie in a tinfoil plate covered with plastic wrap. She handed the bag to me. "What did that, umm, that little girl say to you?"

Connie laughed. "That she needed a trim, which she does. I guess the child was soliciting business for the beauty shop. Does her mother work there?"

Wanda Sue shook her head. "No, her grandmother. Beatrix won a national prize for her cuts. People come for miles."

A reason to talk to Beatrix. "Good. I'll make an appointment as we leave."

Wanda Sue leaned on the old wood kitchen chair at the next table. "Is that your yellow car down the street?"

"Mine," Connie said. "Why?"

Wanda Sue gazed out the window. "I heard you stopped at the Den this morning." She waited a few seconds and then went on. "Cork'd be glad to show you the place. I think he may be willing to drop the asking price—a little, just a little."

Score! I now had a great excuse not only for inspecting the crime scene but also for demanding to read the fire insurance company's report. I went into business mode. "How is the land zoned?"

She straightened. "It's outside the city limits. You can do anything with it you want. The town is really coming back. Since we restored the depot, three LCC faculty members have built new homes here. Beatrix, the mayor, has all sorts of plans."

Careful. No rational person would be eager to buy that property. "Please tell your husband I'd like to see a geological study of the springs. If the one that fed the pond can be reopened, I may consider investing."

Her hand on the chair closed and opened, closed and opened. "I'll tell Cork. He works in St. Jo, so he doesn't come home most nights. He may not have the study right at hand." She paused and licked her lips. "I'm sure there's one in the town records."

Clearly a fabrication. People who can't lie any better than that shouldn't try.

A double buzz sounded from my iPhone. Annalynn rarely called me at noon. Another burglary? "I have to take this call. Excuse me." I hurried toward the door.

"She invests mostly in Eastern European start-ups," Connie said as I opened the door. "She's been looking for something local."

Good follow-up. If she stopped there. She had a tendency to overdramatize. I answered the phone: "Hi. What's up?"

"Where in hell are you?"

My heart raced. Annalynn rarely swore. "A café in Green Springs. What's wrong?"

"Someone tried to kill Achilles."

NINE

I BREATHED DEEPLY to calm myself. "Annalynn, is Achilles hurt?"

"The vet says he's probably okay, but we won't be sure for another hour or so. He may have eaten some poisoned meat."

"I'll be right there." I jerked open the door and motioned to Connie to come. "Where are you?"

"At home. Phoenix, they tried to poison him in my backyard."

I heard Achilles bark at the sound of my name. It sounded like his "hello, I'm here" bark, not his "I'm scared and hurt" bark.

"I'll call you once we're in the car." I disconnected and said to Wanda Sue, "Sorry to rush off. A family emergency." I grabbed the grocery bag from Connie and ran for the car, sorry that I hadn't driven mine.

Connie followed right on my heels. "Is it Quintin or Ulysses?"

"Not my brothers. Achilles. I don't have the details yet." I reached the car and stuck my hand out for the keys.

"No way I'm letting you drive," Connie said. "My Bug wasn't designed for NASCAR racing."

I gave up and got in the passenger seat. Connie pulled out almost as fast as I would have. When I tried to call Annalynn. I couldn't get service. We were in a dead zone. We stayed there until we were a mile or so out of Green Springs. I dialed and turned up the volume so Connie could hear.

Annalynn answered on the first ring. "Achilles seems okay. He keeps running off and coming back with another Frisbee. He must have them stashed all over the house."

"What happened?"

"I'm not sure yet. An hour ago Mr. Thorpe called to say he came home and heard Achilles raising a fuss. I checked the camera and saw him running up and down the garden fence. I could see a dog thrashing around in the garden. I couldn't reach you, so I hurried home. We found that poor old stray dog dead." Her voice cracked.

Annalynn hadn't lost control even when her husband died. I waited for her to pull herself together and go on.

After a moment, she said matter-of-factly, "I assumed the stray died of natural causes, but Achilles went over by the hummingbird feeder and sat the way he does when he smells drugs." She took a deep breath. "He led me to three raw meatballs. The vet came right over. He thinks rat poison killed the stray. He said if Achilles ate even one, he'd—it would show up soon."

Connie pounded on the steering wheel. "I had a premonition that we should take him with us this morning."

I'd had more to go on than that. I'd seen a hooded driver watching Achilles. Ignoring my experience-honed instincts could have cost Achilles his life. My stomach lurched. I forced myself to focus. "Have you checked our security tapes?"

"That's what I'm doing now. The person didn't come onto our properties. I can't spot anyone in the gar-

den either, but I don't know how to zoom in the way
you do."

"Okay. Just play with Achilles. I'll be there in ten
minutes. Bye."

Connie stepped on the gas as we came out of a curve.
"I saw that guilty look. What's going on? What have
you done to put Achilles at risk?"

"I don't know." I'd have to tell Annalynn. I may as
well tell Connie. "This morning on our run, someone
followed us in a black SUV, probably a stolen one. I
dismissed it."

Connie digested this for a mile or so. "No one would
have followed you because of the Bushwhacker's Den
case. Nobody knows we're working on that. Who else
are you investigating?"

"No one." Unless you counted the burglars. "You
said you heard something in Golden Oldies."

"Cork and Wanda Sue Klang have been in financial
trouble for years. When his father died, Cork inherited
the restaurant. He hated fish, so he tried to run it as a
low-cost steakhouse. That went bust after a few months.
He couldn't find a job in Green Springs or Laycock, so
he went to work for his brother as a delivery driver in
St. Jo and came home on weekends. Wanda Sue and the
kids stayed here in his parents' home, which will be his
when his mother passes."

When would Connie reveal something relevant? I
reined in my impatience. "That must have been hard
on the whole family."

Connie chuckled. "Not hard enough. Wanda Sue refused to move to St. Jo. About two years ago Cork
moved back home. He tended bar at Harry's for a couple months. Somehow he got a loan to turn the restau-

rant into a roadhouse. He couldn't make a go of it, so he went back to St. Jo to work and opened the Den Friday and Saturday nights."

We rolled into Laycock. Time to get to the point. "Did you hear anything about the fire?"

"Cork was unlucky that the whole thing didn't burn down. People think he couldn't collect enough to repair the Den because he had the maximum deductible." She glanced at me. "Maybe a prospective buyer can get a look at the insurance policy."

"I'll insist on it."

"What's Annalynn going to say about your sudden interest in real estate?"

"With a little luck, she'll never know about it."

Connie smiled. "Trudy will serve as our early warning system. If she hears you're talking to the Klangs about buying the place, Annalynn soon will. What did you find out? Did brother Leo say anything about the fire?"

"No. He's the strong silent type. Getting anything out of him will take time. He's coming by at five to give me an estimate on fixing my cabinets. I'll work on him then." I reached into my bag for the calendar. "Here's a calendar for you that has a photo of Italian miners. It also has a picture Leo took of Hermione at Christmas. I'm ninety percent sure that he's in love with Jolene. Maybe he'll help make the case against his brother."

Connie turned onto Annalynn's street. "If he didn't help her when she was arrested, he's not likely to now. Neither will Cork's wife. She swore he never got out of bed that night."

"Even so, Leo and Wanda Sue may cough up details they didn't give the police and the fire investigator. If we have only the same information the authorities

had, we're not going to overturn Jolene's convictions."
I thought about it. "It will be a while before we know
whether to continue investigating."

"Bull. The only question is when we tell Annalynn."
Connie pulled into Annalynn's drive. "I'm giving les-
sons all afternoon. See you tonight."

I got out of the car and, a moment later, heard Achilles barking.

The front door opened, and he raced toward me with
his tail at full wag. I knelt to give him an ear rub as
Connie backed out and took off.

He sniffed at the sack, dismissed its contents as not
part of his diet, barked twice, and trotted toward Annalynn's backyard. When I didn't follow, he wheeled,
barked four times, and continued toward the back.

I followed at a jog. I knew that if I didn't, he'd grab
the tail of my top to pull me where he wanted me to go.

Annalynn came out the front door with her keys in
her hand and walked after us.

He led me toward the fence along the side of the
neighbor's garden, which ran about fifteen feet from
the hummingbird feeders. He stopped suddenly and
jumped back.

Bloody hell! The sprinklers used to water the tomatoes every evening came on. Had someone reset the
timer? The water could obscure the intruder's tracks
and scent.

Achilles shook the drops off and went back to the
fence.

I waited for the sprinkler to turn the other way and
joined him. The grass at the edge of the garden was
mashed down. The water hadn't washed away all the

vomit and other expulsions, but it hadn't left the crime scene pristine either.

Annalynn said something under her breath. Then, "I should have marked the garden as a crime scene and disconnected the sprinklers. I didn't want to alarm Mr. Thorpe."

Achilles turned his head toward her, apparently expecting her to give me the details of the stray's demise.

I stroked his head. "I understand. A poor old dog died in misery over there."

Achilles trotted toward the hummingbird feeder. He sat by a little yellow police marker with a one on it and waited for me to come.

"I bagged the meatballs so they can be tested," Annalynn said.

I squatted to examine the grass. No one but Achilles could have found the spot without the marker. We moved on to two other markers, both within five feet of the first.

Then Achilles headed for the fence again, this time with his nose outstretched. He moved along the fence toward the back of the yard and Annalynn's small orchard.

"He's trying to pick up the scent of whoever threw those poisoned meatballs," I said to Annalynn.

"Hey, there," Mr. Thorpe called, coming from behind a big lilac bush. He wore "going out" clothes, a long-sleeved white shirt and black slacks, and his white hair had been slicked down. "I called my bridge club to tell them I'd be late getting back to the tournament. A bunch came over to help me do a grid search. We found a footprint by the compost pile. I put a cardboard box over it to preserve it for you."

Scheisse! Multiple strangers had trampled all over the place. Achilles wouldn't be able to pick out the trespasser's scent, and that footprint could belong to one of the bridge players.

"Thank you," Annalynn said. "Please go on to your tournament. We'll process the footprint." She took out her iPhone and tapped a key. "Gillian, when you come to pick up the meatballs, bring whatever you use to take a cast of a footprint. It's under a cardboard box in Mr. Thorpe's garden."

Achilles barked to get our attention and crept along the fence. He whined and looked back at me and crept forward again.

"He's frustrated by all the scents," I guessed. I pulled up the app to turn off the invisible fence at the back of the orchard. "Let's check out the footprint and see if he can pick up the villain's scent."

We walked out to the sidewalk and then cut across Mr. Thorpe's side yard toward the garden.

Achilles ran back and forth in front of us, pausing momentarily here and there to sniff at a particularly promising scent.

When we reached the thick lilac bush, I stopped. Anyone throwing meatballs from here would be off camera. I saw no signs of anyone having stood there, and Achilles didn't show any interest. "It must be about thirty-five feet from here to where the meatballs landed. How could someone throw a meatball that far? Were they in one piece? Flat?"

"Roundish and whole. I think the burglar heard on the radio that I brought in Achilles to track her yesterday and wanted to prevent him from identifying her."

"I'm not so sure. The poisoner risked being seen.

Maybe the old dog was the target." If not, the poisoner knew way too much about my and our neighbor's schedule for my comfort. I went around the lilac and toward the cardboard box. "The sprinkler's spraying the other way. I'll lift up the box. You take a photo with your iPhone."

"Ready when you are."

I put down my grocery bag and picked up the box. "Good grief. Big Foot in sneakers."

"There goes my theory of the female burglar." Annalynn snapped several photos before the water pushed her to retreat. "Phoenix, who else would want to hurt Achilles?"

TEN

INSTINCTIVELY I REACHED down to stroke Achilles' head. "If I'd had any idea that someone wanted to kill him, I wouldn't have let him out of my sight."

"No, of course not." Annalynn hesitated. "But are you working on anything that you haven't mentioned?"

"Foundation applications. Nothing that involves Achilles." The stalking and the poisoning came before my visit to Green Springs. "I hate to admit it, but I ignored a warning sign. A black SUV pulled out of a parking place when we left on the morning run and showed up on a cross street a couple of blocks later. The driver stopped and turned his head to look at Achilles. I couldn't see the face or the vehicle's license. It could have been that stolen SUV."

Her jaw clenched. "Why didn't you tell me this morning?"

"Because Vernon was listening. Besides, I couldn't think of a reason for anyone to stalk us. I thought I was being paranoid."

A light flush crept up her neck. "Nonsense. You wouldn't have asked me to describe the stolen vehicle if you hadn't suspected something." Her pleasant, calm voice had moved up a note on the scale, bringing Achilles to attention. "I know you, Phoenix. You planned to check it out on your own and tell me nothing."

She'd described exactly what Connie and I were doing

on the Hew case, but not the stalking. I defended myself: "No, I planned to talk to you about it this afternoon— after the LPD did its thing."

She shook her finger at me. "You hesitated. You're holding something back."

The sprinkler turned the other way. Achilles barked and trotted back to the box.

"You know I wouldn't endanger Achilles." I hurried to lift the box for him. "Take a good whiff and remember it." He could remember scents, but I didn't know how long.

He put his nose close to the footprint and traced it inch by inch. He sneezed, growled deep in his throat, and circled the box with his nose to the ground. He crept back toward the lilac bush, moved back and forth over a three-foot area in front of it, and looked back at me. He frowned and moved his feet in place, an indication of frustration and puzzlement.

"Good boy. Good boy. That's where the person stood."

He trotted toward the street with his nose down, moving in a methodical criss-cross search pattern. About halfway to the street, he stopped, raised his head to look back at us, and then trotted toward Annalynn's yard.

"Damn. He can't follow the poisoner amid all those other scents. Besides, something about that footprint doesn't compute."

"Right. It's far too clear and too easy to find. Like someone put down a false scent."

"Yes." I thought about it. "You could pick up an old pair of shoes at a thrift shop and wear those. That would hide your scent, or at least mingle two scents. You also could spray something you had around the house on your shoes."

"Boom sometimes used a scent elimination spray when he went hunting." Annalynn watched Achilles go and then whirled around to face me. "Tell me *exactly* what happened this morning."

A neighbor paused on the sidewalk. I gave a slight nod toward the street. "Nothing more to tell. And we have an audience. Let's talk after we test our theory that the poisoner threw the meatballs from behind the lilac."

She put on her public face. "The only hamburger we have is frozen. We'll have to thaw it before we can turn it into meatballs."

"Of course. The meatballs were frozen. That's why the poisoner could throw them without their falling apart. That means the person rolled them out and froze them before the radio report this morning, so it wasn't the burglars." Who could it be? "Let's simulate the tosses. Achilles, bring me your tennis ball. Annalynn, do you want to throw or watch where the balls land?"

"You throw. Then we'll talk." She marched to the sidewalk and onto her own property.

Achilles brought me a grimy ball from the supply he stored in the orchard for impromptu games of fetch.

"Good boy. Bring me another ball."

He raced off, obviously delighted at this unexpected game. When he'd brought me four balls, all equally yucky, I ordered him to stay and called to Annalynn to be ready to mark where they landed. I positioned myself behind the lilac bush. I couldn't see the hummingbird feeder, Achilles' known hangout. I walked into Mr. Thorpe's garden until I could see the feeder. The cardboard box was about four feet ahead of me.

The poisoner hadn't needed to walk that far to see the target. He/she had walked on to reach bare dirt and create a clear print.

I gauged the distance to the feeder and went back behind the lilac bush. Anyone walking by could see me tossing the balls, so the poisoner probably didn't waste any time. I threw the first ball in a high arc over the lilac bush and then threw the others in rapid succession.

"The first three landed within a few feet of where the meatballs did," Annalynn called. "The last one hit a branch and fell into the garden. Theory proven. Let's go."

Achilles raced into the garden to retrieve the ball there.

I picked up my grocery bag with the pie and cornbread and strolled onto Annalynn's property. I needed a moment to think about how to respond to her inevitable questions about why I'd gone to Green Springs that morning. Annalynn and I had clashed about my need-to-know policy ever since I'd arrived in Laycock. She'd exacted a promise that I wouldn't lie to her. When possible, I kept that promise, but telling the literal truth could hide a lot. Having known me since birth, Annalynn could catch me in lies or evasions faster than anyone else. I'd keep my account of Green Springs short and vague but true.

She had disappeared when I came out of the orchard onto the lawn.

I heard a car pull into her driveway and headed toward it. A car door slammed, and a man's voice mingled with Annalynn's.

Achilles, the tennis ball in his mouth, joined me. As

we reached the garage, he dropped the ball and loped ahead.

LPD Officer Michael Moniteau, a pleased grin on his dark face, bent his lanky frame to reach for the paw Achilles offered. "Hey, there, Deputy Dawg." He straightened. "Good to see you again, Phoenix."

"Michael is working the auto theft," Annalynn said. "Please tell us about the vehicle following you this morning."

Michael took a small digital recorder from the pocket of his light-blue shirt.

I gave them a detailed account. Neither interrupted. I finished and waited.

Michael looked at Annalynn. "You think the stolen SUV and the stalking tie to the attempt to poison Achilles?"

"The timing suggests that. I'd like for you to show Phoenix the vehicle, please. She can fill you in on what we've found here. I'm going to wait for Gillian."

Good. That would give Annalynn time to calm down. "I'll take Achilles with me. Maybe he can pick up something from the SUV." I held out my grocery bag. "Would you mind putting dessert in the refrigerator?"

Annalynn took the bag. "Come straight back, please. We'll have tea and a chat."

I glanced at Michael, wondering whether he realized she'd delivered a command, not an invitation, a sign of how much the poisoning had upset her. The quickness of his move toward the car indicated he had.

Achilles had heard the tension in her voice, too. He licked Annalynn's hand and then glued himself to me, prepared to crowd into the front of the squad car with me.

I opened the back door. "Sorry, Achilles. You'll have to hold your nose and ride in the back seat."

Michael grinned. "Yeah, he's going to smell marijuana, meth, and a few other treats in the perp pad."

I took my place in the passenger seat. "Did you get any prints off the car? Find any witnesses?"

"*Nada*. The perp acted like a pro. A joy rider gets careless, leaves something behind." He backed out of the driveway. "Did anybody tail you after your run?"

"No. I kept an eye out for that."

"I—uh—I remember how that bank robber came after you." He cleared his throat and stared straight ahead. "I have to ask if you've scared some other criminal."

"Not that I know of. I'd think it was the burglar, but your little brother reported that Achilles was on the case just before I left on my run, too late to carry out the poisoning."

Michael's cheeks darkened. "M. L.'s report ran last night, too. I gave him heck, but he said he has the right to report the news." Michael clamped his mouth shut, apparently uncomfortable that he'd revealed personal information. "Fill me in on the poisoned meat."

By the time we reached the block where the SUV had been stolen, I'd told him what little we knew.

Michael pulled over and pointed across the street. "That's where the owner, Newton Nauber, found his vehicle. Right where he left it."

Water ran in the gutter. "And washed it." I stepped out of the squad car and opened the door for Achilles. "If that's not the SUV I saw, it's one very like it." We walked across the street toward the shiny vehicle.

Achilles began to circle the vehicle sniffing for

drugs. When he arrived at the driver's door, he sneezed three times.

I leaned close to the door and sniffed. "Even I can smell a cleaning compound of some sort. The owner cleaned it inside and out."

Michael's shoulders slumped. "Sorry. I shoulda told Newt not to touch it."

"Maybe he didn't. Maybe a family member took it and cleaned it to hide the evidence."

Michael shook his head. "I asked Newt about that first thing. He said his friends and family know they'd pay if they touched his ride. I doubt they'd cross this guy."

That didn't mean they didn't.

Michael shifted his feet. "He worked the night shift, so he's sleeping now. I'll come back later to knock on a few more doors and talk to him."

Good. "Meanwhile let's consider the possibility— the probability—that whoever stole the SUV tried to poison Achilles."

Michael stared at the vehicle and shook his head. "They'd have to buy the meat and the poison. Then they'd have to know they could steal this SUV and when, know where you live and when you run, and figure out how to get the poison to Achilles without being seen by someone or caught on your security cameras." He turned to me. "If somebody went to all that trouble, you got to be really careful."

ELEVEN

WHEN MICHAEL DROPPED me off at the Carr castle, Gillian's blue Yaris sat in Annalynn's driveway. Either a squad car had broken down or the rookie officer, the department's CSI tech, had come from home. I took Achilles inside with me so he wouldn't disrupt her work.

He trotted off when I settled down with my laptop in the old billiards room to study the tape from the security cameras. The giant television screen made the footage as grainy as my grandparents' home movies, but it allowed me to see even shadows. I ran the footage between ten thirty, when I left for Green Springs, and eleven thirty, when the neighbor called Annalynn. I scrolled through the motion-prompted views from my backyard camera. I stopped when the old dog shambled from among the tomato plants toward the fence and gobbled down something on the ground. I backed up the tape fifteen minutes to watch for any movement in Mr. Thorpe's garden or yard. At first I saw nothing other than the tall, dense tomato plants moving in the wind. Then, for no more than an instant, the top of a black hood appeared near the giant footprint. The only person wearing a hood with the temperature in the upper seventies had to be the poisoner and, I'd wager, my stalker.

Seconds later a small round object sailed from behind the lilac. Three more followed in rapid succession. I switched to another camera showing Annalynn's backyard camera's footage and watched three small spheres land.

Annalynn tapped on the French doors.

I let her in, ran the relevant footage for her, and concluded, "The stalker, the car thief, and the poisoner appear to be the same person."

"And most likely the burglar." She had curled up in her late husband's leather recliner to watch the footage. She rose. "For your own and Achilles' protection, you're both officially on duty until we find this person. Please don't go off on your own, and don't leave the house without your Kevlar vests."

Achilles hated wearing the vest even more than I did. "Someone who puts out poison isn't likely to shoot at us."

She frowned. "Can you give me statistics to prove that, Dr. Smith?"

The phone at her elbow rang. "Sheriff Keyser." She listened a moment and smiled. "My appointment ends in a few weeks. Then I'll work full time for the foundation." A long pause. "No, I can't take time off, but this is a great time for Phoenix to go to New York. Here she is." She held out the phone. "Reginald is calling from Vienna."

No way I could leave town now with an aggressive burglar in Laycock and a desperate woman in Green Springs. I took the phone. "*Grüss Gott*, Reg. How are you?"

Annalynn left the room.

"Quite chipper, thank you. Chloe and I saw a delightful new production of *Der Graf von Luxemburg*

Saturday night and thought of you. How are you faring in your musical wasteland?"

"I certainly miss hearing live music, especially now that the season's started."

"Yes, we greatly enjoyed *Lohengrin* two weeks ago. I didn't recognize that distinguished couple sitting in your plum seats."

"My seamstress and her husband." He was stalling. He wanted a big favor. "What's this about New York, Reg?"

"Hank Hollander of J & H has requested—nay, demanded—that you lead Adderly's two-day presentation—nine and ten October—on investing in Eastern European start-ups." He paused. "One of your old flames, my dear?"

"Hardly. I've never met him." Reg and the other men at Adderly had always speculated on my love life. Their gossip had given me cover for my out-of-town CIA missions. "I don't know anyone at J & H. They haven't been active in Eastern Europe."

"I know. It's a wonderful opportunity to build our North American client base." He talked on and on about how my former staff would prepare the proposal and how little work I'd need to do. He concluded, "As a bonus, I'll guarantee you orchestra seats at the Met."

"You know my weaknesses." A tempting offer. That probably meant a weak proposal. "Email me the draft of Adderly's proposal. I'll review it before I decide."

"*Danke, danke.* You will have the preliminary draft within two days. Amend it as you will." He cleared his throat. "We miss you, Phoenix. When you tire of playing peasant, you have a desk reserved in Vienna or New York."

"Thank you, Reg. Give my love to Chloe." I hung up

and used my iPhone to access the Met's website. Hmm. Britten and Bellini to choose from. I clicked through to see the featured singers as Annalynn came back in.

She sat beside me and peered over my shoulder. "You miss Vienna."

"Of course. It's a music lover's paradise."

"Phoenix, I know you'll never love Laycock the way I do." She attempted a smile. "You needn't stay here for me. Even if you can't go back to Vienna, you should reconsider taking that power position at the New York branch."

We'd traveled this ground before. "I don't want to go back to studying numbers half the day and explaining them in meetings the other half." I patted her knee. "Where but Laycock could I have the fun of tracking down criminals and working in a political campaign?"

She studied my face. "You're crazy enough to mean that. But I won't be sheriff much longer, and I may not win the primary, let alone the election. Then what will you do? You're already bored with the foundation's paperwork."

I told the simple truth: "I have no long-term plans. I'll decide my next move after the foundation's operational, your campaign's ended, and my house is ready to sell. A carpenter is coming to give me some estimates on repairing the kitchen cabinets this afternoon."

"Good. That should keep you out of trouble." She glanced at her watch. "Gillian and I are going to the last two houses burglarized for another check. If you don't mind, I'll take Achilles. Maybe he'll detect a scent like that giant shoe's."

"That's fine with me." Great, actually. I'd be free to get an account of the bodybuilder's death from his girlfriend and employer. "Achilles," I called, "bring Anna-lynn your leash."

He barked an acknowledgment. A few seconds later he trotted in with one end of the leather leash in his mouth, whirled the moment Annalynn took it, and darted off.

She listened a moment and smiled. "He's gone to get a drink for the road. Please put the vest on him while I pour myself some lemonade."

He always ran away when she tried to put the vest on him. I retrieved it from the closet under the stairs, took it into the kitchen, and dropped it over Achilles as he lapped water.

He jerked back.

"Stay." I knelt beside him and fastened the vest in place. "I'm sorry, but Annalynn says you have to wear this."

"You're the one who bought it for him," she pointed out. "He understands that wearing it signals he needs to be on the alert." She poured lemonade into her travel cup. "He'll feel safer if you go with us."

I considered a moment. She was worried about exposing him to danger. "No one will try anything when he's with two cops." I needed an excuse. "I promised Reg I'd look at a proposal."

"Okay. Come, Achilles." She walked out of the kitchen.

He looked up at me.

"Guard Annalynn," I said softly. A chill went through me as I remembered how casually I'd left him alone that morning. I reassured myself that no one could know he and Annalynn would be at those houses this afternoon.

I went back to my laptop and Googled Martina Pelben,

the victim's girlfriend. No Facebook page or any other social media connection. No website for Laycock Storage.
No listing on the Vandiver County Chamber of Commerce
site. I found a photo of her playing tennis at a local tournament eighteen months ago. No record of her competing
since Edwin Wiler's death.

I picked up the Vandiver County telephone directory.
Laycock Storage was in the listings but had no ad in the
business section. I flipped to the residential section. No
Pelbens. Not unusual for a young person to have only
cell service.

Almost three o'clock. Time to go. Hand on the doorknob, I remembered Annalynn's caution about the vest
and going out alone. I compromised. I put on the vest
under a long, loose camp shirt that covered my com-
panion, my Glock 27. I wanted Martina Pelben to see
me as a potential customer for Laycock Storage, not a
reserve deputy.

In my childhood, the old motor lodge had stood south
of the city limits on the east-west highway. The city had
annexed that land years ago in anticipation of attracting
a big-box store and fast-food franchises.

Ten minutes after I backed my Camry out of the garage, I pulled into Laycock Storage's shallow parking
lot. It ran along a row of fifteen-by-thirty cinder-block
cabins painted in a color-blind man's version of the
colors of the rainbow. The office building, in contrast,
wore a somber brown. All the cabins had been white
when I was little. They had intrigued me because they
looked like playhouses. I steered between two potholes
and parked to the right of the office door.

Someone moved behind the slatted blinds over the
window. As I approached the door, a lock clicked. Cus-

tomers must be rare. Not many businesses unlocked the
door only when a potential customer arrived.

I'd been wrong. The doorknob didn't turn. The person inside had locked the door. I pulled the rusty chain
on a little bell. It barely clanged. No response from inside. After a half minute, I knocked. Had I interrupted
a burglary? Surely no one would look for money here.
I could dismiss Connie's suspicion of Martina killing
Wiler for his life insurance.

I knocked again. Silence. Uneasy, I drew my Glock
and called, "Hello! Are you open? I'd like an estimate,
please."

A moment later, a woman called, "Just a minute. I'm
finishing a set."

A set of what? I slid my Glock back into the holster
but kept my hand on it as steps came toward the door.

The lock clicked, and the door opened a few inches.
A woman taller than Annalynn, who stood five nine,
looked down on me from an unlit interior and said nothing.

"Hello. I'm having some furniture shipped to Laycock and need to store it a few months. Could I please
see your facilities and your price list?"

"The units are full right now," she said in a breathy,
little-girl voice reminiscent of Marilyn Monroe playing
coquette. "Try that place over in Milan."

Not a typical response. "When will you have space
free?"

"Not until November."

I beamed at her. "That's fine. My things are coming
from Europe by ship."

"I can't show you around. The people who rent storage space have the only keys."

A blatant lie. I smiled sweetly. "Of course. You have to respect their privacy. Could you give me a copy of your price list, please?"

She hesitated a moment and then stepped away from the door. "Sure."

I slipped inside.

The room was dark and chilly, but she wore only a black tank top and running shorts. No perspiration showed on her face or body. Although thin to the point of gauntness, she had bulging calf and shoulder muscles. In the photo I'd seen, she'd worn her dark hair long. Now short and shaggy, her hair shouted all-day bed head.

She brushed past an old but high-quality exercise tower to go behind a battered ante-computer desk. The key boxes on the back wall held nothing but a few ads and coupons. She opened the top drawer of a dented four-drawer filing cabinet and extracted a piece of paper. "No room for your stuff in the castle?"

Apparently everyone in the county recognized me and knew I was staying with Annalynn. "No, and my parents' home now houses a new foundation to assist crime victims' families." I feigned ignorance of her loss to evoke a reaction when I said, "People don't realize how many lives a murder affects."

She handed me the sheet of paper and muttered, "Tell me about it."

"I beg your pardon?"

She pointed to something behind me.

I turned and saw two poster-sized photos, one of a teenage Martina serving a tennis ball and one of Edwin Wiler posing as a bodybuilder. Pay dirt. "A handsome man. Your husband?"

"He was my fiancé. The tramp killed him and then tried to cover it up with a fire." Her soft voice screeched and her hands curled into fists. "You know how much time she got? Six years! The damn bitch took him from me and she got six years!"

"I'm so sorry. You've been through hell." The woman was on the verge of hysteria. She obviously hadn't worked through the stages of grief over the last fifteen months. She badly needed counseling. Not in my skill set, but I had to respond in some way. "Could I get you some water? Brew some coffee?"

She unclenched her fists and ran long fingers through her wild hair. "I don't drink anything defiled with caffeine. It should be banned." She breathed deeply, exhaled, and breathed deeply again. "He was the greatest thing that ever happened to me. He didn't want that tramp, but she wouldn't let him alone. We woulda been married by now." She gritted her teeth. "My family said he was nothing but muscles, but he had lots of great ideas for fixing up this old place. You saw how he painted the cabins?"

"Yes, I noticed the cheerful colors." Give her more of what she wanted to hear. "He must have been a happy, creative person."

"Yeah. He could sing and play the guitar, too." Martina wiped her nose with the back of her hand. "Nobody saw his good qualities. Nobody loved him the way I did."

Unnerving. She'd repeated those two statements like mantras. To keep her talking, I said, "It must be terribly hard for you to stay here and run the business without him."

"You got that right. I'd go back to Springfield in a

minute if I could sell this place." She stared at the poster. "He never liked Laycock, but he came because he loved me." She slapped the counter. "That tramp ruined my life, and she got six years!"

She'd rewound to a regular refrain. I'd had enough of this personal snake pit. I moved toward the door. "My sympathy for your loss."

Outside, I contrasted Martina, the victim's girlfriend, and Beatrix, the accused's mother. The two grieving women had described the bodybuilder and the waitress completely differently. No surprise there. I'd have to judge the truth by the pictures others would draw for me, starting with Leo Klang.

TWELVE

THE WARM AFTERNOON sun felt good on my bare arms after the darkness—physical and psychological—in Martina Pelben's office/exercise room. I risked breathing in the ragweed by lowering the car window to enjoy fresh air.

Driving back to the castle, I couldn't get the young woman out of my mind. Her fiancé had died almost fifteen months ago, but her grieving process had stalled at stage two, anger. Hmm. Maybe she'd never really escaped stage one, denial. She certainly denied that Edwin Wiler attacked Jolene Hew.

Could Martina be right?

Four months ago, I'd thought Annalynn was in denial when she insisted her husband hadn't betrayed her with a younger woman. I'd supported my old friend to comfort her. She'd amazed me and everyone else by wangling an appointment as acting sheriff in order to access the evidence. Once she pinned on the star, she'd thrown herself—and me, and even Connie—into the job. In the last two months, she'd begun the steep ascent out of her grief-driven depression—stage four. She no longer focused only on getting through each day. Stage five, acceptance, appeared on the horizon.

Maybe not. Annalynn hid her emotions even from me. Perhaps I'd read too much into the fact she now slept rather than pacing half the night. The attempt to kill Achilles had revived grief and fear of her loved ones' being hurt. She'd be furious if she knew what I'd been doing today.

And I'd accomplished little. Nothing indicated anyone other than Jolene Hew killed the bodybuilder. On the other hand, nothing proved she had. Beatrix had been convincing when she insisted Wiler was on his feet when she and Jolene left the Den. As Connie had said, a small woman who'd been beaten wouldn't walk back to confront a large, muscular attacker.

I had to convince the close-mouthed Leo Klang to open up. He'd arrived first at the fire and could be protecting his brother—or himself. While Leo inspected my cabinets, I needed to figure out what he wanted and come up with a way to offer it to him. I'd done this hundreds of times in my double career. Almost always greed motivated my target. Leo was an ambitious, hungry entrepreneur. I'd hoped to delete bribery from my toolbox, but I would gladly invest a few thousand in his hotel renovation to obtain vital information.

A pain flashed beneath my right ribs. I pulled into the parking lot of a little strip mall and parked in the nearest space. A hot poker raked across my innards. Sweat drenched me. I closed my eyes and gripped the steering wheel. The poker singed me again. I gasped, clenched my teeth, and held my breath until I had to have air. Then the pain disappeared, leaving me weak and lightheaded. I hadn't had an attack this severe for two months, and nothing half this bad since I'd taken my last magic pill a month ago.

"Phoenix, are you okay?"

I opened my eyes. Trudy, the gossip queen, peered in my window. As usual her gray hair had frizzed into a fuzz ball and her blouse and lipstick proclaimed the glory of pink. "Just trying to remember what's on my shopping list."

She frowned. "From the looks of you, I'd say Percocet."

Bloody hell! She'd tell everyone in the county about my attack. I gave her the approximate truth. "No, I had a flash of pain. That's rare now. The surgeries left a lot of scars."

She reached in and patted my wrist. "Connie told me how weak you were when you came home. I'll walk you in. We'll see what Nell can do for you."

Walk me in where? I glanced up and saw Laycock Pharmacy and Medical Supplies. Trapped by kindness, I got out of the car on rubber legs. "Thanks." I'd have to direct the conversation to forestall her questions. "Connie and I went out to Green Springs for lunch. The woman who runs the café said Beatrix Hew gives outstanding haircuts. Have you heard that?"

"Oh, yes." Trudy grasped my elbow with one hand and her cane with the other. She'd not completely recovered from the broken leg she received in a hit-and-run aimed at me. "If Beatrix had a beauty shop here in Laycock, she'd be rich."

No businesswoman got rich in Laycock. "I don't remember any Hews in high school."

"Green Springs had its own school back then. The Hew boys were wild ones—drinking too much, driving too fast." She nodded to someone coming out of the pizza place. "Beatrix was an Olson, good God-fearing teetotalers. She was an only child. Her mother had polio before they got the vaccine. She couldn't bear another child."

Connie was right. You didn't have to ask Trudy what

you wanted to know. Just get her started and wait for it. "I understand Beatrix is the mayor now."

"And a right jim-dandy one, folks say. Too bad she and Annalynn aren't running the county." She hustled me through the door and let go of my arm so we could walk single file down an aisle full of canes, walkers, and portable potties to the pharmacy in the back. "Nell, Phoenix still hurts from that infection after her gall bladder operation. I found her gritting her teeth and sweating like a harvest hand out in the parking lot. Can you give her something?"

Nell, a pole-thin bottled blond about halfway between Trudy's age and mine, studied me. "What did your doctor prescribe?"

I reached for a pad and wrote it down so Trudy wouldn't know. "My prescriptions ran out in August. I didn't renew them."

"You'll have to call your doctor then. I'm pretty sure I don't have those in stock. I'll check my supplies." She stepped back to a computer.

"I gotta go pick up Tom," Trudy said. "You call me if you need help getting home."

"Thanks. I'll be fine." Asking her to keep a secret was like asking a bee not to buzz, but I had to try. "I'd rather Annalynn not hear about this. My doctor told me not to worry about an occasional pain, and I don't want her to."

Trudy pursed her lips, her reluctance clear. "You know, Phoenix, you really shouldn't keep things from her. It's good for her to know you need her as much as she needs you."

An insight I hadn't expected. "I'll think about that."

My legs solidified again as I waited on a folding chair

in front of the counter. I noted postings announcing that the pharmacy was a gun-free zone and restricted the sale of over-the-counter medications containing pseudoephedrine, a favorite ingredient of meth cookers.

Nell turned from the computer. "I don't have either medication on hand, but I have a weaker pain pill your doctor may approve."

I wanted those magic pills so much that it terrified me. Going off them had required considerable self-discipline. That's why I hadn't renewed my prescription. Better a few minutes of pain than days of temptation. I stalled. "My doctor won't be in his office this late in the day."

"Your color's much better now. You can get by another day." She scribbled the name of the medication on a card. "I don't encourage people to take pills they don't need, especially ones that are habit forming. I don't encourage them to suffer, either. You tell your doctor your symptoms and what I have in stock. He can call me."

I hadn't fooled her. She knew the magic pills scared me. "Thanks, Nell." I walked back to my car. As I started the motor, my cell rang. Quick Fix. "Hi, Leo."

"I can come by your house in twenty minutes."

"Good. See you then."

A little after four o'clock I put my car in the garage and went straight to my office to check for foundation voice mail and email.

Achilles barked at the front door.

I stepped into the hall as Annalynn opened the door to let Achilles rush to me.

She didn't come in. "We didn't find anything else at the burgled houses. Achilles was upset because he couldn't understand what I wanted. He needs your special attention."

I rubbed behind his ears. "He'll get it."

She started to close the door and hesitated. "Michael radioed that no one saw the car thief. He'll run with you tomorrow. We'll map out your running routes when I get home, which may not be until around nine."

When Annalynn closed the door, Achilles darted into her little-used office and emerged with a purple Frisbee.

To calm him, I accepted the disk and led him out the front door.

He tore around the side of the house.

"Achilles, come. We'll play here this time." I tossed the Frisbee high in the air toward Annalynn's lawn. His retrieval gave me a moment to dial Beatrix Hew.

"Bea for Beauty," said a young voice.

"This is Phoenix Smith. Could Beatrix give me a trim tomorrow morning?"

"I'll check." A muffled conversation.

Achilles ran up with the disk. I slung it as far as I could. A pain shot through me.

"Can you come at ten?"

"I'll be there," I choked out. "Thanks."

The pain vanished, but it persuaded me to call my doctor's office, describe the attacks, and give the nurse Nell's suggestion and phone number.

An old white Ram cargo van pulled into my driveway, and Leo Klang waved through his open window.

Achilles dropped the Frisbee he was delivering and whirled to face the intruder.

"It's okay, Achilles." I walked toward the van with him beside me. "Thanks for coming."

The young man stepped out of the van carrying an iPad and small tools on a modern carpenter's belt.

Achilles trotted to the left rear tire, sniffed, and continued around the van.

Leo frowned. "Drug check?"

Scheisse! Everybody knew about Achilles' nose for drugs. Maybe a druggie had tossed out that poison. "His idea, not mine. Come on in."

Achilles joined us, staying at my side as I led Leo through the dining/conference room into the outdated kitchen. "I'll replace the sink, the appliances, and the floor covering, but I want to keep the cabinets. My father and a friend built and installed them in the sixties."

Leo reached up and brushed a red oak door with his fingertips just the way Judge Carr, Annalynn's father, used to. "Nice wood." Leo opened the cabinet doors one by one and then the door under the sink.

Achilles moved forward to protect his toys.

Leo chuckled. "Your stash, big boy?" He shone a small flashlight on the pipes, stared a moment, and then stood back and played on the iPad. "You want a built-in dishwasher?"

"If it's feasible. Would one fit by the sink where the storage cabinet is?"

He nodded. "You want separate estimates for re-hinging the cabinet doors and for installing everything else?"

"Yes, please." Going over the estimates would give me a chance to start a conversation. "While you're doing the numbers, I'll make some lemonade. Have a seat at the conference table." Nothing like food and drink to prolong a conversation.

His shoulders and jaw muscles relaxed. "Thanks."

Hmm. He looked—relieved. The promise of lemonade rarely evoked that. He was booked up for the next two weeks, so he didn't need the work. He wanted an excuse to talk to me. About buying the old Fish House? About writing that grant to help restore his hotel? About Jolene? My spirits rose. Be casual, relaxed. Let him show his hand.

While he made notes in the conference room, I squeezed lemons with Mom's glass juicer, sweetened the juice in her pitcher, and added ice and water. I put glasses and my only food option, mixed nuts, on her Coca-Cola tray to carry to the conference table. Good grief! I'd just done exactly what Mom would have done. I put the tray on the table, handed a glass to Leo, and sat down across from him.

He gulped down half of a glass. "Thanks." He held up a screen showing two estimates for each task. "The top figures are labor with quality materials. The bottom figures are labor with adequate materials. I can email the numbers to you, if you like."

Not too high, not too low. "Yes, please." I gave him one of my email addresses.

He sent the email and brought up a sketch of pipes. "Here's how I could reconfigure the pipes for a dishwasher. If you want that, I'll do an exact measurement when I come to rehinge the cabinet doors. I can do a simulation so you can see exactly what you'll get."

A tech-savvy handyman. "Email that to me, too." I pushed the bowl of nuts toward him. "You're very efficient. Did you study business in college?"

"I took some business courses at State Fair Community College in Sedalia."

And Hermione Hew had been born in Sedalia. "Did you like the town?"

"Yes." He took a few nuts and jiggled them in his hand. "Wanda Sue told me you want to see a geological survey. There's lots of old ones from the mining days."

Okay, straight to the point. "Those aren't likely to tell me whether the spring that fed the pond can be reopened."

He tossed the nuts in his mouth and chewed. "Do you really want to know?"

So he suspected my comment to Wanda Sue was a ruse. Stick close to the truth. "Investing is my specialty. I assure you that your hotel, the restored depot, and anything else in that out-of-the-way town will appeal much more to investors if the springs can be rejuvenated."

He nodded. "I wrote to a professor at Rolla—used to be the School of Mines—asking for students to study the springs to see whether mining diverted the flow or the source dried up. Mom says our spring stopped in the nineties, after the Department of Natural Resources finished the clean-up work on the mines."

"What did the professor say?"

"He'd put it on his list of possible student projects. That's a polite no, I reckon." Leo took another long drink of lemonade and put his glass on the tray. "You went inside the restaurant."

"Yes." Honesty surprised, and disarmed, people. "It was too dark to see much." I poured him a refill to show I expected our conversation to continue.

He picked up and gripped the glass. "Mrs. Hew was all excited about you coming out today. She said you're going to clear Jolene."

So he'd come ready to talk. "I'm exploring the possibilities. I've found nothing yet to verify Beatrix's story."

He sagged like a rag doll.

"I'm talking to people who were there that night and may know something not in the police reports." I paused. "You're at the top of my list."

He held the cold glass against his cheek and his Adam's apple bobbed. "I can email my official report on the volunteers' response to the fire to you."

"Thanks, but I also would like to know what happened earlier. Were you at the Den that Saturday night?"

"Sure. I always went."

Always. I could think of one reason for that. "You went to keep an eye on Jolene."

He nodded and sipped the lemonade.

I couldn't let him remain silent or simply confirm the answers I fed him. Irritating people often elicited the truth. "You didn't want her leaving work with any jackass who flashed cash."

His mouth dropped open. "No! No! Jolene's not like that." He slammed the glass down on the table.

"Then why did you go there?"

He squirmed. "To look after her. I talked Cork into hiring her." His voice had tightened. "I thought she'd earn a little money, and she'd draw people to the place for karaoke. I didn't figure on Wiler—and a few other jerks—hitting on her and bragging about how they were gonna—you know."

A naïve guy. "Now we're getting somewhere. Leo, to help Jolene, I have to learn something the cops never bothered to investigate. I don't know what that may be, so you need to tell me even little things that don't seem important." I reached out and touched his hand. "Will you do that for Jolene? For Hermione?"

He nodded. And drew his hand back.

Okay. He didn't trust me. Smart. Start with easy questions and work up to the tough ones. "First, give me the big picture, what Jolene did at the Den, who came there, a typical night."

He nodded. "She and Cork went to work at six every Friday and Saturday, the only nights they were open. She'd prepare the baskets they used to serve French fries and onion rings and put vinegar and ketchup on the tables." He paused and sipped the lemonade. "On Saturday, she poured the oil they'd used in the deep fryers on Friday through cheesecloth."

Used cooking oil could fuel a fire. Maybe that's why he'd told me. I wouldn't push him on it yet. "What did Cork do?"

"Set up the bar, fix cheese sandwiches to go into two old toaster ovens. Jolene put them in to heat as people ordered them. She or Cork dunked frozen fries and rings in two fryers every half hour starting at seven. That's when they opened."

Odd hours. Late for supper here. "I take it no one came for the food."

"The early crowd, the high school kids, liked the fries and sandwiches. Some older people came to eat Wanda Sue's pies. The drinkers came later." He chewed on some nuts. "Two tables of card players came at seven and stayed until closing. People from the early and the late crowds played pool. Cork loves that pool table."

"Loves? It survived the fire?" I stroked Achilles. He was getting restless.

"Yeah. That, the bar, and a few tables and chairs.

Cork splurged on retardant cloths that protected the pool table and the bar. Sparks burned some holes, but neither one caught fire." He leaned forward to say earnestly, "I don't know who tried to burn the place, but it wasn't Jolene."

Bring suspicions out in the open: "Most people thought your brother did it."

"I was one of them." He shifted in his chair. "It'd be just like Cork to set a fire that wouldn't do more damage than his deductible. He was real upset when we found Wiler's body. Later I asked him outright if he set the fire." Leo's right hand gripped the glass. His left pressed against the table. "Cork denied it, but I didn't believe him. Wanda Sue can't lie worth a damn, so I asked her."

I'd seen that for myself, but she'd lie to protect her husband, the one whose income supported the family. "What did she say?"

"He didn't do it. She swears he never left their bed until I set off the siren. She woke him up. She's a real light sleeper." His hands relaxed. "Jolene finally told me, after she went to prison, that she didn't set the fire. I believe her. I can always tell when she's lying."

No use pursuing this. "Did Cork have any enemies?"

"No. He's a real likeable guy, the outgoing one in the family, a natural bartender."

Brothers didn't always know about enemies. I tried another tack. "Anyone unhappy about the way the bar operated? Serving drinks to teenagers? Letting people drive drunk? Losing money at cards or pool?"

He shook his head. "Cork was real careful."

I couldn't tell whether he was holding back, so I gave a little push. "The lack of other suspects makes Jolene's confession sound credible."

His left hand curled into a fist. "She was addled. Wiler drugged her." He struck the table, making our glasses jump. "Sorry. I don't know why the cops wouldn't believe Mrs. Hew. They confused and scared Jolene, and her stupid lawyer went along. He was real proud of himself."

He and Beatrix agreed on this. Move on. "Okay, but keep thinking about who had a motive to set the fire." He'd had more than a year to come up with a suspect. I had little hope he would now. "Tell me about the late crowd that night."

"The card players, four to six older guys, played Pitch and penny-ante poker. They sat in the back corner and nursed one or two drinks." He leaned back in his chair and stared at the ceiling. "Cork kept space free for karaoke and open mike on the side that burned. Jolene sang a song with the karaoke machine about eight thirty. She tried again a couple of times. No one wanted to pay to sing. Only the other local regulars, three men and two couples, were there until a little before ten. That's when open mike started. It was free."

What a contrast to the crowded tables at the Family Fish House. "Was the Den more a hobby than a business?"

A smile played at the corners of his mouth. "Not on purpose."

"It sounds like your big brother barely cleared enough to pay his electricity bill."

Leo grinned. "He used candles on the tables." He shifted in his chair. "Cork says a candle must have flared up and started the fire. That or a cigar ash."

"Is either one possible?"

"Ask the Laycock Fire Department."

I took that as a no. "Give me a rundown on what happened after ten."

He nodded and leaned forward, ready to talk. "First up was Cork's boy—he's in high school—and his country band, Quantrill's Raiders. Jolene"—his tone softened—"sang two songs with them." He frowned. "Tarzan and the Amazon—Wiler and his girlfriend— came in while Jolene was singing and joined a couple from Laycock. I don't know their names. The Amazon made a lot of noise pulling out her chair."

Rudeness or jealousy? Either would support what Beatrix had said about Wiler going after Jolene on previous occasions. "Were Tarzan and the Amazon regulars?"

"They'd come once or twice. He came by himself sometimes, usually pretty late. He played guitar and sang a couple of cowboy songs one night about a month before that. He stunk. A couple of guys got up and started playing pool during the second song. He stomped out."

Those crayon-color cabins flashed before my eyes. "His musical and artistic talents matched."

"Huh?" A nanosecond later Leo grinned. "Oh, you mean the way he painted Laycock Storage. Jolene laughed about that." He raised his arms in triumph. "You *are* investigating. You've been checking him out. Mrs. Hew said you'd find out the truth."

My snide comment had won him over. Take victory wherever you find it. "What else happened that night?"

Achilles whined and edged toward the hall. Hyperactive, he wanted to go outside to run. Apparently he no longer thought I required a guard.

But he did. I couldn't leave him outside alone, and I couldn't interrupt the interrogation. "Just a moment,

Schatzi." I stood up and refilled the lemonade glasses. "Achilles needs to go out. If you don't mind, we'll take our lemonade to the patio."

"Sure." Leo picked up his lemonade and tablet and followed me.

"Achilles enjoyed playing with Hermione. She's a sweet child." I unlocked the back door and then the reinforced storm door on the enclosed porch.

Achilles, a yellow Frisbee in his mouth, dashed across my yard into Annalynn's much bigger one and straight to the hummingbird feeders. He whirled around them a couple of times, dropped his Frisbee, and darted over to the garden fence. He stared a moment at the spot where the stray had died and then trotted along the fence with his head down.

Leo watched Achilles. "Hermione told me the nice woman with the black hair promised to come back with a dog big as a pony. If she hadn't gone on and on about your dog, I don't think Mrs. Hew would've told me she talked to you."

We walked over to the wrought-iron, glass-topped table on Annalynn's patio and sat facing the backyard.

Leo kept his eyes on Achilles. "Dogs and little kids are pretty good judges of people."

I doubted that. Dogs and kids liked people who gave them treats and attention. "What else happened during open mike?"

Leo edged his chair around to face me.

A good sign. No more avoiding eye contact.

"The kids and their families left. That pretty much emptied the place. Then two or three carloads of LCC students came with everything from maracas to a keyboard. Jolene checked their IDs and took their orders."

He paused. "I've gone over it in my mind so many times that I remember every minute. You want all this detail?"

"Yes." I accepted the Frisbee from Achilles and tossed it high for him to catch.

"Okay. Cork fixed the college kids a pitcher of his Sangria special."

I smiled. "I wouldn't have expected Sangria to be the special at the Bushwhacker's Den. What would Bloody Bill Anderson or William Quantrill think?"

Leo grinned. "Jesse James was too young to drink." He sobered. "Cork uses a cheap red wine and adds frozen raspberries and lemon wedges. Then he dumps in two shots of vodka to give it a kick." He sipped his lemonade. "Cork dropped a pitcher on the floor right about where the fire burned all the way through. Jolene cleaned it up."

I visualized the gaping hole a few feet from the bar. "The Sangria added fuel to the fire."

"Maybe, but alcohol burns real quick. You need more heat than that to reach kindling temperature for wood."

Then Connie's theory of fueling the fire with booze didn't hold water. "The students took over the open mike?" I tossed the Frisbee again, taking care not to twist and waken the beast beneath my ribs.

"No, Tarzan had dibs on ten thirty. He got up with his guitar and introduced himself as a champion body-builder who loved to sing. The LCC crew kept quiet while he sang 'Country Roads,' but when he started another song, they ignored him. You could see he was mad. He asked Jolene to come sing with him, but she skipped off into the kitchen. The Amazon yelled for people to be quiet, but that just made things worse. Tarzan sang one more song and gave up. He and the Amazon stormed out a few minutes before eleven."

"And the couple who shared their table?"

"They didn't leave until later. I don't remember when. I left right before midnight. The only people hanging around by then were the card players." He gritted his teeth and clenched and unclenched his fists. "Wiler strolled in with his guitar five minutes after I left. He ordered a vodka at the bar and talked about getting ready for some competition. Everybody else left. Jolene sang 'Jolene' with him while she cleaned the tables. Cork loaded most of the leftover beer into his pickup to store at home—he did that every week—and then ran Wiler out. That was a little before one." Leo jumped up out of his chair and walked away from me. He stopped a few yards away, his back to me. "If I'd had any idea Wiler would come back…"

I held my breath. Leo definitely could have committed a crime of passion.

He swung around. "You need to know something, but you gotta promise you won't tell Mrs. Hew."

If Leo had attacked Wiler, I couldn't possibly keep that a secret. What else could he be hiding? "I won't tell Beatrix. What is it?"

"Jolene and I had a fight that afternoon over her working there. Mrs. Hew didn't want Jolene to take the job in the first place, didn't want her to be around all that temptation, the drinking and—stuff. I told Jolene that people were saying things that Hermione shouldn't hear." He cleared his throat. "Jolene got real mad. She said she was sick of hearing that self-righteous talk from her dad. She told me to butt out, to keep away from her and stop playing daddy to Hermione." His voice had fallen to barely above a whisper, and his face had reddened.

I knew the anguish of a one-sided romance. "You left the Den early because of the argument?"

"No, well, yeah." He stared at his feet. "The thing is, I came back about one fifteen to apologize and to walk Jolene home, like I usually did. The lights were off, but I heard his guitar and her singing and saw the glow of candles. I looked through a window. They were sitting at a table near the bar. She had a glass of beer and he had a drink in a shot glass. The vodka bottle sat between two candles." He cleared his throat.

Was he working up to a confession? I let the silence drag on.

He rubbed his eyes with the heel of his hands. "I walked away. I watched her take a sip of beer, and I walked away."

THIRTEEN

MY FIRST IMPULSE was to comfort Leo. "What happened wasn't your fault. You had no way of knowing Wiler would attack her."

He cleared his throat again. "I knew he was a braggart and a bully. I knew he flirted with Jolene right in front of his girlfriend. If I'd gone in there, Jolene wouldn't be in prison."

No, but Wiler might have beaten Leo to death with or without Jolene's blessing. "Leo, think a minute. Why didn't you go in?"

"My pride. My damned pride. I thought if she'd rather hang out and drink with that garbage…" He trailed off. "And I was mad. I knew Hermione would wake up expecting her mother to sing to her."

Achilles trotted up to Leo and nudged his hand with the Frisbee.

Leo jumped. A bitter smile crossed his lips. "Dogs and kids love me." He hurled the Frisbee in a high arc all the way to the orchard.

Achilles raced after it.

"Don't undervalue that love," I said. Now back to business. "What did Jolene tell you happened after closing?"

"She won't talk to me about it, or to her mother either. Jolene won't even approve a visitor's pass for her mother. I drive Mrs. Olson—Jolene's grandmother—and Hermione over to the state prison in Chillicothe most Sunday afternoons."

That must be more than an hour's drive each way. "Do *you* get a visitor's pass?"

"Only for the last fifteen minutes. I have to carry Hermione out every time."

I'd heard nothing positive about the prisoner except the child's attachment to her. "Tell me about Jolene."

Achilles raced back to Leo, who obligingly sailed the disk into the orchard.

He paced the edge of the patio. "I've known her since she was two. That's when her family moved in with her grandmother. I didn't know it at the time, but J. J. Hew had lost his job. Jolene's brother, Olson, was in my second grade class. I spent a lot of time at their house up into high school. I thought of Jolene as a cute but pesky little sister. If she wasn't the center of attention, she'd throw a fit." He paused to throw the Frisbee again. "She adored her dad. He always sang her to sleep. He spoiled her. We overheard him and Mrs. Hew arguing about the way he let Jolene get away with stuff." He stopped. "You really want to hear this?"

"Yes. Go ahead." Past family relationships would determine who took care of Hermione if Beatrix died before Jolene got out of prison.

He resumed pacing. "Jolene was a good student, popular. She and Olson sang at their church and community events. Her voice is pretty but kinda light. Their dad always made Olson hold back so people could hear her."

Apparently Jolene drew attention more for her looks and personality than her voice. I tried to move the narrative along: "Why did she leave home the day she graduated?"

"To get away from her mother. The Hews' divorce threw Jolene for a loop. She thought her mother made J. J. leave the house because he couldn't find a decent job."

A different view of Beatrix. "Is that what happened?"

"Not according to my mother. She says Mrs. Hew put up with a lot for years. She pretty much supported the family with a beauty shop in their garage. Mom was getting a cut one afternoon when J. J. came in drunk and yelled at Mrs. Hew for running out of beer. When he left, Mom and another neighbor helped Mrs. Hew pack up his stuff and put it out on the front porch."

I couldn't help but smile. "Good for them."

The corners of his lips lifted a moment. "Yeah, but not for Jolene. Her dad moved into a room in Laycock, and she hardly ever saw him. She messed up to get his attention, and to piss off her mother. Jolene got suspended her junior year for spiking the punch at a school dance. Little stuff like that. Nothing really major, at least in most families."

"When did you stop seeing her as a little sister?"

"After my dad died and I came home from Sedalia to start Quick Fix. She'd come by the shop and hang out after school instead of going home. She turned from a cute kid into a beautiful woman overnight." He grimaced. "She still sees me as an older brother."

But she had an older brother. "What does Olson think of her situation?"

Leo tossed the Frisbee high in the air. "He hasn't had anything to do with her since she came home with a black baby. He's a choir director and youth pastor at a church down in Arkansas. Mrs. Olson says he's afraid the congregation will judge him by his sister."

That eliminated the logical home for Hermione. "Is Jolene still daddy's darling?"

"Hell, no!" Leo's face reddened again. "One day I found her crying. She told me she'd gone to her dad's place to show him his grandchild. The bastard took one look at Hermione and pushed them out the door. He said only the cheapest whores slept with coloreds."

The openness and kindness of my native state had eased my homecoming, but its flip side of narrowness and intolerance alarmed and depressed me. Dreading the answer, I asked, "Did Beatrix welcome Jolene and the baby?"

"She wasn't celebrating, but she didn't think twice about taking them in. She and Jolene argued lots, but never in front of Hermione. Mrs. Olson acted as a peacemaker. You should talk to her. I'm pretty sure Jolene told her grandmother everything that happened that night." He looked at his watch. "I gotta go."

"Anything I should look for in your report on the fire?"

He shook his head. "It won't tell you much that's not in the newspaper. The official LFD report will tell you much more than I can. Thanks for helping us." He strode toward his van.

Achilles trotted after him with the Frisbee in his mouth, disappearing behind my garage for a few seconds and then loping back to me as the van's motor started.

"You're a sweet dog," I told him, a shiver running down my spine as I thought of the poisoned meatballs. After stroking his back and rubbing behind his ears, I headed back inside.

My cell rang. Connie. I answered.

"How's Achilles?"

"He's fine. Annalynn won't be cooking. She's working late."

"Darn. I'm too tired to cook. Let's go to Harry's Hideaway for a burger. I have an incredible story about Jolene and her father to tell you."

"Harry huffs and puffs every time I walk in."

"That's because you're either investigating or arresting one of his patrons. This is the ideal time to go there. He's away visiting family."

The mesquite-grilled burgers were delicious. "Okay. I'll pick you up at six thirty. Bye."

In the house, I went to the supply room and took out a new toy for Achilles, a basket mounted three-quarters of the way up a six-foot pole. I'd bought the game for winter use, but it would keep him occupied inside now that I didn't dare leave him outside alone. I dragged it into the hall near the back door. Then I took the Frisbee from Achilles, walked down the hall, called out "basket," and tossed the disk. It hit the basket rim and dropped onto the floor. On my third toss, it went in. I scored with another throw. When Achilles brought the disk to me this time, I didn't take it from him. Instead I led him down the hall and said, "Basket, Achilles."

He didn't get it.

"Jump, Achilles. Basket. Please."

He stared up at me.

I took the Frisbee from his mouth and dropped it in the basket. "Basket."

When he picked it up, I said, "Achilles, basket, please."

He frowned at my use of an unknown command. I lifted his front shoulders until the Frisbee was on the rim. A pain shot through me. I dropped him and leaned against the wall.

He whined and pressed against me.

I forced myself to stand straight. "I'm okay. You play while I sit in my office."

He followed me into the office, put his feet up on my desk, and knocked the receiver off the telephone with his nose. He barked a command.

I replaced the receiver.

He batted at the receiver with his paw.

"You want me to call Annalynn, don't you?" I picked up the receiver and put my finger on the button. The phone rang. Her cell came up on the caller ID. "Hi, Annalynn."

Achilles barked twice.

"He's upset. What's wrong?"

She'd recognize a lie. "I had one of those pains a little bit ago." Divert her attention with his cleverness. "Achilles knocked the receiver off the phone and demanded I call you."

"Oh, Phoenix, I'm so sorry." She paused a moment. "You call a doctor or I will."

"I already did. Tomorrow I pick up a new prescription."

"Thank goodness. I called to schedule a morning run at six forty-five, but I'm going to cancel it instead."

"No need. I brought on the pain by lifting Achilles to teach him a new trick." But I hadn't lifted anything the first two times. "I'll take it easy tonight. Really."

"Okay. Did Vernon give you access to the newspaper archives?"

I turned on the monitor and opened my local email. "Yes, but I haven't had a chance to explore yet. I have a message from Reg to answer, too."

"If you're not feeling better by the time I'm home, you're off the case. Bye."

Then I had to be—or seem—all well tonight. I opened Reg's email. He'd sent me Gunther's proposal outline. I skimmed it, becoming more and more irritated with each Roman numeral. I sent Reg an uncensored email: "This almost put me to sleep. Adderly has to propose a great new start-up. If Gunther can't profile an exciting project in Hungary (remind him to look beyond Budapest), find an innovator in Rumania or Bulgaria."

I moved on to the next problem. Vernon had sent me a list of pages to visit and a ten-digit password. I memorized it and logged in. I soon saw that neither his notes nor his photos yielded useful new information. Disappointed, I switched to the burglary case, searching for victims' names over the last six months. No hits. I'd have to refine my search. I logged out.

The sound of the ball bouncing in the hall had become increasingly irritating. I should have learned my lesson about noisy toys when I gave my nephews and nieces drums and flutes.

An email from Leo popped up. I opened it and read, "I've attached the estimates and my report on the fire."

I saved the attachments, opened the one on the fire, and found a time line from the 9-1-1 call until the arrival of the county's fire crew. Damn! Nothing on finding the body. I printed the report to share with Connie and studied the last paragraph, "Suspicious Items Noted After the Fire." The list was short: an old metal flashlight and fragments of a broken vodka bottle near the bar and two big metal ashtrays in the hole in the floor. Another disappointment.

A question surfaced from my subconscious. I wrote

Leo, "Thanks. Was the retardant cloth covering the bar at 1:15?"

He replied, "I think so. It was there when we found the body."

He didn't *know*. What did I expect so long after the event? But I needed to be sure. The bar, which looked like a relic of the Wild West, had been the most valuable thing in the Den. Both the floor and ceiling fires had been set far enough away that neither it nor the pool table burned. If I could pin down when the bar had been covered, I might determine whether Jolene Hew set the fire.

FOURTEEN

A DOZEN HEADS swiveled to watch but no one protested as I led deputy dog through the double glass doors of the old garage converted into Harry's Hideaway. For once no one played pool at the three tables that rested on the original car lifts. Tuesday was a slow night.

"Let's take a table by the bar," Connie suggested. "I'll have enough light to read Leo's report." She headed toward the front, waving at the LCC student who had sung in the *Oklahoma!* chorus and now worked as a part-time bartender.

He waved back and beamed.

Achilles went on full alert, his nose in the air and his eyes moving from patron to patron. The only time he'd been here before, Annalynn and I had arrested three punks at gunpoint.

When I took a chair facing the door, Achilles continued to face the bar. His tail twitched in excitement, doubtless at the odor of hamburgers emanating from the kitchen.

"I'm not sure this is a good idea," I muttered to Connie. "He loves hamburger."

"You never eat the whole thing. Give him half of yours. Heck, you can afford to order him his own."

"I fed him at home. I don't want him to expect to eat whenever he smells food."

"Relax. You know he won't take food from a stranger."

She pushed back her chair. "Since you're treating, I'll order. Want one of their German beers with your burger?"

I handed her a twenty. "Water is fine, thanks."

On the way to Harry's, I'd summarized what Leo had told me. When she returned carrying a small bowl of French fries, I said, "We have to talk to Raleigh."

She dipped a fry in a little paper cup of tartar sauce. "First, give me Leo's details."

A disquieting imitation of me. I decided to set an example of being brief but complete.

"Four twenty—Leo received the call and notified the Green Springs volunteers.

"Four twenty-eight—Leo arrived, put on protective clothing, and entered through the kitchen door. He went through the swinging door and sprayed foam from a portable fire extinguisher."

Connie pursed her lips. "I need *relevant* facts."

"Very funny. Here's a fact for you. Leo saw two fires, one on the floor and one overhead." I went back to the timeline. "Four thirty—two other volunteers arrived, gave Leo their fire extinguishers, hooked up hoses, and sprayed water on the roof.

"Four thirty-five—Cork, who had no protective gear, pulled Leo out of the building in fear the roof would cave in."

She dipped another fry into the sauce. "The brothers may not get along, but they took care of each other. Doesn't it seem odd to you that neither one saw the body?"

I tried to imagine the scene. "No. The smoke and foam and steam from the water hitting hot surfaces would have been dense by then." I went back to the report. "Four thirty-nine—the LFD arrived with a tanker truck and took charge of fighting the fire while the Green Springs volunteers sprayed water on nearby vegetation."

Connie pushed the one remaining fry toward me. "Can you come to choir practice tomorrow night?"

What did choir practice have to do with anything? "Why would I do that?"

She grinned. "I'm short on altos." She leaned forward to whisper, "My cousin Raleigh—the firefighter—will be there. We can corner him afterward."

"I'll be delighted to supplement the altos." Careful. She'd maneuvered me into playing piano for auditions for *Oklahoma!* "This one time."

"Maybe you'd better just mime."

A shadow loomed and a hairy hand reached around me to place a huge hamburger with slices of onion and tomato in front of me. "Good evening, ladies. Good to see you."

I looked up at Harry's broad face and shiny dome. To my surprise, he was smiling.

Achilles, who had been stretched out across my feet, rose to sniff the food.

Harry continued to smile. "Would you like something for the canine corps?"

Achilles glanced at him and disappeared under the table again.

"No, thanks. He's not hungry." I salted my tomatoes.

Harry didn't move. "How's it going on catching the burglars? I dreaded opening my front door when we got back from West Virginia today. Guess my security system scared them off."

"You certainly came home in a good mood."

He took that as an invitation to sit down. "We had a great time. We went to Beckley and toured an old coal mine. Beckley's pretty much out in nowhere, but you wouldn't have known it from the crowd of tourists." He leaned his forearms on the table. "When the mine closed, they used lemons to make lemonade. Tourism is good economic development. Right, Phoenix?"

What the heck was he leading up to? "It can be." I glanced at Connie.

She gave a tiny shrug.

Harry leaned toward me. "My mother's grandfather got off the boat in Baltimore, worked in Beckley a year, and came on to Green Springs. I grew up with family stories about mining."

I still didn't know what he wanted from me, but from the gleam in his eyes and the eagerness in his posture, I guessed he was winding up for a sales pitch.

"My ancestors were miners, too," Connie said.

He shifted his gaze to her. "I'll bet you'd love to see where they worked." He turned back to me. "We could make Green Springs a tourist town, too. Fix up an old mine for tours, put a little museum and a souvenir shop in an empty building, open up a family restaurant in the depot. Leo Klang's already renovating the old—the historic hotel."

Pure fantasy. I choked back a sarcastic putdown and said, "So you plan to revive Green Springs?"

He laughed. "Me? Hell, no. We need an investment group, a consortium. Several people in town are interested, but we need somebody with major capital and a knowledge of start-ups."

Bloody hell! Connie's comment to Wanda Sue about my wanting to invest had traveled with the speed of light.

Connie choked on her hamburger. She spat a bite into her napkin and took a drink of my water.

I had to disenchant Harry fast. "I doubt you'll find that investor in Vandiver County."

"Think about it, Phoenix. You and Annalynn will be out of the crime business soon. Your little charity won't keep you busy." Harry stood up, his face grim. "Nobody around here has ever handled big money like you have, but we can see Laycock's going to shrivel up like Green Springs if we don't bring in jobs. You come up with a better idea to jumpstart Vandiver County's economy, I'll back you up."

Achilles popped up from under the table, a low growl in his throat.

Harry strode to the safety of his bar.

His vote of confidence surprised me. Trying to improve the local economy had never occurred to me. I dug into my hamburger.

Achilles settled down at my feet again.

Connie leaned forward to whisper, "Harry hasn't been so friendly to you in—ever. He probably Googled you and realized you're loaded." She fingered a dreamcatcher earring. "He must have extra cash to spend to think of fixing up an abandoned mine. I'm going to talk to him again about my singing here Friday and Saturday nights."

I swallowed my frequently heard discouraging words with a bite of hamburger.

"If he'd hire me, I could afford to direct shows at LCC."

She'd heard nothing I said about accepting a bad contract. "Ask Annalynn what she thinks about compensating for low pay at one job by working another low-paying job."

Two tall women dressed in black came in the door. I didn't know the gray-haired woman, but the younger one was Martina Pelben. They took a table near the entrance to Tequila Junction, the bar area that had been a small grocery store attached to the garage.

"Harry," Connie called as the owner walked past us, "join us for a minute."

He didn't hesitate. "Sure." He motioned to the bartender. "Bring me a bottle of that new German beer. What about you, Phoenix? Like a German beer?"

Hmm. He really, really wanted me to invest. "No, thanks." Curious, I extended a little rope. "You're right that local entrepreneurs have to take the lead in economic development. Have you done any marketing research on Green Springs as a tourism center?"

He took the bottle the bartender brought him and stared at the label. "I've been talking to Beatrix Hew about it since the depot reopened." He sipped the beer. "Green Springs has no resources, and neither does the county. I can't swing an operation that size alone. I don't have the money or the expertise." He put down the bottle. "I understand you have both."

Stringing him on would end badly. "Harry, my specialty is matching Eastern European start-ups with international venture capitalists. You'll have to look elsewhere for a partner." Out of the corner of my eye, I saw Martina walk to the bar to order. Not wanting to advertise that I'd gone to see her, I took care not to make eye contact.

Harry frowned. "Then why did you tell the Klangs you'd be interested in buying the Bushwhacker's Den?"

Think fast. "A stocked spring-fed pond drew crowds to the Family Fish House for two generations. My brothers and I begged to go fish for our dinner. The property is worthless without the spring feeding that pond."

He twirled the bottle in his big hand. "The mines in Green Springs weren't all that deep. It'd be a hell of a lot easier to shore up a couple of tunnels than to restore the springs." He raised his voice. "What were you really up to in Green Springs today, Deputy Smith?"

Bloody hell! He'd attracted the attention of everyone in the place. "It's none of your business," I said, elevating my voice just enough it would carry, "but I went to eat lunch and buy a homemade pie. Have you considered adding Wanda Sue's pies to your dessert menu? You could both profit from that."

He clamped his mouth shut, probably to keep from swearing.

Connie jumped in. "That would draw a new crowd. So would live entertainment, a stand-up comedy open mike one week night and music on Friday and Saturday."

I didn't want to be part of this. "Excuse me, please."

When I pushed back my chair, Achilles rose with me.

"Stay." I grabbed the end of his leash and passed it to Connie. "I'll be back in a couple of minutes." I headed toward the restroom in the back hall.

The light bulb hanging in the two-stall women's room couldn't have been more than twenty-five watts. Even so, the mirror showed me dark smudges under my eyes. The day's events had taken a toll. I fluffed up my hair. It still fell into place, but in another week, it would be so long it would go every which way. If Beatrix Hew didn't wield golden scissors, I might have to attend that meeting in New York to get a haircut.

The door opened. Martina Pelben slipped through it and stood there blocking my exit. "You went to Green Springs and then came to see me. Why? What are you up to, Deputy Smith?"

FIFTEEN

NO WONDER LEO KLANG called Martina Pelben the Amazon. She looked six feet tall blocking the restroom door. Definitely advisable to use brain rather than brawn to get past her. I smiled. "Oh, I'm not a real deputy. The sheriff calls on me when she may need to shoot someone." I patted my holstered Glock. "I'm carrying because of an incident this morning."

She stared at the Glock but didn't move. "I don't like guns. You should learn to defend yourself without one."

I opened my purse and took out some eye cream. I dabbed specks under my eyes and spread it with the tip of a finger. "I'm a little old to learn judo."

She sneered. "Judo's old hat. I do Tai Kwan Do."

So she could use her hands and her feet, and practically everything else. I feigned ignorance. "Is Taiwan Doe good exercise?"

She smirked and then frowned. "You didn't answer my question."

"Really?" She was sharper than I expected. "Sorry. What did you ask me?" I put the eye cream back in my purse and faced her.

She blinked a couple of times, trying to decide—or so I hoped—whether I was evading her question or old and forgetful. Finally she said, "I asked if you went to Green Springs to see where that tramp killed Edwin."

Interesting. She'd revised her question. "Was he your fiancé?"

"You know damn well he was!"

I held out my hands apologetically. "Perhaps you told me that this afternoon, but I'm not good with names. Did he die at the old depot? I went there for lunch."

She put her hands on her hips in exasperation. "No, he passed at the Bushwhacker's Den. Are you investigating his death?"

I gave her my best puzzled expression. "Why would I do that? You said the woman who seduced him went to prison." Give her something else to think about. "Come to think of it, I asked somebody in Green Springs about that half-burned building. He said the woman convicted of arson didn't set the fire. What do you think?"

Her eyes widened. "Of course she did. She admitted it."

I'd shocked the woman. "He never mentioned that." Go a step farther. "He did say Edward—"

"Edwin, not Edward!" She curled her lip and barreled through a stall door.

I beat a quick retreat. Martina Pelben verged on a mental breakdown. *Scheisse!* She was one of the victims we'd set up the foundation to help. I bypassed my table, where Connie and Harry still talked, and walked toward the older woman who'd come in with Martina.

"Good evening." Why was I doing this? I had no idea what to say. "Are you Martina's mother?"

The woman put down a hamburger to give me her full attention. "No, her mother lives in Springfield. I'm her youthful great-aunt."

"Martina and I were talking in the restroom. She's very upset about her fiancé's death." I regretted I'd ever started this, but I couldn't stop now. "I went by Lay-cock Storage to rent some space this afternoon, and she brought him up then, too. I'm concerned about her."

"What do you suggest I do?" Her tone was curious rather than defensive.

"Perhaps you could encourage her to have grief counseling." Not to mention a psychiatric evaluation. "I'm Phoenix Smith. I work with a new foundation providing short-term assistance to crime victims' families. If she qualifies, we could help her pay for some counseling sessions." I waited for an answer. None came. "I thought the suggestion might be better received coming from a relative than from a stranger." Big mistake to interfere with a private matter. Get the hell out of here. "Enjoy your meal."

"Thank you," she said formally as I turned away.

Harry had disappeared. Good.

"I got you a doggie box," Connie said, standing before I could sit. "Let's go."

Achilles trotted for the door, his leash dragging on the floor. I hurried after him, relieved to be getting out of the Amazon's, the great-aunt's, and Harry's sight.

"No luck with Harry," Connie said as we went through the double doors into near darkness. "As soon as you left the table, he asked me if we went to Green Springs to investigate the burglaries."

I unlocked the car doors and opened the back door for Achilles. "And you said?"

"That we went for lunch. Then he said we'd better be catching the burglars. People are scared." Connie put out a restraining hand as I reached for the ignition. "Let's talk a minute. Phoenix, we should postpone the Hew case and work on the burglaries."

She'd be really hurt if she knew Annalynn had shut her out but brought me in. "Connie, we have real leads to follow in Green Springs, and I'll get more tomorrow. Which reminds me, you haven't told me what shocking thing you discovered about the Hews."

"It's family gossip, not facts," she teased. "It has nothing to do with the case."

I wished I could ignore whatever juicy tidbit she'd found, but family interactions would determine Hermione's future. "I'm willing to listen to a quick summary." I started the car.

"Stop me if you get bored." She shifted positions so she could see my profile. "My voice student, Nyoki, knew Jolene in high school. She changed a lot, and not for the better, after her dad moved out."

Old news. "Leo said she blamed Beatrix for the divorce."

"No one else did. Hew finally joined AA, sobered up, and got a maintenance job at LCC. Right before Jolene came back from Sedalia, he married a lay leader at the Power of God's Goodness Church."

"Never heard of it."

"It's an unaffiliated storefront congregation. A year ago last spring, Nyoki went to services there for a month to research a paper for a comparative religion course."

I noted that Connie's voice had changed to stage mode. She had a dramatic story to tell. "And?"

"Jolene came to a Wednesday-night prayer meeting. She went up to her dad and said hello a few minutes before the service. He refused to even look at her. She sat down by Nyoki. The same thing happened the next week. The third week, the preacher prayed for about ten minutes and then asked who felt the spirit. Jolene's stepmother stood up, pointed at Jolene, and called her 'a whore of Babylon and abomination of the earth.' Then Jolene's father prayed that God would drive evil from their midst."

A verbal stoning. Sickening. "What did Jolene do?"

"She sat there with tears streaming down her face and took it. She didn't come back the next week. Nyoki didn't go back after that." Connie sighed. "I hate when people use religion as an excuse for bad behavior." She said nothing for a moment. "Of course, it doesn't have a thing to do with what happened at the Den."

An inexplicable hunch, something from my trusty subconscious, disagreed with that. I tried to figure out why. "Don't be so sure. Two or three months before the fire, the father who had doted on Jolene publicly shamed her. That had to be devastating. Maybe he convinced her it was true. Leo saw her drinking with the bodybuilder."

"What? Are you saying she seduced the guy to prove her father right? If I'd said that, you would've accused me of thinking like a character in a musical comedy."

True. "People are weird sometimes." I braked at a stop sign. "Do you want to go home or come to Anna-lynn's for a piece of cherry pie?"

"Home." Connie sounded hurt. "I have to think about my future, in my Auntie Mame way."

Was it my thoughtless comment about only a fool signing that contract? Or my offer to take her home now? Probably both. "Connie, I wasn't hinting that I wanted to take you home."

"Yes, you were."

Achilles stuck his head over the seat and barked in my ear.

She reached back to rub him under his drooping, bullet-torn right ear. "Thanks, Achilles."

Neither of us said anything until I pulled into her driveway.

Connie rarely kept her mouth shut that long. I had to make amends. "I'm sorry if I seemed to be blowing you off." No reply. "What time is the choir rehearsal?"

"Seven." She opened the door. "When did those burglaries start?"

"More than a month ago, in late August. Why?"

"And here we are in late September. Most of my bills come due the first of the month. Maybe the burglar isn't a teenager. Maybe it's a father who lost his job and can't pay the rent."

Or a single mother. "That's a possibility. I'll mention it to Annalynn."

I stewed all the way home. Connie and I exchanged insults all the time, but she had earned my respect over the last few months. I'd have to find a way to show her that. Go over Annalynn's head and involve Connie in the burglary case? No. Not when I was risking Annalynn's wrath by working secretly on the Green Springs case.

The lights were on in the dining room and kitchen when I turned into my driveway.

Achilles loped ahead of me to the castle and barked.

Annalynn opened the door and made a fuss over him. He turned so his shoulder was by her right hand, his request for her to remove the leash.

I held out my doggie box. "Want half a hamburger?"

"No, thanks. I'm relieved you felt well enough to eat at Harry's." She looped the leash over the doorknob and punched in the security code. "I've spread out the city map on the table. Did you find anything in the newspaper's archives?"

"Not yet. They're poorly organized." I went into the kitchen and put my box in the refrigerator. "Any of the stolen items turn up?"

"No. I've checked with pawnshops and antique stores. Michael has searched online. She's either selling the collectible items privately or holding them to sell later."

I joined Annalynn at the table. "You're sure we're looking for a woman?"

"Not entirely, but I suspect she left that huge footprint to hide she's a woman."

"Harry told Connie and me that the burglaries are scaring people." My chance to insert Connie. "She thinks the timing of the burglaries points to somebody stealing to pay their bills."

"That limits our pool of suspects to half of Laycock, including her and me."

Annalynn's rare sarcasm alarmed me. "Are you worried about money?" She'd never had to until her late husband lost her considerable inheritance in bad investments.

"The bank sent me a reminder that the balloon payment on the summer-home mortgage comes due at the end of the year." She held up a hand. "Don't offer to pay it. I'll call a real estate agent in Branson tomorrow and put the place on the market. I should at least break even."

I knew Annalynn didn't resent our reversal of fortunes, but she didn't relish it either. I leaned over to study colored lines inked on the map. "I take it these lines trace routes through neighborhoods with affluent older residents."

"And with cover provided by topography or vegetation. The red route receives the highest priority. It has the most potential targets. Then orange, blue, and green, in that order. We marked logical running routes of one to two miles. On foot you'll have a better chance of spotting vulnerable homes and places to hide for a stake-out."

I studied the routes. "I don't recognize half of these street names." I pointed to a green line on the south side of town near the turnoff to Green Springs. "This area has deteriorated. The big old family homes have been turned into apartment buildings."

Annalynn tapped on the map. "Except on these two blocks on Harding. Several expensive houses have replaced rundown old ones over the last fifteen years. They're mostly two-income families, established professionals."

The red line ran near the town's northeastern border. "And who lives on—good grief—Stratford and Avon?"

"Our Shakespearean hamlet. LCC staff, retirees, business people. They own a lot of tempting items, and few retirees have security systems." She studied my face. "You've put makeup over the dark circles under your eyes. Are you okay? Michael can run alone."

"No, he can't. Some idiot will call 9-1-1 if they see a young black man running through their neighborhood at daybreak." A tingle of anticipation traveled up my spine. "Besides, I won't miss a chance to help catch the creep who tried to kill Achilles."

SIXTEEN

ANNALYNN BREATHED A sigh of relief. "Then you agree with me that the burglar tried to poison Achilles to keep from being tracked. I was afraid you might be holding out on something else you're involved in." She stepped back from the table. "I'm looking for a connection between the victims. I'll call them while you check the newspaper archives." She smiled. "We can do our homework together in the ladies' parlor the way we did in school."

I brought my laptop from my bedroom and settled down in my usual chair with the hassock. She went behind the carved wood Indian screen separating the parlor from her office to call the victims. Keeping one ear open, I searched for mentions of the stolen collectibles. I'd almost given up when I found an article on hobbyists with a photo of Mr. Carmetti reloading a 44-caliber cartridge for his century-old Colt single-action revolver. I reported to Annalynn.

She came from her desk to read the article and then sat on the love seat. "That ran months ago, long before these burglaries started. It could be a coincidence."

"Or the burglar is a gun enthusiast who clipped the article."

"I hope not." Annalynn stared into space a moment. "Few young people read the newspaper. Our burglar could be the age of the people she's robbing."

"I doubt it. Burglary isn't a common retirement plan."

Achilles trotted in and licked Annalynn's hand. He

whirled, gave a soft bark, walked to the door, and looked back over his shoulder at her. He barked again.

She rose. "What do you suppose he wants?"

"I've no idea. Maybe a ball rolled under your bed."

She followed Achilles, her steps moving through the dining room into the kitchen. I heard the basement door open.

Good. A chance to check Green Springs in the archives for any articles Beatrix chose not to give me. A photo spread on the opening of the train depot popped up. The lieutenant governor had come to cut the ribbon. Beatrix had political clout. Why hadn't she been able to challenge Jolene's confessions? I searched the photos of dignitaries. The county commissioners and Laycock's mayor were there. Boom and Annalynn weren't. I skimmed Vernon's short article, most of it on Beatrix's plans to bolster the local economy. At the end, he noted that it was a dual celebration because July eighteenth was also her forty-ninth birthday. The article didn't mention Edwin Wiler's death in the Bushwhacker's Den only a few days before.

"Find something else?"

I jumped. Closing the page would arouse suspicion. "No. I was curious about the train depot in Green Springs. The stone on the front is the same as your house." I let her see the article and closed the laptop. "Ready to try the cherry pie I brought home?"

"Only a sliver for me." She chuckled. "Achilles wanted me to play with his new toy. He gave me a Frisbee to toss at the basket, and he 'threw' in a tennis ball."

I grimaced. "I can't stand that constant sound of bouncing. I'll put it down in the tunnel tomorrow. Then he can reach it from either house."

Annalynn made coffee while I sliced the pie and poured myself a glass of milk. The map still covered the end of the dining-room table, so we went back to the ladies' parlor.

I cut off a small bite with little anticipation of pleasure. "This is really good, much better than the café's soup."

"Wanda Sue makes her own crust," Annalynn said.

She knew all these people I'd just met, and she'd rejected Beatrix's claim of a false confession a year ago. No, Boom had rejected it. I had to keep going.

My cell rang. A recorded voice from Laycock Pharmacy told me my pills would be ready at nine tomorrow.

Annalynn put her pie on the coffee table and opened a small, leather-covered notebook, her personal calendar. "I'm glad you're taking your health seriously. What's on your schedule tomorrow?"

"The run. The pharmacy. A haircut at ten."

"I'm amazed that you're allowing a beautician in Laycock to touch your hair. Who is the chosen one?"

Careful. Be straightforward and natural. "Beatrix Hew. Do you know her?"

"Yes." She scribbled in her notebook. "We're—we used to be good friends."

I hadn't expected that. "Anything I need to know about why you aren't friends now?"

"No. It's a long, unhappy story. I'll tell you about it some other time."

I couldn't let this chance to get Annalynn's perspective on Beatrix slip away. "Should I cancel my cut?"

"No, no. She's excellent."

"The article gave her credit for reopening the depot. She sounds like a real dynamo."

"She is." Annalynn made a note and looked up.

"She reminds me a little of you. Very bright, very determined, and very energetic. Unlike you, she's also
very religious." She tapped her pencil on the notebook.
"What are you doing the rest of the day?"

"Office work. Nothing I can't put off if we get a lead
on the burglar. I promised Connie I'd go to choir practice
at seven. She's short of altos this week."

Annalynn laughed so hard she had to wipe away a tear.

"*Scheisse!* Connie suckered me, didn't she?"

"I couldn't say." Annalynn clamped her lips shut but
couldn't hide a smile. "She mentioned once she could
use you in the choir."

"And you bet her she couldn't talk me into it." I had
to admire Connie's cleverness. She'd won a bet and
given me cover to talk to Raleigh. I picked up my empty
plate and glass. "I'm tired. I'm going to bed."

"Don't forget to put out the vests that you and Achilles will wear tomorrow."

This time I didn't object, but Achilles did. When I took
the vests from the closet and put them on the steamer
trunk at the foot of my bed, he dashed from the bedroom.

I folded his green blanket into quarters, placed it on the
hooked rug that served as his mattress, and left the door
open wide enough that he could slip back into my room.

Once ready for bed, I opened my laptop to take another look at Vernon's unpublished interior photos. The
retardant cloth, rolled back over the bar above the body,
appeared heavy and awkward for a small woman to
handle. Even if Jolene had the strength—and the lack
of smarts—to walk back to the Den and hit Wiler on
the head, she wouldn't have bothered to cover the bar
before setting the fires. Cork might have, especially if
he'd expected the fire to destroy only part of the Den.

I vaguely remembered hearing that fire insurance paid more if the roof burned. Yes, finding out who put the cloth over the bar could be crucial.

Would Leo have noticed the cloth when he saw Jolene and Wiler together? Or only when firefighters found the body? I'd ask Beatrix, who would be no more reliable than Leo. The two certainly had compared stories long ago and would back each other up. Maybe the official crime scene photos would tell me more. Annalynn could provide those, but I didn't have enough evidence to ask her for them. Connie and I would have to convince Raleigh to give me—us—whatever photos and information he had. I couldn't wait more than another day or two to decide whether to involve Annalynn and to interrogate Jolene. Before I talked to either, I needed facts to refute the confessions and at least a good guess as to why the young woman made them.

Beatrix's veracity was crucial to the whole question of Jolene's innocence. Did Beatrix really have a terminal illness, or had that been a bid for sympathy? I chose a medical site and typed in pancreatic cancer. The information depressed me. Doctors rarely found it at an early stage. The five-year survival rate was dismal, less than one in ten even if found at Stage Two. No wonder she was frantic. Or pretending to be. I had to find a way to verify her claim.

WHEN MY ALARM went off, Achilles rose from his blanket, stretched and yawned, and went out of the open door.

His vest was no longer on the trunk. I smiled—until I thought that vest could save his life. "Annalynn," I called, "Achilles hid his vest. Do you have any idea where?"

"I have it," she answered from across the hall. "He brought it in last night and nosed it under my bed. The morning's foggy and damp. Are you sure you feel up to running?"

"Of course. I slept really well last night." Not a twinge to mar the morning.

She laughed. "You perk up whenever we're investigating. I'll fix a pot of tea so you can have a hot drink before Michael picks you up."

Putting the vest on a squirming Achilles took so long that I'd had only a few sips of tea when Michael pulled into Annalynn's driveway in his red Ford Focus. I downed some water.

Achilles' leash no longer hung on the doorknob. "Leash," I said sternly. "No leash, no run."

He whirled and trotted into the ladies' parlor. He came back dragging the leash.

"Thank you." I curled it up and stuck it in my jacket's roomy pocket.

"He's been hiding a lot of things lately," Annalynn said. "Is that typical?"

"Not that I know of. I think he's bored because I spend so much time in the office." As I had been. "Talk to you later."

Achilles darted out the door ahead of me but hung back as I approached the unfamiliar car. He didn't come when I opened the back door for him.

"It's okay. I'm going, too," I assured him. "Come." I opened the front door. "Good morning, Michael."

Achilles didn't move.

He rarely disobeyed me. He'd hated riding in the back seat of the squad car, but this was Michael's personal car. No time to negotiate. I closed the back door, slid the front seat back as far as it would go, and stepped in.

Achilles jumped in on top of me and thrashed around until he sat between my knees.

Michael laughed. "If he was a kid, I'd say he has separation anxiety."

"He certainly did for weeks after I found him shot on that creek bank last May." I rubbed behind his drooping ear. "I left him alone yesterday, and someone invaded his safe world."

Michael backed out of the driveway. "Is that a Kevlar vest?"

"Yes. Annalynn insists we both wear them. Fill me in on what to watch for as we run."

"The easy targets—places a burglar can break into fast without being seen. You know, trees or bushes to hide behind. No security cameras, and no dogs. A barking dog sends burglars on down the road. Achilles certainly would." The young cop came to a full stop at the intersection. "Watch for doors with glass that a perp could break to reach the locks, and rocks or bricks in flower borders they could use to break glass in a door or window."

"Okay, architecture and landscaping. What else?"

"Signs people may be careless about locking up—open windows and garage doors, toys or tools left outside."

In short, use common sense. "What's your theory about the burglaries?"

"LCC students." He turned onto Stratford. "One keeps watch and drives the getaway vehicle while the other one goes inside."

Old but neat one-story white frame houses with tall trees and untrimmed bushes promised concealment but few rewards for burglars. Puzzled, I held my tongue. When we crossed Taylor Street, the houses on our right were sprawling one-story or narrow two-story houses with open, well-kept yards and no big trees.

"The newer, bigger houses start a block down," Michael said. "I'll park between Oxford and Cambridge. We'll run down Stratford, cut back through the alley, and go down Avon." He grinned. "Several LCC profs live in this area. They like the address."

Even the grander houses didn't appear tempting to me. The vegetation wouldn't conceal an adult, and most houses had signs—possibly fake—announcing security systems.

Michael parallel parked and pointed at a house. "See that big plate glass window with the drapes open? That's like advertising what you got to steal. Those people don't expect trouble. They may not bother to lock up when they go out."

Had I closed the drapes on the picture windows in my house's front rooms last night?

We got out of the car. I turned on the cameras in the back of my cap but left my sunglasses with the special lenses in my jacket pocket. The fog had lifted, but sunglasses still would be out of place. No one else moved on the street, but lights glowed in the houses. "Michael, I suggest we skip the stretches in favor of a slow start."

"Sure. I'll watch the left side of the street. You take the right."

Most of the inspection proved boring for everyone but Achilles, who explored here and there, never going more than a few yards away from me. He found the alley odors particularly interesting and reluctantly followed us onto Avon. I'd written off the run as a waste of time until we neared the end of Avon Street. The last three houses, old brick mansions with tall bushes obscuring their front porches, occupied the sloping bottom of Laycock's highest hill. A shoulder-high wrought-iron fence edged all three front yards. I vaguely remembered coming to an outdoor potluck at one of the houses. Brush and trees on the hill behind the houses offered plenty of cover, but no one would want to carry anything heavy or bulky up it.

I stooped to tie my shoe and put on my sunglasses. "These places look like the owners might have stuff to steal. Isn't there a road on the ridge?"

"Yes, but it's back a ways. That's private property right above."

I dialed the glasses to telescope and spotted a pony by a board fence at the top of the hill. No sign of a trail coming down the hill. I readjusted the glasses and focused on the lock of the nearest house's old-fashioned, wood front door. As far as I could tell, an old lock requiring a giant key—or a deftly applied tool—was the only one on the door.

A beagle rushed through the bushes barking and wove between the trees toward us in little bursts of speed.

Achilles wagged his tail furiously and stuck his nose through the fence.

I stood up. "Let's go."

Achilles didn't catch up with me until I passed the second house. At the third house, our only option was to turn left toward Stratford. Michael had let me set the pace, which I knew was slower than he would have chosen. I lengthened my stride for the last three uneventful blocks.

I was winded by the time we reached the car, but Michael appeared unfazed. This time Achilles went straight to the back door.

Michael turned on the motor. "We should downgrade this area from red to green."

"Except for those three houses with the wrought-iron fence on Avon, or at least the corner one. An old door. No dog or security system. Neighbor on only one side. Plenty of cover. If I knew the owner kept cash or valuables light enough to carry up that hill, I'd go for it." I adjusted the seat belt over my holster. "If you'll send me the owner's name, I'll check for newspaper articles on any collectibles worth going after."

"You want me to send you names from other priority neighborhoods, too?"

I groaned. "Forget it. Checking out all the possible victims could take forever."

He grinned. "Welcome to my world."

SEVENTEEN

I PARKED MY car in front of Laycock Pharmacy at nine thirty and debated whether to take Achilles inside. No one had followed me, but I didn't want to leave him alone. On the other hand, the pharmacy wouldn't welcome him, and I had no idea how he'd react to smelling all those medications. From where I sat, I could see down the aisle to the pharmacy counter. He would be able to see me, and I him.

"Stay," I said, lowering all the windows halfway. "I'll be right back."

He whined but didn't bark.

I hurried inside and down the aisle lined with mobility devices.

Nell appeared at the counter. "Good morning, Phoenix. Your doctor's office asked me to go over your new medications with you."

Was that good news or bad news? "Would you mind talking in the front? My dog's nervous today. He'll bark if I'm out of his sight for more than a minute."

"Surely he doesn't understand someone tried to poison him."

"He knows something bad happened." Odd that Nell knew about the poison but Trudy didn't. "How did you find out?"

"The vet consulted me. We're pretty sure it was rat poisoning. It's so common it's almost impossible to trace the source." She unlocked a shoulder-high door and followed me to the front. She handed me a bag holding a small yellowish bottle. "This is milder than what you had before, but be careful. If you have another attack, take one and go to bed. Don't drive." She handed me another bag. "Take one capsule daily before lunch or supper, whichever is your main meal. Consume no alcohol."

I didn't recognize the name of the medication and had no idea how to pronounce it. "What's this for?"

She hesitated. "I had to look it up myself. It aids in recovery from, uh, liver damage."

Her knowledge cast doubt on my cover story of a rampant infection following gall bladder surgery. "The infection"—otherwise known as a bullet—"necessitated removing a bit of my liver. The pain probably comes from that or adhesions." I flashed back to Beatrix Hew's bottle of pills. That had come from Laycock Pharmacy, and it had been almost empty. "I'm on my way to get a haircut from Beatrix Hew. I noticed Monday that she's due for a refill. I could take her prescription to her."

Surprise flickered across Nell's thin face. "All prescriptions are confidential."

"Of course. Would you mind calling her to ask?" I lowered my voice. "She's beginning to feel uneasy about driving to Laycock."

The pharmacist sighed. "I don't wonder." She caught herself. "Do you know her birthday?"

I never forget a number. "July eighteenth. She's fifty. Her phone number is 656-1212."

Nell relaxed and pulled a cell from the pocket of her white jacket. "I didn't realize you know her so well." She dialed the number. "Beatrix, it's Nell. Phoenix offered to bring out those refills you need." She listened a moment, turned away from me, and walked back toward the pharmacy. "I don't recommend it."

Beatrix had said she had no money for a good lawyer. I guessed she didn't have money for expensive medications either. I walked back considering ways to handle this.

We were the only ones in the place, but I lowered my voice again. "Put whatever Beatrix needs on my credit card." I handed it to Nell. "Tell her they're samples, and let me know when she needs more."

The pharmacist smiled. "That's a wonderful gesture, Phoenix, but the 'samples' could soon come to several thousand dollars."

The money meant nothing to me. "Then you'd better come up with a good story about how you're getting so many free pills. This is confidential, of course."

"Bless you." She unlocked the door and hurried behind the counter. "I'll have them ready in two minutes."

I'd earned a little information. "Do you suppose there's any hope she'll survive?"

A long silence. "I pray for her every night."

Nell had just verified Beatrix's claim of terminal cancer.

Coming back to the counter, Nell handed me a small paper bag with the top stapled shut, showed me the total, and slid my card through. "Are you driving her to Columbia Friday?"

"She hasn't asked me to." Everyone in the area went to Columbia for treatment. I signed the murky screen. "What do you know about her doctor? Should Beatrix get a second opinion?"

"No, Dr. Lysesky is top notch."

The doctor's name was a nice bonus. "I have to go. Thanks, Nell."

"Phoenix," she called as I opened the door, "welcome back to Laycock."

"Thanks." I opened my car door and fended off kisses. "On the floor," I ordered. "We're running late. I have to find you a seat belt. You'll like that even less than the vest." I slid into my seat and checked for anyone sitting in a car. No shadow in sight. I kept watch all the way to Green Springs and saw no one following me.

I parked in front of Golden Oldies, took a fresh chew toy out of the trunk, and walked with Achilles toward the depot.

Hermione waved at us from the shop window. When I waved back, she disappeared. As we crossed the railroad tracks, she peeked around the corner of the entryway.

Achilles barked and loped to her.

She threw one arm around his neck. The other arm clutched her stuffed dog. She kissed the top of Achilles' head. "Pretty dog. Pretty, pretty."

He licked her face.

"Achilles," I scolded, "no kisses on the face. People don't like that."

Hermione frowned at me. "I like dog kisses."

"So do I, *Liebchen*, but not on my face. Watch." I wasn't sure Achilles would perform the trick in front of our audience: Wanda Sue by the café door, a frail white-haired woman in a motorized wheelchair at the depot entrance, and Beatrix by her shop door. "Achilles, be a Viennese gentleman." I held out my right hand, palm down, my fingers curved, my wrist limp. *"Küss die Hand."*

He gazed up at me a moment and stretched forward to lick my hand.

"Good boy," I said. "Now you try it, Hermione." I knelt beside her and guided her hand into position. I whispered in her ear. "Tell him to *Küss die Hand.*"

"Kiss me hand," she said softly.

He licked her hand delicately. Then he swung his head around and gave me a big lick on my cheek.

I jumped up. "Yuk!"

Three women, a child, and a dog laughed at me.

Excellent. His lick had eased the tension. I shook my finger at him. "That's not funny."

He sat down and held up his front right paw.

Good grief. He could milk a laugh as well as Connie. I shook his paw. "Apology accepted."

"What a smart dog," Beatrix said. "He can play with Hermione inside the depot while I cut your hair. Mom will keep an eye on them."

The woman in the wheelchair held out her hand. "Achilles, *Küss die Hand.*"

He gave her a gentle lick and turned expectantly to Wanda Sue.

"How sweet." She held out her hand. "Kiss, Achilles."

He gave a quick lick, and she went back into the café.

He went to Beatrix and extended his nose. His left ear twitched.

I held my breath. He smelled something disturbing. The cancer?

He offered his paw.

She shook it. "He doesn't like the smell of chemicals on my hands."

Mrs. Olson backed her chair through the depot door. "Bring him in here, Hermione."

I handed Beatrix the pills. "I'll be there in a moment." I followed Hermione and Achilles into the depot and watched him begin his usual exploration, Hermione running behind him. I handed Mrs. Olson the chew toy. "Give him this if he gets restless."

Rather than walk outside, I went to the back door of the beauty shop. Achilles raced toward me. "I'll be right here, with lots of smells you don't like. You stay with Hermione." A useless command. He hadn't learned to recognize her name.

She ran up, her face anxious.

"Stay with the pretty girl, Achilles." I smiled at her. "He likes to know where I am." I pointed to the large room. "Go play." I stepped inside the shop, leaving the door open.

He sneezed, licked Hermione's cheek, and resumed his exploration.

Beatrix, dressed in white slacks, white blouse, and a navy-blue vest, stood by the first of three chairs studying a receipt. "Nell billed me for only a few pills but sent the full refill."

"Maybe she had some expired medication."

"Excuse me a moment." Touching the tops of the tall chairs lightly, Beatrix walked to the far side of the shop and went through a door.

The way she touched the chairs reminded me of my mother using furniture to keep her balance as she moved around the house in her last years. Beatrix's makeup had been heavier today than on Monday. She surely couldn't work much longer.

Pull back, I cautioned myself. My sympathy for

Hermione and Beatrix Hew could endanger my objec-
tivity. I focused on the shop, a good size for two beauticians. It was absolutely spotless. Not a smudge on the
mirrors, not a hair on the floor, not a streak on the mats
under the hydraulic chairs. The morning light streamed
in the windows lining the south side and bounced off
eggshell white walls and ceiling. The only things in
the whole place that weren't white were the washbasin
and the chairs. That made the hair products displayed
on the shelves beneath the south windows stand out. I'd
never heard of any of the professional-grade shampoos,
but I recognized an expensive conditioner. A first-class
operation.

I turned expecting to see more products beneath the
large window by the outer entrance. Instead the shelves
held tattered paperbacks, a half dozen ring-binder note-
books, two board games, four plastic cars, four sock
dolls, and five coffee mugs.

With glass on the upper half of three sides, the shop
had little room for the standard large photos of hair-
styles. The only wall decorations hung between the station mirrors. I moved closer to look at framed copies
of Beatrix's license, an award for hair shaping she had
won at a national competition, a black-and-white photo
of an old-fashioned barbershop that had occupied this
same space, and a series of photos of the depot before
and during restoration.

Waiting patrons, or people coming in to chat, could
sit in four black folding chairs at a round white table.
I guessed that the mayor met with constituents here.

I went to the door to check on Achilles. He and
Hermione were playing a version of tag.

"You look much less intimidating when you smile,"

Beatrix said from by the washbasin. She gripped the arm of the chair. "Do you want a shampoo and conditioning, or just a wet down?"

Seeing her fragility, I feared for my hair. "I don't need a shampoo. My real purpose for coming is to go over details with you. Let's sit at the table and talk."

She smiled. "Don't worry. I can manage one more haircut. That's excellent styling. You want the same cut?"

"Yes. I can fluff this up and shake it into place even after I mash it down with a hat." Or a wig worn as a disguise.

She took a deep breath. "I do need to conserve energy. If you don't mind wetting your hair yourself, I'll perch on a stool."

"Certainly." Didn't sitting while cutting violate the beauticians' code?

She snapped a black plastic cape on me and put towels within reach.

Despite the cape, water trickled down my front. I hoped the Kevlar vest would absorb it.

She guided me to the nearest chair and ran her hands through my hair as Hermione had done. "You have healthy hair. Women who have hair this dark often gray early, but I don't think you will." She pulled strands this way and that before opening a drawer and choosing a pair of long, narrow shears from four pairs laid out as neatly as a surgeon's instruments. She leaned against but didn't sit on a kitchen stool. "We'll talk when I've finished." She met my eyes in the mirror and smiled. "Relax. I won't destroy your hair."

I soon believed her. She yanked the hair on top of my head hard enough to hurt once, but she was an artist.

Neither of us spoke as she worked. In the silence I could hear the sound of Hermione's laughter and of six feet running around the depot.

When Beatrix finished blow-drying my hair, she smiled with satisfaction. "How do you like the cut?"

"It's great. You could work in the best salons in the country."

"I wanted to be a Hollywood hair stylist when I was young." She unsnapped the cape and shook it out. "I don't regret my choices." The hands that had been steady now trembled.

I took her arm and guided her to a chair at the table. "I'll clean up. Would you like a glass of water?"

"Yes, please. I'll be better in a minute. I ran out of pills yesterday."

I went into the small back room, found the broom and dustpan, and took these back into the shop with her glass of water. I watched her as I swept up, worried that she would faint. From the nervous movements of her hands on the table, I gathered that she dreaded our talk. She'd called me intimidating. I could use that, but not yet.

I took a quick look at Hermione and Achilles playing fetch with the chew toy before I swept up the last of the hair. "I noticed a teakettle on a hotplate. Would it be okay if I fix us each a cup of tea?" It would give her something to do with her hands and make our conversation appear casual if anyone came in.

"Yes, thank you."

I chose mint tea from assorted bags in a box by the burner. I made the tea in two white mugs and carried them in. We were sure to be interrupted soon. I had to get right to it. "I'd like for you to go through what happened the night of the fire from the time you went out your front door until you heard the warning siren. Any detail you can remember." Start her talking with a simple question. "The street was dark. Did you carry a flashlight?"

Her hands encircled the warm mug. "Yes. A big old-fashioned metal one."

The one Leo had seen on the floor? "Did you see anyone as you walked to the Den?"

"No. No one was around. No lights were on in any of the houses. When I got to that old filling station, I could see a faint light in the Den, so I knew Jolene was there." She lifted the cup with both hands and took a sip of tea. "I switched off my flashlight when I got to the parking lot. I thought if she was talking to Leo, I'd turn around and go back home."

"Umm," I responded, not wanting to interrupt her story.

"I peeked in the window by the door. I didn't see anyone. I opened the front door and still didn't see anyone, just a bottle between two little candles on the bar."

Her speech had quickened. She was repeating a story she'd told many times. I needed to change that. "Was it unusual to see candles on the bar?"

She frowned. "Does it matter?"

"Probably not, but if I'm going to find a way to free Jolene, I need every detail."

"If you say so." She thought a moment. "I suppose it was unusual. Jolene said Cork was really fussy about that bar. He'd let the card players smoke at their tables in the far corner, but he wouldn't let them come near the bar or the pool table with a cigarette or cigar."

A new angle. Cigarettes started a lot of fires, at least

in beds. Maybe the fire had been an accident. But right now I had another lead to follow. "Was anything under the candles?"

"You mean anything flammable, like napkins or a cleaning rag? Ahhh. You think the candles could have started the fire." She closed her eyes. "No, I don't remember seeing anything like that." She opened her eyes and stared into her cup. "I heard a noise and turned on my flashlight and saw that man over Jolene on the floor." She covered her face with her hands. "I couldn't see her face, couldn't see that he'd hit her. I yelled at her. I said, 'Jolene, what are you doing?' She didn't answer. He sat back on his knees, straddling her. Then I saw the blood on her mouth. I hit his head with the flashlight as hard as I could."

Whoa! Monday she'd said she threw the flashlight, not that she hit him. I decided not to challenge her on it yet. She'd given me a much less detailed account two days ago.

She lowered her hands, revealing a contorted face. She spat out, "He laughed at me. He said, 'You want some, too?'" She took a series of shallow breaths. "I picked up a chair—an old wood kitchen chair—and tried to hit him with it, but he grabbed the legs and tossed it over the bar. He jumped up and knocked over the table right by me. I jerked back, sure he was going to hit me."

The threat to her was new, too. "Did he?"

"No. Jolene moaned and tried to sit up." Beatrix wiped away a tear. "She said, 'Mama?' He backed off then." Her hands clasped the mug, and her face became composed. She smiled wryly. "I guess he was too much of a coward to take on the two of us. That's when he told me to take her home."

A strange account. That didn't mean it wasn't a true one. I should ask a question to verify her story. I couldn't think of one. I moved on. "Was Jolene fully conscious? Could she walk on her own?"

"She walked like she was drunk. I put my arm around her waist and her arm over my shoulder and practically carried her. We fell down once. I had a bruise on my knee the next morning." She turned her face away. "God forgive me, I thought she was drunk. I thought what happened was her fault. I was proud and self-righteous. I sinned against her and against God." She faced me. "Help me, Phoenix. Help me lift the burden of others' sins from Hermione's shoulders."

EIGHTEEN

Was Beatrix's plea for the child calculated to conceal Jolene's guilt? I squeezed Beatrix's hand sympathetically to mask my skepticism. "I'll do whatever I can to help Hermione." I didn't hear her and Achilles. "I better check on the playmates." I hurried into the depot.

Hermione stood against the ticket booth hiding her eyes while Mrs. Olson counted.

She waved at me and pointed to a wood bench from the original waiting room. The tip of Achilles' tail stuck out from behind it.

I chuckled. "They're playing hide and seek. He always sniffs me out in an instant. Fortunately he doesn't know his tail sticks out."

Beatrix came to see for herself. "I wouldn't have believed it. She rarely plays with children."

"They're having a great time. Let's go through some other points." I ran through a mental checklist as we went back to our chairs. "What's the last thing you saw when you left the Den?"

"Wiler standing at the bar pouring himself a drink."

Back to the blow she struck. "You hit him with a flashlight. Was he bleeding?"

"Not that I could see. I heard him playing his guitar as we walked away. He certainly didn't act hurt."

She'd verified Leo's account that Wiler brought the

guitar back with him. Where was it? "I didn't see the guitar in the newspaper photo. Did it burn?"

"I don't know. That must be in the fire department's report."

"I'll check there." If Raleigh could be persuaded to let me read it. "What time did you and Jolene get home?"

"A little before two. When I started to clean her up, I realized she must be groggy from more than liquor. The doctor always told us to keep the kids awake at least an hour after a head bump. I didn't let her go to sleep until three."

"Where were you?"

"In the living room. We couldn't make it up the stairs. She was on the couch. I stretched out in the recliner."

"Was she fully clothed?"

"Yes, or I thought she was. She wore a blouse with a scooped neck and a strapless bra to work. They found the bra with the body. She didn't remember him pulling it off."

"Did you hear a vehicle between the time you left the Den and the fire alarm?"

"No."

Yet a passing motorist had called in the alarm. She must have dozed.

She added. "We have window air conditioners. Those drown out the sound of a motor."

The woman was sick, but she wasn't stupid. I had nothing specific left to ask. "Can you think of anything—anything—you haven't told me about that night?"

She didn't reply for several seconds. "Jolene swore she did nothing wrong."

Wrong is in the eye of the beholder. I decided to

throw Beatrix an unexpected question: "Did Cork Klang set that fire to collect the insurance money?"

She twisted her hands together. "I wish I could say yes. I thought so at first. I went to him and begged him to come forward when Jolene accepted that plea bargain. He denied that he'd set it. So did Wanda Sue, on her Bible." Beatrix smiled wryly. "I didn't ask Cork if he killed Wiler. He wouldn't have had the nerve to take on a man that strong."

"Don't underestimate what a person desperate for insurance money will do."

Beatrix glanced over her shoulder. "Wanda Sue confided in me that Cork never filed a claim. When he closed the steakhouse and opened the Den two nights a week, he amended his policy to cover only a major catastrophe. The policy didn't pay anything unless fifty percent of the place was destroyed. She was so upset that he had such a bad policy that she asked me to help her choose a life insurance policy last spring."

I knew nothing about small business insurance, but the policy for the Den sounded odd. "Did she show you the policy Cork had on the Den?"

"No. Cork handled that. He made the decision to open the place and to close it for good. He had nightmares about the fire. He said he couldn't work where a man died. He sold that old saloon bar to Harry's Hideaway to put in Tequila Junction and the kitchen equipment to a church. The tables and chairs that didn't burn are in the café."

If this hearsay could be believed, Cork had nothing to gain from arson. I'd suspend my judgment for now. "Who do you think started the fire?"

"It had to have been Wiler." She paused as laughter

rang out in the depot. "I don't know how on earth you can prove it, but I think he got drunk, blacked out, and knocked the candles onto the floor. It had been soaked with liquor and grease for years."

Her theory had one gigantic flaw. "Did he also kill himself?"

Her shoulders sagged. "If I could prove Jolene didn't kill him, I wouldn't have bothered you."

Achilles trotted in the door and straight to me for some stroking.

"Good boy," I said, rubbing behind his ears. He and the child both needed a playmate.

Hermione raced in and cuddled against her grandmother.

Beatrix smiled, but tears welled in her eyes. "Did you have a good time?"

Hermione hid her face in her grandmother's shoulder a moment and then lifted her head to say softly, "Can we go outside?"

Beatrix glanced at me. "Achilles has to go home now. Ask Grammy to take you."

"I'm chilled, and it's windy today," Mrs. Olson said. "I need to go home, too."

The child puckered up and hugged Achilles.

What the heck. "Beatrix, would it be okay for Hermione to play with Achilles and me in the park a little while? I'll walk her home from there."

The child nodded vigorously and grabbed my hand.

The two women exchanged surprised glances.

"Thank you," Beatrix said. "I'll be here if you need me."

I stood and handed her a folded fifty. "Thanks for the excellent cut."

Hermione tugged at my hand. "Let's go."

Wanda Sue waved frantically from her café as we walked by.

"Wait, Achilles," I said, sure the child would stay with him. I opened the café door. "The cherry pie was delicious."

She smiled, rearranging the premature lines on her face. "I made blackberry pie today."

"My favorite." My mouth watered. "I'll be back for lunch in a few minutes."

I took Hermione's hand and made a point of looking both ways before crossing the train tracks to the block-wide grassy park. On the far side, a statue of a World War I soldier stood between two large maples with red-tipped leaves. A set of children's swings occupied a spot behind Golden Oldies near the senior center, and a two-bench glider swing and a water fountain welcomed passersby to step off the cracked sidewalk.

Achilles dashed toward the water fountain.

"Come," I called. "I'll get your water bowl from the car."

He came back, giving Hermione a quick lick on the cheek before trotting to my car.

When I opened the trunk to get his bowl, he put his front paws on the edge, stretched his neck to reach a purple Frisbee, and loped with it toward the water fountain.

After filling his bowl, I steadied Hermione as she mounted a step and drank about a third as much water as she got on her nose and chin. Achilles was neat by comparison.

He nudged me with his Frisbee.

"Let's play three-way catch," I said to Hermione. "You and Achilles go over there by the swings. I'll throw it to him, he'll give it to you, and you throw it to me." I hoped my tosses wouldn't reawaken the monster.

After a few harmless collisions between child and dog, the game worked well. Then Achilles dashed after a pair of squirrels sprinting between the maple trees. They scrambled up a trunk well ahead of him and chattered while leaping from limb to limb. He watched their acrobatics, running under the limbs they landed on.

Hermione shivered as the wind gusted.

"Come sit with me in the glider until Achilles gets tired of the squirrels," I said, not sure she would do it. "I'll share my warm jacket with you." I sat on one of the benches and waited.

The child watched me for a moment, her brown eyes wide and uncertain. Then she ran to join me.

I opened the left side of my jacket so she could sit up against me and it would cover her shoulders. "Do you like my new haircut?"

She leaned forward and twisted around to study my hair. "Grammy Bea gives a great cut."

I picked up a pigtail and tickled Hermione's nose with the end of it. "Grammy Bea makes a great braid, too."

Hermione picked up the other pigtail and tickled my nose. "Your hairs are black like my hairs."

"Yes. And we both have brown eyes, too."

She peered into my eyes. "Why you got brown eyes?"

"Two of my grandmothers had brown eyes." Beatrix and Mrs. Olson both had blue eyes.

The child thought this over. "Was you a ninny? A little ninny?"

Strange question. "My big brother thought so." Wait a minute. Had I understood her? "Did someone call you a ninny?"

She nodded. "Grampa. In the Hy-Vee. Know what? Grammy Bea got mad. She told him, 'You bite your tongue.'"

A light dawned. He'd called her a pickaninny. Hiding my fury, I said, "He was joking, and your grandmother didn't think his joke was funny."

"Why?"

Not a question I cared to answer.

Achilles saved me by nudging me with his Frisbee.

"It's time for me to take you home, *Liebchen*." I stood up. "We'll play again soon."

She slid off the bench and took my hand. "Why you call me lee chin?"

"*Liebchen*. It means—umm—little loved one or sweetheart."

"Mommy sings the sweetheart song. Know what? She can't come home now. She's in school. Know what? When Mommy comes home, we make cookies and sing, sing, sing."

She prattled on and on about songs and games she and her mother would play as we walked the block to her home. I understood only about half of what she said. She stopped talking and let go of my hand only when I tapped the heavy brass knocker on the front door.

She flung her arms around Achilles' shoulders and kissed the top of his head. "Come back soon." She ran inside the moment the door opened and flung herself on the stuffed dog sitting in a miniature rocking chair.

Mrs. Olson and I exchanged the usual courtesies, and I headed back to the café weighted with the child's need for her mother. Whatever mistakes Jolene had made, she'd earned her child's love.

NINETEEN

I HEADED BACK to the café for another go at Wanda Sue
Klang. Despite her oath to Beatrix that Cork didn't leave
the bed until the siren went off, I couldn't discount him
as the possible arsonist. How should I handle the pie
maker? She was so beaten down that she'd be easy to
intimidate. The thought repelled me. I'd spread honey
to attract revelations from the pathetic woman this time.

As I crossed the street, the door to the senior center
opened and the activities director, clad in another floral blouse, bustled out with a red umbrella in her hand.

Trapped. On second thought, lucky. Connie's fan
could tell me all about the Hews and the Klangs and
everyone else in Green Springs. I'd save time and effort if I could come up with her name. I smiled as it
surfaced. "Good morning, Louise."

She beamed. "Hi, Phoenix. Did you realize you had
an audience for your Frisbee game?"

Scheisse! I hadn't noticed anyone. "No. Who?"

"The knitting group. They love to watch children in
the park." She fell into step beside me. "Your dog looks
fierce, but he was a teddy bear with Hermione. She usually won't let Beatrix or Ursula out of sight."

An opening: "I suppose she's afraid they'll disap-
pear the way her mother did."

"Very perceptive. Do you have any idea why the
child won't talk?"

She'd certainly talked to me. "I don't know much about kids. I just heard her mother's in prison for setting the fire at the Bushwhacker's Den. What happened?"

"A man came in after closing and tried to rape the girl. She was working there as a waitress. Beatrix went down to find Jolene and stopped him." The woman opened her umbrella against a few sprinkles. "After that, we really don't know what happened. The next day Jolene confessed to hitting the man in self-defense and then panicking and setting the fire. Beatrix insists Jolene was coerced to confess, that she didn't kill the man or set the fire."

An excellent summary. I suspected Louise had anticipated my question. "Why would Jolene confess if she didn't do it?" I pulled up my jacket's hood as the sprinkles proliferated.

The woman stared straight ahead. "Are you asking me as an officer of the law?"

Would I learn more with a yes or a no? I tried for the middle: "I'm an occasional volunteer, not a deputy. Besides, the case is closed. What concerns me is the child."

Louise nodded. "I could see that." She cleared her throat. "I've heard hours of speculation about the confession. Most people say Jolene confessed because she did it. A few of us think she was protecting someone else, probably Hermione's father. Whoever that is." She lifted her umbrella high enough to see my face. "Annalynn will reopen the case if you think Jolene is innocent."

I told the truth. "Only evidence can persuade Annalynn to reopen a case."

The woman sighed. "I don't know where you'd find

any new evidence now. A real investigation then might have, but not now."

Louise had waylaid me and probably knew, or guessed, why I was here. Did she want to give or receive information? Let her tell me in her own time. "Who do the observant women in the knitting circle suspect?"

She chuckled. "The romantics think a tall, dark, mysterious stranger, not Beatrix, saved Jolene from a fate worse than death. Then he killed Wiler in a fair fight and knocked over a candle—with his cape, I suppose—as he exited into the night. I call that the Scarlet Pimpernel theory." She waited for my reaction.

I smiled and said nothing.

"Then we have the TV detectives. They're convinced Leo killed Edwin Wiler to avenge Jolene and set the fire to cover up the crime." She glanced at me and added, "Neither explanation makes sense. No strangers come through Green Springs during the day, let alone at night, and Leo would never let Jolene go to prison for something he did."

She'd omitted one obvious suspect. "Anyone think his brother might have set the fire?"

"Not with Wiler in there, dead or alive. I saw Cork when they found the body. He fainted, or at least fell to his knees. He went into shock. He's never really come out of it. He was always a chubby, happy-go-lucky, glass-half-full kid. The class clown. An impulsive guy who'd pop his cork one minute and hug you the next."

As Leo had said, the brother everyone liked. I made no comment.

The rain came down in earnest, and we hurried into the café.

My phone vibrated while we waited at the counter. I

pulled it out. The screen announced Edwin Wiler. Dead man calling. I couldn't miss this call. "Phoenix Smith."

"This is Martina Pelben. I want to apply for victim's assistance."

The great-aunt had taken my suggestion. I moved away from the counter. "The foundation's guidelines and application form are online. Go to www—"

"I'll come by to fill out the paper."

Excellent. She'd handed me an opportunity to question her.

"Phoenix," Wanda Sue said, "do you want potato soup or cheese and broccoli?"

I lowered the phone. "Potato, please." I glanced at my watch before raising the phone. "I'm at lunch now. Can you come by my office on Franklin Street at three? It's the little brick house next to the Carr castle."

"I'll be there." She disconnected.

As I turned to join Louise at a table, the phone vibrated again. Annalynn.

"Phoenix, where are you?"

Achilles barked a greeting at the sound of Annalynn's voice.

"We're at the café in Green Springs. What's up?"

"Someone in a hooded sweatshirt tried to open the padlock on a back gate on Avon. The neighbor's dog scared her off, and its owner called 9-1-1."

I remembered the deep-voiced beagle. "Do you want me to bring Achilles?" I stroked his head.

"No, it's more important to anticipate her next target. I'd like for you to drive the green route on your way home. I'll email you an image of that route. Please write down the addresses of the likely targets. We'll decide where to go from there."

We lacked the officers to stake out more than four or five houses. "You expect another"—I became aware of my audience—"another visit today or tomorrow?"

"This is the third in four days. Wouldn't you?"

"A sensible person would wait a few days."

"Phoenix, this person tried to poison Achilles. She is *not* sensible."

"Agreed. I'll leave now."

"No, no. Finish your lunch. Call me when you reach Laycock. If you see anything suspicious today, please, please stay in the car and call 9-1-1. Promise me, Phoenix, that you won't be foolhardy."

"Of course not. Thanks for the call." I disconnected and strolled to the table by the window where Wanda Sue was serving my and Louise's soup, cornbread, and water. My interest in buying the Den had prompted table service.

Achilles sniffed appreciatively.

I knew Wanda Sue wouldn't dare object to his presence, but her customers might. "I can take my food as carry-out if Achilles is a problem."

Louise smiled. "We saw how gentle he was with Hermione. Besides, everyone knows he's a deputy, too."

Face solemn, Wanda Sue nodded agreement.

I sat down at the table, and Achilles stretched out beside me.

Wanda Sue shifted from one foot to the other. "Would you like me to heat your pie and serve it with vanilla ice cream?"

I smiled to relax her. "Thanks. That sounds wonderful. And I'd like a cup of coffee with it, please."

"Let me know when you're ready." She stood there, rotating the round tray in her hands.

I gave her what she wanted. "When will Cork be ready to discuss that matter?"

The crease disappeared from her forehead. "Tomorrow at three at the Den?"

Poor choice. Smarter to give me a pitch about the property's potential before showing me what a mess it was. "I'll be there."

She scurried back to her inner sanctum.

Louise said, "I heard you're considering buying the Bushwhacker's Den."

Of course she had. Trudy probably knew by now, too. Neither confirm nor deny. "I noticed the For Sale sign." I sampled my soup. Tasty and hot, a good meal for a chilly, rainy day. The cornbread was warm, too. I gave Achilles a bite containing no onion. "I remember how clear the pond was when my family fished at the Family Fish House. I never saw the other springs. Do you know where they were?"

"The biggest one was at the end of Spring Street, about three blocks from here. It, and several small ones, petered out in the twenties when coal mining was at its peak." She buttered her cornbread. "I have a small one in my backyard. I use it to water my flowers."

"Do you live in Green Springs?"

"No, three miles southeast of here in what used to be the Lone Star School. When my mother went to school there, they used the spring for drinking water."

"Do you know of any recent geological surveys that trace the sources of the springs? Explain why they dried up?"

She glanced toward the counter. "None that's reliable." She leaned forward. "Back in the eighties, a man named Cratchit—like Scrooge's bookkeeper—came to town with a map showing the underground sources of the springs. He claimed he could drill into an aquifer and start a company that would provide dozens of jobs bottling medicinal water. All he needed was the town's permission to drill." She paused and waggled her eyebrows. "Plus fifty investors willing to put in five thousand a share."

An old-fashioned con. "I don't remember hearing about that. Did people bite?"

"About a dozen did, including the Klangs. People here are honest. They don't expect to be cheated."

Hogwash. "Yet someone killed a man in a bar and set the place on fire."

She frowned. "It must have been an outsider, someone from Laycock, or maybe some old enemy of Wiler's from Springfield. He got in bar fights there."

I didn't point out that an outsider wouldn't have known Wiler had gone to a rundown roadhouse after hours. Neither would a local—except one with a reason to go there. Like Leo.

Wanda Sue came toward us with two brown mugs and a pot of coffee.

"Good timing," I said. "I'll be ready for dessert in about three minutes." Time for a neutral topic. "Is the rain letting up yet?"

In farm country, you can always talk endlessly about the weather. We dwelt on it through the truly delicious dessert. I paid my bill and hurried toward my car through a soft rain while Louise enjoyed another cup of coffee and, I assumed, Wanda Sue's latest gossip.

Leo drove past me in his white van and waved before turning toward Laycock.

I covered the front passenger seat with a beach towel

reserved for Achilles. He gave a shake that wet me more than the rain had before hopping up on the towel. When I got in, he put his head in my lap.

I stroked him. "What's wrong, *Schatzi*? You liked playing with Hermione."

When we reached the edge of Laycock, I pulled over, opened Annalynn's email showing the nearby green route, and texted her that I'd arrived. I pulled down the visor and placed my iPhone on the grip so I could see the screen and handle calls with voice commands. I drove past Laycock Storage and a block of modest but well-kept homes toward Harding Street.

Achilles popped up to look out. He barked a request for me to lower the window.

I lowered it a couple of inches. The rain guard I'd installed would shield the interior.

He stuck his nose in the crack and whined.

"It's wet out there!" What did it matter if the rain came in? Between exterior damage from a bomb and interior deterioration from Achilles' paws, my used Camry approached clunker status. I kept a blanket in the trunk to spread over the front seat when a person rode with me. Worse, everyone in town recognized the car I'd chosen because it was inconspicuous. As soon as I figured out where to go from Laycock, I had to buy a car fit for human passengers. I lowered the window three more inches, my usual concession to Achilles.

My phone buzzed. "Hi, Annalynn. What's up?"

"A white cargo van, a 2008 Chevrolet Astro, was stolen near the high school between ten thirty and eleven forty-five. The license plate is XML-358."

Two or three blocks from where the black SUV had been stolen. "Our burglar." I pulled over in front of an old frame house that had moldy white vinyl siding on the front and peeling white paint on the side. "I'm a block from Harding Street. Where do you want me?"

"Stay in that area for now. Gillian and I will patrol on the west side of town while the LPD handles the east." The police radio sounded in the background. Annalynn's voice but not her words came through for a minute. "Phoenix, don't disconnect. Tell me every turn you make."

Achilles stretched his head toward the phone to bark a greeting.

"And don't let Achilles out of the car," she ordered. "Are you both wearing your vests?"

"Yes. Why?"

"Michael found one of the two bullets the burglar fired at the house on Avon. He thinks it's from that old six-shooter stolen Monday. Our burglar is armed and dangerous."

TWENTY

"BLOODY HELL! THE burglar shot at the neighbor's beagle." Now I worried about Annalynn's safety. When we'd encountered armed criminals, she had insisted on giving them a chance to surrender rather than being sensible and shooting them. Gillian, four months on the job, would be little help. "Be careful. If you see any signs of this nut, wait for backup." I checked the street for traffic and pulled out. "Where are you? I'll join you and we'll drive parallel streets."

"Stick to the team plan, Phoenix. I won't let Gillian take chances."

True. Annalynn always watched out for others. I relaxed, a little. "Okay. I'm turning left onto Harding." Rain pelted the windshield, and I punched on the air conditioner to clear the fog. I drove slowly down a block of large two-story frame houses built in the booming twenties. A few years after I left Laycock, a real estate company divided two of them into spacious apartments with parking in the back. I'd visited one of my former high school teachers on this block. The coming of Laycock Community College had prompted someone to renovate them and create small student apartments, unlikely places to find cash and collectibles.

I turned my wipers onto full power as I cruised the next block. Here sagging one-story white frame houses from before the Second World War mingled with post-war ranch houses. The most likely collectibles here would be salt and pepper shakers.

Achilles whined. He wanted to go home. I glanced at the clock. Ten after one. I opened the console and found one of his treats. He took it and barked for another. I gave it to him and drove onto the next block.

On my left were solid two-story brick houses in five similar designs, and all featured old-fashioned, spacious front lawns. Plenty of room to play croquet or badminton, if anyone still did. Dogwood trees lined both sides of the street, providing beauty in the spring and a privacy screen in the summer. When I was little, housewives in such a neighborhood would have noticed a strange car. Today no one was home.

I pulled over in front of a distinctive two-story stone house that dated from an earlier era. A blue tarp covered most of a motorcycle parked in an abbreviated driveway. An elaborate metal wind spinner hung on a shepherd's hook in front of a bay window with no drapes. Valuable items outside, possessions on display inside. I took my sunglasses from the console and put them on telescopic vision. "Down, Achilles. You're blocking my view."

"Phoenix," Annalynn said, "what are you looking at?"

"A possible target, a stone house at 1608 Harding." I strained to see what lay behind the bay window, but rain and gloom hid the room. "No lights on. No security sign. The driveway extends only a car length from the street, and I see no garage. Is there an alley?"

"Yes, an alley runs between Harding and Coolidge. On the older houses, detached garages open to the alley, and open breezeways run from the garages to the back doors."

"Sounds promising. I'm going to take a right at the next corner and drive down the alley."

"If you see anything, get out of there. We're only five minutes away."

"Gotcha." The odds against my finding a burglar were astronomical.

The rain let up as I pulled out. I counted four houses before I took a right at the corner and another right into a narrow alley cratered with potholes. When I passed the third house, I saw an open garage door behind the stone house. I slowed to a crawl. "Mayday! A white van is parked in the garage facing out." I lowered my window to listen. "The motor's running."

"Get out of there! Gillian, step on it!"

I rolled forward to see the license plate. "It's the stolen van. I'll park the Camry in front of it and—"

"No! Leave!"

Scheisse! I considered disobeying the frantic command but elected to compromise. "I'm backing into the neighbor's driveway and parking behind a row of lilacs."

"For God's sake, Phoenix, be careful."

"I will." Now to get out of the car to peek through the lilacs without Achilles following me. I gave him the hand signal for stay, put the car in park, opened my door, and put my left foot out.

Achilles barked and lunged after me.

"Phoenix! What's going on?"

A door slammed. I drew my Glock and pushed my way between two interlocked bushes.

A figure in a dark hooded jacket raced from the breezeway into the garage.

I backed out of the lilacs, grabbed Achilles by the collar, and propelled him to my car as the van's motor roared and tires squealed. I fastened my seat belt, shifted, and shot into the alley. "We're in pursuit. Going east. Down, Achilles, down."

The van bounced over potholes, rocketed into the turn, and swooshed sideways on the wet street. The driver regained control.

"Turning left out of the alley." I skidded around the turn and stepped on the gas.

A dark car sped toward us on the narrow street. I hit my horn.

Brake lights flashed a split second before the van swerved to turn right onto Coolidge. Its rear end skidded and slammed into the oncoming car's front door. The car spun half around and slid toward me.

TWENTY-ONE

I SWERVED TO the right and stepped on the gas to evade the oncoming missile. It whacked the back of my car. I stomped on the brake as my Camry left the narrow street and plunged into a dense head-high line of Rose of Sharon. The airbag exploded in my face. The motor died.

Achilles yelped and scrambled up to me.

I exhausted my supply of German swear words as I pushed the deflated bag away and hugged him. My iPhone remained in place. Amazing that I'd heard nothing from Annalynn. I took a deep breath and spoke calmly: "The van turned right onto Coolidge. I'm no longer in pursuit." Greenery blocked my front doors and obscured my view. I checked the rearview mirror but couldn't see the dark car.

Annalynn finally responded: "Are you both okay?"

"Yes, but I'm wedged in a hedge just off Coolidge. The driver who hit me may be in trouble." My door wouldn't budge more than an inch, and the greenery looked even thicker on the passenger side. I stuck the mobile in my jacket pocket, reclined my seat, climbed over it into the back, and opened the door. Spotting the dark car in a yard, I retrieved my mobile and said, "We're out. The other car hit a dogwood."

I hurried to the car. A young blond man slumped over the steering wheel, his face resting on his right arm. No airbag and no seat belt. "Call an ambulance. He's unconscious." I opened the door and reached for his left wrist.

The kid moved his head slightly to look at me. His eyes widened. "What happened? I can't move my left arm."

A fire engine's siren sounded on Coolidge. "Stay still. Help is coming."

The engine turned the corner and stopped at an angle, blocking the street. Four men in heavy brown pants and blue t-shirts jumped out of various doors. I focused on the two beefy men running toward us carrying first-aid bags.

Achilles growled and pressed up against me.

"It's okay, boy." I grabbed his collar and moved away from the car. "The driver was unconscious maybe a minute. He can't move."

"Please step back, ma'am. We'll handle it," the older man said.

A slender but muscular forty-something man with close-cropped brown hair took my arm. "I need to check your vitals, deputy." He guided me to the engine and out of view of the action, seated me on a running board, and draped a blanket around my shoulders.

"I'm fine. I don't hurt anywhere." I put one end of the blanket over Achilles' shoulders. He was shivering against my left leg.

The firefighter shone a small flashlight into my eyes. "Looks okay." He took my wrist to check my pulse. "A little fast but not bad."

I waved away a blood-pressure kit. "I'm fine. Did you see a white van with a damaged rear end as you came down Coolidge?"

"No."

A strong, silent type. "How did you get here so fast?"

"We'd just finished a call at Tenth and Madison."

A car stopped behind the engine and two doors slammed.

Achilles barked and raced to greet Annalynn. Gillian glanced at me as she ran past me toward the dark car. I disconnected our call.

Annalynn walked toward me with her hand on Achilles' head and her public face obscuring her emotions. "What happened here?"

I told her and the attentive firefighter and added, "The van must have turned off Coolidge in a couple of blocks or the firefighters would have seen it." I looked at him for confirmation.

He nodded and left in response to a summons from a firefighter at the car.

Annalynn scribbled something in a small notebook. "Did you see her face?"

"No." I stood up to assure her I was okay. "I couldn't even tell whether it was a man or woman. Maybe the kid in the car saw the face."

An ambulance screeched to a stop behind the injured driver's car. A civilian car stopped behind it.

Annalynn moved to block my view of the action. "We'll call a tow truck to pull your car out of the hedge and to a garage."

I folded the blanket and walked over to inspect the damage. "The hood took as big a hit as the trunk." A chill made me shiver.

A flash went off. "A photogenic haircut, Phoenix," Vernon said. "Did you catch the burglar?"

Annalynn put her hand in front of his camera. "You

know Phoenix doesn't want her photo in the paper. Could you take her home, please? She'll give you her usual terse off-the-record summary. Jim or I will give you the official report later this afternoon."

"Of course." He lowered his camera. "You look cold, Phoenix. Let's get you and Achilles into my car."

I couldn't suppress another shiver. "I have to take personal items out of the Camry."

"I'll take care of that," Annalynn said. "You have a choice: Vern's car or the ambulance."

"Thanks for the ride, Vernon." I turned and almost ran into Gillian.

Her light-skinned face rosy and her short ginger hair frizzy from the dampness, she jumped back. "The driver is Brett Fairley, nineteen, an LCC student. He doesn't remember what happened. He's got a dislocated shoulder and probably a concussion. The ambulance is taking him to the hospital."

We'd get no help from him. I walked toward Vernon's car as the firefighters returned to their engine. "Thanks, guys."

Vernon opened the car door for me. Achilles pushed his way in and settled himself between my knees with his nose on my left forearm.

"You were chasing the stolen cargo van?" Vernon turned on the motor and put the heat on high.

"Only half a block." Give others the credit. "Annalynn and Jim mapped out likely target areas. She assigned me to cruise this one."

The fire engine drove by us.

Vernon backed up a few yards and turned into the alley. "Where did you see the van?"

"Inside the garage with the open door."

He stopped the car near the garage. "I know that house. Clarence Fop, the owner, died a week ago. The burglar reads obituaries." Vernon lowered his window and took a photo of the garage. "Clarence installed good locks on the house but nothing on that old garage door. Did the burglar break into the house?"

"I don't know. Achilles barked and someone ran from the back door. The van hit the kid's car at the intersection, and it hit me." I buried my cold hands in Achilles' hair.

Vernon drove on down the alley.

I held my breath as the tires rolled in and out of potholes, afraid the jolting would awaken the dormant pain.

He turned left and left again, driving down Harding. He stopped in front of the stone house. "What tipped you off to check this particular house?"

"The fancy wind spinner, the motorcycle, the—"

"What motorcycle?"

"The one that"—I stared at a blue tarp covering nothing. I grabbed my phone and called Annalynn. "A motorcycle's gone from the front of the late Clarence Fop's house. Looks like the burglar ditched the van nearby and doubled back to steal the cycle."

"She took a big risk," Annalynn said.

"So was staying in that van."

"Right. Did you see the cycle's license number?"

"I didn't see anything but a bit of a tire under a tarp."

Vernon said, "Clarence didn't own a motorcycle."

"Maybe a neighbor does. I'll let the LPD know," Annalynn said. She disconnected.

As Vernon drove, I watched for the van and brought him up to date. He volunteered to preview obituaries, vacations, special events, and anything else that might leave a house unoccupied and attract the burglar.

He pulled into Annalynn's driveway a little before two thirty. "I'll let you know what I come up with tonight after I file my story. I know you went to Green Springs. Have you found anything to support Beatrix's claims that Jolene is innocent?"

"No, the events and the people are as murky as that old pond. I heard a new theory this morning: that an outsider from Wiler's wild past tracked him down at the Den and killed him."

He snorted. "Wishful thinking. People would much rather blame strangers." He smiled. "You look like you could use a hot toddy. Take care of yourself."

"I will." I hurried into the castle and gave Achilles some of his favorite food. I didn't have time to warm up under the shower, but I changed into a wonderfully soft and warm rust-colored cashmere sweater.

At two fifty I hurried through the basement tunnel to my house with Achilles at my side and went to my office to check phone messages. Nothing but charities asking for donations.

I opened an "urgent" email from my boss at Adderly. He wrote, "I agree that Gunther's plan is woefully inadequate. Phoenix, our proposal requires your full attention. Please be so kind as to fly to New York tomorrow to consult with our office there and proceed to Vienna Saturday. I'll be most grateful."

I read it again, confirming my initial impression that Reg had issued an ultimatum: Give Adderly all of my time or none of it. My comfortable consulting role, allowing me to accept or reject assignments, no longer met the company's needs. I calculated the time difference. Late Wednesday night in Wien. Reg would be at the Staats Oper or cuddling with his wife. I had a few hours to rethink whether to cut my ties to Adderly and, consequently, to the prestigious and profitable corporate career I'd built during and after my years as a covert operative. I didn't need the money. I didn't relish the power. I didn't owe Adderly my expertise. So why was I hesitating? Because I didn't know what else to do with my life.

The doorbell chimed. I checked the outdoor camera to be sure it was Martina. I hadn't designed a strategy for questioning the grim-faced young woman and didn't anticipate an easy time. I opened the door and almost jumped at the sight of a white cargo van. The license plate told me it wasn't the stolen one. Besides, it was a Ram rather than an Astro. I fashioned a warm smile. "Come in, Martina."

Achilles sneezed and backed away.

She stared at me from hostile light-brown eyes a long moment, hands in the pockets of a huge red jacket. "You got a haircut."

"Yes, I did. You're very observant." Certainly her eyes functioned far better than her nose. She reeked of perfume. No, not perfume, men's cologne, undoubtedly the cheap stuff favored by her late lover and, I surmised, the jacket's original owner. Not wanting to endure the cologne in my office, I motioned to the conference table. "Please have a seat. I'll print an application for you to fill out."

She remained standing in the open door, her gaze on Achilles. "I didn't bring a pen."

"I'll provide one." Her breathy, little-girl voice reminded me of her somewhat juvenile behavior the night before. Could arrested development be part of her inability to move on with the grieving process?

Achilles followed me toward the office but waited in the hall to keep an eye on our visitor. I ran out the two-page application and grabbed a couple of pens from my desk.

She'd pulled a chair well away from the table and sat sideways as if she expected to run for the door. "Would you put that huge police dog outside, please? He makes me nervous."

I handed her the application. "He's a Malinois, a Belgian shepherd. I'm sorry, but I can't put him out in this weather." I searched for an excuse. "He's taking a cold."

Achilles sneezed as if on cue.

He disliked the cologne far more than I did. "I'll give him a chew toy to play with in my office." I went into the kitchen and let him select from his collection. I didn't recall smelling the cologne at Laycock Storage or Harry's. Then I remembered Annalynn burying her face in Boom's robe. Martina wore her lover's jacket and cologne to comfort her.

I shivered. I had to get rid of this chill. Hot tea should help. "Martina, I'm making tea. Would you like a cup?"

"No. I never consume caffeine." A pause. "Thank you for offering."

I opened the refrigerator. Slim pickings. "Perhaps you'd like a glass of cranberry juice?"

Silence. Then, "Yes, thank you."

I put Mom's old teakettle on the stove, shook loose Irish breakfast tea into a tea ball, and took one of the delicate Augarten cups I'd given Mom from the cabinet. Then I poured a glass of cranberry juice and took it and a napkin to Martina. "Go play, Achilles," I said.

He trotted into the hall with his toy. A moment later he peeked out from behind the piano.

She stopped writing and frowned. "Why should I tell you my annual income?"

"The level of assistance is based partially on financial need."

She wrote down a figure. "I make good money, but Edwin's death involved a lot of expenses. His mother took the car because she co-signed the loan." Her voice was bitter.

"His mother didn't help with the funeral and burial expenses?"

A long silence. She cleared her throat. "She insisted on cremation." Her face contorted. "I don't understand how she could destroy that beautiful body."

"Umm," I said, attempting to convey sympathy without commenting. Ashes to ashes, dust to dust. Did it really matter? I suspected his life cost Martina more than his death. "List any death-related expenses on the back of the sheet, please. We'll take that into account."

My kettle whistled. I poured the water into the Augarten pot. The china delighted my eyes and enhanced the tea. I put extra sugar into my cup. Then I put everything on the tray and took it to the conference table.

"I'm done." Scowling, she leaned back and jammed her hands in the pockets of the giant jacket.

His jacket. His cologne. His attitude? "I'll go over the application with you to be sure we have everything the board needs." I'd have to tie my questions to the form. I sat down across from her and poured my tea before picking up the paper. Her handwriting was full of girl-ish swirls but quite legible.

She gave her income as thirty-five thousand a year, almost certainly gross rather than net, and requested four hundred dollars a month for grief therapy. "We'll need the name of the counselor or therapist, the fees, and the anticipated duration of treatment."

"You sound like a banker, not a philanderer—uhh, one of those people with money to give away." She squirmed. "My aunt said you would tell me about counselors."

"I see." A reasonable expectation, but one I couldn't meet at the moment.

Martina reached for the cranberry juice with her left hand, but she'd written with her right. Odd. She swished the juice around and licked her lips but didn't take a drink. Tension flowed from every movement. I'd asked nothing yet. Why was she so tense? "We can research the counseling for you, of course, but that will delay implementation."

She smirked. "Just fix me up with the shrink the sheriff goes to." She glanced toward the kitchen where the old linoleum floor was visible. "Did you really live in this little house?"

"I grew up here, but I've worked in Europe a long time."

"My aunt says you made a mountain of money."

By Laycock standards. "I have more than I did grow-ing up." The applicant sounded like a curious child, but her narrowed eyes indicated calculation rather than cu-riosity.

She leaned forward. "I guess you lived in a real castle over there, not a pretend one like that place next door."

I smiled. She'd never be named Miss Charming. "I lived in an apartment in Vienna." I read the section on the victim. "You say the cause of death was smoke inhalation. I understood that he died from a blow to the head."

"No, no! He would have recovered from that. Smoke killed him." She bounced in her chair and flailed her hands, knocking over her cranberry juice. "That tramp admitted she set the fire that killed Edwin. I don't need a grief counselor. What I need is for Jolene Hew to get what she deserves—the electric chair."

TWENTY-TWO

I ELECTED NOT to point out to Martina that Missouri no longer used the electric chair. Instead I hurried into the kitchen and brought a sponge to wipe up the juice while I pondered how to handle her vehement assertion that her fiancé died of smoke inhalation. "I'm sorry to upset you, Martina, but the newspaper said Edwin died from blunt force trauma." Now take her side. "Come to think of it, I didn't see you quoted in the article."

She scowled. "That old man didn't print anything I said."

True. Vernon hadn't quoted her. "What did you tell him?"

"The truth. The tramp got Edwin drunk to seduce him. They had rough sex, and she killed him so her Jesus freak of a father wouldn't find out what she'd done."

That defied logic, but Hew's public humiliation of his daughter gave Martina's imaginative theory a modicum of credence. Go along. "Was Jolene afraid he'd disown her?"

"He did that right in church when she came home with a black baby." She watched me from under lowered lashes. "Aunt Sybil says he's got no right to be casting stones. He's been born again so many times he's copyrighted his repentance prayer."

Chalk one up for Aunt Sybil. "It's a shame that the

newspaper didn't print your side of the story. Perhaps you'd feel better if you tell me what really happened that night."

She drew back, guarded.

Retreat and coax her to follow me. "It's completely up to you. How the victim died has nothing to do with the application." I sipped my tea to give her a moment to think it over. When her shoulders relaxed, I said, "It helped Annalynn to tell me what happened when her husband died. The newspaper got that one wrong, too."

Her shield dropped, and color rose in her pallid cheeks. "That's right. He died in that motel with a young woman. Nobody but you believed the Queen of Laycock." Martina took a deep breath, rested her elbows on the table, and, for the first time, met my eyes. "It's awful. I have nightmares about him surrounded by flames. I forget to eat. I start to add a column and forget where I am." She twisted her hands together. "Sometimes I feel like I'm going nuts."

Pity for the young woman overrode my quest for information. "That's all natural when you face such a sudden, terrible loss, but you can't endure so much pain forever. A grief counselor can help you move on to the next step." And the next, and the next.

"That's what Aunt Sybil said. She insisted I fill out your application." Martina's right hand edged toward the paper. Then she pulled it back. "Who counsels the sheriff?"

No one. Annalynn hid—even suppressed—her grief much of the time. I couldn't say that to this distraught woman. "She and her minister pray together. Mainly Annalynn talks to me."

"Not to her family?"

"No." How to explain this without invading Anna-lynn's privacy? "She doesn't have any family in Lay-cock, and she refuses to burden her son and daughter. With me, she doesn't have to pretend she's fine. Do you talk to your aunt or your mother? Or a sibling?"

"No." She ducked her head. "They don't—didn't ap-preciate Edwin."

From what I'd heard, no one but Martina did. I guessed physical attraction had defeated common sense. "Does Edwin have friends you can share your grief with?"

"Not really. We hadn't lived here long. I didn't much like his drinking buddies in Springfield. That's one rea-son I insisted we move here."

"Could one of them have come up here to hurt Edwin?"

She scowled. "That's ridiculous! It was the tramp."

I was losing her. "I was thinking, Martina, that some-one jealous of Edwin's success as a bodybuilder, or with you"—may as well toss in a little flattery—"could have lured him to the Den. It's hard to see how a petite woman like Jolene Hew managed to hit a strong man like Edwin over the head. Do you think she could be covering for some man?"

She half rose. "You've been listening to her mother. She gave you that haircut, didn't she?"

"Yes, and she swears that her daughter is innocent. It occurred to me that the girl had an accomplice. Didn't you ever wonder about that?"

She eased back into her chair. "Yeah, before she con-fessed. I thought that plumber set the fire."

"You mean Leo Klang? People say he kept the fire from burning down the whole place."

She snarled, "He sure didn't rescue Edwin." She moistened her lips. "What does the sheriff talk about to you?"

I groped for an appropriate reply. "Ways to move on without her husband."

"You must be wicked good. Aunt Sybil says the sheriff is finally coming into her own." Martina fingered her empty glass. "Sorry about the spill. Could I have some more, please? My mouth's really dry."

Uncomfortable as I was being mistaken for a counselor, I moved fast to refill her glass and gain time to probe.

"Thank you," she said primly in her soft little voice. She picked up the glass with her right hand rather than her left this time. "You play piano?"

"Yes. It relaxes me. Do you play an instrument?" Right hand on the table, good. Right hand in her pocket, bad. What in hell did she keep in that pocket? A tape recorder? A rabbit's foot? A cell phone?

"I'm not musical. Edwin loved to play his guitar and sing. He was real good. That's what started the whole thing." She stared into her glass. "Not much to do in Laycock. My cousin talked us into going to that grungy roadhouse. The tramp flirted with Edwin from the time he came in the door until we left. She asked him to sing karaoke with her. She practically begged him to bring his guitar and sing with her on open-mike nights."

"Umm." Martina and Leo had seen events differently. Not all that unusual.

"We met my cousin and his girlfriend there that night. By then the crowd was drunk and real rude. Besides, those old geezers playing cards stunk up the place with their cancer candy—their cigars. We left right after Edwin finished his set."

The cigar smoke bothered her but not that awful cologne. "What time was that?"

"I don't know. We got home about eleven." She gazed intently at a ragged fingernail on her right hand.

Sure she was wording a lie in her head, I asked the obvious: "When did he leave?"

She put her right hand in her pocket but didn't lift her head. "When I went to take a shower and wash that cigar smoke out of my hair." She raised her head and looked me in the eye. "He went to get some—uhh—cigarettes."

People thought you would believe them if they met your eyes. Okay. Give her a little rope. "You mean weed?"

She fidgeted, an exaggeration of nervousness. "Yeah."

A lie to cover a lie. "Because you had a fight?"

She slapped the table with her left hand. "The tramp called him to come out there after everybody left."

But he had arrived at the Den well before closing. He had to have left within minutes of the time he and Martina arrived home. "How do you know that she called?"

She scowled. "I heard him talking to her when I stepped out of the shower." She covered her face with her hands. "I told him to stay away from her or stay away from me. That made him so mad that he left. If he'd only listened, he'd be alive and we'd be married now."

The fight might explain her inability to move on. "You said the right thing. I've had more than one man cheat on me. After the first time, I learned to walk away."

She clenched her fists and shouted, "I couldn't walk away! I loved him."

Achilles sprang from the hall and growled.

"Quiet, Achilles. Go play."

He backed into the hall, his eyes on Martina.

"That dog is scary! Can't you put him outside?"

"It's okay. You frightened him when you shouted." I needed to pull her back on track. "We always feel a loss more when our last words were full of anger rather than love. You have to forgive yourself."

Hands back in her pockets, she hunched over the table. "I can't. I just can't."

I had no answer. I lacked the knowledge or the temperament to go through an emotional trauma with this or any other applicant. "That's why you need a grief counselor." Finish the interrogation and be free of her. "What did you do after he left?"

She didn't look up. "I dried my hair and went to bed. I didn't know he hadn't come home until I woke up about eight."

Words spoken by rote after multiple repetitions. Annalynn had told me about Boom's death in much the same tone. "How did you hear what happened?"

"Sheriff Keyser, the man not the woman, came by our cabin about nine. I thought they'd made a mistake. He took me to the hospital to identify Edwin. That's when the sheriff told me they were questioning a person of interest. I knew it had to be the tramp."

"What do you think happened at the Den?"

"I *know* what happened." She'd raised her voice. She glanced over her shoulder to make sure Achilles hadn't responded. "Edwin was upset about our fight, so he went to her for sympathy. Instead she got him drunk on vodka to seduce him. He was used to beer, not the hard stuff." Martina leaned forward, tense and earnest.

"The tramp's father was right. She's a Jezebel, one of those ninjamaniacs who like kinky sex."

Ninjamaniac? I interpreted the word as a mesh of *ninja* and *nymphomaniac*. "How do you know that?"

Martina glared at me. "It's a hundred percent obvious. She slept with so many black soldiers she didn't even know which one was the father. She liked her sex rough. That's why she had that cut lip she used to claim self-defense. She left him drunk and went home to clean up." The words tumbled out. "She came back for more. She saw him on the floor all bloody. Then she set the fire to hide what she'd done."

A story to fit the grieving woman's emotional needs. On the other hand, I could assume the same about Beatrix's version of what happened.

"You think I'm making all this up, don't you?" Martina jumped up, strode to the door, and yanked it open. She paused on the threshold and pointed her finger at me. "You don't believe me? Read the tramp's confession!"

TWENTY-THREE

I WATCHED THE troubled young woman stride to her van, slam the door, and roar out of my driveway. Martina desperately needed a skilled counselor and a patient friend. I wasn't either of those. Most of what she'd told me about Jolene seducing Edwin Wiler struck me as delusional, but Martina's demand that I read the confession made sense. The catch was that Annalynn wouldn't give it and the rest of the file to me without solid evidence.

Achilles nudged me with a tennis ball.

I took it. He'd stayed quiet but on guard while Martina was here. He deserved a reward. I tossed the ball from the front door toward the basket again and again, and he leapt to intercept it, more often by blocking than catching. While he chased the ball, I thought about how to persuade Annalynn to let me see the files. None of my observations and informal interrogations reached the level of evidence. All I had was Beatrix's account, discounted by Boom, and my growing conviction that Jolene, despite her confession, hadn't set the fire. I needed something concrete from Raleigh to substantiate that.

I switched my attention to Reg's request that I go to New York. I had to answer him. I gave Achilles the ball and resigned myself to listening to bounces as I worked. I could understand Reg's position. If I wasn't coming back to Adderly full time, the company needed to hire someone else with my expertise. Reg probably issued his veiled ultimatum because he'd recruited someone and had to act or lose him. Him? I ran through a short list of possibilities. Yes, almost certainly a man, one who would make sure Adderly never called on me again.

Would I regret severing my professional ties after Annalynn settled in on the Hill? I couldn't stomach politics. No way I would stay in Laycock and run the foundation. Stuart had tunneled his way into my affection while we were investigating Annalynn's husband's death, but I couldn't envision a happy-ever-after ending with me playing stepmother to his resentful teenagers every weekend. Damn! I really missed him, but he would remain incommunicado for four more days and unavailable for another week.

The basement door creaked open, and Achilles barked a greeting.

Annalynn walked into my office, her face anxious. "Are you two okay?"

"I expect to see some bruises when I put on my pajamas tonight and to be a little stiff in the morning." I swiveled to face her. "As far as I can tell, he's no worse off than I am. How badly hurt is my car?"

She handed me a piece of paper. "The garage will give you a diagnosis and an estimate next Monday. I left the bag with your stuff in your room."

At least five days with no car. "Did you find the stolen van? Or any new evidence?"

"No. She didn't get in the house and left no prints, hand or foot. What's so important that you're working instead of resting?"

"Adderly's proposal for that potential client in New York stinks." I had to tell her the rest. "Reg wants me to fly to New York tomorrow and on to Vienna Saturday."

"Even if the CIA says you can leave the country, you can't possibly go." She paused. "I mean because of your flare-up, not because of the burglaries." She thought a moment. "I could tell Reg you were in a car accident and can't travel. That's the truth."

Or close to it. Her offer surprised me. She hated such obfuscations. I'd been a bad influence. "I have a few hours. Let me think about it." I needed to prepare her for my findings on Jolene Hew's case. "By the way, we need to review applications for grants soon."

She waved a dismissive hand. "I trust your judgment. Besides, I can't focus on anything except these burglaries. Jim is coming over tonight to plan our squad car deployment for the next few days." She rose. "I missed lunch. Let's eat whatever's on hand while you give me your read on this afternoon's attempt."

The three of us went back to Annalynn's house through the tunnel. I grilled ham-and-cheese sandwiches—a comfort food for her—while she made a tossed salad and fed Achilles. At the table, I took one of my new pills and, at her insistence, recounted every moment from the time I spotted the burglar's target house until I spoke to the kid in the wrecked car.

Annalynn's worry lines deepened. "Two aborted attempts in one day, and definitely alone on the second one. She'll try again soon. If we don't catch her, she may kill someone."

"I'm surprised she hasn't tried to sell some of the collectibles online."

"Jim says we're dealing with amateurs, probably a

man and a woman who've lost their jobs and don't know where to fence stolen items. He gave Vernon and the radio station a list of things for homeowners to do to discourage burglars. We've stressed that anyone seeing suspicious activity should call 9-1-1, not check it out themselves. The problem is that the LPD spends so much time answering calls that it can't handle much else."

The phone rang two short rings. Annalynn jumped up and hurried to the hall phone. "Maybe the LPD found something." A few seconds later, she went into the den to talk.

I cleared the table.

Annalynn came into the kitchen as I turned on the dishwasher. "Our burglar left the stolen van, wiped clean, in an apartment building's parking lot two blocks from the accident. No sign of the stolen Harley yet. The kid across the street owns it. He left the key in plain sight."

I admired the thief's daring and execution. "It took steady nerves to sneak back there and nick that cycle with us and the firefighters right around the corner."

Annalynn glanced at her watch. "I'll give you a ride to the church, if you still plan to go."

Achilles barked at the word *go*.

"I can't take him to a choir rehearsal. He would howl through the whole thing."

Annalynn reached out to stroke him. "He can stay with me."

"Then I'll drive your Mercedes, if you don't mind. Why don't you sell it to me? You won't want to own a Mercedes when you run for the House." And she needed the money.

"Boom bought that car for me." She sighed. "I'll think about it. For now, I'll take you in the SUV. Please, for my peace of mind, don't go out alone until we catch the burglars. If you're not too stiff and sore tomorrow, we'll patrol together in a squad car."

I liked the idea of riding with her. She might need my protection. "Okay. Connie can bring me home from rehearsal."

"I'll meet you at the door in ten minutes. Wear your vest and a blouse that covers your holster."

By the time we left, the rain had stopped. We monitored the LPD's radio calls as she drove. She pulled up to the First Methodist's front steps, and I jumped out and closed the door before Achilles could scramble after me. I ran up the steps to avoid hearing his howls of protest at being left behind. He'd settle down once Annalynn got him home.

Going into the simple but elegant sanctuary, I enjoyed a moment of peace. My family had attended services here. The grandiosity of cathedrals had shocked me after growing up with austere off-white walls and small symbolic scenes—lots of lambs—painted on the large but not massive windows. Here I'd exchanged wedding vows with the handsome lawyer who broke them two years later.

Connie came through the side door off the choir that led to the robe room. About twenty people, two-thirds of them women, moved to take their places behind the preacher's lectern. I recognized a former classmate at the organ, three college students from Connie's *Oklahoma!* production, and the firefighter who had checked me at the accident scene. He must be cousin Raleigh. I greeted the students, nodded to him, and took a place among the altos in front of him and to his left.

I hadn't sung with a choir since I left Laycock. In Vienna, a city filled with professional singers, I played the piano at parties and kept my mouth shut. Connie's warm-up exercises told me I'd lost three notes in my upper range, not to mention tonal quality.

Rehearsing an unfamiliar hymn and a song Connie called Christian pop, I sang the right notes softly enough not to call attention to myself.

"We'll end with a song everyone knows, 'Swing Low, Sweet Chariot,'" Connie announced. "We'll do it *a cappella*. Everyone sing the refrain. Then hum softly while Shawna takes the first verse. Raleigh, you sing the second. Caryn, the third."

Our trio had sung that song at the church a dozen times. Connie always insisted on singing the verses while Annalynn and I hummed backup. I'd objected, but Connie and Annalynn outvoted me. It still rankled.

The teenager next to me said, "I don't know the words to anything but the refrain, Miz Diamante."

"Oh. Well, you'll learn them after a couple of rounds. Phoenix, you sing verse one the first time through."

Scheisse! If I sang, Raleigh and everyone else would realize I wasn't here because of my voice. "I don't remember it."

Connie frowned. "It will come back to you. We sang that song a hundred times. You never forget anything."

"I remember that you always sang all the verses while Annalynn and I hummed."

Someone giggled, and Ed, the organist, guffawed. "She's got you there, Connie."

Color crept up her neck, but she said calmly, "Give

us the pitches, Ed. We'll try it with everyone singing the verses before we go to solos."

Why had I been so childish? My remark was going to cost me with Connie, and quite possibly with her cousin. I glanced his way as we began the refrain. He grinned and winked at me. I relaxed. After he sang his solo in a pleasant tenor voice, I gave him a thumbs up.

Connie soon dismissed the choir. The LCC students crowded around her, leaving me to corral Raleigh.

He took my extended hand and smiled. "How are you? Any sore spots?"

"I'll take a long, hot soak tonight. Do you know how the young man in the car is doing?"

"He'll be okay in a few days." The firefighter leaned in. "Connie used to make all the cousins sing backup for her at family reunions." He drew back. "How did she talk you into joining the choir?"

"She was short of altos tonight." Out of the corner of my eye, I saw the students file out through the choir door and Connie walk toward us. "After I promised to be here, I found out she bet Annalynn twenty dollars I'd come to a choir rehearsal."

He chuckled.

Connie glared at me. "Why were you such a pain in the apse tonight?"

Raleigh grinned. "You two are a hoot."

"I'm glad you're enjoying yourself." She took his arm and led him down the three steps to a front pew. "We need to talk to you."

"On foundation business," I added, following them but remaining standing as they sat sideways facing each other. "We've had an application for assistance that involves a fire you extinguished."

He crossed his arms over his chest. "I can't talk about my work."

A rule follower. Use it. "This fire also is related to an investigation."

He wrinkled his brow. "The burglaries?"

"No, this is an old case." I couldn't hide my work on the burglaries much longer. "We've uncovered some new evidence." How far did I dare stretch the truth? "Our findings raise doubts that Jolene Hew set that fire at Bushwhacker's Den."

He said nothing.

"You don't look surprised," Connie said.

He rested his hands on his knees and stared at the floor. "The sheriff hasn't asked us for additional information on that fire."

I was ready for that. "The sheriff hasn't officially reopened the case yet. That's why I'm handling it. You may remember that Boom, the prosecutor, and the defense attorney all bragged about what a great job they'd done. Annalynn won't go public until we can provide definitive evidence she can take to the court."

Connie added, "She leaves office in a month. We have to move fast."

Head still down, he muttered, "They moved too damn fast convicting that girl."

We had him. Now to reel him in. "It's critical that we see your fire investigation report, including your photos."

"It's not mine to give you. Besides, we never really finished the investigation." He raised his head. "It was July. We were working overtime on brush fires. After the Hew girl confessed, the chief said to write up what I found that morning and hold off on testing the samples until we knew what the county would pay for."

I didn't get it. "Doesn't the law require a complete investigation report on any arson?"

He grimaced. "Complete is a matter of opinion. The county can't afford to staff local fire departments, just three volunteer units with secondhand equipment. One's in Green Springs. The county pays the Laycock Fire Department a set fee based on time and mileage whenever we take our trucks outside the city limits."

"Let me get this straight," I said. "The county refused to pay for a detailed report."

"The sheriff's department said they couldn't afford to pay for unnecessary gas chromatography analyses. The confession gave them what they needed."

Connie patted his knee. "Raleigh, I know you didn't leave the Den until you knew what caused that fire. When we inspected the place yesterday, the first thing I noticed was that someone set two fires, one on the floor and one in the attic. Right?"

He blinked. "You're really serious about investigating the fire." He ran his hand back over his short hair. "Yeah, it's no secret. Two incendiary incidents."

I nodded to Connie to go on.

"Did someone spill liquor on the floor and light it?"

"No, but the floor had plenty of liquor soaked into it." He hesitated. "And lots of oil from all those dropped fried fish and—stuff."

He'd hinted at cooking oil as the accelerant. Leo had mentioned the oil Cork used to make French fries every half hour. Convinced Raleigh would tell us what we needed to know if we asked the right questions, I jumped in. "Cooking oil served as an accelerant for both fires?"

"No, at least not by itself. The arsonist had to mix it with something more volatile, like gasoline. That's what the Hew girl claimed." He hesitated. "Cleaning fluid would work, too." He squirmed and looked heavenward. "You can't prove what it was without a headspace-GC test of samples from both areas."

Then the test must still be possible. "Do you have the samples you took that day?"

"Yeah. Six of them in airtight containers. No chain-of-evidence problems." He spoke with professional pride. "We could still send the samples to the lab, if the county pays for it, but we might not get the results for weeks." He leaned back against the pew. "Besides, identifying the accelerant doesn't tell you who put it there. That's why we didn't insist on tests."

"I get that." Connie rose to pace in front of the pews to my left. "The question is whether a small woman who's just been beaten up could have put any—umm—fuel on the ceiling."

"Right." Raleigh jumped up to pace in the other direction. "That's always bothered me, especially since the accelerant was on top of the ceiling, like somebody tossed it through that panel in the kitchen ceiling."

So that's how the fire started. Stepping back to give them room to cross paths, I said, "You'd need a ladder to do that. Was there a ladder at the Den?"

"No," Raleigh said, passing Connie.

That left the method of ignition. "How fast would whatever junk and insulation was on the ceiling catch fire if you tossed a cigar on them?"

"A cigar isn't hot enough." He halted in front of me.

"Cork said the card players smoked cigars that night. We found an ashtray and some cigar stubs right by where the fire burned through the floor. I told the deputies those weren't a likely source of ignition, but I couldn't say what was."

Good. Raleigh had recognized a plant. I confirmed it. "Cork made the smokers sit in the back corner, no-where near where the fire started."

Connie stopped pacing to join us. "Phoenix, what time did Beatrix take Jolene home?"

"About two. Raleigh, what time do you estimate the arsonist set the fire?"

He thought a long time. "Well after three. I couldn't pin down how long it took the heat source to ignite the fuel and the roof to reach kindling temperature. The variables—"

Connie interrupted. "Stop talking like Dr. Smith."

I said softly, "She'll understand if you pretend you're talking to kids."

He grinned. "Okay. The fire didn't flare up instantly, at least not on the floor. You know how long it can take to start a fire in a fireplace. Overhead, it took any-where from a few minutes to more than an hour before the flames burned hot and high enough that the roof caught. The place woulda burned to the ground if that doctor on an emergency call hadn't reported the fire. A half hour later, the Green Springs crew never woulda managed to contain it until we got there."

Connie raised her eyebrows. "The volunteers put the fire out with garden hoses?"

Raleigh reared back. "No way. The LFD put out the fire—with water from our tanker truck." He relaxed. "Gotta say the vols did a good job, especially Leo. He slowed down the fire inside with foam while the other two hosed down the roof and kept sparks from spreading the fire. We all thought that old building would collapse. That's why we didn't go in until we were down to smoke and hotspots."

"No one is questioning your judgment, Raleigh." Connie perched on the front pew. "What I can't understand is why no one saw the body sooner."

Raleigh frowned. "You have any idea how dark it was in there with all that smoke? Besides, the guy was dressed in black and right up against the bar, and he was half under a big retardant cloth. Cork said he always threw it over the bar when he closed."

But did he do it then or later that night? I thought of Martina's claim smoke inhalation had caused the death. "One person told me Wiler would have lived if the firefighters got him out of there sooner."

"You mean Martina Pelben," Raleigh growled. "She's dead wrong. He was alive when the fire started, but just barely. Smoke inhalation didn't kill him. That whack on his head did. Read the autopsy report."

I had almost enough to convince Annalynn to let me do that. "How could you tell he died almost immediately from blunt force trauma?"

Raleigh's mouth dropped open. "Who said I did?"

"If you hadn't, you would have evacuated the body and attempted resuscitation the minute you saw it."

He gave an almost imperceptible nod before pressing his lips together.

I'd have to find a safe way for him to give details. "I assume you're trained to tell whether a victim was alive when the fire started."

"Sure. Basic stuff." He jammed his hands in his

pocket and stared at his feet. "When the victim has black smudges around his nose and mouth, he's been breathing smoky air."

Connie grasped Raleigh's forearm. "And you didn't see smudges on Wiler's face."

"He had a few smudges." The firefighter took a deep breath. "You can't tell anybody you heard this from me. He had some burns on his left arm. If he'd been alive, those burns woulda blistered. Besides, I doubt he coulda moved with his head bashed in like that."

"We won't tell anyone." Connie pointed to a large-print Bible on a reading stand. "As God is our witness."

He grinned. "Who can lie in a church?"

Millions of people. "Thank you, Raleigh. Anything else you can tell us? Or show us in photos?"

"I can't give you anything official, but I'll email Connie some photos of my kids that I took on my personal phone on July Fourth, a year ago." He looked at me. "You understand what I'm saying?"

"Yes. Thanks." His email would include photos taken a few days later at the fire. "I'd love to see your kids' photos."

"Most of 'em didn't come out too good. Still, maybe you'll see something nobody else did. I'll sure feel better if you do."

TWENTY-FOUR

CONNIE LOCKED THE side entrance to the church as her cousin hurried toward his pickup. "Phoenix, why did Raleigh think you're working on the burglaries?"

Careful. "When I was driving home this afternoon, Annalynn asked me to watch for a van the burglar stole. I saw it, followed it, and ended up in a hedge. Raleigh was one of the firefighters who responded." I cut off her exclamation. "I'm fine, but my car's in the body shop. Could you give me a ride home, please?"

"Of course. Thank God you weren't hurt. Trudy must be slipping. I hadn't heard a word about it." She unlocked her car doors. "Don't you want to come to my house to see the photos?"

"From what Raleigh said, I doubt we can tell much on your laptop. Forward the photos to me. I'll enhance them on the big monitor downstairs after Annalynn goes to bed and email them to you. If they show what I think they will, I—you and I—can ask Annalynn to reopen the case."

"Okay, I'll drop you off." A frown line emerged. "You've been working with Annalynn on the burglary investigation since Monday night, haven't you?"

I fastened my seat belt as I chose my words. "She's talked to me about it."

Connie said nothing for a block. "Did you tell Annalynn to keep me out of it?"

"No." Naturally Connie blamed me. I reined in my impatience. She'd always been crushed if Annalynn excluded her for any reason. "Jim suggested the investigation should stay within the law enforcement community. I'm a reserve deputy."

Connie slowed as we approached Annalynn's. "You wouldn't be anywhere on the Jolene Hew case without my help."

A typical melodramatic overstatement. Nevertheless, she deserved—and needed—credit. "You did a great job coaxing Raleigh to share information on the arson."

She sighed. "Don't be nice to me. It's unnatural. We both know you're the one he expects to handle this."

Good grief! Now I had to massage her bruised ego. I called on my better self. "Connie, he knows you as his singing cousin." Don't be too nice. "His much older cousin. I'm the mysterious stranger who almost caught the burglar this afternoon."

"And a sharpshooter." Her voice had brightened. "One of the reasons I can coax people to give me clues is that I don't carry a gun."

True, but annoying. As she turned into Annalynn's driveway, I noticed Jim's car sitting in front of a neighbor's house. Was I a big enough person to coddle Connie? Barely. "Jim and Annalynn are still working. We can go into the basement office from my house, download the photos, and go through them together."

Achilles barked from the dining room window.

"We obviously can't sneak in." Connie turned off the motor and opened her car door. "We don't need to. Leave it to me to handle Annalynn."

"Be careful. These burglaries have her on edge." The muscles in my back felt uncomfortably tight as I got out

of the car. I wanted to go straight to a hot bath instead
of that chilly basement office.

The front door opened, and Achilles raced to me.

I knelt to give him a good stroking. He probably
ached, too. I stood when he tried to lick my face. "Where
are your manners, Achilles? Say hello to Connie."

He loped to her, accepted a pat on the head as she
went in the door, and trotted back to join me.

I hurried in to hear what Connie would say to Annalynn.

Connie pointed to intersecting red and blue lines on
a city map, one of three spread out on the dining room
table. "Do I live in one of the burglar's favorite neighborhoods?"

"No," Annalynn assured her, "but keep all your windows and doors locked even when you're home."

"Turn on your radio and a lamp when you leave,"
Jim added. "Give the impression you're home. Turn
outdoor lights on at night whether you're there or not."

"Thanks for the suggestions," Connie said. "Annalynn, a choir member is emailing me some photos. Do
you mind if I download them on the big monitor downstairs so Phoenix can edit them for me?"

I couldn't have obscured our purpose better myself.

Annalynn studied me. "Connie, I don't think Phoenix
is up to that. She needs a hot soak and an early night."

"I'm okay." I headed for the basement. "The photos
will take only a few minutes."

"Enough time for you to chill," Annalynn said. "Take
the pashmina shawl in the den." She turned her attention back to the maps.

I grabbed the soft shawl and wrapped it around my
shoulders when I reached the office.

"Here's the email," Connie said, rising from the big ergonomic chair that had fit Annalynn's late husband much better than any of us. "Go to it."

I perched on the chair and downloaded twenty-three low-resolution photos into a program written for just such problem images. Five photos of kids in shorts and eighteen dark blobs. I clicked on the first blob to expand it to screen size. A dozen shades of gray and black, two horizontal straight edges, one strong vertical, and a dozen or so irregular shapes.

Connie peered over my left shoulder. "Oh, Lord. I hope the others are better than that."

"So do I, but even this isn't hopeless, or at least it's not if we can orient ourselves, figure out where he stood when he took the picture."

"He was standing at the front door, taking a wide shot. You can tell by the light."

"Good eye." The lines still didn't make sense. "I'll run through them all first to see the quality and the sequence. We may need to enhance only certain ones." I brought up each one. Four close-ups of the dead man's head and upper body were the clearest of a murky set.

Connie averted her eyes. "I can see the blood without any enhancement. Phoenix, what do you expect these pictures to prove? What are we looking for?"

I expanded the first shot and worked with it. "Beatrix said a bottle of vodka and candles were on the bar when she went in. No cloth. She heard Wiler playing the guitar as she and Jolene walked away. Leo heard the guitar and saw the candles and the vodka on the table. He thinks the cloth was on the bar. Either of them could have remembered wrong. Raleigh said a retardant cloth on the bar hid the body. He must have thrown the end of it up over the bar to get to Wiler." I zoomed in on the top of the bar. "Nothing there but the cloth after the fire."

"Umm. It hangs down about a yard. I can't imagine Jolene taking time to spread that big thing over the bar before lighting a fire."

"She or Cork could have done it as part of the closing routine." I shivered and pulled the shawl closer. "When and who put the cloth on is a wash. Everyone accepts the vodka bottle as the weapon. That leaves the question of what happened to the guitar."

Connie moved away to pace the small office. "The wood would burn. Plastic strings would melt. Steel ones wouldn't. The frets and the truss rod would resist heat, maybe even fire. We'll never be able to see things that small in these photos."

"It's worth a try. The odds are that the guitar would have been on the bar or near the body, possibly out of reach of the flames."

She paused in front of the desk. "What does it prove if we find it?"

Good question. "Nothing. It proves a lot, though, if it wasn't there." I saw her frown. "If it's not there, somebody took it between the rape and the fire. Someone other than Jolene."

Connie pumped her fist. "Of course! Just what I've been saying from the beginning. A false confession. Someone else killed Wiler, took the guitar, and set the fire."

"That's my guess." But who? A jealous Leo? Hermione's missing father? An unknown lover? "First, we have to determine whether the guitar was there."

A pain shot under my ribs. I sat straight and still, dreading a sequel. Would I never be free of this?

Achilles, draped across my feet, jumped up and whined.

"Phoenix, what's the matter?"

"This chair is uncomfortable. Give me a minute." I stroked Achilles and rubbed behind his ears. No pain. I took a deep breath. Not even a twinge. For now. "Let's focus on the key photos."

I expanded the fourth photo, one taken standing almost over Wiler's body and showing it between the bar and the overturned table that had shielded him from the flames. I trimmed the edges and fiddled with the contrast until we had a hazy view. Ashes, charred bits of ceiling, and smoking pieces of chairs and tables littered the floor visible behind the overturned table and beyond Wiler's head. Ashes dotted his black clothing. On the floor between him and the table, bits of light reflected from the flash. "Glass. Pieces of the vodka bottle. There's the neck. No sign of a guitar."

I moved on to the best close-up of Wiler's head and shoulders. I worked on it until I could make out ashes flecking the dried blood that matted his hair and almost covered his neck, left ear, and lower jaw.

Connie bent to look. "All that blood—it makes me sick."

"The blood vessels are close to the skin, so head wounds always bleed a lot. I can't be sure, but it looks like the blood dried before the ashes fell on him. That would indicate the fire started a while after he was hit."

Connie gripped my shoulder. "What's that around his neck?"

I zoomed in and strained my eyes until I figured it out. "Jolene's strapless bra."

"How weird is that!"

I smelled cocoa.

"Weird indeed," Annalynn said, putting a tray with three mugs on the desk. "Why are you two looking at those awful photos?"

Connie jumped back from the computer.

I reached for a mug. "We're researching an application to the foundation. This one requests assistance for a victim's little girl." I took a sip. "Thanks for the cocoa."

A flush crept up Annalynn's cheeks. She stared down at me for several seconds. Then she focused on Connie. "Those are photos of the victim at Bushwhacker's Den."

Achilles popped up in front of the desk. He watched us, his expression anxious.

Connie wiped a deer-in-the-headlights expression off her face and said casually, "Yes. We've been doing— research. We're almost positive Jolene Hew gave a false confession."

Annalynn's flush drained away, and her eyes darkened.

Achilles swiveled his head between Annalynn and me and whined.

Connie cleared her throat. "Calm down, Annalynn. We decided not to worry you about the case unless we could find evidence that Jolene's innocent."

"Evidence? Neither one of you knows or cares about evidence." Annalynn towered above us like a wrathful valkyrie. "Do you two crave excitement so much that you go behind my back on a closed case? How dare you attack my husband's integrity and judgment!"

"We are not questioning his integrity," I said. He'd proved repeatedly that he had bad judgment. Her face told me she'd read my thought. "Mistakes happen. Innocent people go to jail all the time."

"Despite all your promises, Phoenix, you've deceived me and involved Connie in a case you know nothing about. You've reverted to—" Annalynn clamped her left hand over her mouth.

Bloody hell! She'd almost told Connie I'd been in the CIA.

Annalynn headed out the door. "Connie, please go home. Phoenix, go to hell."

TWENTY-FIVE

ACHILLES DIDN'T KNOW the words, but he recognized the tone. He whined in distress.

"Go with Annalynn," I said softly. She needed his comforting presence more than I did. Besides, I'd goofed by not telling her what we were doing before she caught us at it.

Connie followed Achilles to the office door and stood uncertainly, blinking away tears. "Shouldn't we go after her to apologize?"

"She's in no mood to listen right now. She'll think it over tonight and calm down by tomorrow." I hoped. Maybe I should give her a few days, go to Vienna to work on the presentation. Surely by now the CIA knew who had shot me and why and would lift the hold on my passport.

"I knew she'd be upset, but I've never ever seen her so mad." Connie plopped down in the folding chair on the far side of the desk and fiddled with her left earring. She brightened. "Annalynn blames you, not me."

Because I could have stopped the investigation cold. But I couldn't then or now. I clicked on the next photo, a close-up of Wiler's face, and zoomed in on the mouth and nose. Raleigh had said the smudges there indicated Wiler had been alive when the fire started. I had to take the firefighter's word for it.

Connie frowned. "She doesn't respect me. She thinks

I'm just hitching a ride on the back of your broom. For the fun of it."

For Pete's sake. First Connie had been relieved that I took the brunt of the anger. Now she resented it. "Connie, Annalynn reacted so strongly partly because she has to acknowledge another one of Boom's big mistakes." And another instance of my keeping secrets. "Besides, she didn't expect us to work together on anything without her as an intermediary. Maybe she'd feel better if you tell her I led you astray."

"A generous offer, one I must refuse. She may not listen to *me*, and she may not listen to *you*, but she'll listen to *us*." Connie popped up to pace again. "Annalynn can't leave that poor girl in prison for something she didn't do any more than we can. We have to come up with more evidence. The question is how." She paused in front of the desk and glared at me. "Come on, you're the big brain."

I didn't bother to deny it. "I'll get something out of Cork tomorrow afternoon. He's the most likely person to have set the fire. Jolene would have gotten off on self-defense if she hadn't confessed to arson." I brought up a photo of the smoldering hole in the floor. It told me nothing. "These photos aren't much help. You said Raleigh is thorough. Ask him if he found the remains of a guitar. If he says no, ask him if he could testify no guitar was there." I clicked on a photo focused on an object eight to ten inches long up against the overturned table. I fooled with the software until I made out an old-fashioned metal flashlight, surely the one Beatrix carried.

Connie slapped the edge of the desk. "Phoenix, we're going at this all wrong. Raleigh said he couldn't understand how Jolene could have hit the guy so hard. We should be concentrating on other suspects—somebody enraged by what Wiler did." She leaned forward. "My money's on Leo, the classic rejected lover." She returned to pacing. "He was angry. He waited nearby to have it out with Jolene. He saw Beatrix go into the Den. Then he saw her and Jolene stagger home and heard Wiler's guitar."

Connie darted outside the office. A moment later, she peered through the door. Her face contorted in anger. "The bodybuilder bends over to pick up the bra, his trophy." She rushed to the desk, grabbed a stapler, and crashed it down on empty air. She gasped and stared at the floor. "What have I done?" She ran out the door.

Hmm. Beatrix almost certainly left the door open. The newspaper story said the firefighters broke the door down. Someone closed the door. Did the firefighters batter it down because it was too hot to handle or because it was locked?

Connie tiptoed back in and, her hand extended, knelt on the floor in front of the desk. "I've killed him. I've got to cover this up. But how?" She stood up. "What do you think?"

Careful. Don't dismiss her reenactment out of hand. "Your theory that Leo, or at least someone, saw what Wiler did to Jolene and went after him makes sense. From what I've seen of Leo, though, he wouldn't have let Jolene go to jail for him."

Connie sighed. "From what I've heard about Jolene, she wouldn't have gone to jail for anyone." She perched on the edge of the chair. "What if she stayed at the Den because she was meeting someone else that night? A lover we don't know about."

Possible. "Could you talk to your voice student who knows Jolene again? Maybe the girl heard rumors of another love interest."

"I think she told me all she knew, but everyone in town must have been talking about Jolene a year ago." Connie paced back and forth in front of the desk. "I'll have to mine Trudy's memory for nuggets without tipping her off that we're investigating."

Tricky, but Connie did tricky well. "I'm afraid so."

"Anything else I should ask Raleigh about besides the guitar?"

"Yes. Ask whether the front door was locked."

"Right. Not many people would have had keys." Connie began to tick off possibilities on her fingers. "Leo did. He told you he unlocked the back door. Jolene did, because she closed up. Cork did, and probably Wanda Sue. Those four have to be the main suspects for setting the fire."

"I'd thought the fire was set for the insurance, but maybe Boom was right. Maybe the motive was to cover up the blow to the head."

"We're not going to figure it out tonight. I need to go home, and you need to go to bed." Connie hesitated at the door. "Aren't you coming? I'd rather not face Annalynn alone."

As I would have to do tomorrow. "I'll go up with you."

Neither of us spoke as Connie led the way upstairs and eased open the door to the back hall. Not a sound, not even of paws.

Connie tiptoed through the kitchen and paused to study papers on the abandoned dining room table. "The

burglar reads the newspaper to find out when homeowners will be gone?"

"Probably."

She pointed to a yellow legal pad. "Lucky you.
You're patrolling with Annalynn tomorrow morning."

Not a fun way to start the day. "I'm afraid nothing
we have so far will convince her to reopen the case.
Please ask Raleigh about that guitar."

"I will. I'll call you on your cell tomorrow morning."
She motioned for me to follow her back into the kitchen.
"I almost forgot. I met J. J. Hew at the college today.
That is one handsome, sexy man. Charming, too. If I
hadn't heard how he humiliated his daughter in church,
I would've been blown away."

No one else had mentioned this. Maybe a man-
deprived two years in Laycock had lowered her standards. "What happened?"

"I was giving a voice lesson in that icy practice room.
I called maintenance to adjust the temperature, and Hew
responded. He sympathized, said he understood what
cold air could do to a singer's voice box."

I made a spinning motion with my hand to signal
her to get to the point.

She frowned. "Either you want every detail or you
want a telegram. Okay. I told him I'd met his beautiful
granddaughter. I held up my phone with the picture I
took of you and Hermione." She paused and waited.

I hadn't seen Connie take a photo. First things first.
"How did he react?"

"He stared at the photo a long time. At first his expression was soft. Then it went hard. He said, 'Who's
that woman with her?' I don't know who he thought
you were, but I didn't give him your name. I said I'd

gone to Green Springs to have lunch and saw you and the child. Then he was all charming again. He invited me to attend a big sing-along tomorrow evening at the Freewill Baptist Church."

I pondered his reaction. "He won't accept his grandchild but doesn't like it when someone else does." I had another issue. "Why did you take that photo?"

"To show Annalynn. It helps explain why you're investigating." She hurried out of the kitchen to the front door, waved good-bye, and opened and closed the door with care.

I locked it behind her and set the security system for the night. My shoulders ached. Resisting the temptation to immerse myself in a hot bath, I went back downstairs to the computer and worked on three other photos. I learned nothing. I emailed the enhanced photos to Connie and to myself and turned off the computer.

As I turned out the light to the office, I reflected that morning would bring two uncomfortable confrontations, one on the phone with my ex-boss and current client and another in the car with Annalynn. I decided to take care of one right now. I went to my foundation office to email Reg. Soften a no by giving a solution, not an explanation. I wrote, "Sorry, but circumstances preclude my flying to New York tomorrow and to Vienna Sunday. I suggest you bring in Clyde from London and Eszter from Budapest. They lack experience, but each has part of the requisite knowledge and the right mindset."

Could I fly to Vienna if I wanted to? I hadn't heard anything from either my official or unofficial CIA contacts for weeks. The shooting in Istanbul's spice bazaar had been almost six months ago. Surely Operations knew whether the shooter had targeted me specifically or I'd been collateral damage. If the shooter had targeted Phoenix Smith, covert operative, returning to Vienna posed a real problem. Still, at some point I had to empty my apartment there of both personal and professional items.

No point in asking Jerry about the shooting, even though he'd hired me for the mission. He'd been reassigned three months ago, an obvious demotion. My best bet was my handler during my final years as a covert operative. We'd used comments on blogs to pass messages since my retirement. I plugged in my special hard drive and began the worldwide journey to an Australian academic's Emily Dickinson fan blog.

Achilles barked four times at the basement door.

"Coming." He wasn't usually so vocal. I let him in, stroked him, and went back to the computer.

He came with me and stood at my side staring at the screen.

"Go play."

He didn't move. He whined softly.

"I'm almost done." I continued to type.

He barked his "come" bark and trotted to the office door.

"Just a minute." He didn't seem alarmed, just determined that I should leave. I finished the message and unplugged the hard drive.

He grasped the end of my shawl in his teeth and tugged.

"What's the matter? Did Timmy fall in a well?" I shut down the computer and turned off my office light.

Achilles trotted ahead of me, waiting impatiently when I stopped at the dining room table to check the map and the patrol schedule. After a few seconds, he barked his disapproval.

Uneasy now, I followed him up the stairs. He sat down at Annalynn's closed door and barked. He grinned the same big grin that appeared when he found a stash of marijuana.

Convinced she had sent him after me, I knocked softly on her door. No answer. "Annalynn, you know Connie and I aren't looking into the Bushwhacker's Den case on a whim, and we certainly don't mean to blame Boom for a false confession."

Silence.

"Are we okay?"

"I'm too angry to talk to you. Now for God's sake go to bed before you collapse."

That was a big improvement over telling me to go to hell. I went into my room across the hall and into my bathroom to run the water.

When I took my pajamas out of the dresser, Achilles stretched out on his old green blanket. "Good boy," I crooned. I stroked his back and sides, careful not to rub hard. He surely had bruises just as I did.

I saw how many when I got in the tub. None hurt unless pressed, but I made a mental note to wear a long-sleeved blouse tomorrow. After relaxing in the water a couple of minutes, I turned my mind to planning what to say to Annalynn. First, an apology for not telling her sooner. Then the facts of the case. Plus my interpretation of them. No lies, no evasions. Except that I'd keep my promise to Beatrix not to tell Annalynn that her old friend had terminal cancer.

By the time I made my way to bed, Achilles was

asleep, an old beach towel draped over him for extra warmth.

Annalynn remained furious with me, but she had worried about Achilles and me.

TWICE DURING THE night I heard the double ring that signified a call from the sheriff's department.

When the grandfather clock chimed seven and forced my eyes open, the beach towel lay atop the green blanket. I got up and looked out into the backyard. Annalynn was sipping a cup of coffee and reading the newspaper at the patio table while Achilles inspected the orchard for intruders. A normal morning.

Except for one thing. A navy windbreaker covered her shoulders and hung down so far the sleeves touched the patio. It reminded me of Martina in Wiler's red jacket. I'd never seen Annalynn wear any of Boom's clothing before. Damn! Questioning his handling of the arson case had pushed her backward. Dreading talking to her, I dressed quickly in brown slacks, my Kevlar vest, a green t-shirt, and a beige blouse almost the same color as Annalynn's uniform.

I peeked out the window. She accepted a grimy tennis ball from Achilles and threw it toward the orchard. She usually refused to touch those dirty balls. She was stalling, putting off coming inside to face me. I hurried downstairs, poured a cup of coffee, toasted a cinnamon raisin bagel, and went through the tunnel to my office.

Too soon for a reply to my coded query on the blog, but I could expect something from Reg. I opened my email. One from Reg and another from Eszter. I opened his first. "Forgive me for asking you to travel so soon after your auto accident. I hope you weren't badly hurt and will be able to lend us your expertise in New York in a fortnight. I've acted on your suggestion, but even two future stars don't burn as brightly as you."

Bloody hell! He or someone else at Adderly must be monitoring me on Google and found Vernon's article on yesterday afternoon's car chase. Hmm. Reg was too ambitious to let our friendship stand in the way of replacing me. I had underestimated my value to Adderly.

Eszter's flowery note expressed her thanks for my recommending her and pledged to live up to my faith in her. She also said how much she looked forward to my leadership during the presentations in New York.

My mobile buzzed. Connie. I answered.

"Can you talk?"

"Yes, she's avoiding me by playing with Achilles out back." I picked up my bagel. Connie would give me plenty of time to chew.

"Raleigh raked through the ashes at the Den before he had to leave. He didn't find anything resembling part of a guitar. He plays one, so he would have recognized it. He doesn't know whether the door was locked. He can't give us anything else without an official request."

Remarkably succinct for Connie. "Good enough, for now. He must think we're right."

"He always did, but his wife—and the chief—told him the confession settled it, to let it go. Now he feels guilty that he gave in." She paused. "We have to protect him, Phoenix."

"Of course. Annalynn has learned not to question me too closely about my sources." I might not get the usual pass this time.

"One other thing. One of my voice students is singing this morning at a charity brunch at the country club. It's not in the morning newspaper, but she told me her name is on announcements posted at the library, Harry's, and a bunch of other places. The burglar could have seen it."

"Could be. Do you know who's chairing the brunch?" I dropped the last of my bagel on the plate and Googled the country club.

"No. Annalynn did it last year, and the year before, etc. She may know."

I clicked through to the club's events page. "Here it is online. Rita Ellison chairs a committee of five. I don't know any of them or where they live."

"Annalynn has probably been in all their homes for meetings or parties."

"Right." I hit Print and looked out the window. "I don't see her or Achilles. I better get going in case she plans to leave without me. Bye."

I grabbed the sheet from the printer and ran. I heard Achilles bark as I started up the stairs and slowed down. Opening the door into the back hall, I greeted him with a rub behind his ears. "Good morning," I said stepping into the kitchen.

Annalynn emptied the coffee pot into a thermos and said nothing.

Achilles darted away and came back with one end of his leash in his mouth.

"No run this morning, boy. We're going on patrol with Annalynn."

She poured milk in the coffee. "I don't want to take you away from your hobby for a mere burglary investigation."

My hobby? I bit back a retort. Annalynn hated confrontations. Now she was trying to push me into one. Arguing while patrolling would interfere with our task. No matter what she said, I wouldn't fight with her. "When do you want to leave?"

"In five minutes."

"I'll be ready." I dropped the sheet onto the map on my way upstairs. Determined to be ready in five, I brushed my teeth and strapped on my holster. I grabbed Achilles' vest and ambled down the steps to the front door with seconds to spare.

Eyes focused on the brunch announcement, Annalynn said, "Is this your hunch of the day?"

"Connie mentioned this notice is posted around town. Any of the committee members look like possible targets this morning?"

She glared at me. "I asked you not to involve Connie in the burglaries."

The irony of my defending Connie's involvement made me smile. "I didn't, but she was sharp enough to recognize the possibility and volunteer the information. It's up to you to evaluate it." I fastened the vest onto Achilles.

Annalynn folded the paper and tucked it into the map. "Please tell me she's not out patrolling with some LCC criminal justice student."

Considering Connie's thirst for drama, that wasn't as farfetched as it sounded. "She's busy making a living today." I needed to coax Annalynn out of her sulk to concentrate on business. "We investigated Beatrix's application on our own because we didn't want to disturb you with it unless we found her claims had merit. We meant to spare you, not hurt you. We're not sorry we investigated. It needed to be done. I am sorry our secrecy hurt your feelings."

She ducked her head, hiding her reactions. When she

faced me, she wore her public face. "Phoenix, I have to concentrate on this burglary case. We'll talk about the 'application' after we've caught the burglar." Sheriff Keyser picked up a set of keys and a tote bag. "I'll drive. We're taking a squad car rather than my SUV. I want people to see the department is on the job." She sighed. "And call off Connie, for God's sake. She'll get herself in real trouble trying to play true detective."

"That's my line." I'd said something similar to Annalynn a dozen times.

She didn't smile. "I have water and treats for Achilles. Do you want to add a snack or anything to my bag?"

Achilles trotted to her and dropped in a green Frisbee.

"You're so smart, Achilles," Annalynn said, stroking his head.

Had he understood her question, or did the bag remind him of his new game? Either way, he'd pleased Annalynn. I went into the kitchen. "I'll peel a banana to eat as we go. Any sign of that stolen motorcycle yet?"

"No. We'll watch for it on patrol." She pulled a small pad from her blouse pocket. "It's a small model, a 2007 Harley Sportster, cobalt blue, license G2G53."

We went out to a squad car parked in her driveway and coaxed Achilles into the back seat filled with unpleasant odors left by former passengers, usually drug addicts or drunks.

I finished my banana, put on my seat belt, and made sure I could reach my Glock quickly. "I saw the patrol schedule. How long can the city and county keep that up?"

"We'd planned on four days, but I don't know

whether our staffs can handle that. People are report-
ing so many suspicious incidents that they're running
Jim's officers ragged." She backed out with her usual
caution and drove toward the northwest corner of town
where houses sat on both sides of the city line. "I have
a theory. I think our burglar gets a thrill from stealing
collectibles that the victims value for personal reasons,
not for their dollar value."

Greed motivated most people. "I doubt she's robbing
surrogates for her parents or in-laws. Criminals—burglars
to bankers—prey on people who are vulnerable."

"Surely no one steals towels because they need towels. They must be trophies."

"Awfully modest ones. What does Jim think about
your thrill-seeker theory?"

"I wanted to test it on you first. You're addicted to
action, to the adrenaline rush that comes from taking
chances."

Be honest, Phoenix. "I do get bored with routine,
but I never take a risk without a cost-benefit analysis."

"You're rationalizing. You've been rushing to find
and conquer new challenges your whole life. It's who
you are."

Was that so bad? I glanced at my watch. Only eight
fifteen. "What are our challenges today? We surely
aren't going to drive around two square miles all morning."

"No, you're going to look for likely targets, ones
worth staking out. You obviously think like a burglar."

Compliment or criticism? I didn't ask.

Forty-five minutes later I'd seen nothing that ap-

peared ripe for burglary. Achilles and I both were grow-
ing impatient.

Annalynn used her cell rather than the police radio
to talk to Jim. "I'm leaving sector five to check out
Phoenix's hunch, the Ellison house by Big Bass Lake.
Please send a car to the Jablonski place on Pierce Street.
Both owners will be at the country club this morning."

Good. She hadn't dismissed Connie's tip. "I don't
remember Big Bass Lake."

"It's a giant pond in the hills off Western Road outside
Laycock. In the late eighties four families bought the land,
dammed a creek, and put up houses in the timber around
it. Those trees offer burglars ample cover."

A tingle went down my spine. A perfect set-up. I put
on my sunglasses with the adjustable binocular lenses
and scanned the brush on the right side of the road. As
we approached a private gravel road, the sun reflected
off metal. "Stop! I see something odd down that road.
What's it lead to?"

Annalynn braked hard. "No homes." She backed up
a few feet to make the square turn. "A couple of shacks
that church groups rent for overnight campouts." She
drove slowly down the rutted road.

"Look left! Behind that gooseberry bush. It's a motorcycle." I let the sunglasses fall on their chain and
drew my Glock. "It's black, but I'll bet it's the right one."

"How on earth did you see that from the road?" She
stopped the car.

I jumped out and opened Achilles' door. When he
loped into the woods and left his mark on a tree, I lowered my Glock.

Annalynn, her service weapon at the ready, crept to

the cycle. "Right make, wrong color, and wrong license number." She bent for a closer look and gasped. "No! This is it. She painted it black and changed a *G* to a *C* and a three to an eight. We've found her!"

TWENTY-SIX

I PUT MY sunglasses back on, adjusted the lenses to infinity, and moved around the motorcycle to stare toward the Big Bass Lake development. Trees and undergrowth blocked my view. "How close are we to the Ellison house?"

"A quarter of a mile as the crow flies," Annalynn said softly. "I'll call for backup." She walked toward the squad car talking on her cell phone.

I touched the rocker box covers on top of the engine. Not even warm. The burglar would already be in the house. If we moved fast, we might catch her there. And if we missed her? I opened a tiny blade on my keychain, reached under the tank, and cut the wires going to the coil. I joined Annalynn. "We can't wait for backup."

"Gillian will be here in eight minutes. LPD will send a car when it can."

The rookie crime scene investigator would be no help. "Tell her to watch the motorcycle in case the burglar gets past us. We'll go on foot."

While Annalynn conveyed the orders, I moved our squad car down the gravel road around a corner and rejoined her. Her service weapon was in its holster. "You have a round in the chamber?"

"Yes, but don't shoot unless she displays a weapon."

"Okay. Let's go. Quiet, Achilles." I jogged through

the woods with Achilles ranging ahead and Annalynn close behind.

In three or four minutes we reached an open area and the development's one-lane paved road. A thirty-foot-wide strip between the pond and the road looked as well maintained as a golf course. On the side next to the main road, trees and brush obscured the houses, which had been built up against a steep hill. I could see only the closest house through the foliage. "Achilles, come. Quiet. Stay with me. Annalynn, where's the Ellison house?"

"It's the last of four on this side of the pond. We can go behind the houses and keep out of sight."

"We'd better check the back doors in case the burglar went into another house." I listened for the sounds of movement outside or occupation inside. Nothing. "Okay. Let's hotfoot it across the road into the woods behind the first house." I took a deep breath and ran.

Achilles stayed right by my side. Annalynn caught up with me when I slowed to a walk in the shelter of the woods. The three of us approached the first house, a two-story natural-wood modern. No sign or sound indicated a person or a pet.

Annalynn pulled a glove from her Sam Brown Belt and tried the back door. Locked with a good deadbolt.

We moved on to the next two houses. Two cats, one black and one white, watched us from a window of the third house. They vanished when Annalynn tried the back door. Locked.

I crept to the corner of the house, this one a light stone with matching patio, and peeked at the Ellison home, another two-story natural-wood modern. A four-foot-high stone wall separated the narrow, tree-less yards. A form moved by an upstairs window.

I jerked back out of sight. "Either they have a giant cat or a visitor." Accosting an armed burglar in an unfamiliar house struck me as foolish. "We'll get the drop on her as she comes out. Maybe by then we'll have backup. I'll watch the windows while you and Achilles run for that wall. You cover the front door from there. When you're in place, I'll go cover the back door."

Achilles stood alert, his shoulder against my left leg.

"Quiet, boy. Go with Annalynn."

He looked up at me, and she moved between him and me to put her hand on his collar.

I studied the windows. I couldn't see anyone. "Go!"

Annalynn ran to the wall and ducked down. She crept along it to the end with Achilles at her side, knelt on one knee, and drew her Glock.

A door banged against the back wall of the house. A figure in dark blue leapt atop a three-foot-high stone retaining wall and plunged out of sight between bushes.

"Stop! Police!" I shouted, racing after her. I jumped onto the wall and shouldered my way through the bushes only to face a hill as steep as stairs. Legs in blue jeans vaulted up the hill with the ease of a bobcat. I holstered my Glock so I could use both hands to scramble after her—or him. That worked for about ten feet, then my foot slipped and I fell. A stick dug into my stomach, and pain almost made me black out. I turned onto my back and grabbed a sapling to slow my slide down the hill.

Achilles bounded up the hill to me. He barked and snarled but didn't follow the burglar.

"Go on after her," I gasped out as Annalynn emerged from the bushes.

She hesitated a moment before beginning to climb.

Achilles licked my face and whined. He refused to go.

I fought to stay conscious, dimly aware of Annalynn struggling up the hill.

Then I heard a motor roar and the squeal of tires on the main road.

Bloody hell! The burglar had outrun and outsmarted us.

TWENTY-SEVEN

I SAT UP and warded off Achilles' kisses as Annalynn half slid back down the hill.

"Phoenix?"

"I slipped. I'll be okay in a minute." Please let it be true. "Did you get a look at the burglar or the vehicle? All I saw was a figure in jeans and a blue hoodie."

"I didn't even see that. I sent out the alarm and told Gillian to go after her."

A car raced by on the main road and screeched around a corner.

Annalynn offered a hand to pull me up. "Gillian is too far behind to catch the getaway car, or even to see which way she went at the crossroads."

I reached out for Annalynn's hand, but pain changed my mind about getting up. "I need another minute. You and Achilles take a look around."

"Please let me call an ambulance, or at least a doctor."

"Definitely not." We'd gone through this before. A medical exam would shatter my cover story of recovering from gall bladder surgery.

Achilles stretched out close to me and put his snout on my shoulder. He licked under my chin.

Annalynn knelt on my other side. "He's not leaving you, and neither am I." She studied my face. "Your color is coming back. That's always a good sign."

The sharp pain turned into a dull ache. I sat up, felt no repercussions, and reached out for a hand up. "I'm all better. Well, mostly better." I inched my way down to the wall. I didn't relish the idea of hopping off the retaining wall into the small patio as I normally would have. Instead I perched on the wall and faced the open back door. "Look at that. She dropped the trophy towel and some jewelry." I tried to remember the blur of blue leaping onto the wall. "I'm not so sure the burglar's a woman. Whoever it was rocketed up that hill like a mountain goat. The hill on Avon is almost as bad. Are there any rock-climbing clubs here?"

"I don't know of any." Annalynn brushed dirt off her slacks. "It had to be two people today, one to ride the motorcycle and one to drive the getaway car. Michael has always thought it's LCC students. Maybe he's right." She extracted a fresh pair of gloves from an attachment on her twenty-five-pound belt and began to pick up the jewelry. "Could there have been two people in the stolen van yesterday?"

"I didn't see a second person, but it's possible."

Annalynn picked up a necklace of dark pearls. "This would sell for less than a hundred dollars in a department store. None of these pieces would bring more than a few dollars at a flea market or pawnshop. Most women would know that. Maybe the burglar's a man after all."

"Taking costume jewelry doesn't fit the pattern. Surely you steal collectibles either for a specific buyer or to sell by the piece. Does the owner have a special collection?"

"I'll find out when she gets here." Annalynn paused to answer her cell. "No, come back here to process the crime scene, please." Pause. "Leave the motorcycle to the LPD. That's their case." She signed off, placed the jewelry in the center of the towel, folded it, and put it on the wall. "You go rest on the front deck while I check the hill for footprints."

I started to object, but sitting in the sun a few minutes sounded good for what ailed me, an expression my mother had used when she forced unwelcome potions down our throats.

Achilles came with me to the front of the house. I sat on the deck in a swing glider so that he could join me.

He put his head in my lap for me to stroke.

I rolled up my sleeves to my elbows and tried to relax in the late September sun. I couldn't. "That's twice I've not moved fast enough, Achilles. Three strikes and you're out. No, third time's a charm. If I'm going to be trite, I might as well be positive."

He raised his head to stare toward the pond. He scrambled out of the glider, dashed across the grass, and plunged into the water.

"What the heck?" I walked toward the bank as he swam farther out.

He veered to his right, grasped something in his mouth, and paddled toward me.

A black Malibu turned into the property and raced toward the house. It turned into the driveway, and a tall woman with short, curly, orange-red hair rushed to the front door and let herself in.

Achilles splashed ashore. Something yellow protruded from his jaws.

I held out my hand to take his prize. A rubber duck. I jumped back as he shook water off of him and onto me.

The front door opened, and Annalynn came out on the deck. "What did he find?"

"A bathtub toy. What did *you* find?"

"Nothing so far."

The redhead spoke behind her, but the words didn't carry.

Annalynn said, "How much?"

I couldn't hear the reply. I walked toward the deck. "What is it?"

"Two hundred dollars disappeared from the cookie jar," Annalynn said. "We're going upstairs to check there." She pointed toward the pond, where Achilles was swimming again. "I can't bring him in the house wet. How long will it take for him to dry off?"

"A few minutes. I'll take him around back. Maybe he can identify the scent on the towel and follow it."

"Why? We know where she—or he—went."

"If Achilles knows the burglar's scent, he may recognize it another time." I thought of our other attempts at tracking. "He tracks us on his own, but he doesn't really understand tracking a stranger."

"Worth a try." Annalynn watched him a moment. "He loves the water."

A squad car sped toward us. A green Buick followed more slowly. Gillian pulled over, waved to me as she took her CSI bag from the trunk, and hurried to the house. Vernon got out of the Buick.

The redhead let Gillian in and yelled, "No photos, Vernon Kann. I don't want to advertise my home to burglars. This is private property. Get yourself out of here."

"Now, Rita, I—"

Annalynn stepped in front of the woman to interrupt him: "Could you take Phoenix home, please?"

He glanced at me and took a step toward Annalynn. "I need the *official* story by eleven thirty."

She held up a restraining hand. "Phoenix will give you the basics. Call me at eleven fifteen with any questions."

I heard Achilles give a giant shake and felt sprinkles on my back. "What about Achilles?"

"Let him sniff the towel and see whether he can pick up the scent on the road as you leave." Annalynn stepped inside and closed the door.

I couldn't ask Vernon to put a wet dog in his meticulously clean car. "I'll finish here and meet you at the main road." He'd never leave without photos. "No, I'll meet you on the road to the campground—by the stolen motorcycle."

He grinned and opened his car door. "Thanks. Take your time."

Achilles gave another shake.

"Come." He trotted all around me but never more than a few feet away as I walked to the back. The light-blue towel was still on the wall. I didn't have any gloves with me, so I took a light hold on Achilles' collar and brought his nose near the towel. "Find, please."

He stared at the towel and then looked up at me for clarification.

I pushed his nose closer.

He sneezed and pulled away.

I lowered my head to sniff. Perfumed laundry soap. "Okay, we'll pass on this." I went to the door to inspect the lock. A good one, and no scratches or gouges indicated it had been forced.

Gillian opened the door. "I came to get the stolen items. Could Achilles pick up the scent?"

"No. I suspect the owner forgot to lock the door."

Gillian stepped onto the little patio. "I'll tell the sheriff. This lady acts like the burglary was our fault. She's a real pain."

"Annalynn will placate her. I'm getting out of here." My pain now gone, I jogged to the road by the so-called lake.

Achilles loped to the bank and along beside it parallel to me.

Discomfort under my ribs warned me to slow to a walk.

Achilles whined and came to my side.

"I'm okay."

He trotted back toward the house, barking three times to get Annalynn's attention.

"Come," I called. Annalynn had enough on her hands without worrying about me. I walked on, taking care not to jolt my upper body. "We're going home."

The word *home* brought him back to my side. He stayed there until my tense shoulder muscles loosened and I moved freely. Then he loped into the woods the way we'd come.

A couple of minutes later, a man called, "Phoenix?"

"Coming." I saw a blue uniform running toward me. "Hi, Michael. What's wrong?"

He waited for me to reach him. "Just making sure you're okay. Sheriff Keyser said you're to go straight home. How in heck did you find the motorcycle?"

"The sun glinting off the metal caught my eye. You'll find my prints on it. I cut some wires to disable it."

Vernon joined us. "How did you know the burglar would hit the Ellison house? We killed the brunch announcement so the burglar wouldn't see it."

Give Annalynn the credit. "The sheriff thought one

of the organizers might be targeted, and the Ellison house seemed the most vulnerable."

Michael and Vernon exchanged glances, and Michael said, "Those burglars must think you're psychic, Phoenix. You've called the last three. What's your next prediction?"

"I have no idea, but common sense says to expect a change in M.O.—an earlier or later time, a different target group, entrance through the front rather than the back."

Vernon shook his head. "How do you know how criminals operate?"

Careful. "I don't, but I've spent my life analyzing facts and statistical probabilities."

Vernon smiled. "Here's a probability for you: Annalynn will have my hide if I don't get you home. She called and asked me to stay with you an hour or so to make sure you're okay. And she would like for you to remind Connie it's her turn to cook tonight."

I breathed a sigh of relief. Annalynn had signaled a truce, or at least a debate. "Let's go, but on the way I want to see where our rock-climbing burglar came out of the woods and where the getaway car was parked."

"Check the trailhead around the next curve," Michael said. "When my church group camped out here, we'd hike along the old railroad tracks and follow a trail to the top of the hill."

Vernon and I walked to his spotless Buick, which was parked by the main road. I checked Achilles and his vest for dampness. Not dry enough to lie on the back seat. "I'll wrap Achilles in my shirt and let him sit between my knees, if that's okay with you."

"Of course. I'll slide the seat back to give you more room."

Achilles loved this arrangement. He barked a protest when Vernon pulled over near where the burglar ran out of the trees onto the road.

Vernon peered into the trees. "He sounds unhappy. What's wrong?"

"Nothing. He wants to go home." I coaxed Achilles out and, after insisting Vernon not photograph us, walked up and down the edge of the wood. I saw no footprints or broken twigs or those handy shreds of garments so common in TV cop shows. Achilles showed no interest in tracking a scent. When he trotted back to the car and sat by the door, I gave in.

At the trailhead pullout, I learned nothing except the thick brush would have hidden the getaway car from any passersby. I walked across the gravel to a dirt path zigzagging down a long hill to the railroad tracks. Halfway down a narrow dirt road ran through scrubby trees. On the far side of the tracks, a woman with a black-and-white collie strolled along a path toward the Laycock city limits.

A peaceful scene. Yet the burglaries had disturbed the peace of the whole community.

We drove down the hill, crossed the unused tracks, and turned left at a four-way stop. The getaway car had a choice of escape routes. We drove through a neighborhood of nicely landscaped houses built, Vernon said, in the nineties.

I filled him in on what had happened. Chagrined that I had allowed the thief to escape, I used the sight of the brightly painted buildings of Laycock Storage to change the subject. "I didn't read any quotes from Martina Pelben in your articles or your notes on the Hew case."

"There's a reason for that. I hadn't heard such swearing since Vietnam. I would have risked libel charges if I'd printed what she said about the Hew family, the sheriff's department, and the prosecutor. The Pelbens are known for hot tempers. Hers never cooled down."

She hadn't sworn much when she talked to me. Maybe she thought I'd be shocked. "Do you know her family well?"

"I knew her uncle—her great-uncle that would be— fairly well. He bought the old motor lodge twenty years ago for next to nothing. He expected to sell it to some big-box store or fast-food franchise for a huge profit."

"When did he convert the cabins to storage?"

"After LCC opened. He renovated one unit to rent to students as a test. No one would live in a place that small. He didn't make back his investment. He didn't make much on the storage either, but he didn't work all that hard at it. He didn't need the money. Sybil, his wife, sold her share in the family farm when land prices were sky high." He stopped at a light and glanced at me. "Have you found out anything to help Beatrix yet?"

"No, but I expect to prove Jolene didn't set the fire. Did you see the remains of a guitar in the Den?"

"If it's not in my photos, I didn't see it. Have you told Annalynn what you're doing yet?"

"Sort of. She caught Connie and me looking at photos on the computer last night. I've rarely seen Annalynn so angry."

"The jail administrator's write-in campaign has upset her, too."

News to me. "That misogynistic jerk is running against Jim for sheriff?"

"Not officially. It's too late to file. Yesterday three people told me that he's using the unsolved burglaries as an excuse to start a word-of-mouth campaign. He claims Jim is nothing but Annalynn's toady, and neither is competent. He wants to bring them both down." He stopped at another light and twisted in the seat to face me. "Phoenix, I'm the one who sent Beatrix to you, but you need to postpone work on her daughter's case and catch these burglars. Annalynn's future in politics may depend on it."

TWENTY-EIGHT

VERNON'S PLEA TO postpone work on the Hew case to catch petty criminals struck me as both ill-timed and ill-advised. "I've set things in motion in Green Springs that I can't stop without scuttling the investigation. As far as catching the burglars goes, I'm strictly a foot soldier, an extra pair of eyes for two understaffed police departments."

"But you've identified the last three targets."

"No, I didn't." This time I refused to take credit, fearing undeserved praise would raise unrealistic expectations. "Michael showed me what attracts burglars. Annalynn sent me to Harding Street to patrol, and I applied Michael's criteria. Connie told me about the brunch, I mentioned it to Annalynn, and she decided to go to the Ellison house."

Vernon turned off the motor. "I see. You had absolutely nothing to do with anything."

Sarcasm didn't become him. "Thanks for the ride." I opened my door, and he opened his. "You don't need to walk me to the door, Vernon."

He smiled. "Sorry, foot soldier, but the general gave me strict orders." He opened the back door to get his laptop. "We can both work."

Achilles loped toward Annalynn's backyard.

"Come, Achilles," I called, uneasy about letting him

stay outside alone. "Vernon, please come in and sit a spell," I said with my grandmother's intonation. "You can explain to me how Jim's election affects Annalynn's bid for the House."

"He's her candidate. He has a weak opponent. If she doesn't have enough influence to make Jim the next sheriff, donors will discount her as a candidate in the primary campaign."

I didn't know how seriously to take this. "Is the new write-in candidate spending his money or someone else's?"

"I don't know. All he's done so far is talk and order yard signs and bumper stickers." The newsman's mouth flew open. "My God! You suspect somebody is financing a write-in campaign to lame Annalynn at the starting gate?" He shook his head. "No, no. People expect her to take over the new foundation. No one knows she's planning to run."

"She's had great publicity for her work as sheriff. Any ambitious idiot could figure out she's a good candidate." I unlocked the door, pushed it open, and held it for him.

"I'll ask around. Would you mind if I listen to the local news? I want to hear what my competitor reports."

"Good idea." I hurried into the kitchen to turn on the radio. "Have a seat at the dining room table. I need coffee. Would you like something?"

"No thanks. Just water. I've had my caffeine for the day."

Achilles rubbed his Kevlar vest against my leg.

"Sorry, boy." I removed it and draped it over a kitchen stool. Then I turned on the radio and started the coffee.

A man said, "After many years of farms becoming larger and larger, we've seen a move toward small farms, many of them raising organic produce for local markets. Some farmers supplement their incomes by engaging in agrotourism. For example, they give children, or whole families, a chance to tend a garden or feed chickens or milk goats."

When I'd done such chores on my grandparents' farm, we'd called it work.

"Congratulations on your award for encouraging agrotourism, William Cadoni," said the interviewer. "Pleased stay tuned for 'News at Eleven.'"

My coffee was ready by the time the news came on.

"We have breaking news," the station owner said. "Sheriff Annalynn Carr Keyser interrupted a burglary this morning at the home of Rita Ellison, Big Bass Lake. The burglar eluded Sheriff Keyser and a deputy. We'll have a report from the sheriff on 'Noon News.'"

"Damn," Vernon muttered. "How in hell did he pick that up? Annalynn and Jim have been using phones to keep everyone from following them on their police scanners."

"How did *you* hear?"

"My daughter covered the brunch. Rita announced a burglary-in-progress before making a dramatic exit." He pointed a finger at me. "I need something the station won't have to post on our website."

"Like a photo of the recovered motorcycle?"

"Thanks. I forgot to upload that."

With Vernon occupied, I took my coffee into Annalynn's office and dialed Connie's home number.

When she answered, I said, "Annalynn said to remind you it's your turn to cook tonight."

"Thank goodness. That means she's forgiven us. I'll

come over right after my last voice lesson." A woman singing an exercise slightly flat sounded in the background. "Are you on patrol now?"

"No, I'm home while Annalynn searches for prints at Rita Ellison's house. You were right about the brunch."

"Yes! Kinsey Milhone, eat your heart out. See you tonight."

Who in heck was that? I didn't remember any Milhones in Laycock.

"Phoenix," Vernon called, "can you explain to me why the burglars had both the motorcycle and a car?"

"I can only guess." I returned to the dining room. "You saw the pathetic effort to disguise the motorcycle. They might have realized it was safer to ditch it." I joined him at the table. "Or maybe they wanted the inside man to have an escape vehicle in either direction." I remembered how surely those feet—in white running shoes—had gone up the hill. "Do you know of any rock climbers in Laycock?"

"No." He leaned forward to peer at the screen of his laptop. "I'm posting a photo with Michael dusting for fingerprints and a close-up of the altered numbers on the license plate." He leaned back. "How are you feeling?"

"I'm fine." I took the Frisbee Achilles offered me. "He missed his run. I'm going to take him out back to play."

Vernon closed his laptop. "Then I'll go to the paper to call Annalynn and post my story."

"Thanks for the lift." I escorted him to the front door and then went through the former billiards room and out the French doors leading to the backyard. To my relief, Achilles raced to the hummingbird feeder to check on his charges and, after circling it half a dozen times at full speed, loped over to the garden fence and walked along it with his nose in the air. He paused to lower his nose as he made his way into the orchard.

Had he detected the scent of the poisoner at the Ellison house?

Vernon and Annalynn were right. We had to solve these burglaries fast. So what did we know about the B&E gang?

Smart. Smart enough to select and hit a series of houses without being seen or getting caught fencing the items stolen. Smart enough to have two options for escape this morning. Smart enough to recognize that the sheriff's K-9 could pose a danger and to toss poison in his yard. I shivered at the thought.

Fit enough to sprint up hills. The recklessness of repeated attempts and the daring to steal the motorcycle also hinted at someone young. Smart, athletic, young, daring. Not exactly a profile, but it fit Michael's theory of LCC students.

Achilles raced up to me with a Frisbee.

Afraid long throws would aggravate my tender spot, I tossed it high for him to catch.

My mobile buzzed. Annalynn.

"Phoenix, this is a conference call with Jim and Michael. We want your take on what to anticipate."

The question, or rather my inability to answer it, annoyed me. "I'm not the one to ask. Jim and Michael know much more about how burglars operate than I do."

"Nobody else operates like this pair," Jim said. "You got a real knack for getting inside criminals' heads."

A rare, but not rare enough, compliment.

"Brainstorm with us," Michael said. "Say anything that occurs to you."

He'd taken one too many classes on creative management. "Okay. But first bring me up to date. Annalynn, did you find anything useful at the Ellison house?"

"Gillian lifted a partial fingerprint—probably not enough for a match—from an empty cookie wrapper in the jar with the cash. She says the pattern indicates the burglar is a woman."

Back to Annalynn's theory of a female burglar. "Any collections in the house?"

"Not unless you count a library of VHS tapes featuring Lucille Ball," Annalynn said.

Jim added, "Years ago someone told Rita she resembled Lucy."

That explained the orange-red hair. "What did Rita say about the back door?"

"She swore it was locked," Annalynn said. "Her daughter called and reminded her to lock it and turn off the coffee pot right before she left. She did both."

That hadn't been an easy lock to pick without leaving any marks. "Are there any locksmiths in town who could run up that hill?"

"No," Jim said. "Nobody in our recent arrest records either."

We had no way to identify this person. "Let's look at the time of day. All took place in the afternoon except yesterday morning and this morning."

"The attempt to kill Achilles was in the morning, too," Annalynn said. "The flexible schedule indicates someone unemployed or LCC students. When do you expect them to try again?"

What would I do if I desperately needed money and had narrowly escaped being caught four times in a row? The sensible thing, the expected thing, to do would be to take a vacation. "I'd watch out for another attempt soon, maybe this afternoon. This time it may be the home of young professionals rather than retirees." Laycock must have a few.

After a short silence, Annalynn said, "I'll ask Vernon and the radio station to urge citizens to be on high alert."

Jim said, "I'll extend shifts so we can keep more cars on the streets."

Good ideas, but short term. Hmm. "The burglars may change times again." When would I go burgling? "I doubt they'll risk breaking in at night when people are home. So maybe either right after people leave for work or right after people go out in the evening. Today's Thursday. What's likely to draw people out of their houses tonight? Bingo? Eastern Star? A baseball game?"

"Early evening sounds right to me," Jim said. "We need to make some changes, too. Annalynn, what would you say to patrolling prime targets from six to eight in unmarked cars?"

"A good idea," she said. "We'll patrol as planned this afternoon while we figure out where to focus this evening. Phoenix, do you feel well enough to patrol with me?"

"I wouldn't miss it."

"Please pick me up at the office in the SUV at five forty-five. Oh, and let Connie know we'll be eating supper late."

"Will do. Bye." Good. I could devote the afternoon

to the Hew case. Almost three hours before I was to meet Cork Klang at the Bushwhacker's Den. Time to talk to the other prime source, Jolene Hew.

to find low rate. Almost once there, ... was ...
... Cooke ... lodge at the Barnwidener's Den. Now, to
fill ... the other prime source, Jolene Hew.

TWENTY-NINE

ACHILLES GAVE ME his sad face but obeyed my call to
come back into the house. I opened a new "bone" as a
consolation and went to my foundation office to leave
a message of a late dinner for Connie and look up the
Chillicothe Correctional Center's procedure for talking to prisoners.

Skimming the CCC site, I saw that neither a phone
call nor a visit would be all that quick and easy to ar-
range. Visitors had to fill out forms and go through
background checks. Phone calls had to be initiated
by the prisoner or approved by prison personnel as an
emergency call, and the prison recorded all telephone
conversations. Unlike most of the world, the prisoners
weren't allowed to use email. The website urged family and friends to write lots of letters. Good news for
the U.S. Postal Service.

I couldn't make the case that my call constituted an
emergency. My only option was to persuade Jolene's
caseworker to encourage the prisoner to call me collect. I dialed the general number, identified myself as
the Coping After Crime Foundation's chief financial
officer, and asked for the name and extension number
of Jolene's caseworker.

The operator put me on hold for three minutes.

"Ms. Smith," a woman finally said, "Jolene Hew
told me earlier today that you might call. She does *not*

wish to speak to you or to add you to her visitors' list. Good-bye."

"But—" Dial tone shut me up. In Russia, I would have assumed the caseworker, not Jolene, dictated that message. In Missouri, I had to assume it came from Jolene. Leo had said she didn't talk to Beatrix, so surely he or Mrs. Olson had given Jolene my name. Why wouldn't she talk to a person trying to reunite her with her child?

The most logical explanation: guilt.

Could she have bashed in Wiler's head with that vodka bottle? She was used to lifting a toddler. If she came up behind a drunken Wiler while he sat in a chair, she could have done it.

And then brought a tall ladder and an accelerant, set two fires, and carried away the ladder, an accelerant container, and the guitar. No way. But I could see her telling someone she'd bashed in Wiler's head and that person setting the fire. Who could she have told?

Beatrix. She would have been much stronger fifteen months ago, but she would have had little time to prepare—psychologically or physically—to set a fire in two places.

Leo. He knew how to set a fire, but he wouldn't have doused ones he'd ignited.

Her boss. Was Cork a man she would have turned to? I'd find out this afternoon.

I scoured my brain for other suspects, people Jolene might protect from sharing her time in prison. Who else might protect Jolene by starting the fires but let her go to prison for it? Her brother? No. He feared association with her and her fatherless, biracial child. Besides, the arsonist had to live close by. The fires started soon after the fatal blow. Jolene's father? He'd publicly condemned his daughter and rejected his grandchild. Did a desperate plea reawaken his parental love? Less than a fifty-fifty chance.

I recalled Connie's theory of an unknown lover coming for a rendezvous that night. Jolene had come home to Green Springs roughly eighteen months before the fire. She'd had plenty of time to become involved with someone.

Or for Hermione's undeclared father to complete a deployment and reappear.

Jolene's refusal to talk to me indicated she was hiding something or sheltering someone. So try to get through to her again. I'd recruited scores of reluctant assets by appealing to their greed, their pride, and even their patriotism. If this caseworker hadn't burned out, she would relish helping free an innocent young mother. I dialed the CCC number again and asked for Jolene's caseworker. This time my call went through immediately, only to be answered by a recorded statement: "I am out of the office. Please leave a message. If you require a reply before Monday morning, please call the central number and request assistance."

Scheisse! Plan B. Go to a secondary source, Jolene's grandmother. I dialed the number.

It rang only once before she answered.

"Mrs. Olson, this is Phoenix Smith. I'm coming to Green Springs this afternoon. Would it be convenient for me to bring Achilles by to play with Hermione?"

"How kind of you. She would love that. What time?"

I glanced at my watch: twelve twenty. "One thirty?"

"That's fine. See you then."

All set. Except for one thing. My Camry would be

in the repair shop for days. I didn't have time to rent a clunker. Connie needed her car. Annalynn had asked me to pick her up in her SUV this evening. I'd use that.

WITH A FEW minutes to spare, I drove past Big Bass Lake to check on the burglars' possible escape routes. At the four-way stop where Vernon had turned left to return to Laycock, I went straight ahead. As I'd expected, the getaway car could have turned left three times and right twice before running out of options. I turned left at the T intersection, the final option, and picked up the road to Green Springs half a mile later.

My cell rang. Annalynn. I answered.

"Where are you?"

"In the SUV south of town. Do you need me?"

"You're on your way to Green Springs to talk to Cork Klang about buying that burnt-out bar, aren't you?"

Outstanding detective work. Or Connie had told all. "Yes."

"Oh, Phoenix! How can you be so reckless? If you think Cork started that fire, you shouldn't meet him alone."

"I'm not alone, Annalynn. I have Achilles." And my Glock.

He barked a greeting.

"Are you wearing your vests?"

"I am. He will be when we talk to Cork." Was I being foolish? Not from what I'd heard about Cork. "I'll be careful." Not reassuring. "Everyone in Green Springs knows we're meeting. He won't try anything." No answer. "Annalynn, I have to do this to be certain we have grounds to reopen this case. I won't take unnecessary chances."

"It's what you consider *necessary* chances that worries me." She sighed. "You'll be in a no-service cell zone most of the time. Report in by radio every half hour." She hung up.

I turned on the radio. Not much chatter today. As Vernon had said, Annalynn and Jim used the radio sparingly to avoid giving away their movements.

A red Ford pickup with a dented back fender sat in the Den's parking lot. Plywood no longer covered the windows and entrance, and an old door salvaged from somewhere leaned against the wall. The Klangs were cleaning up the property to show.

Half a minute later I parked in Mrs. Olson's driveway. I waved at Hermione and her grandmother sitting in the porch swing.

Hermione jumped down, put her stuffed dog in the swing by her grandmother, and raced toward me.

I let Achilles out and followed with a Frisbee as he trotted toward her, his tail raising a breeze.

She hugged him and kissed the top of his head. "Pretty dog." She let him go and flung her arms around me. "Thank you for coming to play."

I hadn't expected to be included in their games. "Hi, *Liebchen*. I'll talk to your grandmother for a little while first. Achilles would like for you to show him around the yard. He likes to explore."

"Come, Achilles," she said in a remarkable imitation of my command tone.

I walked on to the porch. "Good afternoon. A lovely fall day."

"Please join me." She patted the place Hermione had vacated. "Hermione and Beatrix are both very taken with you. Please don't disappoint them."

Her directness surprised me. I decided to match it. "I don't intend to, but I need to fill in some blanks about what happened the—the night of the fire. Jolene has refused to take my call. I understand she talks to you."

Mrs. Olson didn't feign surprise. "I called her last night. I thought she'd be happy when I told you were investigating. Instead she said for me to tell you to butt out."

She gripped the arm of the swing with her right hand and stared at her granddaughter. "I've told you." She licked her lips and turned her head to face me. "Please promise me you'll find out why she confessed to crimes she didn't commit." She stopped, fighting for control.

"You have my word." I asked the big question: "Who is Jolene protecting?"

Mrs. Olson threw up her hands. "I don't know. She won't tell me. The most I ever got out of her is that what happened was her fault and she must pay for her sins."

Not my cup of tea, but the attitude fit with what I'd learned about the Hew family's beliefs. Surely Mrs. Olson must know the possible beneficiaries of Jolene's confession much better than I did. "Who do you *suspect* she's protecting?"

She drew a shuddering breath. "It must be someone from Sedalia. I can't believe anyone I know would let her go to jail for what they did."

"You mean Hermione's father."

The great-grandmother didn't answer at first. "It can't be. He died in Afghanistan several months after Hermione was born. He'd paid part of the bills, and he'd promised to divorce his wife when his deployment ended." She blinked hard. "Jolene came home because she couldn't make it alone emotionally or financially.

Nobody else here knows about him, not even Beatrix. You mustn't tell anyone."

I couldn't give this woman a false promise. "I won't tell unless it's absolutely necessary." A stranger from Sedalia, or anywhere else, defied common sense. "Leo could have killed Wiler."

"Yes, he could." She'd regained her composure. "But he couldn't have let Jolene go to prison for his crime."

"Was Jolene seeing anyone else?"

"No, she said no one could measure up to her soldier. That's one reason she was so upset that Leo wanted to be more than friends, wanted to be Hermione's father." She sighed. "I've had a year to think about this. I can't find an answer."

Try another approach. "Did Jolene start the fires?"

"No. That morning before the police came and got her, she thought that man, that Edwin Wiler, was so drunk that he knocked over those cheap candles and passed out."

"That's definitely wrong. It was arson."

Mrs. Olson twisted her gnarled hands together and studied them as though her fingers were intertwined snakes. "At first I thought Cork burned the Den for the insurance, but he didn't collect. That made Beatrix and me wonder about his fire insurance policy." Mrs. Olson pushed a wisp of white hair back from her forehead. "The insurance agent's mother is a good friend of mine. She wouldn't talk to me about the insurance when it happened. I called her again yesterday and asked why her son didn't give Cork any money. Her son took a lot of heat, so she told me. Cork couldn't collect because his policy said he wouldn't serve food cooked there, only drinks and snacks he brought in. Her boy said he could smell the cooking oil when he went out to look at the place after the fire."

Good grief. "Is Cork dumb enough to fuel a fire with oil he wasn't supposed to be using?"

She took a long time to answer. "Let's say he's not the type to pay attention to the fine print. Even the big print." She shook her head. "I just can't say. I've known him his whole life. He was a happy-go-lucky kid, very likeable, a little lazy. He got into all sorts of minor scrapes because he didn't think ahead. He couldn't make a go of the Family Fish House, but maybe nobody could have these days. His mother says she wouldn't believe Cork and Leo are brothers if she hadn't been there when they were born." She twisted her hands together again. "I can't believe Cork would let Jolene go to prison for a fire he set."

We were going around in circles on Cork, and Hermione and Achilles would demand attention soon. I switched to specifics. "Did Jolene know Wiler was coming back to the Den after closing?"

"No. When he knocked on the door, she thought it was Leo and unlocked it. The man had his guitar and said he wanted to sing with her a little while, so she let him in. She and Leo had a fight earlier, and she hoped seeing her with another man would show Leo she wasn't interested in him."

Or make him jealous. "And then what?"

"She finished cleaning up while he played the guitar. She poured him a vodka. She sat down with him and drank a beer. That's when he drugged her. That's all she remembers until the police came."

How convenient. "Do you believe she's forgotten everything?"

"No, but I'm sure she didn't leave the house that night." Again Mrs. Olson twisted her fingers together. "I heard Beatrix bring her in and put her on the sofa. Like Beatrix, I thought Jolene was drunk. She has no tolerance for alcohol. As soon as I saw her face, I knew someone had hit her. Jolene asked me to stay with Hermione and not let her see her mother that way. I didn't sleep much that night. Beatrix came in a little after three to let me know Jolene was asleep. We decided to tell Hermione her mother fell down walking home in the dark."

A new possibility. "Could Jolene have called someone while Beatrix was talking to you in your bedroom?"

"I suppose so, but she wasn't there more than two or three minutes."

Achilles trotted up to me, took the Frisbee from my lap, and gave it to Hermione.

The child smiled shyly at me. "Time to play now? Please."

"Go ahead." Mrs. Olson patted my hand. "She's afraid of most people, but she likes you. I'll gather my thoughts and see if I can remember anything else."

"Okay." I glanced at my watch. Time to check in with Annalynn. I tossed the Frisbee across the yard, and both my playmates ran after it. "I'll be with you in a moment." I jogged to the SUV.

Achilles raced after me.

"Calm down, boy. I'm just contacting Annalynn." I left the door open as I radioed the dispatcher. "Any messages for me?"

"Proceed as instructed," she replied.

I closed the SUV's door.

Hermione stood with her hand on Achilles' neck. "Annalynn is your little girl?"

"No, she's my friend. Let's play keep-away. You go over there, we'll put Achilles between us, and he can try to catch it when we throw the Frisbee back and forth."

Achilles and Hermione loved the game even though her throws were wild and her catches few. We spent most of our game chasing the disk. I hadn't seen such pure joy in years. As caring as Beatrix and her mother were, this child needed her mother.

A white van stopped on the street.

"Leo," Hermione called.

But the van wasn't Leo's. Martina Pelben gave me the finger and turned left toward the railroad station. She parked in front of Leo's shop and got out.

"Who's that?" Hermione pressed against me. "Leo's friend?"

"No, and she's not Grammy Bea's friend either." What in hell was Martina doing? Was she going to accuse Leo of setting the fire?

She tried the door, peered through the glass, and then stepped back. She turned her head toward us for a split second and then sauntered across the street and walked toward the depot. Today she wore an oversized black t-shirt and baggy black running pants.

I didn't like it. She obviously felt I'd sided against her. Would she go curse out Beatrix? "Hermione, could you please get Achilles some water to drink? I'll be back in a minute. Achilles, stay with Hermione."

I jogged to the depot, my unease rising and my pace quickening as I went. I slowed to a walk when I reached Bea for Beauty and looked in the window. Beatrix watched from a stool as a young woman set an older woman's hair. I went on to the café. Martina, eating a piece of pie, occupied a window table. She'd seen me run to check on her.

Bluff it out. I opened the café door. "Hi, Wanda Sue. I was afraid you would close before I got here. Do you have a peach or apple pie to spare?"

Wanda Sue smiled. "Hi, Phoenix. I got half a cherry pie. You want it in a box?"

"Yes, please."

When Wanda Sue disappeared into the back, I turned to Martina with a smile. "What brings you to Green Springs?"

She smiled back. "I came out to look for space to rent. I'm expanding my storage business." She pointed to my holster. "Do you wear that gun everywhere?"

"I do when I'm on call as a reserve deputy."

"You must be pretty hard up to work a second job like that."

Apparently she hadn't Googled me. "You know how it is. My dog eats a lot." I went to the counter to take the pie and give Wanda Sue a ten. Almost time to meet Cork. At the door I threw out a casual, "See you later."

Wanda Sue waved.

Martina snarled, "Not if I see you first."

My sentiments exactly.

THIRTY

ACHILLES AND HERMIONE met me at the edge of Mrs. Olson's yard. I went to the SUV to report to the sheriff's department and get a treat for her to give to him.

The dispatcher said, "Proceed as instructed."

I walked to the porch to wind up my conversation with Mrs. Olson.

She clutched the stuffed dog. "Who was that woman you followed?"

"Martina Pelben. She's still—umm—overwrought about Edwin Wiler's death. She didn't like it when she saw me here."

Mrs. Olson nodded. "I remember her. I never heard such swearing from a woman. Did she scream at Beatrix?"

"No, but that's what I expected. Martina is eating cherry pie in the café. She went to Leo's shop first, but he's closed." I didn't want to frighten the great-grandmother, but Martina hadn't come to eat pie or rent storage space. "I have to leave in a couple of minutes. I suggest you keep Hermione inside until Martina leaves town."

"Yes, the poor child already hears too much from the haters."

Like J. J. Hew. "Is it possible Jolene called her father and told him Wiler attacked her?"

"No. She knew J. J. would blame her." The woman's

eyes misted. "Jolene adored him. She blamed Beatrix for his many falls from grace. Even after Beatrix welcomed Jolene and Hermione home and J. J. called his daughter—uh—a woman of the evening, Jolene still lashed out at Beatrix and pleaded for her father's understanding. Those first months after she came home were some of the most difficult in my adult life."

I remembered Beatrix's first thought at the Den had been to blame Jolene. "But Beatrix and Jolene reconciled?"

Mrs. Olson's shoulders slumped. "Not really. For Hermione's sake, and for mine, they maintained a fragile truce."

"Was your grandson here at the time? Could Jolene or Beatrix have called him?"

"No. He lives in Arkansas. He didn't enter this house from the time Jolene came home until the Thanksgiving after she went to prison." Her voice had cracked. "And not since."

I risked reopening a raw wound. "Why is that?"

"He demanded Beatrix put Hermione up for adoption." Mrs. Olson's voice rose in a gentle woman's fury. "I told him not to come back until he learned to live, not just preach, the words of Our Savior."

No wonder Beatrix was desperate to bring Jolene home. I could think of no comforting words. "Tell me about Jolene, what kind of person she is."

Mrs. Olson smiled. "Shakespeare could've been writing about her when he said, 'She loves not wisely but too well.' From the time she was tiny she loved or despised people and things, no middle ground. I hoped she'd learned a lesson about human weakness when she found out her noble soldier had a wife and two small children. And again when her misunderstood father treated her like a leper."

My life now seemed quite simple and untroubled. "Jolene sacrificed years away from Hermione to protect someone. Please call me if you figure out who that is." I rose to leave.

She grasped my hand. "Bless you, Phoenix."

Hermione sobbed when Achilles hopped into the SUV.

"We'll come see you again, and you can visit us," I promised. I called him out of the SUV and let her help me put on his vest. All the while I talked about Achilles' hummingbirds. To demonstrate good faith, I left a Frisbee there for our next visit. She wiped away a last tear when I suggested she practice throwing and catching with Leo in preparation for our next keep-away game.

I pulled into the Den's parking lot a few minutes after three. As I let Achilles out, a short man with receding brown hair, long on the sides and back, stepped out the open door, ground out a cigarillo with his heel, and stretched out his hand. He wore a chambray work shirt tucked into baggy khakis held up by a pair of red suspenders. A missing bicuspid marred a pleasant smile.

"I'm Phoenix Smith." I shook his hand. "Sorry to be late. I was visiting with Mrs. Olson while Hermione played with my dog." I saw him stiffen at the child's name. Sympathy or guilt? "She cried when we left. She still cries for her mother every night."

His smile became forced. "Wanda Sue tells me you used to fish for your supper at the Family Fish House."

"Yes, the water was remarkably clear then. We came on Saturday nights because Fridays were so busy."

"Lots of Catholics came to eat fish on Friday even

after the pope said they didn't have to." He motioned toward the open door. "A successful restaurant demands long, long hours. I gave it up after my daughter was born."

And he went broke. I glanced inside. Light from the door and newly uncovered windows showed that he'd cleaned up the debris and put a six-by-eight piece of plywood over the hole in the floor. "Was Bushwhacker's Den a restaurant?"

"No, barely a bar. I didn't even have a telephone. I had a liquor license so I could serve alcohol, but I ran the Den like a social club. You know—cards, karaoke, conversation."

That must have been the line he gave the insurance agent writing the policy. I pointed to the ragged hole in the ceiling. "The fire did a lot of damage. Has the building been condemned?"

"No way. The structure is sound, and it's historic. The back part was old when my grandparents bought the property. I hate to let it go, but even with the tax write-offs for historic preservation, I don't have the capital to develop it."

He'd prepared his pitch well, mixing family history and tax-deduction fantasy. The floor was damp. He'd probably swept or shoveled the debris into the hole and mopped the floor. I pointed at an empty light fixture. "Are the plumbing and electricity up to code?"

"Almost. They need a little work."

Starting from scratch, I'd bet. "Do you have contractors' estimates?"

"Not with me. I can get 'em for you." He knelt to pick up a long sliver of blackened wood. "Some of the estimates wasn't in writing. I got notes on those."

Or you will by tomorrow. "I'd like to see the historic section."

"Sure. That's now the kitchen." He hustled to the swinging door and held it open for me. "The brick walls, the tin ceiling, the brick floor—all historic." His voice changed tone—from salesman to proud owner. "I planned to put a modern kitchen on the back and turn this into a private dining room for family parties— birthdays, anniversaries, graduations."

Now I could see the guy everyone liked, a guy who dreamed modest but impractical dreams. I turned my attention to the ceiling. "Is that an entrance to an attic up there?"

"Yup." He opened the back door. "You probably remember my dad cleaning the fish out here on this slab."

I wasn't about to let him distract me from that ceiling. "Is there a drop-down ladder?"

"No. If I need to go up there, I bring a ladder from home." He stepped outside. "The property goes back to that row of trees, three hundred yards from the road. I own the old filling station, too. Plenty of room to expand. If you take both properties, I'll sweeten the price a tad."

Achilles trotted into the tall grass, sniffed the air, and came back to my side. He'd had bad experiences in the great outdoors. He whined softly, a sign he wanted to go home.

His impatience mirrored my own. I'd listened to enough of Cork's deceptive sales pitch to seem a legitimate prospect. "I'm not interested in these properties at any price unless the spring can be restored. Do you have an up-to-date geological or hydrological survey indicating what's blocking the source?"

"Yes, of course, but I need a table to spread it out. I thought we could do that at the café over some pie and coffee. Wanda Sue closes at three so we won't be interrupted."

The survey intrigued me. "What a nice thought. Wanda Sue's pies are wonderful."

He beamed. "I'll lock up and meet you there."

"Great." Except that the newly installed front door had a broken lock. I doubted that the door even fit the frame. I walked around the side of the building to the SUV.

Out of long habit, I surveyed the area. The usual quiet scene. I let Achilles in the car, backed out into an empty road, and drove toward the depot.

Martina's van still sat in front of Leo's closed shop. I parked across the street in front of Golden Oldies and saw her watching me from inside the store.

I radioed in again and received the same reply: "Proceed as instructed."

Cork drove past me and turned onto the narrow cement strip—barely a lane wide—between the railroad tracks and the depot. He turned left to go behind the depot.

I waited for him to have time to unlock the café. A battered white Corolla drove from behind the depot and stopped at the sidewalk. Wanda Sue sat at the wheel.

Beatrix emerged from the front entrance and got into the passenger seat. Both of the women turned their heads to look at Martina's van as they drove past it. Wanda Sue pulled into Mrs. Olson's drive and drove up to the garage. Beatrix got out and walked slowly to the front door. Wanda Sue backed out.

"Grammy Bea is losing strength every day," I told

Achilles. "I have to find out if Cork started that fire *now.*"

He cocked his head, waiting for orders.

"Let's go." I opened the door and, not looking toward Golden Oldies, strolled with Achilles to the depot. Cork didn't strike me as smart or brave. I decided to give him another opportunity to lie to me about the property. If he did, I would use his lies to intimidate him and elicit information about the arson.

Beatrix's shop had a neat, hand-lettered sign on the door: Closed Until Tuesday. I hoped that would prove true. I doubted she'd have the strength to work next week.

I pushed open the door to the café.

Cork put a cup on the counter. "Wanda Sue left you a piece of peach pie. How d'ya like your coffee?"

Wanda Sue's coffee had been quite weak, a common local failing. "Just a drop of milk." I walked over to a sheet of paper spread out on two small tables pushed together and held in place by napkin holders. I'd seen only two such maps in my life. This one far exceeded my expectations. I acclimated myself by locating Robert E. Lee Avenue and the two major mines to the northeast and southeast of town.

Cork put the coffee and pie down on an adjoining table. "That big shaded area, that's Bevier coal field. It played out here years ago, but they're still mining over in Randolph County." His finger traced a line. "That's an underground stream. It don't look like much, but it flooded a mine in the twenties."

I remembered a photo in the town calendar showing rescue work. I looked for a date. The corner of the map with the printed identification had been smudged with water. Hours ago, I judged. "Did that stream feed the spring at your pond?"

"No." He pointed to an even smaller line. "Our water come from there. The surveyor said mine explosions blocked it and rerouted it into a creek. All you gotta do is follow the creek back and blow out the block."

Hogwash. If it were that easy, he'd have done it. "That's quite encouraging. How old is the survey?"

"Four or five years. I don't remember." He bent over the table, moved a napkin holder, and held up the smudged corner. "I can't make it out."

I pulled out my keys and turned on my flashlight. "Let me take a look." The date and almost everything else had disappeared, but I made out a *C* at the beginning and a *t* at the end of the surveyor's name. When Louise and I had lunch in the café, she had said a con man called Cratchit used a fake survey to defraud the Klangs and others. Cork's attempt to con me with that same survey proved both his willingness to cheat and his inability to foresee consequences. He'd erased my doubts that he'd started those fires expecting to collect insurance money.

I smiled. "Let's sit over at that corner table and talk."

He beamed. "Great. I'll just get me a glass of water."

"No coffee for you?"

"No, I got ulcers. I can't drink it anymore."

Guilt-induced ulcers? I took my pie and coffee and sat so he would have to take the chair up against the back and side walls. I wanted him to feel trapped when I interrogated him. I took a bite of the pie. Really good.

Achilles stretched out near me where he could watch Cork. My backup knew something was up.

Cork slid into his chair and leaned forward, his eyes

shining. "Once the spring is restored, the property will triple in value. I wish I could afford to do the work myself, but I got kids to feed. I can let you have the spring property for seventy-five thousand and the one next to it for thirty-five thousand."

Connie had told Wanda Sue I had money to invest, but the man was delusional to start the negotiations for his worthless property at such a high price. "The deed is in your name, and your name only?"

"Sure." His smile faltered. "Well, not exactly. My mother owns a share. She's ripe to sell. She's staying at my brother's house in St. Joseph this week."

A little more rope. "And she knows you're showing me this survey?"

"Oh, yeah. Sure." He took a sip of water. "She told me where to find it."

Gotcha. "I'm sorry to hear that. Prison will be terribly difficult for a woman her age."

He reared back, whacking his chair against the wall. "What? Whatta you talking about?"

"I'm a Vandiver County deputy sheriff, and you've just named your mother as a co-conspirator in this fraud. I assume your wife knew about the Cratchit survey, too. Maybe they can share a cell."

He tried to push his chair back and stand.

"Sit down."

Achilles encouraged cooperation with a growl.

The man sank into the chair, his face drained of blood, his body shriveled. "They didn't know I still had it." He covered his face with his hands. "Please, I can't go to jail. I got a family to support."

Fatigue settled over me. I'd dealt with unprincipled losers like Cork for years, often in ongoing relationships that had to be maintained to facilitate my work. I'd had enough of that, but I had to carry through. "What you've done is despicable."

He lowered his hands from his face. "I'm sorry I tried to fool you. You can have both properties for forty-two thousand. That's what I owe on my mother's house." He extended his hands palms up and pleaded, "It's nothing to you, but losing the house would break my mother's heart and leave my kids without a roof over their heads."

When all else fails, ask for mercy in the name of the loved ones you've hurt. "You expect me to buy useless property to save you from your paying for your crimes?"

He stared at me like a wounded puppy. "Wanda Sue said you're a kind, generous woman."

"Anyone who would marry you is a poor judge of character." Rein yourself in, Phoenix. Get to the point. "You let a young mother go to prison for a crime you committed."

His mouth opened in surprise. He gasped for air. "I didn't kill Edwin Wiler. Jolene did. She confessed."

"She confessed to starting the fires, too, but we both know that she didn't. You used cooking oil from your illegal French fries and"—I risked a guess—"cleaning fluid as accelerant for two fires."

"No, no, the floor was soaked with grease from years of fried fish. Jolene knocked over a candle and set the fire." His voice had gained assurance as he repeated familiar words. "She admitted it."

I leaned forward and pointed my finger at him. "No one knocked over a candle on the roof side of the ceiling. What time did you go to the Den to set those fires?"

"I didn't go there until the fire alarm went off."

He pulled back his shoulders as he retold a tested lie. "Wanda Sue will tell you. She's a light sleeper. She woulda heard me leave."

I made a guess: "If you hadn't drugged her."

Panic flitted across his face. "I didn't kill that man. I made him leave so he wouldn't bother Jolene. I had no idea he'd come back."

Finally a bit of truth. "What did you do with his guitar?"

His brow creased. "What guitar? I don't know what in hell you're talking about."

"The guitar Wiler brought with him."

"I never seen no guitar anywhere." He struggled to his feet. "I don't care if you are a deputy. You got no right to talk to me this way."

Achilles bristled and growled.

Cork sat down. "You can't force me to say I did somethin' I didn't do."

His forced confession wouldn't do Jolene any good. Bluff. "No, but we can test samples of the accelerants to prove you set those fires." I softened my face and my voice. "Since you didn't file an insurance claim on the Den, a good lawyer can get you a suspended sentence on the arson charge. If I charge you with trying to defraud me out of a hundred thousand, that's a major felony. No lawyer will be able to keep you from years in prison." Confident he'd bought it, I poured some honey on the table. "For your family's sake, I'm going to give you a chance to hire a lawyer and turn yourself in for arson." I stood up. "Be in Sheriff Keyser's office by noon tomorrow ready to give a detailed statement on how and when you set those fires."

I lifted the napkin holders pinning down the fake survey. The weight gone, the sheet rolled up. I tucked the fat tube under my left arm. "If you show up at the sheriff's office on time and sign a statement, I'll burn this. If you don't, it will be Exhibit A at your trial for fraud."

A strangled cry came from his throat as Achilles and I left the Chew-Chew Café.

THIRTY-ONE

MARTINA'S WHITE VAN was no longer parked in front of Leo's shop. I strolled to Annalynn's SUV, opened the back, and pulled a large garbage bag from the official supply. Leo came out of the Quick Fix and walked toward me as I rolled the loose tube tighter.

"Hi, Phoenix. How did your meeting with Cork go? Are you really considering buying the Family Fish House?"

Did he have any idea his brother tried to pull a con? "The survey showing the source of the spring really piqued my interest." I focused my attention on putting the tube in the bag without tearing the edges.

Silence.

I closed the door and turned to face him.

His right hand splayed against his chest, he stared at the depot. "I didn't know he had a survey. Was it a new one from the Department of Natural Resources?"

"No. Water or coffee had spilled over most of the surveyor's name. It started with a C."

Red rose up his neck to his cheeks. "Cork's a real optimistic guy. He's convinced himself an expert could bring back the spring with a few sticks of well-placed dynamite." He jammed his fists in his pockets. "You might want to—uh—to check with the DNR."

I was relieved. Without ratting on his brother, Leo had warned me of Cork's "optimism."

Achilles barked at the driver's door, telling me he was ready to go.

"Just a sec," I told him. "Leo, when you went in the Den to fight the fire, did you see anything on the bar?"

He stared at me blankly. "What? Oh, the bar. I don't think so. I didn't pay much attention to it. I had my eyes on the fire."

"Of course. When the Laycock firefighters broke down the door, did you go inside?"

"Sure. Raleigh called me in to identify the body."

"Think back carefully. After you identified Wiler, did you look around the place to check the damage before you went outside again?"

"Sure."

"Sometimes talking about an event brings back additional memories. Try to visualize what you saw." I gave him a moment. "What was on the bar?"

"Nothing." He closed his eyes. "Nothing. Raleigh threw the cloth back so he could get to the body." He opened his eyes. "What did you expect to be on the bar?"

"I'm curious." Telling him would risk slanting his memory. "Did you see anything on the floor that didn't belong there?"

He answered promptly. "The broken bottle." He ducked his head. "Jolene's bra looped around Wiler's neck. It was so bloody and dirty that I couldn't tell what it was at first. Later we found a couple of ashtrays near the front windows. They shouldn't have been there."

"You helped the LFD go through the place?"

"Until the sheriff ran us out."

He surely would have seen the remains of a guitar. Not mentioning it didn't mean he didn't. I had to be careful how I asked. "How badly damaged was Wiler's guitar?"

He frowned. "His guitar? I don't remember seeing it." He closed his eyes and slowly swept his left hand, palm down, from left to right. His eyes opened wide. "His guitar wasn't there." His voice rose in excitement. "Not even a piece of it! My God! Whoever killed the bastard took his guitar. That proves Jolene didn't do it."

"Calm down." Leo had received Cork's share of the family brains. "The guitar could have burned to the point it wasn't recognizable. Did anyone look for Wiler's guitar?"

"No. Why would they?" He breathed deeply and barely exhaled.

I wondered if I should get him a paper lunch sack, the department's official evidence bag, to breathe into.

He grasped his head with both hands. "Let me think. Raleigh ran a rake through the ashes on the floor and in the hole. He would've found something." Leo dropped his hands. "Nobody said a word about a guitar. I sure as hell didn't think about it."

I waited as he rocked back and forth and clasped and unclasped his hands. If he'd been older, I would have worried about a heart attack.

"Jolene must've told the police. They questioned her for hours and hours. Beatrix talked to the sheriff that afternoon, but she couldn't have known they didn't find the guitar. A couple of deputies came out here with a search warrant. They took Jolene's clothes, a computer, and a journal. They searched the house and the garage and the yard. They looked in the yards between the house and the Den and out back, too. We wondered what they were looking for. Maybe it was the guitar."

"Let's hope so."

He lunged at me, and I dropped my hand to my Glock. He enveloped me in his arms. "Thank you, thank you."

I patted his back. "You're a little premature with those thanks, but I have enough information to persuade Annalynn—Sheriff Keyser—to reopen the case." I stepped away, wondering how Leo would feel when he learned his brother had let Jolene take the fall. Cork would be safer in jail for a day or two. "By the way, I saw Martina Pelben's van in front of your shop earlier. Did she talk to you?"

"Yeah, she claimed she wanted to rent two or three of my unrenovated rooms in the hotel for additional storage." He smiled grimly. "Right before she left, she asked me how 'the tramp' likes living with all those women."

"What do you think Martina wanted?" I feared she suspected Leo of killing Wiler.

"I don't know. She started out all polite in that little-girl voice. She flipped through the calendar and said, 'What a pretty child on the rocking horse.' Then she asked me if Hermione is your grandchild. She said, 'They both have a dark side.' I said no and let it go."

Odd. I thought of an explanation. "She saw me playing with Hermione a few minutes ago, and she knows Beatrix cut my hair. Martina doesn't know I don't have a son who could be Hermione's father. By the way, yesterday she talked to me about what happened the night Wiler died. She claimed smoke inhalation killed him."

Cork's pickup raced along the side of the depot, careened onto Robert E. Lee, and whizzed past us. He didn't wave or turn his head toward us.

"She's a nut," Leo said. "Every family's got one. Tell the sheriff I'll help any way I can."

THIRTY-TWO

A MILE OUT of Green Springs I pulled over in response to Achilles' pawing the button to lower his window, a new trick he'd learned all by himself. I let him into the back seat so his drool would fall on less of the SUV and lowered the window for him. Before pulling out again, I radioed in and received the same reply. Then I checked my mobile and found a voice mail followed by three text messages from Connie. I played the voice mail: "Good news. Klimton snagged twenty-five thousand from the Missouri Arts Council. Now LCC can pay me a decent salary. Later."

I opened the first text message: "screwed. $ for production but not me." The second read: "$ to *** elf. i quit."

Good for Connie. We'd clashed with Frank Klimton, an LCC administrator, and the elf, a petite dance instructor, during *Oklahoma!* rehearsals. I opened the third text: "talking to fk at 4:30."

At least he was willing to negotiate. Not her strong point. Hmm. I put my mobile on the SUV's holder and, as I pulled out, called Vernon to ask what he knew about the grant.

"Phoenix, when you have information I want, you force me to make a deal. What can you offer me for my invaluable knowledge?"

Touché. "Do you want the scoop on who really set the Den on fire?"

"You found evidence?" His high voice had risen two notes.

"No evidence yet, but I expect the arsonist to come forward by noon tomorrow. If he doesn't, I'll have a different scoop for you."

A long silence. "Careful, Phoenix. Last night Cork stopped by Harry's for a beer and bragged that he was selling the Family Fish House to a sentimental rich woman. Harry thinks that description of you is so hilarious that he's telling everyone. If Cork confesses tomorrow, most people will assume you tricked him into it. You have to follow the letter of the law."

"I'm close enough." *Scheisse!* The eyes of Laycock were upon me. "Right now I need to know what's in the grant that Connie can use to negotiate a fair contract."

"Give me a moment to check my files." A minute later, he said, "The proposal cited the high-quality direction of *Annie Get Your Gun* and the goal to maintain that quality this year. The LCC press release says half of the grant will go to a local dance studio for choreography. Your favorite dance instructor and her sister own that studio."

In short, the elf was getting Connie's money. "Could you please email copies to me?"

He didn't reply for a moment. "What do you have on Cork that would make him step forward after all this time?"

No point in denying Cork started the fires. I would need Vernon's help again. "Strictly off the record—I have tangible evidence of attempted fraud."

"Which, of course, you won't tell me about." He

sighed. "People are such fools. I took great pleasure in exposing stupidity and corruption as a young reporter. Now it depresses me. I'm sending the documents now."

"Thanks, Vernon. Bye."

I drove straight to Laycock Community College's ugly new Arts Building, arriving only two minutes before Connie's appointment. Not bothering to pick up Achilles' leash, I hurried with him into the building and checked the directory to locate Klimton's office.

The security guard burst out of an unlabeled door. "Ma'am, you can't bring a dog in here." He stepped back. "Or a gun."

"We're both sheriff's deputies. Where's Klimton's office?"

"Sorry. Didn't recognize you, Deputy Smith. Second floor, far end on your right."

"Thanks." I hurried up the steps with Achilles sticking close, curious but cautious in this unfamiliar place. He trotted ahead as we approached the open office door.

"Achilles," Connie said, "what are you doing here?" She reached out to stroke him, saw me at the door, and arched her eyebrows.

The young woman at the desk smiled at Achilles and at me.

I judged her to be friendly and nosy. I motioned for Connie to come into the hall.

She rushed out. "What's wrong? Is Annalynn okay?"

"She's fine. I found out something you can use in negotiating a better contract." I stepped farther away from the door and opened Vernon's email on my phone. "Klimton cited your first production in his grant application. He has no right to allot money to the elf's studio for choreography." I handed Connie the phone. "Read the proposal and the press release."

"Ms. Diamante," the woman called from the office, "Dr. Klimton is free."

Connie took a step toward the door and whispered, "Stall him while I read this." She grabbed my wrist and pulled me into the reception room with her. "Good afternoon, Dr. Klimton. You've met Dr. Smith, my business manager." She picked up a turquoise tote bag that matched her jewelry and the swirls in her skirt. She subtly conveyed the world of show biz.

Klimton, an unprepossessing middle-aged man who probably lacked fiber in his diet, gave me a strained smile. "A pleasure to see you again, Dr. Smith."

An obvious lie considering our run-in over his son. I smiled and shook hands. I was here on business today. "Frank, this is Achilles, a K-9 reserve deputy. We're on call."

Achilles didn't offer his paw.

Klimton ushered Connie and me to two uncomfortable office chairs and sat in an expensive leather chair behind a large paper-clogged desk. "Faculty members rarely have business managers."

Connie's eyes were glued on my mobile, which she concealed behind her tote.

I was on. "Ms. Diamante isn't a faculty member. She's never taught a class here."

He pursed his lips. "I don't believe you understand American education today, Dr. Smith. While she never taught an old-fashioned chairs-in-a-row class, she served as an adjunct faculty member. That's standard in colleges and universities today."

His condescension ticked me off. "I'm quite familiar with how higher education has increased high-paid administrative staff and saved money by hiring part-time faculty. Some short-sighted colleges devote scarce funds to peripheral items, like leather chairs and out-sourced choreography."

He took off his glasses and rubbed his eyes. "With the funds we're allotted, tenured faculty have become a luxury." He put his glasses back on and sat up straighter. "Besides, adjunct instructors bring our students up-to-date, real-world experience. I, for one, greatly value that."

Score one for him. "You're certainly right about the value of Connie's extensive theater experience. Students and parents recognize that. She's received compliments on both her productions from theater departments all over the Midwest." A slight exaggeration. "The leads in *Oklahoma!* came to LCC rather than a four-year col-lege because of the reputation she established in direct-ing *Annie Get Your Gun* last year."

Connie looked up. "You don't need to tell him that, Phoenix. He described the production's value to the stu-dents, LCC, and the community in the grant proposal."

I hid a smile. Her timing was impeccable.

He played with a black tie that had lemon-yellow books tumbling down it. "I have no options. I can't pay one adjunct faculty member more than another."

"But Dr. Klimton," Connie said, "I'm not a faculty member. I'm—tell him, Phoenix."

"She's an independent contractor, a consultant, the kind of specialist the grant covers." I smiled at Connie. Now she had to speak for herself. I should have sug-gested a character for her to play.

"I realize that LCC can't offer the money or prestige

I'd earn at Stephens or Northwestern," Connie said, her posture relaxed, her voice casual. "I love working with the students. Unfortunately, the adjunct position takes far too many hours away from my other work." She rose and strode toward the door. "Thank you for your time." She delivered her exit line over her shoulder. "And thank you for your compliments in the grant proposal."

Achilles and I followed her.

"Wait," Klimton called. "Ms. Diamante! Connie!"

I moved slowly enough that he caught up with me at his office door a split second after Connie disappeared through the exit. She needed time to decide how much to ask for. "I'm sorry, but she had to rush off to an appointment."

He attempted a smile. "Please tell her I'll see what I can do about a special contract. I'll need, uh, to discuss figures with her."

"Of course." Let him sweat. "Her schedule is full tomorrow. She'll call you Monday." I strolled to the stairs.

Connie was waiting for me in the first floor hall. She handed me my mobile. "Thanks. How much should I ask for?"

"That's up to you. You're to call him for an appointment Monday." We walked toward the front door.

Her smile wavered. "I'm like the dog who caught the car and doesn't know what to do with it. I don't want to ask too little and cheat myself or too much and lose the contract."

"I can't give you that magic number." I thought a moment. She needed general rules, not complicated calculations. "Try this. Figure your costs—what you would earn from your top-paying gigs. Directing is more complex than performing, so add a reasonable amount—

say twenty percent. Then add thirty percent to that and round out the figure. That number gives you wiggle room. Make sense to you?"

The frown lines vanished. "Yes, I can do that, especially if you check my figures."

"One other thing. Don't undervalue yourself. If you do, he will, too."

Her smile returned. "I'm not the one who undervalues me." She paused at the hall leading to the practice rooms. "I'm giving another lesson. What happened in Green Springs?" She rolled her eyes. "Trudy wants a report."

Scheisse! What did I want Trudy to spread around town? Nothing. "Tell her Cork finally put a front door on the Den. I'll give you details at dinner. Annalynn and I should finish the evening patrol by eight thirty."

"I can't wait that long. Give me a twelve-word summary."

I hated it when she used my words against me, but I responded to the challenge. "Cork set the fires. He didn't kill Wiler." I thought a moment. "Jolene didn't either."

Connie marked a point for herself in the air. "Just like I said."

THIRTY-THREE

I DROVE STRAIGHT home to feed Achilles, pack snacks to carry on patrol, and check foundation messages. By five thirty, the sun and the temperature were easing down. I took along my rain jacket.

When I pulled into Annalynn's parking place, she emerged from the building wearing gray slacks and a blue blazer. She carried a leather shoulder bag with a gun pocket and her belt loaded with police paraphernalia. A Bluetooth device on her ear signaled continued reliance on cell phone communication.

Achilles, in the back seat, barked his welcome.

She greeted him before opening the passenger door. She nodded to me but said nothing as she put her belt on the floor beside the small cooler with our snacks and climbed in.

I put the SUV in reverse. "Where to?"

"Do you have any recommendations?" Her tone was polite, professional.

"No. I thought you and Jim had mapped out our routes."

She concentrated on fastening her seat belt. "Have you thought about this case at all this afternoon?"

We'd have a rough ride. "I drove out by Big Bass Lake to see where the burglars could have gone from there." I'd dismissed the case from my mind on the road to Green Springs.

"We'll start with that quadrant." She reached down and fiddled with the radio controls. "The LPD had eight 9-1-1 calls about suspicious activity this afternoon. All false alarms. I had five calls asking whether you're buying property in Green Springs. I was struck by who didn't call me: Vernon Kann. Have you told him what you're doing?"

His opinion carried weight with Annalynn. "More or less. He's the one who sent Beatrix to—the foundation."

"To you, in other words. You're both convinced Jolene's innocent." Annalynn rubbed her right temple. "If you can prove Jolene Hew didn't set the fire, of course I'll reopen the case."

I couldn't prove it yet, so I said nothing.

"Well, Phoenix? PUSU."

I smiled at her use of our childhood shorthand for put up or shut up. "You'll have proof tomorrow morning. Cork Klang is having a crisis of conscience." Prompted by our talk. "I suggested that he call a lawyer and come to see you." I turned left.

"Pull over, please!"

Achilles whined.

The moment we stopped Annalynn shifted in her seat to face me. "You know that Jolene Hew confessed to hitting that man and setting the fire."

"Of course." I put on the blinkers. "I also know she didn't start the fires—two fires, not one." I may as well drop the bomb. "I'm almost certain that she didn't kill Wiler, that she confessed to protect someone."

Annalynn raised a skeptical eyebrow. "Who?"

"I don't know, but it has to be someone she loves deeply. She wouldn't leave Hermione otherwise. Maybe the interview tapes will give us a clue. Who interviewed her?"

"George Brendan, but Boom sat in on most of the interrogations."

I kept my mouth shut. Annalynn knew my opinion of her late husband's chief deputy. I'd been more than glad to see the last of him.

Annalynn faced front. "I'm sorry I accused you of entertaining yourself with the investigation, but I'm still furious that you didn't tell me. Tonight let's focus on the burglaries." She opened a map. "We'll drive the city-county line. We didn't find any big events to take people out of their homes tonight. We have no new leads."

I checked traffic and pulled out. "I wouldn't say that. We know that the one who goes into the houses is athletic—and young. Only the young would be daring enough to steal that motorcycle while we're a block away."

"Really, Phoenix? Only the young? You're still the most daring person I know."

True, but I felt compelled to defend myself. "I calculate the rate of return for everything I do."

Annalynn shook her head. "You need a new calculator. Turn left at the next street. I want to check that old dirt road between the railroad tracks and the road that runs past Big Bass Lake. Maybe the burglars will stay in that neighborhood."

The bumpy, rutted road had nothing along it but an ancient trailer and an abandoned house.

For more than an hour we roamed the outskirts of Laycock. Most of the time Annalynn talked to her deputies or LPD officers and left spotting potential targets and crimes in progress to me. I struggled to stay alert.

Achilles and I both wanted a break by the time I turned onto a winding blacktop road that followed the low ridge north of town. The few homes ranged from a double-wide trailer on cement blocks to a mock Tara with horse-country white fences. Almost every place had a couple of dogs. I pulled into a roadside overlook where high school kids parked to neck. "Achilles needs out. I brought seedless grapes and mixed nuts, if you want a snack."

We got out. Achilles trotted over to mark a tree while Annalynn and I surveyed the town in the dusk. I flashed back to a view of the Danube from a restaurant on a high point in the Vienna Woods. I'd loved to go there before sunset, order a local wine and a mixed grill, and watch the city light up.

Annalynn offered me the bag of nuts. "My mother said coming up here with a young gentleman was low class. What's going on at the Freewill Baptist?"

"A sing-along." And a chance to assess J. J. Hew. "That must attract older people. Want to go down and check the crowd for a singer with a house worth burglarizing?"

"Are you serious?"

"Just a thought."

"You're the one with insights on breaking and entering. Let's go."

I walked back to the car. "You'll need an explanation for showing up."

"You wanted to attend a sing-along."

I opened the door for Achilles. "They wouldn't appreciate his tenor. I'll stay outside with him."

"You come up with an excuse. You're much better at that than I am."

A zinger, but an accurate one. "You could give a little speech about preventing burglaries."

"You scare me. You don't need a second to come up with a story." She carried her belt to the back of the SUV and put it in the cooler. "I can't go in armed, and you should put on your jacket to hide your holster."

Annalynn got in, buckled up, and pulled out her phone. A few seconds later she said, "The sing-along rotates among four churches. What a coincidence. J. J.'s wife is an elder in one of those."

Caught. "I've never met either of them. Was she a factor in the Hews' divorce?"

"No. He was a faithful drunk. She didn't even live here then. She bought that florist shop south of the square right before your mother died. But you surely know that."

"All I know about her is that she called Jolene a whore during a service."

Annalynn gasped. "That's horrible! Boom said J. J., and a lot of others, didn't welcome Jolene home. Working in a bar didn't improve her reputation either."

I couldn't believe my ears. "Annalynn, forty percent of the children in this country are born out of wedlock. Surely you don't think those mothers are all on a no-exit road to hell."

"Of course not, but I do believe they've shown bad judgment."

Hard to dispute that. "Jolene's 'reputation' may explain why George and Boom and the prosecutor encouraged a confession that defied logic."

"That's enough!" Annalynn's explosion brought another whine from Achilles. "If you had devoted as much time to identifying the burglars as you have to proving Boom made a mistake, we might have caught these thieves by now."

Her illogical accusation told me how much recalling her late husband's incompetence cost her, but she needn't take it out on me. I held my tongue as I turned into the church's parking lot.

She touched my forearm. "I'm sorry, Phoenix. That—that outburst was inexcusable. I know you set out to right a wrong, to bring Jolene home to her child."

"Please remember that." I stopped at the walkway. "I'll park and wait outside with Achilles."

After she got out, I found a pull-through parking place, put on my jacket, and picked up Achilles' leash. I fastened it to his collar and walked with him to a big evergreen tree by the lot. It had been the town's biggest Christmas tree when I was a kid. As usual, Achilles stayed at my left side, leaving my gun hand free. "Sit, boy. Quiet." We would be at the edge of the streetlight, but I'd have a clear view of everyone going into the church.

A moment later a little boy pulled away from his mother and ran toward Achilles shouting, "Doggie, big doggie."

Achilles managed to lick the boy's face before the mother caught him, glared at me, and hauled the wailing boy inside.

A trim man with salt-and-pepper hair and a thirty-something ash-blond woman hurried from the parking lot. She waddled with the gait of a woman well along in pregnancy. With each step, a large gold cross with three glittering diamonds bounced below the ruffled neck of a white blouse. The man, some twenty years her senior, held her elbow with the solicitude of a father to be. He nodded to me, did a double take, and veered away from the walkway toward me.

The woman came with him reluctantly. Gold crosses dangled from each ear and from a bracelet on her right wrist. "J. J., we're late."

"You go on in, sweetheart," he said in a beautiful baritone voice. "I'll be there in one minute."

Connie had overrated him, probably because of the voice. He reminded me of a musical comedy star—Robert Goulet?—she'd drooled over as a kid.

He waited ten feet away from me until she went in the church door. Then he stalked up to me and leaned in, hands on his hips. "Who are you? Why are you here? What do you want?"

Achilles growled, and J. J. Hew jumped back.

His reaction intrigued me. Who did he think I was, and why didn't he want his wife to overhear our conversation? "That's not a very friendly greeting."

"As far as I'm concerned, you can take the child. Beatrix will fight you for her, but I won't. I don't want to ever see her again."

Hmm. My dark complexion, a melding of my Cherokee and Italian genes, had prompted him to mistake me for Hermione's paternal grandmother. I went along. "You say that now, but you may change your mind as Hermione gets older. I understand Jolene was her daddy's girl."

"That was before the angel turned into a devil." He raised his hand to shake a finger at me and dropped it to his side as Achilles bared his teeth. "Tell Jolene to stop writing to me." He had lowered his voice. "I'm starting a new life with a new baby daughter. We won't allow evil into our house."

I wanted to break his nose, but I smacked him with words instead. "I hope that she'll have a better father than Jolene did."

"Yes, I sinned." He had raised his voice. "My God is a loving God. He has forgiven me my sins."

"If God can forgive your cruelty to your prodigal daughter, certainly God can forgive Jolene's love for a man."

He stormed off, pushing his way through a group that included Martina and Sybil Pelben.

Sybil addressed a young man, "Save me a seat, Newt. You know where I prefer to sit." She strolled over to me, her eyes on Achilles. "A beautiful animal. I understand he's right smart."

He offered his paw, and she bent over to shake it.

Surprised but pleased by both of them, I said, "You should hear him sing."

She checked to be sure her group had gone inside. "You impressed Martina with what you said about her not having to endure pain forever. Please find a counselor fast. She's been getting worse since last July, the anniversary of that awful man's death."

Her attitude encouraged me to be frank. "I'm afraid she needs more than a few weekly sessions with a grief counselor. We may not have anyone qualified in Laycock."

Sybil nodded. "I've tried to talk her into going back to Springfield. She won't listen to me. She's mad because I refuse to lie and say Edwin was wonderful. She came tonight only because her cousin practically dragged her out of that miserable cabin."

The buzz from the church quieted.

"I have to go in. Thanks for your help." She hurried inside.

I wondered whether her home met the burglars' qualifications. With no one else arriving, I removed the leash to let Achilles sniff around the tree. He trotted toward the church when Annalynn's voice carried to us. I called him back and walked into the parking lot with him.

He began to check for drugs, moving from car to car in the dim light.

An organ played a few notes, and the singers began a hymn I'd never heard. Achilles raised his head to listen. Then he joined in.

"Achilles! No singing." He didn't recognize the command. "Quiet!"

He hung his head.

Annalynn hurried out the door talking on her cell, and he ran to meet her. She waved to me and pointed toward the lot.

I brought the SUV to the walkway and lowered my window to listen to her conversation.

"Do you want me to meet you at the jail?" Pause. "Okay. Call if you need me. Bye." A smile erased her worry lines. "Jim and Michael caught a young couple carrying stolen items out of a house on Oak Street. We've caught the burglars."

THIRTY-FOUR

ANNALYNN FASTENED HER seat belt. "Congratulations, Phoenix. You were right about the burglars changing time and tactics."

"What happened?"

"A neighbor noticed a light moving in the house across the street and called 9-1-1. Michael and Jim caught a young man and woman carrying a big flat-screen television out the back door. They also had three hundred dollars in cash in their pockets."

The tactics had changed a bit too much. "This is the first time they've taken a TV."

"I noticed that. Maybe they expected this to be their last job."

"Who are they?"

"They won't say, and they weren't carrying IDs. The LPD will check the vehicles in the area for any that don't belong and talk to neighbors."

I put on my left-turn signal. "Then we can go home."

Achilles barked his approval.

Annalynn reached back to pet him. "After I pick up some files at the office. Excuse me while I reassign my deputies."

When I parked the SUV in her space, she opened her door. "Please tell Connie to expect us in fifteen minutes. After dinner, the three of us will work together on Jolene Hew's case." She closed the door and hurried toward the building.

I delivered her message and disconnected. Now that Annalynn was ready to focus on Jolene, I couldn't stop thinking about the burglaries. Nothing about this one fit the pattern. Could this pair be opportunists hoping their theft would be blamed on someone else? Only the police knew that the burglars never took TVs. Still, the victims surely told their friends what had been taken. Trudy could probably give me a full list.

My unease grew. What if tonight's burglars hadn't been the ones who tried to kill Achilles?

Annalynn came out carrying a cardboard box and put it in the back before taking her seat.

I turned on the motor. "Did the pair Jim caught take a towel?"

"I don't know yet. He'll fill me in after the LPD processes them. Right now I want to hear the executive summary of why you think Jolene Hew didn't kill Wiler or set the fire—the fires."

Where to start? "I'll take you through what various people have told me about what happened. First, Wiler bombed during open mike. He and Martina left in a huff. He came back alone an hour or so later with his guitar and asked Jolene to sing with him. At quarter to one Cork ran him and other stragglers out, closed, and left Jolene alone to clean up. Right after one o'clock, Wiler—guitar in hand—knocked on the door. She let him in."

"How do you know she let him in?"

"She told her grandmother. At one fifteen, Leo came to walk her home. He heard Wiler playing the guitar and, through the window, saw them sitting at a candle-lit table, her with a beer and Wiler with a drink. Leo left."

"Are you sure Leo was there? That's not in the case notes," Annalynn said.

"Because no one asked him. He feels guilty that he didn't go in. Besides, what Beatrix told me she saw confirms what Leo said. About one thirty, she walked to the Den with a flashlight looking for Jolene. She—Beatrix—saw candles and a vodka bottle on the bar. She walked in and found Wiler crouched over Jolene. Beatrix saw blood on Jolene's mouth, hit Wiler with her flashlight, and tried to hit him with a chair. He grabbed it and threw it behind the bar."

"Interesting story, if true. Go on."

"Beatrix half carried Jolene home, cleaned her up, and stayed with her in the living room all night. Well, almost all night. Around three, Beatrix went into Mrs. Olson's room briefly, not long enough Jolene could have walked to the Den and back, but long enough Jolene could have called someone."

Annalynn sighed. "Phoenix, any mother would lie to save her daughter from a murder charge. Jolene told officers that she walked back to the Den after her mother went to sleep."

I slowed for the only four-way stop on the way to the castle. "Beatrix also said Jolene was drugged, that Wiler put something in her beer."

"He didn't," Annalynn snapped. "Boom had tests run. No drugs, and not enough alcohol to be legally drunk." She paused. "You'd have known that if you had come to me in the beginning."

A valid point, but I made another one: "That test was run at least eight hours after Beatrix rescued Jolene."

"Boom said she obviously had a hangover. They wouldn't have believed her story that Wiler attacked her if she hadn't had bruises on her face and arms." Annalynn rubbed her temple. "Jolene *may* have had a light concussion. You don't know all the facts, Phoenix."

"That's why we need to go through the official files." I took a moment to regroup. "Annalynn, it's not only Beatrix's statement that Jolene never left the house. A woman who has been beaten unconscious doesn't walk two blocks in the dark to confront the bodybuilder who'd beaten her. Could a small woman hit a tall man on the head hard enough to kill him?" Hmm. Yes, but only if he saw no threat. "And carry a ladder from somewhere, climb up it to spread and light an accelerant, start another fire on the floor, and put a fire-retardant cloth over the bar? Oh, and carry the ladder away."

Annalynn remained silent for a several seconds. "Yes, it's hard to believe, but people get a surge of adrenaline and perform unexpected physical feats." Another pause. "Alcohol or a concussion could have prompted her to act illogically."

Despite Annalynn's rejoinder, I'd established reasonable doubt. I moved on to another point. "That arsonist mixed cooking oil with something more volatile, so the fires were planned, not a panicked reaction. I'm sure Cork, who's a dimwit, set the fires."

"Phoenix, you have no proof! This is one of your theoretical scenarios—brilliant when you're right, forgotten when you're wrong."

Her criticism didn't bother me. I'd heard it before. "I have one other thing supporting my 'scenario.' Leo and Beatrix both heard the guitar. The fire department found no sign of a guitar. When I asked Cork about it, he had no idea what I was talking about. Boom's deputies searched Mrs. Olson's house and grounds and the area in between there and the Den. Where's Wiler's guitar?" I pulled into the driveway, punched the garage-door opener, and parked the SUV beside the Mercedes.

"The search turned up ladders at every house," Annalynn said. "I don't remember Boom mentioning a guitar. He talked about this case with me every night for at least two weeks. He felt sorry for the girl. He didn't question her confession." She opened her door. "I brought copies of her statement, the official photos, the autopsy report, and George's summary of the interviews. If we need to listen to the tapes or look at anything else, we'll have to do it at the department."

Her "we" raised my spirits but didn't lower my fatigue. This had been a long, full day.

Walking toward the house with her box and her equipment belt, Annalynn said, "Let's relax over our food before we dig into the files. I haven't had a minute off all day. I told the office to call me tonight only if there's an emergency."

"Okay with me, but Connie is going to have questions."

Connie opened the front door. "Hi, I just heard on the radio that Jim caught the burglars."

"We know, but we don't have any details." Annalynn took the box into the ladies' parlor. "I'm going up to change."

"I'll put the food on the table," Connie said.

I followed her to the kitchen. "Is that baked sweet potatoes I smell?"

"Yes, with turkey breast, green beans, and salad.

Sorry, no cranberries." She pointed up toward Anna-lynn's room and arched an eyebrow.

"She's touchy and a bit defensive," I whispered. "She brought the Hew files for us to go over, but she doesn't want crime on the dinner menu." Connie could be entertaining if you gave her the right topic. I opened the refrigerator and brought out a bottle of cranberry-grape juice. "We could talk about which musicals you're considering."

"Okay. The first criterion: Which ones have the most singing and the least dancing."

"Cut the dance teacher off at the pass." I chuckled at the thought. "Have you thought of doing an operetta—*The Merry Widow* or *The Desert Song* or *The Gypsy Princess*?"

Our discussion of the merits of American musicals versus Austro-Hungarian operettas carried us through the meal.

Annalynn took her last bite and folded her napkin.

Connie took that as a signal. "While I was waiting for you two, I Googled false confessions and the Innocence Project. Did you know that twenty-five percent of more than three hundred people exonerated by DNA evidence had confessed?"

"No, I didn't." Annalynn rose. "I'll make a pot of tea. Connie, since you've read up on confessions, you read Jolene's statement and the summary of her interrogation, please. I'll review the officer's notes on the crime scene. Phoenix, you go through the photos and the autopsy report. Let's see where we stand in an hour."

Connie beat me to the box. She grabbed her files and went to rummage through Annalynn's roll-top desk. "I need a highlighter."

I found an unlabeled DVD and the autopsy report and headed for the basement with Achilles at my heels.

"Phoenix," Annalynn said as I sped through the kitchen, "remember we're not playing a game. This involves a young man's violent death."

I stopped short. This investigation had proved to be a stimulating challenge, but the stakes exceeded those for any game. How could I explain my sense of urgency? I'd long avoided philosophical reflection on my actions, but my lifelong friend had questioned my motives. "Annalynn, my major concern isn't the body-builder's death. We can't do anything about that. What drives me is the ongoing aftermath, the way his death continues to bring misery and destroy lives." Enough of that. I waved the DVD at her. "What I find—or don't find—in these photos could change a young woman's and a little girl's future."

THIRTY-FIVE

MY HOPES WERE high but my expectations low as I opened the photo file. Anticipation mounted when the slide show revealed clear shots. The photographer had used a first-class camera that showed the distinctions among the many shades of black and gray after the fire. In rapid succession I opened, expanded, and closed almost two hundred photographs, many of them including the little yellow numbered evidence markers. No guitar or pieces of a guitar appeared in any of them, but a kitchen chair was behind the bar right where Beatrix said Wiler threw it.

Annalynn put a cup of tea on my desk. "How's it going?"

"Great." I pointed to the screen. "Here's the chair Beatrix told me about. That proves she was there."

"Oh, Lord. Boom didn't believe her." Annalynn rubbed her temple. "Connie showed me the picture of you with Hermione. Phoenix, are you sure your concern for the child isn't influencing your judgment?"

"My judgment about what happened, no. My hope that her mother's innocent, yes."

"Fine." The corners of her mouth twitched. "Can we trust Connie's judgment on false confessions?"

I usually asked such questions. "She's been researching them since she read the application." Three days ago. "She's found statistics." Numbers can lie. "Trust but verify."

Annalynn left. Achilles, a Frisbee in his mouth, trotted after her.

I went back through the photos, bringing up and studying only the ones that showed the floor around and near the body. Nothing resembled a guitar, but Connie might recognize something I wouldn't. I emailed the key photos to Annalynn and me for study upstairs.

Then I went back to the photos taken, apparently, right after the firefighters found the body. The first showed two of them kneeling by Wiler. Tendrils of smoke wafted up on their left. The cover on the bar had been thrown back. The next shot looked down on Raleigh with his gloveless right hand on Wiler's carotid artery. The third, taken from a different angle, showed only the victim, the left arm bent above his head, the body up against the bar, the left leg bent slightly. He wore a black t-shirt, black pants, and black shoes.

The guy looked huge: bulging biceps, broad shoulders, thick thighs, big feet. He had to have been very drunk or very cocky for anyone to come close enough to swing that bottle with deadly force.

I opened the autopsy report. The first page gave his size: six foot, one hundred ninety-seven pounds. I flipped through the report until I found "Conclusions: Cause of Death." It read, "Blunt force trauma to the head with a fracture of the occipital cranium, cerebral contusions and lacerations, intracranial bleeding. The configuration of the injury conforms to the shape of the bottle found on the scene. The fatal blow hit the skull straight on, not at an upward or downward angle."

Interesting. Either Wiler had been bent over and the

blow came from above or he was sitting and the blow came parallel to the floor. Either way, he had turned his back on the attacker.

I read the next paragraph. "One half hour to three hours before death (prior to the aforementioned fatal blow), the victim suffered a minor lateral hematoma from a blow with a different object. That blow did not contribute to expiration. Neither did a scratch on his left cheek, inflicted with a writing utensil containing blue ink."

Almost certainly the bruise came from Beatrix's blow with the flashlight and the scratch from Jolene's ballpoint pen.

The final paragraph read, "The limited traces of soot (see Internal Examination) within the lungs establish that the fire did not cause expiration. Smoke *may* have hastened death."

Martina definitely had been wrong about the cause of death. I ran my finger down the page to "Time of Death: 2:30 to 4 a.m. (see Internal Examination: stomach contents)." Wiler suffered the blow after the Hews left the Den and before a fire started. He lived long enough, barely, to breathe smoke.

I went to the section on stomach contents and read: "No undigested food; small quantity of undigested vodka (indicates consumption within less than two hours of expiration)." What did this tell me? Wiler had been a little high but not drunk when he was struck. He didn't fear his killer. Or he'd fallen asleep.

Bloody hell! I still had more questions than answers.

I skimmed the entire report but found nothing to tell me what had happened that night. I ran through the photos one more time, this time lingering on the ones with police markers. The biggest clusters were around Wiler and the broken bottle. The other major ones showed the flashlight, the ashtrays, and bits of debris that, I assumed, pointed to arson. The last photos had been shot from the trap door in the kitchen ceiling. The sun shone through a big gap in the roof and lighted the hole in the ceiling and mysterious black and grey mounds.

Chagrined at my inability to interpret what I saw, I closed the photo file. At least I'd confirmed someone had taken the guitar between the time the Hews left and the firefighters arrived. Cork's confusion convinced me he hadn't done it. I gathered up my stuff and went upstairs.

Achilles met me in the kitchen to lead me into the den. He liked to have his people together.

Connie and Annalynn sat on the love seat in front of the paper-strewn coffee table.

Connie shook a highlighter in Annalynn's face. "You have to listen to the tape. I'll bet Deputy Brendan threatened her with the death penalty to get her to confess. Why else would she deny everything for three hours and suddenly cave?" Connie pointed to a sheet of paper. "This wording came straight from a cop, not from a teenage girl."

"She was twenty-two," Annalynn said. "But you're right. The statement reads more like an incident report than a distraught young woman's confession."

I reached for it.

Annalynn slapped her hand down on it. "Later. We divided the files to save time. Connie and I both read the confession and George's summary of the interrogation."

Connie bounced up to pace. "It's the classic case. A young person amazed and confused by an unfair accusation. Cops keeping her isolated from her family and telling her they have evidence of what she did and how she did it. Threats of life in prison for her and her accomplice. Promises that if she identifies who helped her she'll get a lighter sentence. No inkling of her rights to a lawyer—or even that she needs one—until it's too late."

"You left out that she had a splitting headache from being beaten." I'd have taken Connie's accusations more seriously if Annalynn had made them. "Connie, is that what you assume, or what the summary implies?"

"It's inconclusive," Annalynn said. "We'll have to listen to the tapes to know for sure. Did you see remnants of the guitar, Phoenix?"

"No, and these photos were excellent."

Annalynn smiled. "Boom took them."

Lucky that I'd praised them. "Connie, you would recognize the guts of a guitar when I wouldn't. I'd like for you to double check seven photos in case I missed something."

"Later," Annalynn said, "after you tell us about the autopsy report."

"Wiler definitely died from blunt force trauma, a straight-on blow." How would I have hit that big, powerful man? "Maybe the killer dropped something and hit Wiler when he bent down to pick it up."

Connie settled into the chair across from the love seat. "You said 'the killer.' You're sure Jolene didn't do it."

"Almost. If Beatrix is telling the truth, and I think she is, she was keeping Jolene awake at the time Wiler received the fatal blow." I sat down in my regular chair and put my feet on the hassock. "We haven't heard your report on the case notes yet, Annalynn."

"They were shorter than I expected." She reached up to release her French roll, a pre-bedtime ritual. "After the fire a deputy interviewed the neighbors, the driver who reported the fire, and the Green Springs volunteers. No one saw anything."

Not surprising at that time of night. "No one interviewed Cork?"

"George interviewed him on the scene. He was incoherent, so George talked to him the next day. Cork admitted that hot cooking oil was in the kitchen when he left and that he had allowed old friends to smoke cigars."

Connie sprang to her feet. "That's it? Holy crap! George decided that Jolene, barmaid and single mother, was guilty and stopped investigating."

Annalynn ran her hands through her long hair to smooth it out. "In George's defense, he also called Cork's insurance agent and verified that Cork didn't have a valid claim. His policy didn't allow any cooking."

It had taken me three days to find that out, and then I only had hearsay.

Connie was pacing the length of the long room. "What do we do now?"

Annalynn turned to me. "Well, Phoenix?"

"This afternoon I encouraged Cork to admit he started the fires. Tomorrow he'll sign a statement. If we're lucky, he knows something that will help us identify the person who attacked Wiler. If not, we listen to the tapes of Jolene's interrogation to figure out what scared her into confessing."

Annalynn nodded. "You think she confessed to protect someone else."

Connie shook her head so hard her curls bobbed.

"Sorry, but I don't buy it. Anyone Jolene loved that much wouldn't have let her go to jail."

"Unless they would have served a much longer sentence," I said. "We don't have a crowd of suspects to choose from. No one knows of a boyfriend other than Leo, and he would have come forward. Hermione's father was"—I couldn't tell them he was dead—"out of the country." I could think of one man who would have taken Jolene's sacrifice as his due, but I wanted to see whether Connie and Annalynn did. "Anyone else Jolene loved?"

"Her father," Connie said. "No way that man would have lifted a hand for her. Her big brother?"

Annalynn said, "He was at a church camp in Arkansas with his three kids and pregnant wife."

Connie picked up her purse. "You're overthinking this. It's obvious who killed Wiler."

Annalynn and I waited.

Connie walked to the door and wheeled dramatically. "The bodybuilder fell asleep. Cork snuck in. He knew the place so well he didn't need a light." She turned off the table lamp by the door. "He threw around liquor and cooking oil to fuel the fire without seeing Wiler." She pantomimed the action in the exaggerated style of silent film. "Then Wiler woke up and caught him. Cork said, 'Sit down, my friend. Have a drink on the house. Can I offer you a few hundred dollars to keep your mouth shut?' Wiler replied, 'A few hundred? Make that a few thousand.' Then Cork whacked him."

She bowed and waited for applause we didn't give her. "You'll see. Goodnight." She pranced out of the room and the front door.

Annalynn and I sat in silence a moment.

She began sorting the papers on the coffee table. "You know, Connie could be right."

"It doesn't explain the false confession." I stretched, ready to go to bed. "We'll know tomorrow. If Connie's right, Cork won't show up in your office. He'll run."

THIRTY-SIX

THE TWO SHORT rings that signaled a call from the sheriff's department woke me the next morning. I could hear the murmur of Annalynn's voice in her bedroom but not the words. I dressed quickly and went down to the kitchen with Achilles. I started the coffee while he lapped water and then took him out the back door to conduct his morning business in my backyard.

A touch of fall chill reminded me we'd be seeing yellows and reds in the trees soon. I loved the fall, but I didn't look forward to the Missouri winter. What's the point of snow if you can't ski?

"Phoenix," Annalynn called from the door, "please come in, and bring Achilles."

He loped toward the door at the sound of his name. She usually fed him his breakfast.

I followed more slowly. Her tone had hinted at bad news. "What's up?"

Annalynn poured two cups of coffee. "The kids stealing the television set aren't the ones who broke into the other places. The girl is a high school senior who babysits for last night's victim. The boy attends LCC part time and plays video games full time."

I wasn't surprised. "Back to patrolling."

"We're not announcing that the kids face only one charge. Jim and I expect the burglars to take advantage of the heat being off and hit somewhere this morning. What do you think?"

"They won't be able to resist the opportunity. Do you want me to patrol with you?"

"No. One of the burglars followed you and Achilles before. I think they may watch this morning to see whether you've gone back to your routine rather than hunting for them." She dropped bread into the toaster. "Gillian is going to pick me up in a squad car and drive me to the office. They'll see you're not with me. When you take Achilles for a run, use your Bluetooth so you can call immediately if you see anyone. Remember, they stole guns." She took plates from the cupboard. "Is your cell fully charged?"

"Yes." I scavenged butter and jam from the refrigerator and took it to the table marveling at how much confidence and savvy Annalynn had gained since she became acting sheriff in May.

She brought our coffee and plates into the dining room on the silver tray. "I think the burglars will go for a big score today, something really valuable. Do you have any idea where that might be?"

How on earth could I? "None, but I'd bet they'll follow the pattern—affluent older person's unoccupied house. You and Jim have been studying potential targets all week. Pick the top ones. After all, you can't be everywhere."

"Unfortunately. We talked about sending out another alert, but that would warn the burglars. And load us down with false reports." She buttered her toast lightly. "I skimmed the morning paper and didn't see any events today."

"Don't forget that Cork and a lawyer are coming in to your office to confess."

"If I have to go out, I'll leave instructions to keep them there."

A squad car pulled into the driveway.

Annalynn made a toast sandwich and wrapped it in a napkin. "Would you mind cleaning up, please?"

"Go. I'll talk with you later."

She grabbed her heavy belt and hurried out the front door.

I smoothed a thick layer of raspberry jam on my toast and turned on the radio to listen for news of last night's burglary. A brief report on the LPD's capture of two unidentified burglary suspects led the news. The weather—sunny in the mid-sixties this morning and the high seventies this afternoon—received twice as much time. When the stock market report came on, I got up to switch off the radio. Stock here meant cows and hogs, not Dow Jones. As I reached for the button, the reporter announced that William Cadoni received an award for his work on agrotourism in Chicago last night.

Hmm. He wouldn't be home until this afternoon. I had turned on the news to hear about the burglaries. Maybe the burglars had, too. I opened the regional phone book, slimmer than an issue of *Smithsonian*, and found Cadoni's address. I'd noticed the place, a modern log cabin, during our patrol last night. The house number had been outlined in river rocks at the edge of the front lawn. The two-story cabin stood on the street above the railroad tracks near where a woman walked her collie yesterday morning.

My hunch was such a long shot that I decided not to mention it to Annalynn. She and Jim might pull their resources from other areas and ignore the real target. In any case, the trail was a good place for our morning run. And I'd better not dally. I crammed the last of the toast into my mouth and hurried upstairs to put on the vest and change into green slacks and a matching t-shirt that would blend into the leaves. I grabbed Achilles' vest and ran downstairs, anxious to be settled into a good viewing point before the neighborhood emptied out and the burglars broke in. "Leash, Achilles," I called. "I hope you're willing to sit quietly for an hour or so."

I got the vest on him easily this time. He was getting used to it. I grabbed a daypack from the hall closet and dropped in the leash, a bottle of water, a plastic bowl, some chicken-based treats, and a new chew toy.

I drove a circuitous route initially, going around blocks to be sure no one followed me. As an extra precaution, I took the road that went past Big Bass Lake and stopped at the pullout to make sure no getaway vehicle was parked there or, as far as I could tell, on the old dirt road halfway down the long, wooded hill. With my binocular sunglasses, I spotted the log cabin above and to the left of a cleared section of the trail. Boundary Street, two blocks up, crossed the tracks, offering a good place to go onto the trail.

By the time I parked Annalynn's SUV on a side street half a block from Boundary, my watch said eight forty. I strapped on the daypack, leaving Achilles unleashed in case of trouble.

The streets here didn't have sidewalks. I jogged along the street's edge, turned left toward the tracks, and a block later turned left again onto the trail. I didn't see a single person, didn't hear voices or music, didn't smell bacon.

Achilles, too, stayed on high alert, using his eyes and nose to check the strange surroundings and never straying more than ten feet from me. We both looked back when a car slowed to cross the tracks. A late model gray Acura, not a likely getaway car.

The burglars had always approached houses from the back, so I paid particular attention to the old dirt road. It provided a good vantage point and parking spot for the burglars.

I jogged through the clearing. The rise on my left was steep. Someone had planted dozens of old-fashioned orange daylilies to hold the soil. I called Achilles to me and ducked into the woods as soon as the trees and bushes thickened enough to hide us from anyone watching from the houses or the dirt road. The rise here wasn't so steep. I walked up it at an angle until I saw the top of the cabin thirty yards to my left. I went on up until I could see the top half of the back door. I found a stump to sit on while I watched.

Achilles sniffed the air and, puzzled, turned to me for orders.

"Come, stay," I whispered. I slipped off the daypack and gave him his chew toy.

My phone vibrated. Diana, Annalynn's sterling admin assistant. Instead of answering I sent her a text saying I couldn't talk, to text me the message.

A minute later she texted: "wife says cork missing. where u?"

Damn! He'd run for it, and he hadn't had the guts to tell his wife. I texted, "on trail by rr tracks. need me?"

"no. stay lck."

Lck? Laycock. Where would Cork go? St. Jo? Only long enough to borrow money from his brother or mother. He might try to hide out in some little town in the west, but odds were he'd head for Canada and try to cross the border on an unguarded road in North Dakota.

Achilles dropped his bone and rose to face the trail.

I put my hand on his shoulder. "Quiet." I heard nothing for almost a minute, but he remained alert.

A dog barked only yards below us. Through the leaves I saw bits of black and white, the border collie who'd been on the trail yesterday.

"Shush, Angus," a woman said.

I stayed absolutely still. A car started at a house above us and drove off.

Achilles relaxed and stretched out to gnaw on his toy.

With the woman walking her dog as a deterrent, the burglar wouldn't come here soon. I checked my email. Reg had sent me a series of questions. I scrolled through them. My reply could wait until I got back to the office and had a standard keyboard.

An unfamiliar email address caught my eye. The combination of letters told me it was my CIA contact. Odd that she was answering me this way. I opened it: "I hear it's a lovely place for a vacation, but the climate is still chilly. It should be better in the spring."

Vienna would have to wait. I heard a vehicle somewhere on the other side of the tracks. It stopped.

Achilles nudged me with his nose.

The collie barked below us.

"Come, Angus," the woman said.

Achilles and I stayed motionless for a couple of minutes before going back to our respective toys.

Five minutes later my phone vibrated. A new text message from Diana: "AK wants u at gs café asap."

Not good. I replied, "on way. eta 20 min."

I stuck Achilles' toy in the daypack, shrugged into the shoulder straps, and put the mobile in my pocket. "Let's go," I whispered even though that made no sense now that we were leaving. Even so, I stepped lightly going through the trees to the trail.

Achilles shared my unease. He stayed close to my left leg.

"Don't doubt our instincts," I murmured as I approached the clearing. I stopped at the edge and put on my binocular sunglasses to scan the area across the tracks. Seeing only leaves and hearing nothing, I took a deep breath. "Go!"

We sprinted toward the limited cover fifty feet away. Halfway across, I felt like an idiot. Then I heard the pop of a pistol and saw a daylily fall off its stem a yard ahead of me. A bullet dug into the ground on my left and another into the trail right ahead of us. As I gave thanks that the burglar was a lousy shot, a bullet hit my backpack with enough force to throw me off stride. I plunged into the brush and hid behind the nearest tree. "Down, Achilles, down!"

I hugged the tree for support as pain rocketed through my old wound. After a few seconds the pain subsided. I drew my Glock and peeked out. I could barely see the hillside through the leaves, let alone anyone moving there. I adjusted the sunglasses. Binoculars don't see through leaves. The shots had sounded as though they came from below the dirt road. I calculated my position in relation to the trail zigzagging up the hill and fired four shots, each about five feet apart. The odds against hitting anyone were astronomical, but my return of fire might convince the burglars to move. I listened for sounds to guide my next shot.

A motor roared. A vehicle gunned down the old dirt road. I couldn't see the shape or color, but I heard the vehicle turn left to take the same route as yesterday's getaway car. The burglars would vanish before I could get back to the SUV to give chase. I dialed the dispatcher and reported shots fired at me, probably with the stolen Colt, and a getaway vehicle that could be headed into southwest Laycock. Not much to go on, but lots of crooks get caught because they break traffic laws.

Dampness on my back scared me. I pulled off the daypack. Water, not blood, dripped from it. I threw up my toast and jam, washed out my mouth with what hadn't drained from the bullet hole in the water bottle, and then jogged with Achilles to the SUV.

Why had the burglars shot at us? We were leaving the scene, giving them access to the home, posing no threat. Two shots were low. Those could have been intended for Achilles. The other two rounds definitely were meant for me. Why would the burglars fear me? Simple. I'd interrupted the last three attempts. I'd become burglar enemy number one.

THIRTY-SEVEN

IN THE SUV, I put my mobile on the holder, pulled out, and called Annalynn's cell to update her and find out why she wanted me at the Chew-Chew Café. The call went to voice mail. She probably was in a dead zone. I left word I was on my way. Better to tell her face to face that a round had missed me by two inches.

The shortest route to the Green Springs Road took me past Laycock Storage. Martina was hosing down her white van out front as I sped by. Her counseling would have to wait a little longer.

I ordered Achilles to the floor and accelerated after turning onto the two-lane blacktop road leading to Green Springs. I tried Annalynn's cell again.

She answered on the first ring: "Give me a moment."

Definitely something bad happening. I sped up.

She came back on. "Cork went to Harry's last night around eight thirty. He had a black eye. Just a sec."

Leo had been furious when I'd talked to him. Had he confronted his brother about the fake map and the fires? More important, had Cork admitted setting the fires? If he had, Leo wouldn't have let him run.

Annalynn returned. "Harry says Cork drank several beers, called you the b word, and asked for the name of a good lawyer. He received a text between nine thirty and ten and left." She spoke to someone before coming back on the phone. "He never came home. When Wanda

Sue opened the café, she found a chair smashed. That's when she called me."

I groaned, fearing that Leo had blacked Cork's eye and come back for another whack at him. "Is Leo there?"

"He came over from Quick Fix when he saw the squad car. I sent him and Gillian to senior housing to ask if anyone saw activity at the café last night. Wanda Sue walked home to see if Cork had packed any clothes. I'm treating the café as a crime scene, but I didn't want to say that to his family. Where are you?"

"Five minutes away. I'll check to make sure Cork isn't in Bushwhacker's Den."

"No need. The door was ajar so I looked in as we came by. Come straight here."

"Okay. I'm almost to the dead zone. Bye." Annalynn followed the rules. She would never have gone through that door if she hadn't feared the worst.

No one was in sight when I turned onto Robert E. Lee Avenue. I parked next to the squad car and, with Achilles at my side, strolled to the café. I didn't want to alarm any of those curious seniors sure to be watching out their windows.

Annalynn, wearing plastic gloves, opened the door to the café for me and handed me a matching pair. "I checked the kitchen. Nothing seems out of place there."

Achilles trotted over to sniff at a leg that had come off one of the old chairs. He began a circuit of the room, a low growl in his throat.

"Too bad he can't talk," Annalynn said. "What or who do you think he smells?"

"I've no idea. He didn't react that way to Cork yesterday." I studied the room. "Except for the broken chair and that saucer turned into an ashtray—cheap cigar, from the smell—the room is the same as it was yesterday afternoon."

Achilles barked by the door that led into the depot. I forced the gloves onto my hands and opened it.

He lowered his nose and moved confidently to the matching back door of Bea for Beauty.

Scheisse! Whose scent was he following?

Annalynn tried the knob. "It's locked."

The depot's entry doors were closed, making this section dusk dark. I went back through the café and across to Beatrix's glass door. I peered around the Closed sign into the sun-lit salon. A picture book lay on the floor. The drawer at Beatrix's station extended out a quarter of an inch. A foot-long scuffmark, the kind a dragging shoe makes, marred the pristine floor. The three blemishes in the super-neat shop shouted trouble. I tried the door. Locked. Securely locked. The lock on the back door would be easier to pick.

Annalynn joined me. "What do you see?"

An invitation to come in. "That back door is jammed. You stay here, and keep Achilles with you." I went back through the café to the locked door and opened it in seconds. Avoiding the scuffmark, I walked past the stations to the back room. I took a deep breath before I opened the door, anticipating Cork's body on the floor inside. Wrong. The room looked as it had when I fixed tea there. I went to Beatrix's station and eased the drawer open. I'd noted how she had lined up four pairs of shears with surgical precision. I stared down at three.

Annalynn tapped on the glass door. "What did you find?"

"What someone wanted us to find. A pair of Beatrix's shears is missing. I'm afraid we'll find a blade in Cork's body." I closed the drawer to its previous position.

Annalynn froze a moment. Then she went into the café and, a moment later, stepped into the salon. "Show me."

"Don't step on the scuff mark," I cautioned as I pulled the drawer open.

Annalynn bit her lip. "Oh, Phoenix, no. Furious as Beatrix would have been at Cork for not admitting he set the fires, she surely wouldn't have killed him."

"Not only wouldn't but couldn't. She's so weak she can't stand up to cut hair. She's being framed." By whom? Leo might have hurt Cork for letting Jolene go to prison, but he'd never blame it on Jolene's mother. "The killer left the scuff mark and the drawer open a fraction of an inch to draw my—your—attention."

Achilles barked twice and, nose down, walked out the door.

"Coming." I followed him through the big room to a heavy metal door leading outside. I opened it enough to peek out. Cork's pickup was parked to the left of the door. I hurried out to check the cab and bed. Both were empty.

Achilles ignored the pickup. Instead he sniffed around a space about fifteen feet from the depot door. He moved into the street, turning right and searching in ever smaller circles. He yelped in apparent frustration and trotted to me.

"Good boy." I knelt to stroke him. I heard Annalynn step outside and said, "Whoever Achilles was following got in a vehicle and drove away, probably with

Cork's body. Did you see any more scuff marks? Any sign of dragging?"

"No, but I found this cell phone with a cork cover on the floor." She turned it on and hit a couple of buttons. "Beatrix isn't the only one being framed." She held up the phone so I could read a text message: "we need talk. meet me at 10 in café. p smith."

THIRTY-EIGHT

I STUDIED THE message I hadn't written. "A frame, or simply a way to get Cork to the café." Another possibility occurred to me. "A clever man would leave signs of his own murder to cover up his disappearance." I rebutted that. "Cork's not clever." I remembered something else. "His wife took out a life insurance policy on him. He's worth more dead than alive."

"Don't assume the wife did it," Annalynn admonished me. "The *assumed* killer dropped the cell phone on purpose just as he left a scuff mark in the beauty shop." She walked into the middle of the street and revolved slowly. "No houses near enough to see someone entering or exiting. If anyone in senior housing was up at ten o'clock, they were watching the news. Leo said none of the hotel's apartments face the depot."

I discounted the likelihood of witnesses. "I've known Beatrix four days. Why frame her and me?"

"That's what I was about to ask you. We need to talk to her. Please lock the back door while I secure the crime scene." She hurried back inside the depot.

I checked the area one more time before going inside. "Come, Achilles." I closed the door and turned the lock, an industrial-strength one. Cork must have opened it with a key.

"Gillian and Leo are walking back from the senior

center," Annalynn called. "Please go out and talk to Leo while I give Gillian instructions."

"Right." I stripped off and pocketed my gloves before walking into the street. "Anyone see Cork?"

Gillian and Leo both shook their heads. She reached down to stroke Achilles. When she moved on, he cozied up to Leo.

He absentmindedly petted Achilles' head. The young man had circles under his eyes. A white line above his lip indicated his tension.

I casually blocked his way. "Cork's pickup is out back. Did you hear any vehicles last night after, say, nine o'clock?"

His Adam's apple bobbed. "No, I was watching a Cardinals' game." He ran his right hand back over his cropped hair. Two of his knuckles were bruised. He motioned me to follow him a few steps from the door. "I didn't want to talk to Cork in front of his family. I had him come to the shop after supper." His fists clenched. "He admitted it. He admitted he tried to burn down the Fish House. He swore on our father's grave he had no idea Wiler was on the floor."

Leo had verified Jolene's innocence and his motive for hurting his brother. And an even stronger motive for keeping Cork alive. But Leo could have killed Cork by accident. I kept my tone light: "Did his confession come before or after you blacked his eye?"

He ducked his head. "About a nanosecond before. I didn't know I could be so mad." He jammed his hands in his jeans pockets and shuffled his feet. "He cried. He thought she would get off on self-defense. When she didn't, he was too scared to say anything." Blood flooded his cheeks. He raised his head. "Actually, that's when I hit him in the eye. The first time I punched him in the stomach." He crossed his muscular arms and clasped his elbows as though to restrain himself. "He promised to turn himself in today. Where in hell is he?"

Leo's voice and his body language almost convinced me that he was telling the truth. I had to be sure. Subtly. "Did he tell Wanda Sue that he could have saved Jolene from prison?"

"No. They don't talk much anymore. She thought he went to Harry's to drink and didn't want to come to bed drunk. She expected to find him asleep on the couch this morning."

Wanda Sue surely had guessed Cork started that fire. But she could be in denial. "Do you suppose he ran for the border?"

Leo shook his head. "No, not that he wouldn't want to. Mom and Wanda Sue never give him enough cash for more than one tank of gas. Wanda Sue cut up his credit cards years ago."

Annalynn joined us. "Leo, do you have the key to the depot's front door?"

"No. Beatrix has one. Would you like for me to go get it?"

"No, thank you. I understand your brother is a sociable man. If you don't mind, I'd like for you to swing through town and see if he's chatting with someone."

"Sure," Leo said with little enthusiasm. "Maybe he slept in the pickup and went to the convenience store for coffee." He focused on me. "You'll take care of—you know—even if Cork won't come forward?"

"Yes. The sheriff has agreed to reopen the case."

He stepped forward to hug me. "Thank you." He released me and jogged down the street.

Annalynn smiled and strode toward the Hew/Olson home. "I take it you don't think Leo killed Wiler or Cork."

"No." I amended that. "At least not on purpose. Cork admitted he set the fires."

"Leo wouldn't kill the person whose testimony can free Jolene. On the other hand, Leo might kill Cork to keep him from testifying that Leo killed Wiler. Oh, Lord. I'm spinning wild scenarios the way you do."

"I always look for information to support or disprove my fact-based theories."

"Have you concocted a scenario that features Beatrix as Cork's killer? Say, Leo told her Cork set the fires." She mimicked my tone. "She texted Cork pretending to be you and asked him to confess. He said no. She grabbed her shears and stabbed him. She's certainly smart enough to drop that phone to frame you."

An impossible scenario based on what I knew, good reasoning based on what she knew. "Not many people would know his cell number. Beatrix might." I'd kept the secret of Beatrix's illness. Did I break my promise now? I compromised. "It can't be Beatrix. She's quite ill, too weak to carry a man through the depot to a vehicle."

"Leo could have helped her."

"If you'd killed a man, would you ask his brother to help move the body?"

"Perhaps not." She watched Achilles detour into the park and, when we didn't follow, come back to trot ahead of us. "I've sent out alerts and called a deputy to lead a search. The town has at least a dozen abandoned buildings. Achilles will be a big help. He obviously knows Cork's scent."

I stopped. "If Cork is dead, he didn't leave a trail out of Beatrix's salon for Achilles to follow. Either Cork's alive or Achilles was tracking his killer."

Annalynn grabbed my arm. "And Achilles is tracking someone whose scent he knows, someone he doesn't like."

"He likes Leo."

Achilles barked and stopped at the street as he'd been taught.

Hermione ran across the lawn waving both arms.

No cars moved on the streets. "Go, Achilles."

Annalynn said, "I didn't realize you know the child so well."

"She's dog crazy, and he likes playing with her." Their exchange of hugs and kisses continued until Annalynn and I approached them.

Hermione hurled herself at me, giving me my second unexpected embrace. I knelt to hug her back. Much more satisfying than hugging a tree to keep from collapsing. I rose. "Hermione, this is my friend Annalynn. She has a granddaughter your age."

The child edged behind me and hid her face against my back.

"You play with Achilles while Annalynn and I talk to Grammy Bea."

The child ran toward her toy car with her hand on Achilles' back.

Beatrix, dressed in slacks and a fleece jacket, waved at us from the porch swing. She held a picture book, and the stuffed dog was beside her in the swing.

"This isn't an official interrogation," Annalynn murmured as we walked toward the house. "Tell her as little as possible, and please back off if I take the conversation in another direction. Okay?"

"I'll follow your lead, Sheriff Keyser." Not the right time to remind her that I had a lot more experience coaxing information from people than she did. I angled off to bring a rocking chair to the swing. My detour let Annalynn take the lead.

"Good morning, Beatrix. Your granddaughter is lovely." Annalynn took the rocking chair on the other side of the swing. "She and Achilles certainly adore each other."

"Yes." Beatrix smiled. Makeup didn't conceal her ashen color or the deep shadows under her eyes. "Hermione was so excited when she saw the SUV parked down the street. What's happening at the depot?"

Annalynn hesitated, so I answered, "A break-in at the café. They broke a chair but didn't take anything. Wanda Sue is very upset. Did you see a light down there last night? Or see a car behind the depot?"

"No. I went to bed early. You can ask my mother, but she doesn't see very well." Beatrix shifted to face Annalynn. "I've been expecting you. Are you ready to arrest me?"

Annalynn kept a poker face. "On what charge?"

"Murder." Beatrix twisted the stuffed dog's arm. "Surely Phoenix has found proof that I'm the one who killed him."

How could she possibly have taken Cork's body out of the depot? Keeping my face neutral, I nodded to Annalynn to follow up.

She sat quiet for a moment. "We're reviewing the evidence, but it takes time. It will speed up the process if you tell me what happened."

"I don't know what more I can add to what I told Phoenix." She turned to me for support. "I saw that big man on my daughter and hit him with my flashlight."

Light dawned. Beatrix was confessing to killing Edwin Wiler, not Cork. Was she expecting me to support a false confession? A big mistake, especially when she didn't need to do that to clear her daughter.

Annalynn arched an eyebrow.

I elected to stick to the truth. "I read the autopsy report last night. The flashlight bruised him. It didn't kill him."

Beatrix shrank into a little old woman. "But who else could have done it?" Then she rallied. "I hit him with the chair, too. This cancer is my punishment for not confessing my sin immediately."

She'd asked the relevant question: Who else could have done it? Odds and ends floating around my brain fell into place. The motive for the fatal blow. A reason for Jolene's false confession. The connection between my being shot at on the trail and my being framed for Cork's murder. And I'd been blaming Boom and his staff for overlooking the obvious. "You didn't kill him, Beatrix. Neither did Jolene." A sense of urgency hit me as my new perception of the past clarified the present and forecast the near future. "Annalynn, we have to go." I leapt off the porch and ran toward the SUV. Seeing Hermione, I stopped long enough to call, "Beatrix, keep Hermione inside. Keep your whole family inside until I give you an all clear." I ran full tilt.

Achilles caught up with me. Annalynn didn't. I hopped into the SUV and picked her up at the corner.

"You've figured out who killed Wiler?"

"Wiler and Cork." I stepped on the gas and ignored

Annalynn's questions to crystallize my thinking and anticipate the killer's next move. I had to brake hard to turn into the Bushwhacker's Den parking lot as another likelihood occurred to me. "If Cork's body is here, I'll know I'm right." I jumped out and rushed to the half-open front door.

Annalynn followed me. "Gillian and I already looked inside."

I pointed to the plywood covering the hole in the floor. "Help me move this."

Achilles thrust himself in front of me, attempting to push me back.

Annalynn raised the nearest corner a foot and pushed. I evaded Achilles and grabbed the other corner. A flash of pain compelled me to let go.

"There he is," Annalynn said. She dropped the board and rushed to the front door to breathe deeply. She pulled a fresh pair of gloves from the packet on her belt and returned to push the plywood back another foot. "The killer wrapped duct tape around his arms. A blade from the shears is sticking in his chest."

I ignored the throbbing under my ribs and moved over to look in the hole. The body lay in a bed of ashes and charred debris. I forced myself to kneel and study the torso and head, the only parts fully visible. "The blade didn't kill him. If it had, he'd be covered with blood." I flinched as I studied the contorted face. "That's a burn on his cheek. Made with his own cigar probably." I averted my eyes. "His red suspenders are missing. They're probably the murder weapon."

A car screeched to a stop outside and pulled into the parking lot.

"That's one of mine," Annalynn said.

"Good. He can handle this. We have to go."

"Where?"

The answer sprang from my subconscious. "To J. J. Hew's house." I hurried outside.

"We found Cork's body in there," Annalynn told the deputy as I climbed into the SUV. "Close off the depot and this entire property as crime scenes." She opened the passenger door. "I'll call Gillian, Diana, and the medical examiner on my way to town. When you have both crime scenes secure, tell Leo Klang you've found the body and go with him to notify Cork's wife."

Achilles leapt into the SUV to settle himself at Anna-lynn's feet.

I backed out and hit the gas hard. "You won't be able to make any calls for a minute or two." And Edwin Wiler couldn't have received a call from the Den that night. No landline and no cell service.

"Enlighten me, Phoenix. What makes you think Jolene's father killed these two men?"

"I don't."

"Then who did?"

I answered with a question: "Who would be furious that Edwin Wiler took Jolene's bra as a trophy?" Wrong question. It had too many possible answers. I narrowed down the possible suspects with another question: "Who also would be furious that Cork started a fire—fires—with Wiler in the building?"

Annalynn said nothing for a long time. "I can think of one person, Martina Pelben. But, Phoenix, whoever killed Cork had to have his cell number. She wouldn't."

It took me a mile to come up with a possible reason she would. When Annalynn disconnected from her call to her admin assistant, I said, "Call Harry again. Ask him if Cork gave anyone at the bar his number. If he did, who could have seen or heard it?"

She placed the call. "This is Sheriff Keyser. Let me speak to Harry, please. It's urgent." A long, long pause. "Did Cork Klang give you or anyone in the bar his cell number last night?" Pause. "Who was there?" A long pause. "Thanks, Harry." She disconnected. "I hope this tells you more than it does me. Cork asked for the name of a lawyer and gave his number to Harry and to two men at the pool table. Several people could have heard him, including a group who came in for cheesecake after the sing-along."

That cinched it. "Martina must have been part of that group." Now to confirm my other conclusion. "Did you see anyone in the church who seemed a good target for a burglary? You got the call about Jim catching the burglars and didn't say."

Annalynn frowned. "Why on earth do you ask that now?"

"I want to see if you come to the same conclusions I have. Two heads, etc."

"Okay. The wealthiest older person there, by far, was Sybil Pelben, but no one would break into her house. She has two Rottweilers and the best security system in town. Running a storage place, her late husband knew all about locks."

Another missing piece slid into place. He'd passed on his tools to his great-niece along with Laycock Storage. "Did you notice that J. J.'s wife was wearing a lot of gold?"

"Everyone noticed that. I still don't understand why we're going to their house." Annalynn clapped her hands. "You're linking the murders and the burglaries. For Pete's sake, spell it out for me."

"This morning the burglar shot at me as I left a potential victim's house. Why? Not because of the burglary. She heard Cork asking about a lawyer last night at Harry's and realized I'd identified Cork, not Jolene, as the arsonist. Logic would tell her my next move would be to figure out who crushed Wiler's skull. That's why she framed me and Beatrix. The way Cork's killer picked that lock at the salon tipped me off that the killer and the burglar could be the same person." I became even more convinced that I was right as I spoke. "She saw me running. She surely guessed I'd gone to look for Cork. What better time to break in for one last haul?"

Annalynn frowned. "Yes, but you have no proof she's the killer or the burglar."

"We will if we catch her red-handed and get a search warrant."

"To find the stolen items plus Wiler's missing guitar. The Hews' house is certainly worth a try. I'll get the address."

The Hews lived on Harding Street two houses down from where I'd spotted the stolen van.

I turned off Green Springs Road and approached Laycock from the west, guessing the burglar would expect any officers on patrol to come from downtown rather than from the county. To make Annalynn's SUV inconspicuous, I parked between cars on Coolidge, the street parallel to Harding and to the alley. I dislike wearing Bluetooth devices, but I hooked mine up so Annalynn and I could communicate by voice and have our Glocks in our hands.

Annalynn racked a round into the chamber of her service weapon. "How do we do this?"

"The same way we did at Big Bass Lake. You and Achilles sneak through the neighbor's yard and hide where you can watch the front door. I'll go up the alley, hide in the lilac bushes, and guard the back for anyone coming or going."

She took a deep breath. "If my mother could see me now. Let's go."

We walked down the street with Achilles trotting ahead of us. His head went up as we entered the alley. I didn't know whether he recognized the place or detected our quarry's scent. We drew our weapons. "Quiet, boy," I said softly.

He pressed against my leg, tense and uneasy.

I expected to see Martina's van parked in the garage where she'd left the stolen van before, but the garage stood empty. Had I been wrong about her going after Mrs. Hew's jewelry? We'd soon find out. "Go through the yard here," I whispered. "It's the next house on your right. If you see any sign she's there, tell Achilles to speak. That should send her running out the back. Stay in place until I yell at her."

Annalynn nodded. "If you're right, she's killed two people. Don't take any chances."

"Ditto. Achilles, go with Annalynn. Guard Annalynn."

He whined, but he went.

Once Annalynn and Achilles were out of view behind the neighbor's house, I walked to the Hews' garage and crept along the side until I reached a wall of dense lilac bushes. A footprint showed distinctly in the grass-free soil between two bushes. A humongous footprint. Just like the one in the neighbor's garden. Like one Edwin

Wiler's shoes would make. Those oversized shoes would slow her down if she ran.

I called Annalynn and whispered, "Bigfoot is here. Are you in position?"

"Give me one minute."

I peeked through the thick leaves at a cement patio with a white plastic table and two white plastic chairs. They afforded no cover. Bullets would go right through the plastic. Blinds covered both the downstairs and the upstairs windows on the back. No basement. She had to come out the front or back door.

And she would have that pistol in hand. I needed better cover than the lilacs. I measured the distance between the bushes and an old ash tree. Twelve unprotected feet separated me from that sanctuary. It had no low limbs to conceal me. Or her. "Annalynn, in thirty seconds, tell Achilles to bark. And hold on to his collar."

I counted to ten and raced to the tree. Flattened against it, I strained my ears but heard nothing.

Achilles barked four times. Then he snarled.

Something crashed in the house. I made myself small behind the tree.

Achilles barked again, frantically this time. He knew the person inside the house endangered me. He intended to come after her.

The storm door opened with a metallic squeak. I waited two seconds for her to look around and step out. I heard her stumble in the big shoes.

I peeked out enough to aim the Glock. A hood covered her head. A skull mask covered her face. Her right hand was in her pocket—a bad sign when I'd interrogated her. "Police! Hands on your head! Drop to your knees!"

She did neither. Instead she pulled the pistol from her right pocket and, using an amateur's awkward grip, pointed it at me.

Annalynn, not yet in sight, shouted, "Drop that gun!"

Achilles, snarling, dragged her around the corner of the house.

Martina flinched but kept the six-shooter aimed at me.

Annalynn couldn't hold Achilles back long. Secure behind my tree and sure I could shoot Martina before she could aim at them, I gave her a choice. "Drop it or Achilles will tear you apart."

A siren wailed nearby. Annalynn had called for backup.

"Call that beast off!" Martina lowered the pistol.

Annalynn holstered her gun and grabbed Achilles' collar with both hands. "An LPD unit will be here in seconds."

I repeated my order: "Drop your weapon, Martina. Don't make me shoot you."

Instead she raised the six-shooter to her own head. "Let me go or I'll shoot myself."

An idle threat. She'd emptied the Colt of its hand-loaded cartridges while shooting at the beagle on Avon and at me on the trail. "Go ahead. It will save the county the cost of trying you for the murders of Edwin Wiler and Cork Klang."

She threw the gun at me and sank to her knees as it bounced off the tree. She pulled off the skull mask and glared at me. "I didn't kill Edwin. That stupid Cork did. It was all that tramp's fault." She lowered her head to her knees and curled up with her gloved hands covering her hooded head.

Coming up: an insanity plea. Hard to make a Missouri jury buy that. If they did, someone else would have to find her counseling.

A siren stopped in the alley. A moment later Jim crashed through the lilacs.

I holstered my Glock and hugged my frantic dog.

THIRTY-NINE

JIM HAD NO shackles with him to supplement the handcuffs, so Achilles and I accompanied him to book Martina for breaking and entering. Meanwhile Annalynn requested a search warrant and drove to Green Springs to report the impending murder charges against Martina in person. Annalynn didn't say so, but I expected her to apologize to Beatrix for Boom's role in Jolene's arrest and conviction. I wondered if Annalynn had thought of the political boost both she and Jim would get by catching the burglar and murderer. The disgruntled jail administrator's write-in campaign for sheriff would evaporate by evening.

With Martina behind bars, Achilles and I went off duty. I gave him a drink of water and a treat before we started home for lunch. What a morning. I declined a ride. We both needed to run off the tension.

Vernon Kann phoned me when I was halfway home. "Phoenix, I know Klang's death relates to Jolene's imprisonment, but I don't know how. Fill me in."

I owed Vernon, but this case had become too big for me to talk about with anyone from the press. "Sorry, but you have to get this story from Annalynn."

"She said you'd outline what happened." He sighed. "Off the record."

I debated what to tell him.

"Phoenix, this is a complex story. We have only a few

hours to gather and write the breaking news and pull together the back story readers need to understand it."

He had a point, and he'd prompted the investigation by sending Beatrix to me. "Okay. I'll give you the expurgated version. We haven't acquired all the evidence yet, so don't print anything without Annalynn's verification. Understood?"

"Of course."

"First, Wiler's murder. Martina Pelben found her lover alone at the Den with Jolene's bra and hit him with a handy vodka bottle. Cork came to the Den about an hour later. He didn't turn on a light so he didn't see Wiler against the bar. Cork started the fires for the insurance money, but he'd violated his policy on cooking food so he couldn't even file a claim."

"I hope you can prove this. Go on."

"Martina convinced herself smoke inhalation killed Wiler. Jolene confessed—I don't know why—so Martina blamed her for the arson and Wiler's death." I forced myself to acknowledge my role in Martina's attack on Cork. "My investigation alerted Martina to the likelihood that Cork started the fires. She lured him to the café last night and killed him."

"My God! I knew you caught her during a burglary. I would never have guessed she killed Wiler. She put on a convincing show of grief."

Vernon had ignored my guilt. "She wasn't acting. She didn't intend to kill him, and she went into denial. That gives me hope that she didn't destroy the physical proof." Had she taken the guitar that night as a hostage? "The police are searching for it now."

"What physical proof?"

"You'll have to wait for Annalynn to release that." I disconnected. My phone rang again half a block later.

Diana said, "Thank goodness I reached you. Annalynn said your houseguest will be at the castle in twenty—make that ten—minutes. Bye."

Houseguest? Surely Annalynn's admin assistant had misunderstood. I called back and got voice mail. I suspected Annalynn had instructed Diana not to tell me any more than she had.

I didn't recognize the blue Chevy Malibu that pulled into Annalynn's driveway as I prepared to open the castle's front door. I walked toward the car.

Beatrix lowered the front passenger window. "I can never thank you enough for clearing Jolene. God brought you to us and will bless you for your good work and kindness." She touched a small gold cross at her neck. "I'm so grateful that you volunteered to take care of Hermione while I'm in Columbia."

Annalynn had flat-out lied to Beatrix. The wonder of it almost left me speechless. I finally came up with, "I'm happy to do it. Hermione and Achilles adore each other."

"God bless you," Mrs. Olson said from the far side of the back seat. "We might be back tonight, but it's such a relief to have Hermione with you in case the"— she glanced at Hermione—"the oncologist wants Beatrix to stay."

Annalynn was punishing me for keeping secrets by compelling me to babysit. I smiled a welcome and opened the door for the child. Shrinking back, she clung to the sides of her car seat. I held out my hand to her. She shook her head no and scooted down behind her stuffed dog.

Achilles wriggled past me and barked a welcome.

What do you say to a justifiably terrified little girl? "Hermione, Achilles wants to show you his hummingbirds. He plays with them every day. They'll be happy to have a new friend."

She craned her neck. "Where the birdies?"

"In the backyard. That's where Achilles, you, and I will play keep-away."

She thrust her stuffed dog at me, unfastened her seat belt, and hoisted herself out of the car seat. She took my hand to jump out of the car.

"Give me some sugar, sweetie," Beatrix said.

Hermione kissed her grandmother's cheek and ran after Achilles toward the backyard.

The trunk popped open, and Louise—now wearing a short-sleeved blue sweater rather than her usual floral top—got out of the driver's seat. "I never thought we'd get out of here without a river of tears, including some of my own." She walked to the trunk and took out a small rolling suitcase.

Beatrix said, "We brought enough clothes to last the weekend, Phoenix. If you should need anything from the house or any help before we get back, call Leo." She handed me a piece of paper. "This is the number for Louise's sister. My mother will stay there, if need be. I'll call you from the hospital as soon as I have a number."

Definitely a weekend visit. At minimum.

Hermione ran to me as the car backed out. Her face puckered and tears flowed, but she didn't wail. Pressed against me, she waved and waved even after the car drove out of sight.

Achilles licked away her tears.

She hugged him. Then she smiled up at me. "Know

what? Mommy comes home soon. Know what? We throw a big, big party. Want to come? Achilles likes parties." She wheeled around and skipped toward the hummingbird feeders, one hand on Achilles' back.

What a wonderfully resilient child. I hadn't realized how depressing the day had been until I saw the joy on her face. Occasionally *Sturm und Drang* surrenders to sweetness and light.

MY RESPECT FOR my late mother grew over the next eight hours. My two brothers and I had been more active—and combative—than Hermione. By the time I tucked her into bed—my bed, regrettably—and tiptoed downstairs to join Connie and Annalynn in the ladies' parlor, I was exhausted.

"Here's Grandma Phoenix," Connie said, gesturing with a half-full glass of white wine.

Annalynn poured me a mug of cocoa from a thermal pot. "Beatrix called with good news while you were singing 'Swing Low, Sweet Chariot' upstairs. She's been accepted in a clinical trial. She said you'd understand."

"Yes." She hoped to prolong her life at least a few more months. I changed the subject. "You didn't say where you found the guitar, Annalynn."

"On Martina's bed, with the neck on a pillow. It was creepy. Apparently she slept with it there. Her cabin, the purple one, had a tiny living room, a minuscule kitchen, and a bedroom behind a half wall. The place looked ready for a time traveler from the forties." Annalynn sipped a scotch, an indulgence she rarely allowed herself as sheriff. "Martina furnished the green cabin as a shrine to Wiler. She had a computer there with love

notes to his email account. Gillian is reading them to
see if Martina wrote about the homicides or the burglaries."

Not likely. "What about the stolen collectibles?"

"She hid most of them in the only two cabins being
used for storage. The towels were folded neatly in her
bathroom."

In our first conversation, Martina had told me the
storage units were full. In the interview, she'd exaggerated her income. "Then the need for money prompted
the burglaries."

"Yes, but her aunt says Martina also may have
wanted to get back at people who criticized Wiler."
Annalynn's lips twitched as she suppressed a smile.
"By the way, Michael spoke again to Martina's cousin,
Newton Nauber." She waited for my reaction.

It took me a moment to place the name. "The owner
of the stolen SUV that followed me?"

"Right. Martina knew where he hid the key."

Connie shifted impatiently. "What about her accomplice, the one who drove the getaway car at Big Bass
Lake?"

"Martina had no accomplice." Annalynn didn't
bother to hide her smile this time. "She even fooled
Phoenix. We're fairly certain Martina used a ramp that
she carried in her cargo van to load and unload the stolen motorcycle."

A good time to mention the shots she fired at me.
"Annalynn, you may want to send Gillian to the patch
of day lilies along the trail a block or so from Boundary.
She'll find a bullet from Martina's stolen pistol embed-
ded in the soil behind a clipped-off stem."

Annalynn made a note on a yellow legal pad. "Where did the other shots hit?"

"I can't pinpoint those." I relived the panic I'd felt diving into the woods. No need to share that with Annalynn now or ever. I'd get rid of the daypack with the hole in it. "What still puzzles me is why Jolene Hew confessed to killing Wiler and to arson."

Annalynn arched an eyebrow. "Why didn't you ask her?"

"Because she wouldn't talk to me. Strangely enough, prisons don't force prisoners to talk to strangers." My tired brain woke up. "But they have to talk to the law."

"So they do," Annalynn said. "As acting sheriff of Vandiver County, I called Jolene and told her we'd found proof Martina Pelben killed Edwin Wiler. Once Jolene stopped crying, I asked why she confessed." Annalynn took a moment to compose herself. "She said that at first she couldn't think clearly, didn't know exactly what she'd done. The deputy's questions convinced her that either she'd killed Wiler or she'd driven her mother to commit a sin. Jolene thought Beatrix had gone back to get the bra, encountered Wiler, and attacked him."

Connie marked a point for herself in the air. "Like I said, police interrogators confuse young people and convince them they committed a crime." She frowned. "But why would Jolene think her mother would risk confronting a big, mean, drunk man?"

I speculated. "That also describes Jolene's father, and Beatrix took him on. Besides, Jolene woke up while Beatrix was in Mrs. Olson's room." Don't blame Boom. "When the deputy questioned Jolene, she assumed Beatrix went back to the Den. After all, no one else knew Wiler was there."

Annalynn said, "And once Jolene accepted the plea deal, no one believed her when she said she was innocent." She closed her eyes and shook her head. "From what Jolene told me, at first she refused to talk to Beatrix out of guilt for the anguish she'd caused her. Then Jolene became angry and, well, disillusioned, that her mother didn't come forward to save her—again, as she had at the Den and when Jolene brought home a baby."

My mind turned to a more practical reason for Jolene accepting the plea deal. "Beatrix's income supported all of them. Jolene confessed both to protect her mother and to provide for her daughter."

"For Pete's sake, Phoenix," Connie protested, "Jolene's choices show she reacts to emotions, not economics. She's the type to rationalize her actions to make herself heroic, a martyr."

Quite possible. How would we all survive without finding excuses for our mistakes? "In any case, those false confessions led to pointless tragedy."

Face drawn, Annalynn drank the rest of her scotch. "If Cork had admitted to arson when Jolene confessed, Boom would have rejected both her confessions. She would have gone free, and Cork would still be alive." She turned to me. "People cause a lot of anguish when they keep secrets. Don't you agree, Phoenix?"

And sometimes when they tell them. "Honest communication is critical," I said piously.

Connie hooted, and Annalynn threw up her hands.

What could I say? "I will never, ever tell either of you all of my secrets, and I certainly don't want to be bored by yours."

Connie raised her glass. "Here's to less boring secrets. I was afraid Laycock would put us to sleep when Annalynn turns in her star. Judging from what happened this week, I predict the foundation's applicants will provide plenty of excitement."

"I hope not," Annalynn said fervently.

I sipped my cocoa and wondered what else Vandiver County could throw at me.

* * * * *

ABOUT THE AUTHOR

CAROLYN MULFORD WRITES the award-winning *Show Me* mystery series featuring an ex-spy who applies her tradecraft honed in Eastern Europe to solving homicides in rural Missouri. In April 2014, the first book, *Show Me the Murder*, received the Missouri Writers' Guild's Walter Williams Major Work Award. DearReader.com named *Show Me the Deadly Deer* a Mystery of the Week. *Show Me the Gold* won MWG's Best Book Award in December 2015. Carolyn served in the Peace Corps before working as a magazine editor in Vienna and Washington, D.C. She survived for decades as a freelance writer/editor before changing her focus from nonfiction to fiction. Her first novel, *The Feedsack Dress*, was Missouri's Great Read at the 2009 National Book Festival. To read excerpts from her books, visit carolynmulford.com.

Get 4 FREE REWARDS!

We'll send you 2 FREE Books plus 2 FREE Mystery Gifts.

Get 4 FREE REWARDS!

We'll send you 2 FREE Books plus 2 FREE Mystery Gifts.

Harlequin® Romantic Suspense books feature heart-racing sensuality and the promise of a sweeping romance set against the backdrop of suspense.

FREE
Value Over
$20

Get 4 FREE REWARDS!

We'll send you 2 FREE Books plus 2 FREE Mystery Gifts.

FREE
Value Over
$20

Both the **Romance** and **Suspense** collections feature compelling novels written by many of today's best-selling authors.

YES! Please send me 2 FREE novels from the Essential Romance or Essential Suspense Collection and my 2 FREE gifts (gifts are worth about $10 retail). After receiving them, if I don't wish to receive any more books, I can return the shipping statement marked "cancel." If I don't cancel, I will receive 4 brand-new novels every month and be billed just $6.74 each in the U.S. or $7.24 each in Canada. That's a savings of at least 16% off the cover price. It's quite a bargain! Shipping and handling is just 50¢ per book in the U.S. and 75¢ per book in Canada.* I understand that accepting the 2 free books and gifts places me under no obligation to buy anything. I can always return a shipment and cancel at any time. The free books and gifts are mine to keep no matter what I decide.

Choose one: ☐ **Essential Romance**
(194/394 MDN GMY7)

☐ **Essential Suspense**
(191/391 MDN GMY7)

Name (please print)

Address   Apt. #

City   State/Province   Zip/Postal Code

Mail to the Reader Service:
IN U.S.A.: P.O. Box 1341, Buffalo, NY 14240-8531
IN CANADA: P.O. Box 603, Fort Erie, Ontario L2A 5X3

Want to try 2 free books from another series? Call 1-800-873-8635 or visit www.ReaderService.com.

Get 4 FREE REWARDS!

We'll send you 2 FREE Books plus 2 FREE Mystery Gifts.

Love Inspired® Suspense books feature Christian characters facing challenges to their faith... and lives.

FREE
Value Over
$20